Roger Ingleton, Minor

by
Talbot Baines Reed

Roger Ingleton, Minor
by Talbot Baines Reed

Copyright © 2024

All Rights reserved.

No part of this publication may be reproduced, stored in a retrieval system, or transmitted in any form or by any means, electronic, mechanical, photocopying or Otherwise, without the written permission of the publisher.
The author/editor asserts the moral right to be identified as the author/editor of this work.

ISBN: 978-93-63054-37-0

Published by

DOUBLE 9 BOOKS

2/13-B, Ansari Road
Daryaganj, New Delhi – 110002
info@double9books.com
www.double9books.com
Tel. 011-40042856

This book is under public domain

ABOUT THE AUTHOR

Talbot Baines Reed was an English author of boys' fiction who lived from April 3, 1852, to November 28, 1893. He created a type of school stories that lasted until the middle of the 20th century. The Fifth Form at St. Dominic's is one of his most well-known works. He often and regularly wrote for The Boy's Own Paper (B.O.P.). Most of his writing was first published there. Reed became a well-known typefounder through his family's business. He also wrote the standard work on the subject, History of the Old English Letter Foundries. John Reed was a colonel in Oliver Cromwell's army during the English Civil War. The Reed family came from him. Their home was in Maiden Newton, which is in the county of Dorset. They moved to London at the end of the 18th century. Andrew Reed (1787–1862), Talbot Reed's grandpa, was a minister in the Congregational Church and the founder of many charitable organizations, such as the London Orphan Asylum and a hospital for people who could not get better. He was also a well-known hymn writer. His "Spirit Divine, attend our prayers" can still be found in many hymnals today. Talbot Baines Reed grew up in a happy family where Charles Reed was very religious and thought that tough outdoor games were the best way to raise boys.

CONTENTS

Chapter One
A Summons 7

Chapter Two
The Living among the Dead 17

Chapter Three
A Missing Inscription 27

Chapter Four
Acquaintances New and Old 36

Chapter Five
A Churchyard Cough 47

Chapter Six
A Case of Eviction 57

Chapter Seven
Mr Armstrong puts down his Foot 67

Chapter Eight
Two Ends of a Rope 76

Chapter Nine
The Captain relieves Guard 86

Chapter Ten
Robert Ratman, esquire, Gentleman 95

Chapter Eleven
Awkward Questions 104

Chapter Twelve
A Windfall for the Captain 114

Chapter Thirteen
    A Voice from the Dead 122

Chapter Fourteen
    What a Horsewhip discovered 132

Chapter Fifteen
    Strong Hearts and Weak Tempers 142

Chapter Sixteen
    Roger sees a little too much Life 150

Chapter Seventeen
    "When the Cat's away—" 159

Chapter Eighteen
    Miss Jill Oliphant At Home 168

Chapter Nineteen
    A Feeble Clue 177

Chapter Twenty
    The Ghost of Hamlet 184

Chapter Twenty One
    Sharks by Land and Water 191

Chapter Twenty Two
    Mr Ratman visits his Property 199

Chapter Twenty Three
    Captain Oliphant pays one of his Debts 209

Chapter Twenty Four
    The Billiard-marker at "l'Hôtel Soult" 219

Chapter Twenty Five
    The Heir of Maxfield comes of Age 227

Chapter Twenty Six
    Missing Links 235

Chapter One
A Summons

The snow lay thick round Maxfield Manor. Though it had been falling scarcely an hour, it had already transfigured the dull old place from a gloomy pile of black and grey into a gleaming vision of white. It lodged in deep piles in the angles of the rugged gables, and swirled up in heavy drifts against the hall-door. It sat heavily on the broad ivy-leaves over the porch, and blotted out lawn, path, and flowerbed in a universal pall of white velvet. The wind-flattened oaks in the park were become tables of snow; and away over the down, to the edge of the cliff itself, the dazzling canopy stretched, making the gulls as they skimmed its surface in troubled flight appear dingy, and the uneasy ocean beyond more than ever grey and leaden.

And the snow was falling still, and promised to make a night of it. At least so thought one of the inmates of the manor-house as he got up from his music-stool and casually looked out of the fast-darkening window, thanking his stars that it mattered little to him, in his cosy bachelor-den, whether it went on a night or a fortnight. This complacent individual was a man at whom one would be disposed to look twice before coming to any definite conclusion respecting him. At the first glance you might put him down for twenty-five; at the second, you would wonder whether you had possibly made a slight miscalculation of twenty years. His keen eyes, his smooth face, his athletic figure, his somewhat dandified dress were all in favour of the young man. The double line across his brow, the enigmas about his lips, the imperturbable gravity of his features bespoke the elder. Handsome he was not—he was hardly good-looking, and the nervous twitch of his eyebrow as it came down over his single eye-glass constantly disfigured him. What was his temper, his character, his soul, you might sit for a month before him and never discover. But from his deep massive chest, his long arms, his lithe step, and the poise of his head upon his broad shoulders, you would probably conclude that his enemy, if he had one, would do well not to frequent the same dark lane as Mr Frank Armstrong.

This afternoon, as he draws his curtain and lights his lamp, he is passably content with himself and the world; for he has just discovered a new volume of Schumann that takes his fancy. He has no quarrel, therefore, with the snow, except that by its sudden arrival it will probably hold his promising pupil, Master Roger, prisoner for the night at Castleridge, where he and his mother have driven for dinner. The tutor has sufficient interest in his work to make him regret this interruption of his duties, but for the present he will console himself with Schumann. So he returns to his music-stool—the one spot in creation where he allows that he can be really happy—and loses himself in a maze of sweet sound.

So engrossed is he in his congenial occupation, that he is quite unaware of the door behind him opening and a voice saying—

"Beg pardon, sir, but the master wants you."

Raffles, the page-boy, who happened to be the messenger, was obliged to deliver his summons three times—the last time with the accompaniment of a tap on the tutor's shoulder—before that *virtuoso* swung round on his stool and demanded—

"What is it, Raffles?"

"Please, sir, the master wants you hinstanter."

Mr Armstrong was inclined to compliment Raffles on his Latin, but on second thoughts (the tutor's second thoughts murdered a great number of his good sayings) he considered that neither the page nor himself would be much better for the jest, and spared himself.

He nodded to the messenger to go, and closing the piano, screwed his eye-glass in his eye, ready to depart.

"Please, sir," said Raffles at the door, "the governor he's dicky to-day. You'd best have your heye on 'im."

"Thank you, Raffles; I will," said the tutor, going out.

He paced the long passage which led from his quarters to the oak hall, whistling *sotto voce* a bar or two of the Schumann as he went; then his manner became sombre as he crossed the polished boards and entered the passage beyond which led to his employer's library.

Old Roger Ingleton was sitting in the almost dark room, staring fixedly into the fire. There was little light except that of the flickering embers in his dim, worn face. Though not yet seventy, his spare form was bent into the body of an old, old man, and the hands, which feebly tapped the arms of the chair on which they rested, were the worn-out members of a man long past his work. He saw little and heard less; nor was he ever to be met outside the confines of his library, or, in summer weather, the sunny balcony on to which it opened. Only when he talked were you able to realise that this worn-out body did not belong to a Tithonus, but to a man whose inward faculties were still alert and vigorous, whatever might be said of his outward failure. Could he but have been accommodated with the physical frame of a man of fifty, he had spirit enough to fill it, and become once more what he was twenty years ago, a complete man.

"Sit down, Armstrong," said he, when presently his dim eyes and ears became aware of the tutor's presence. "There's no need to light the lamp, and you need not trouble to talk, for I should not be able to hear you."

The tutor shook the eye-glass out of his eye, and seated himself at a corner of the hearth in silence.

Mr Ingleton, having thus prepared his audience, looked silently into the fire for another half-hour, until the room was dark, and all the tutor could see was a wan hand fidgeting uneasily on the arm of the chair.

Then with a weary effort the Squire turned his head and began, as if continuing a conversation.

"I have not been unobservant, Armstrong. You came at a time when Roger needed a friend. So far you have done well by him, and I am content with my choice of a tutor. What contents me more is to think you are not yet tired of your charge. I rather envy you, Armstrong. I came to grief where you succeeded. I once flattered myself I could bring up a boy—he happened to be my son, too—but—"

Here the old man resumed his gaze into the fire, and the room was as silent as the grave for a quarter of an hour. The tutor began to be uneasy. Perhaps he had yearnings for his piano and Schumann. For all that, he sat like a statue and waited. At last the Squire moved again.

"I dreaded a repetition of that, Armstrong. Had he lived—" Here he stopped again abruptly.

The tutor waited patiently for five minutes and then screwed his eye-glass into his eye.

As he did so, the old man uttered a sound very like a snore. Mr Armstrong gave an imperceptible shrug of his shoulders and inwardly meditated a retreat, when the sound came through the darkness again. There was something in it which brought the tutor suddenly to his feet. He struck a match and hastily lit a candle.

Squire Ingleton sat there just as he had sat an hour ago when the tutor found him, except that the hand on the chair-arm was quiet, and his chin sunk a little deeper in his chest. The tutor passed the candle before the old man's face, and then, scarcely less pallid than his master, rang the bell.

"Raffles," said he, as the page entered, "come here, quick. The Squire is ill."

"I said he was dicky," gasped the boy. "I knowed it whenever—"

"Hold your tongue, sir, and help me lift him to the sofa."

Between them they moved the stricken man to the couch, where he lay open-eyed, speechless, appealing.

"We must get Dr Brandram, Raffles."

"That'll puzzle you," said the boy, "a night like this, and the two 'orses at Castleridge."

"Is there any chance of your mistress returning to-night?"

"Not if Tom Robbins knows it. He's mighty tender of his 'orses, and a night like this—"

"Go and fetch the housekeeper at once," said the tutor.

Raffles vanished.

Mr Armstrong was not the man to lose his head on an emergency, but now, as he bent over the helpless paralytic, and tried to read his wants in the eyes that looked up into his, he found it needed a mighty effort to pull himself together and resolve how to act.

He must go for the doctor, five miles away. There was no one else about the place who could cover the ground as quickly. But if he went, he must leave the sufferer to the tender mercies of Raffles and the housekeeper—a prospect at which Mr Armstrong shuddered; especially when the latter self-important functionary entered, talking at large, and proposing half a dozen contradictory specifics in the short passage from the door to the sick-couch.

Mr Armstrong only delayed to suggest meekly that his impression was that a warm bath would, under the circumstances, be of benefit, and then, not waiting for the contemptuous "Much you know about it" which the suggestion evoked, he set off.

It was no light task on a night like this to plough through the snow for five miles in search of help, and the lanes to Yeld were, even in open weather, none of the easiest. But the tutor was not the kind of man to trouble himself about difficulties of that sort, provided only he could find the doctor in, and transport him in a reasonable time to Maxfield.

As he passed the stables, he glanced within, on the off-chance of finding a horse available. But the place was empty, and not even a stable-boy could be made to hear his summons.

So he tramped out into the road, where the snow lay a foot deep, and with long strides carved his way through it towards Yeld. Half a mile on he overtook a country cart, heavily laden and stuck fast in the snow.

"Ah! Hodder," said he to the nonplussed old man in charge, "you may as well give it up."

"So I are without your telling," growled the countryman.

"Very well; I want your horse for a couple of hours. The Squire's ill, and I have to fetch the doctor."

And without another word, and heedless of the ejaculations of the bewildered Hodder, he began to loose the animal's girths.

"I'm blamed if you have a hair of him," said the yokel.

"I don't want one. Here!" and he pitched him a half-crown. The man gaped stupidly at the unharnessing of his beast, and began to pump up for another protest.

But before the words were ready, Mr Armstrong had led the horse out of the shafts and had vaulted on his bare back.

"Eh," sputtered Hodder, "may I—"

"Good-bye and thanks," said the tutor, clapping his heels to the animal's flanks; "you shall have him back safe."

And he plunged away, leaving the gaping son of the soil, with his half-crown in his hand, to the laborious task of hoisting his lower jaw back into its normal position.

Dr Brandram, in whose medical preserves Maxfield Manor lay, was solacing himself with an after-dinner pipe in his little cottage at Yeld, when the tutor, crusted in snow from head to foot, broke unceremoniously on his privacy. An intuition told the doctor what was the matter before even his visitor could say—

"The Squire has had a stroke. Come at once."

The doctor put down his pipe, and, with a sigh, kicked off his cosy slippers.

"He has chosen a bad night, Armstrong. How are the roads?"

"A foot deep. Shall you drive or ride?"

"I never ride."

"You'll need both horses to get through, and I can lend you a spent third."

"Thank you. How did he look?"

"He knew what had happened, I think, but could not speak or move."

"Of course. Suppose you and I do the latter, and postpone the former till we are under weigh."

In less than ten minutes, the doctor's gig was trundling through the snow, with three horses to drag it, and Mr Armstrong in charge of the reins.

"Yes," said the doctor, "he's been leading up to this for a long time, as you have probably observed."

"I can't say I have," said Mr Armstrong.

"Ah! well, you've only known him a year. I knew him twenty years ago."

"Ah!" replied the tutor, chirruping encouragement to the horses.

"Roger Ingleton's life twenty years ago was a life to make an insurance company cheerful," said the doctor.

"What changed it?"

"He had a scape-grace son. They fell out—there was a furious quarrel—and one day the father and son—ugh!—fought, with clenched fists, sir, like two—two costermongers!—and the boy did not get the best of it. He left home, and no wonder, and was never heard of since. Faugh! it was a sickening business."

"That explains what he was saying this afternoon about a son he had once. He was telling me about it when he was struck."

"Ay! that blow has been owing him for twenty years. It is the last round of the fight, Armstrong. But," continued he, "this is all a secret. No one knows it at Maxfield. I doubt if your pupil so much as imagines he ever had a brother."

"He has never mentioned it to me," said the tutor.

"No need that he should know," said the doctor. "Let the dead bury his dead."

"Is he dead, then?"

"Before the Squire married again," said the doctor, "the poor boy went straight to the dogs, and they made an end of him. There! let's talk of something else. I don't know why I tell you what has never passed my lips for twenty years."

"I wish you hadn't," said Mr Armstrong shortly, whipping up his horses.

The two men remained silent during most of that cold, laborious journey. The doctor's few attempts at conversation fell flat, and he took refuge finally in his pipe. As for the tutor, he had his hands full, steering his team between the lane-side ditches, and thinking of the wrecked life that lay waiting at the journey's end.

It was nearly ten o'clock before the dim lights of Maxfield Manor showed ahead. The snow on the home-drive was undisturbed by the wheels of any other vehicle. The mother and son had not returned, at any rate, yet.

As the two men entered, the hall was full of scared domestics, talking in undertones, and feeding on the occasional bulletin which the privileged Raffles was permitted to carry from the sick-room to the outer world.

At the sight of the doctor and Mr Armstrong, they sneaked off grudgingly to their own territories, leaving Raffles to escort the gentlemen to the scene of the tragedy.

Old Roger Ingleton lay on the sofa, with eyes half-closed, upturned to the ceiling; alive still, but no more. Cups and wine-glasses on the table near told of the housekeeper's fruitless experiments at restoration, and the inflamed countenance of that ministering angel herself spoke ominously of the four hours during which the sufferer's comfort had been under her charge.

The tutor, after satisfying himself that his mission had not been too late, retired to the fireplace, where he leaned dismally, and watched through his eye-glass the doctor's examination.

After a few minutes, the latter walked across to him.

"Did you say Mrs Ingleton and the boy will not be back till the morning?"

"Probably not."

"If so, they will be too late; he will not last the night."

"I will fetch them," said Mr Armstrong quietly.

"Good fellow! you are having a night of it. I shall remain here; so you can take whichever of my horses you like. The mare will go best."

"Thanks!" said the tutor, pulling himself together for this new task.

Before he quitted the room, he stepped up to the couch and bent for a moment over the helpless form of his employer. There was no recognition in the glazed eyes, and the hand, which he just touched with his own, was nerveless and dead already.

With a silent nod to the doctor Mr Armstrong left the room, and was presently once more ploughing on horseback through the deep snow.

It was well this man was a man of iron and master of himself, or he might have flagged under this new effort, with the distressing prospect awaiting him at his journey's end.

As it was, he urged doggedly forward, forgetful of the existence of such an individual as Frank Armstrong, and dwelling only on the dying man behind and the mourners ahead.

The clock was chiming one in Castleridge Church when at length he reined up his spent horse at the stable entrance to the Grange. Here for a weary quarter of an hour he rang, called, and whistled before the glimmer of a lantern gave promise of an answer.

To the stable-boy's not altogether polite inquiry, Mr Armstrong replied, "Mr Ingleton of Maxfield is ill. Call Robbins, and tell him to put the horses in immediately, to take his mistress and Mr Roger home; and get some one in the house to call them. Don't delay an instant."

This peremptory speech fairly aroused the sleepy stable-boy, and in a few minutes Mr Armstrong was standing in the hall of the Grange talking to a footman.

"Take me up to his room," said he, pushing the bewildered servant before him up the staircase.

The man, not at all sure that he was not in the grip of an armed burglar, ascended the stair in a maze, not daring to look behind him.

At the end of a corridor he stopped.

"Is that the room? Give me the lamp! Go and tell your master to get up. Say a messenger has come with bad news from Maxfield; and look here — put some wraps in the carriage, and have some coffee or wine ready in the hall in ten minutes."

The fellow, greatly reassured by this short parley, went off to fulfil his instructions, while the tutor, with what was very like a sigh, opened the door and entered his pupil's bedroom.

Roger Ingleton, minor, lay sound asleep, with his arms behind his head and a smile on his resolute lips. As the light of the lamp fell on his face, it looked very pale, with its frame of black curly hair and the deep fringe of its long eyelashes; but the finely-chiselled nostrils and firm mouth redeemed it from all suspicion of weakness. Even as he slept you might judge this lad of nineteen had a will of his own hidden up in the delicate framework of his body, and resembled his father at least in this, that his outer man was too narrow a tenement for what it contained. Almost at the first flash of the light his big black eyes opened, and he started to a sitting posture, bewildered, scared.

"Oh! why, hullo, Armstrong! what's the matter?"

"I'm sorry to disturb you, Roger, but—"

The boy bounded out of bed and stood facing his tutor in his night-dress.

"But I want you to dress as sharp as you can. Your father is unwell."

"Unwell?" repeated the boy, shivering. "You do not mean he is dead?"

"No—no; but ill. He has had a stroke. Dr Brandram is with him. I thought it better not to wait till the morning before fetching you."

"Mother—does she know?"

"By this time."

"Why ever did we not go back?" groaned the boy. "Is there *any* hope, Armstrong?"

"Some—yes. Go to your mother and tell her so. The carriage will be ready in five minutes."

In five minutes the boy and his mother descended to the hall, where already their host and hostess were down to bid them farewell. It was difficult to imagine that the slender dark-eyed handsome woman, who stood there and looked round for a moment so white and trembling and bewildered, was really the mother of the young man on whose arm she leant. Even under a blow such as this Mrs Ingleton belied her age by a decade. She was still on the sunny side of forty. You and I might have doubted if she was yet thirty.

Captain Curtice and his wife had the true kindness to attempt no words as they sympathisingly bade their visitors farewell. When the hall-door opened and let in the cold blast, the poor lady staggered a moment and clung closer to her son's side. Then abandoning composure to the wintry winds, she found her best refuge in tears, and let herself be led to the carriage.

The tutor helped to put her in, and looked inquiringly at his pupil.

"Come in too, please," said the latter; "there is room inside."

Mr Armstrong would fain have taken his seat beside Robbins on the box. He hated scenes, and tears, and tragedies of all sorts. But there was something in his pupil's voice which touched him. He took his place within, and prayed that the moments might fly till they reached Maxfield.

Scarcely a word was spoken. Once Roger hazarded a question, but it was the signal for a new outburst on his mother's part; and he wisely desisted, and leant back in his corner, silent and motionless. As for the tutor, with the front seat to himself, he nursed his knee, and gazed fixedly out of the window the whole way.

What weeks those two hours seemed! How the horses laboured, and panted, and halted! And how interminably dismal was the dull muffled crunching of the wheels through the snow!

At length a blurred light passed the window, and the tutor released his knee and put up his eye-glass.

"Here we are," said he; "that was the lodge."

Roger slowly and reluctantly sat forward, and wrapped his mother's shawl closer round her.

Raffles stood on the door-step, and in the hall beyond Mr Armstrong could see the doctor standing.

As he stepped out, the page touched him on the arm.

"No 'urry," whispered he; "all over!"

Whereupon the tutor quietly crept away to the seclusion of his own room.

Chapter Two
The Living among the Dead

The household of Maxfield, worn-out by the excitement of the night, slept, or rather lay in bed, till hard on midday.

The tutor, as he slowly turned on his side and caught sight of the winter sun through the frost-bespangled window, felt profoundly disinclined to rise. He shrank from the tasks that awaited him—the task of witnessing the grief of the widow and the pale looks of the orphan heir, the dismal negotiations with undertakers and clergymen and lawyers, the stupid questions of the domestics, the sickly fragrance of stephanotis in the house. Then, too, there was the awkward uncertainty as to his own future. What effect would the tragedy of last night have on that? Was it a notice to quit, or what? He should be sorry to go. He liked the place, he liked his pupil, and further, he had nowhere else to go. Altogether Mr Armstrong felt very reluctant to exchange his easy bed for the chances and changes of the waking world. Besides, lastly, the water in his bath, he could see, was frozen; and it was hopeless on a day like this to expect that Raffles would bring him sufficient hot, even to shave with.

However, the tutor had had some little practice before now in doing what he did not like. With a sigh and a shiver, therefore, he flung aside his blankets and proceeded to break the ice literally, and take his bath. After that he felt decidedly better, and with the help of a steady ten minutes grind at the dumb-bells, he succeeded in pulling himself together.

He had reached this stage in his toilet when a knock came at the door.

"Come in, Raffles," said Mr Armstrong, beginning to see some prospect of a shave after all.

It was not Raffles, but Dr Brandram, equipped for the road.

"I'm off, Armstrong," said he. "I'd ask you to come and drive me, only I think you are wanted here. See the boy eats enough and doesn't mope. You must amuse him if you can. You understand what I told you last night was not for him. By the way,"—here the doctor held out a sealed packet—"this was lying on the old man's table last night. It was probably to give it to you that he sent for you in the afternoon, and then forgot it. Well, good-bye. I shall come to-morrow if the roads are passable. I only hope, for my sake, all this will not make any difference to your remaining at Maxfield."

Mr Armstrong finished his toilet leisurely, and then proceeded to examine the packet.

It was a large envelope, addressed, "Frank Armstrong, Esquire," in the old man's quavering hand.

Within was another envelope, firmly sealed, on which the same hand had written these words—

"*To be given unopened into the hands of Roger Ingleton, junior, on his twentieth birthday.*"

The effort of writing those few words had evidently been almost more than the writer could accomplish, for towards the end the letters became almost illegible, and the words were huddled in a heap at the corner of the paper. The sealing, too, to judge from the straggling blots of wax all over and the ineffective marks of the seal, must have been the labour of a painful morning to the feeble, half-blind old man.

To the tutor, however, as he held the missive in his hand, and looked at it with the reverence one feels for a token from the dead, it seemed to make one or two things tolerably clear.

First, that the contents, whatever they were, were secret and important, else the old man would never have taken upon himself a labour he could so easily have devolved upon another. Secondly, that this old man, rightly or wrongly, regarded Frank Armstrong as a man to be trusted, and contemplated that a year hence he would occupy the same position with regard to the heir of Maxfield as he did now.

Having arrived at which conclusions, the tutor returned the packet to its outer envelope and locked the whole up in his desk. Which done, he descended to the breakfast-room.

As he had expected, no one was there. What was worse, there was no sign either of fire or breakfast. To a man who has not tasted food for about twenty hours, such a discovery could not fail to be depressing, and Mr Armstrong meekly decided to summon Raffles to his assistance. As he passed down the passage, he could not forbear halting for a moment at the door of a certain room, behind which he knew the mortal remains of his dead employer lay. As he paused, not liking to enter, liking still less to pass on, the sound of footsteps within startled him. It was not difficult, after a moment's reflection, to guess to whom they belonged, and the tutor softly tapped on the door.

The only answer was the abrupt halting of the footsteps. Mr Armstrong entered and found his pupil.

Roger was standing in the ulster he had worn last night. His eyes were black and heavy with weariness, his face was almost as white as the face of him who lay on the couch, and as he turned to the open door his teeth chattered with cold.

"I couldn't leave him alone," whispered he apologetically, as the tutor laid a gentle hand on his arm.

"Of course—of course," replied Mr Armstrong. "I guessed it was you. Would you rather be left alone?"

"No," said the lad wearily. "I thought by staying here I should get some help—some—I don't know what, Armstrong. But instead, I'm half asleep. I've been yawning and shivering, and forgotten who was here—and—" Here his eyes filled with tears.

"Dear old fellow," said the tutor, "you are fagged out. Come and get a little rest."

Roger sighed, partly to feel himself beaten, partly at the prospect of rest.

"All right!" said he. "I'm ashamed you should see me so weak when I wanted to be strong. Yes, I'll come—in one minute."

He walked over to the couch and knelt beside it. His worn-out body had succumbed at last to the misery against which it had battled so long, and for a moment he yielded himself to his sorrow. The tutor waited a moment, and then walked quietly from the room.

For a quarter of an hour he paced restlessly in the cold passage outside; then, as his pupil did not appear, he returned to the chamber of death. Roger Ingleton, as he expected, had fallen asleep where he knelt.

The wretched days between the death and the funeral dragged on in the usual dismal fashion. Mrs Ingleton kept her room; the domestics took the occasion to neglect their work, and Roger Ingleton, minor, passed through all the stages from inconsolable misery to subdued cheerfulness. Mr Armstrong alone went through no stages, but remained the same unimpassioned individual he had been ever since he became a member of the Maxfield household.

"Armstrong," said the boy, the day before the funeral, "do you know, I'm the only male Ingleton left?"

"I didn't know it. Have you no uncles or cousins?"

"None on our side. Some distant cousins on, mother's side, but they're abroad. We were going over the lot yesterday, mother and I; but we couldn't scrape up a single relation to come to-morrow. We shall have to get you and Brandram and fathers solicitor to come to the funeral, if you don't mind."

"Of course I shall come," said Mr Armstrong.

"And, by the way, it seems rather queer, doesn't it, that I shall have charge of all this big property, and, I suppose, be master of all the people about the place."

"Naturally. Amongst your humble and obedient servants the present tutor of Maxfield will need to be included."

"Oh, you!" said Roger, smiling; "yes, you'll need to look out how you behave, you know, or I shall have to terminate our engagement. Isn't it queer?"

Queer as it was, the tutor winced at the jest, and screwed his eye-glass a little deeper into his eye.

"Seriously, though," said Roger, "I'm awfully glad I've got you here to advise me. I want to do things well about the place, and keep square with the tenants, and improve a great many things. I noticed a whole lot of cottages to-day that want rebuilding. And I think I ought to build a club-room for the young fellows in the village, and give a new lifeboat to replace the 'Vega,' What do you think?"

"I'll tell you this time to-morrow. Meanwhile what do you say to a ride before dark? It would do you good."

They had a long trot through the lanes and along the shore, ending with a canter over the downs, which landed the heir of Maxfield at home with a glow in his cheeks and an appetite such as he had not known for a week.

Next day the funeral took place in the family vault at the little churchyard of Yeld. The villagers, as in duty bound, flocked to pay their last respects to the old Squire, whose face for the last twenty years they had scarcely seen, and of whose existence, save on rent-day, many of them had been well-nigh ignorant.

Many an eye turned curiously to the slim, pale boy, as he stood alone, the last of his house, at the open tomb; and many a speculation as to his temper and prospects occupied minds which were supposed to be intent on the solemn words of the Burial Service.

Roger himself, with that waywardness of the attention which afflicts us even in the gravest acts of our life, found himself listening to the words in a sort of dream, while his mind was occupied in reading over to himself the names of his ancestors inscribed on the panels of the vault.

"John Ingleton of Maxfield Manor, who died ye ninth day of June, 1760, aetat 74."

"Peter Ingleton of Maxfield Manor, his son, obiit March 6, 1794."

"Paul Ingleton, only son of above Peter; born January 1, 1790, died September 20, 1844."

"Ruth, beloved wife of Roger Ingleton, Esquire, of Maxfield Manor, who died on February 14, 1865, aged 37."

Now a new inscription would be added.

"Roger Ingleton, son of the above-named Paul Ingleton, who died January 10, 1885."

And when that was added, there would yet be space for another name below.

Roger shuddered a little, and brought his mind back with an effort to the solemn act which was taking place.

The clergyman's voice ceased, and the fatherless lad stooped to get a last view of the flower-covered coffin. Then, with a heart lonelier than he had ever known it before, he turned away.

The people fell back and made a silent lane for him to pass.

"Poor lad," said a country wife, as she looked after him, "pity knows, he'll be this way again before long."

"Hold thy tongue," said another; "thee'd look white and shaky if thee was the only man of thy name left on earth—eh, Uncle Hodder?"

"Let un go," said the venerable proprietor of the tutor's borrowed horse last week, "let 'un go. The Ingletons was all weaklings, but they held out to nigh on threescore and ten years. All bar the best of them—there was naught weak about him, yet he dropped off in blossom-time."

"Ay, ay, poor lad," said the elder of the women in a whisper, "pity of the boy. He'd have taken the load on his shoulders to-day better than yonder white child."

"Hold thy tongue and come and take thy look at the old Squire's last lying-place."

Roger overheard none of their talk, but wandered on, lonely, but angry with himself for feeling as unemotional as he did. He told the coachman he would walk home, and started along the half-thawed lanes, hoping that the five miles solitary walk would help to bring him into a frame of mind more appropriate to the occasion.

But try as he would, his mind wandered; first to his mother; then to Maxfield and the villagers; then to his pet schemes for a model village; then to Armstrong and his studies; then to a certain pair of foils that hung in his room; then to the possibility of a yacht next summer; then to the county festivities next winter, with perhaps a ball at Maxfield; then to his approaching majority, and all the delights of unfettered manhood; then—

He had got so far at the end of a mile, when he heard steps tramping through the mud behind him.

It was Mr Armstrong.

The boy's first impulse was to put on an air of dejection he was far from feeling; but his honesty came to his rescue in time.

"Hullo, Armstrong! I'm so glad it's you. You'll never guess what I was thinking about when I heard you?"

"About being elected M.P. for the county?" asked the tutor gravely.

"How did you guess that? I tried to think about other things, you know, but—"

"Luckily you chose to be natural instead. Well, I hope you'll be elected, when the time comes."

The two beguiled their walk in talk which, if not exactly what might have been expected of mourners, at least served to restore the boy's highly-strung mind to its proper tone, and to make the aspect of things in general brighter for him than it had been when he started so dismally from the graveyard.

"Now," said he, with a sigh, as they entered the house, "now comes the awful business of reading the will. Pottinger is sure to make an occasion of it. It would be worth your while to be present to hear him perform."

"Thanks!" said the tutor; "I'll look to you for a full account of the ceremony by and by. I'll accompany it to slow music upstairs."

But as it happened, Mr Armstrong was not permitted to escape, as he had fondly hoped, to his piano. Raffles followed him presently to his room and said—

"Please, sir, Mr Pottinger sends his compliments, and will be glad if you will step down to the library, sir."

Mr Armstrong scowled.

"What does he want?" he muttered.

"He wants a gentleman or two to say 'ear, 'ear, I fancy," said the page, with a grin.

Mr Armstrong gave a melancholy glance at his piano, and screwed his glass in his eye aggressively.

"All right, Raffles; you can go."

"What does the old idiot want with me, I wonder," said he to himself, "unless it's to give me a month's notice, and tell me I may clear out? Heigho! I hope not."

With which pleasant misgivings, he strolled down-stairs.

In the library was assembled a small but select audience to do Mr Pottinger, the Yeld attorney, honour. The widow was there, looking pale but charming in her deep mourning and tasteful cap. Roger was there, restless, impatient, and a little angry at all the fuss. Dr Brandram and the Rector were there, resigned, as men who had been through ceremonies of the kind before. And a deputation of dead-servants sat on chairs near the door, gratified to be included in the party, and mentally going over their services to the testator, and appraising them in anticipation.

"We were waiting for you, Mr Armstrong," said the attorney severely, as the tutor entered.

Mr Armstrong looked not at all well pleased to be thus accosted, and walked to a seat in the bay-window behind Mr Pottinger.

The man of the law put on his glasses, took a sip of water from a tumbler he had had brought in, blew his nose, and glancing round on his audience with all the enjoyment of a man who feels himself master of the situation, began to make a little speech.

There was first a little condescending preamble concerning the virtues of the deceased, which every one but Roger listened to respectfully. The son felt it as much as he could put up with to sit still and hear it, and began to fidget ominously, and greatly to the disturbance of the speaker. When Mr Pottinger, after a few reproachful pauses, left this topic and began to discourse on his own relations with the late Squire, it was the turn of Dr Brandram to become restless.

"This is not the occasion for dwelling on the gratification I received from—"

Here the doctor deliberately rose and walked across the room for a footstool, which, as deliberately, he walked back with and laid at the feet of Mrs Ingleton. "Beg pardon—go on," said he, meeting the astonished eye of the attorney.

"The gratification I received from the kind expressions—"

Here a large coal inconsiderately fell out of the fire with a loud clamour. Raffles, with considerable commotion, came from his seat and proceeded to restore it to its lost estate.

Mr Pottinger took his glasses from his nose and regarded the performance with such abject distress, that Roger, catching sight of his face, involuntarily smiled. "Really," exclaimed the now thoroughly offended friend of the family, "really, my boy, on an occasion such as this—"

Here the Rector, to every one's relief, came gallantly to the rescue. "This is very tedious, Mr Pottinger," said he. "The friends here, I am sure, will prefer that you should omit all these useless preliminaries, and come to the business at once. Let me read the document for you; my eyes are younger than yours."

At this terrific act of insubordination, and the almost blasphemous suggestion which capped it, the lawyer fell back in his chair and broke out into a profuse perspiration, gazing at the Rector as he would at some suddenly intruding wild animal. Then, with a gasp, taking in the peril of the whole situation, he hastily took up the will and plunged into it.

It was a long, tedious document, hard to understand; and when it was ended, no one exactly grasped its purport.

Then came the moment of Mr Pottinger's revenge. The party was at his mercy after all.

"What does it all amount to?" said the doctor, interpreting the perplexed looks of the company.

"I had better perhaps explain it in simple words," said the attorney condescendingly, "if you will give me your attention."

You might have heard a pin drop now.

"Briefly, the provisions of our dear friend's will are these. Proper provision is made for the support in comfort of the widow during her life. Legacies are also left, as you have heard, to certain friends, servants, and charities. The whole of the remaining property, which it is my impression will be found to be very considerable, is left in trust for the testator's only son, Roger, our young friend here, who is to receive it absolutely on reaching the age of twenty-one. The conditions of the trust are a trifle peculiar. There are three trustees, who are also guardians of the heir. The first is Mrs Ingleton, the widow; the second is Edward Oliphant, Esquire, of Her Majesty's Indian Army, second cousin, I understand, of Mrs Ingleton, and, in the event (which I trust is not likely) of the death of our young friend here, heir-presumptive to the property. His trusteeship is dependent on his coming to this country and assuming the duties of guardian to the heir, and provision is made accordingly. The third trustee and guardian is Mr Frank Armstrong, who is entitled to act so long as he holds his present post of tutor to the heir, which post he will retain only during Mrs Ingleton's pleasure. It is also provided that, in the event of any difference of opinion among the trustees, Mrs Ingleton (as is most proper) shall be permitted to decide; and lastly—a curious eccentricity on our dear friend's part, which was perhaps hardly necessary to insert—in the event of Roger Ingleton, previous to his attaining his majority, becoming a felon, a lunatic, or marrying, he is to be regarded as dead, and the property thereby passes to the next heir, Captain Oliphant. I think we may congratulate ourselves on what is really a very simple will, and which, provided the trustees named consent to act, presents very little difficulty. I have telegraphed already to Captain Oliphant. Mr Armstrong, will you do me the favour, at your convenience, of intimating to me your consent or otherwise?"

Mr Armstrong made no response. It was indeed doubtful whether he had heard the question. For at that precise moment, gazing about him in bewilderment at the unexpected responsibility thus thrown upon him, his eyes became suddenly riveted by a picture. It was a portrait, partly concealed behind the curtain of the window in which he sat, but unveiled sufficiently to disclose the face of a fair-haired boy, younger by some years than Roger, with clear blue eyes and strong compressed mouth, somewhat sullen in temper, but with an air of recklessness and determination which, even in the portrait, fascinated the beholder. Mr Armstrong, although he had frequently been in his late employer's study, had never noticed this picture before. Now, as he caught sight of it and suddenly met the flash of those wild bright eyes, he experienced something like a shock. He could not help recalling Dr Brandram's sad story the other day. Something seemed mysteriously to connect this portrait and the story together in his mind. Strange that at such a moment, when the fate of the younger son was being decided, his guardian should thus come suddenly face to face with the elder!

Mr Armstrong was not a superstitious man, but he felt decidedly glad when a general break up of the party allowed him to get out of range of these not altogether friendly eyes, and escape to the seclusion of his own room.

Chapter Three
A Missing Inscription

A week later, Mr Pottinger, as he trotted into his office, found a letter and a telegram lying side by side on his desk.

He opened the telegram first and read —

"Bombay, January 17. Consent. Am starting, Oliphant."

"That's all right," said the lawyer to himself. "We shall have one competent executor, at any rate."

He endorsed the telegram and proceeded to open the letter. It too was a very brief communication.

> "Sir, I beg to say I accept the duties of trustee and guardian conferred on me by the will of the late Roger Ingleton, Esquire.
>
> "Yours, etcetera,
>
> "Frank Armstrong."

"Humph!" growled the attorney. "I was afraid so. Well, well, it's not my affair. The Squire knew my opinion, so my conscience is clear. An adventurer, nothing less — a dangerous man. Don't like him! Well, well!"

To do Mr Pottinger justice, this opinion of his was of no recent date. Indeed, it was of as long standing as the tutor's first arrival at Maxfield, eighteen months ago. It was one of the few matters on which he and his late client had differed.

Calmly indifferent as to the effect of his communication on the lawyer, Mr Armstrong was at that moment having an audience with his co-trustee and mistress, Mrs Ingleton.

"Mr Armstrong," said she, "I hope for all our sakes you see your way to accept the duties my dear husband requested of you."

"I have written to Mr Pottinger to notify my consent."

"I am so glad. I shall have to depend on you for so much. It will be so good for Roger to have you with him. His father was always anxious about him—most anxious. You know, Mr Armstrong," added she, "if there is any—any question as to salary, or anything I can do to make your position here comfortable, you must tell me. For Roger's sake I am anxious you should be happy here."

"Thank you, madam. I am most comfortable," said Mr Armstrong, looking anything but what he described himself. He had a detestation of business interviews, and wished profoundly he was out of this.

"I am sure you will like Captain Oliphant," said the widow. "I have not seen him for many years—indeed, since shortly after Roger was born; but we have heard from him constantly, and Mr Ingleton had a high opinion of him. He is a very distant cousin of mine, you know."

"So I understand."

"Poor fellow! his wife died quite young. His three children will be quite grown up now, poor things. Well, thank you very much, Mr Armstrong. I hope we shall always be good friends for dear Roger's sake. Good-bye."

Roger, as may be imagined, had not waited a whole week before ascertaining his tutor's intentions.

He had been a good deal staggered at first by his father's will, with its curious provisions; but, amongst a great deal that was perplexing and disappointing in it, he derived no little comfort from the fact that Mr Armstrong was to be one of his legal protectors.

"I don't see, you know," said he, as he lounged against his tutor's mantelpiece one evening. "I don't see why a fellow of nineteen can't be trusted to behave himself without being tied up in this way. It's my impression I know as well how to behave now as I am likely to do when I am twenty-one."

"That is a reflection in advance on my dealings with you during the next two years," said the tutor with a grin, as he swung himself half round on the piano-stool so as to get his hand within reach of the keys.

"I don't mind *you*," said the boy, "but I hope this Cousin Edward, or whoever he is, won't try to 'deal' with me too."

"I am informed he is virtue and amiability itself," said the tutor.

"If he is, all serene. I'll take my walks abroad with one little hand in yours, and the other in his, like a good boy. If he's not, there'll be a row,

Armstrong. In anticipation of which I feel in the humour for a turn at the foils."

So they adjourned into the big empty room dedicated to the manly sports of the man and his boy, and there for half an hour a mortal combat raged, at the end of which Roger pulled off his mask and said, panting—

"Where did you learn foils, Armstrong? For a year I've been trying to run you through the body, and I've never even yet scratched your arm."

"I fenced a good deal at Oxford."

"Ah! I wonder if I shall ever go to Oxford? This will cuts me out of that nicely."

"Not at all. How?"

"Well, you can't be my tutor here while I'm an undergraduate there, can you? I'd sooner give up Oxford than you, Armstrong."

"Kind of you—wrong of you too, perhaps. But at twenty-one you'll be your own master."

"I may not be in the humour then. Besides, I shall have my hands full of work here then. It's hard lines to have to kick my heels in idleness for two years, while I've so many plans in my head for improving the place, and to have to ask your leave to spend so much as a halfpenny."

"It is rather tragic. It strikes me, however, that Cousin Edward will be the financial partner of our firm. I shall attend to the literary part of the business."

"And poor mother has to umpire in all your squabbles. Upon my word, why couldn't I have been treated like a man straight off, instead of being washed and dressed and fed with a spoon and wheeled in a perambulator by three respectable middle-aged persons, who all vote me a nuisance."

"In the first place, Roger Ingleton, I am not yet middle-aged. In the second place, I do not vote you a nuisance. In the third place, if you stand there much longer like that, with your coat off, you will catch your death of cold, which would annoy me exceedingly."

This was one of many conversations which took place. It was difficult to say whether Mr Armstrong took his new duties seriously or not. He generally contrived to say something flippant about them when his pupil tackled him on the subject, but at the same time he rarely failed to give the boy a hint or two that somewhere hidden away behind the cool, odd exterior of the man, there lurked a very warm corner for the fatherless heir of Maxfield.

For the next week or two the days passed uneventfully. The manor-house settled down to its old routine, minus the old man who had once been its master. The villagers, having satisfied themselves that things were likely to be pretty much the same for them under the new *régime* as the old, resumed their usual ways, and touched their caps regularly to the young Squire. The trampled grass in Yeld churchyard lifted its head again, and a new inscription was added to the family roll on the door of the vault.

"Armstrong," said the heir one day, as he stood inspecting this last memorial, "I have a good mind to have my brother's name put on here too."

This was the first time the tutor had ever heard the boy mention his brother. Indeed, he had, like Dr Brandram, doubted whether Roger so much as knew that he had had a brother.

"What brother?" he inquired vaguely.

"Oh, he died long ago, before I was born. He was the son of father's first wife, you know," pointing to the inscription of Ruth Ingleton's name. "He is not buried here—he died abroad, I believe—but I think his death should be recorded with the others. Don't you?"

"Certainly," said the tutor.

"I must try to find the exact date," said Roger as they walked away. "My father would hardly ever talk about him; his death must have been a knock-down blow to him, and I believe it broke his mother's heart. Sometimes I wish he had lived. He was called Roger too. I dare say Brandram or the Vicar can tell me about it."

Mr Armstrong was a good deal concerned at this unexpected curiosity on the boy's part. He doubted whether it would not be better to tell him the sad story at once, as he had heard it from the doctor. He disliked secrets extremely, especially when he happened to be the custodian of them; and painful as the discovery of this one might be to his ward, it might be best that he should know it now, instead of hovering indefinitely in profitless mystery.

It was, therefore, with some sense of relief that, half-way home, he perceived Dr Brandram in the road ahead. The doctor was, in fact, bound for Maxfield.

"By the way, doctor," said the tutor, determined to take the bull by the horns, and glaring at his friend rather fiercely through his eye-glass, "we were talking about you just now. Roger has been telling me about an elder brother of his who died long ago and thinks some record of the death should be made on the vault. I think so too."

"I was saying," said Roger, "my father never cared to talk about it; so, except that he died abroad, and that his name was the same as mine, I really don't know much about him. Did you know him?"

The doctor looked uncomfortable, and not altogether grateful to Mr Armstrong for landing him in this dilemma.

"Don't you think," said he, ignoring the last question, "as the Squire did not put up an inscription, it would be better to leave the tomb as it is?"

"I don't see that," said the boy. "Of course I should say where he really did die. Where was that, by the way?"

"I really did not hear. Abroad, I understood your father to say."

"Was he delicate, then, that he had to go away? How old was he, doctor?"

"Upon my word, he was so seldom at home, and, when he was, I saw so little of him, that my memory is very hazy about him altogether. He can't have been more than a boy of fifteen or sixteen, I should say. By the way, Roger, how does the new cob do?"

"Middling. He's rather lumpy to ride. I shall get mother to swop him for a horse, if she can. I say, doctor, what was he like?"

"Who?—The cob? Oh, your brother! I fancy he was a fine young fellow, but not particularly good-looking."

"At all like me?"

"Not at all, I should say. But really, as I say, I can recall very little about him."

The doctor uttered this in a tone which conveyed so broad a hint that he did not relish the subject, that Roger, decidedly mystified, desisted from further inquiries.

"What on earth," said the former to Mr Armstrong, when at last they had reached Maxfield and the boy had left them, "what on earth has put all this into his head?"

"I cannot tell you. I rather hoped you would tell him all you knew; it would come better from you. If I know anything of Roger, he will find it out for himself, whether you like it or not."

"Nice thing to be a family doctor," growled Dr Brandram, "and have charge of the family skeletons. Between you and me, Armstrong, I was never quite satisfied about the story of the boy's death abroad. The old man said he had had news of it, and that was all anybody, even the poor mother, ever got out of him."

"Really, Brandram," said the tutor, "you are a most uncomfortable person. I wish you would not make me a party to these mysteries. I don't like them, they are upsetting."

"Well, well, old fellow," replied the doctor, "whatever it was once, it's no mystery now; for the poor fellow has long ago made good his right to an inscription on the tombstone. You need have no doubt of that."

A letter with an Indian post-mark, which arrived that same evening, served for the present, at least, to divert the thoughts of Roger as well as of his tutor to other channels.

The letter was from Captain Oliphant addressed to Mrs Ingleton.

"My very dear cousin," it read, "need I say with what deep sympathy I received the news of our dear Roger's sudden call? At this great distance, blows of this kind fall with cruel heaviness, and I assure you I felt crushed as I realised that I should no more grasp the hand of one of the noblest men it has been my privilege to call by the name of friend. If my loss is so great, what must *yours* be? I dare not think of it! I was truly touched by our dear one's thought of me in desiring that I should join you in the care of his orphaned boy. I regard this dying wish as a sacred trust put upon me, which gratitude and love alike require that I should accept. Ere this letter reaches you, I shall myself be nearing England. The provision our dear Roger has made has emboldened me to resign my commission, so that I may devote my whole time without distraction to my new charge. You know, dear cousin, the special bond of sympathy that unites us; your boy has been robbed of a parent; my children long since have had to mourn a mother. I cannot leave them here. They accompany me to England, where perhaps for all of us there awaits a community of comfort. I bespeak your motherly heart for them, as I promise you a father's affection for your boy. I will write no more at present. The 'Oriana' is due in London, I believe, about February 20, and we shall, I need hardly assure you, not linger long before bringing in our own persons to Maxfield whatever sympathy four loving hearts can carry amongst them.

"With love to the dear boy, believe me, dear cousin, your loving and sympathising fellow-mourner,—

"Edward Oliphant."

Mrs Ingleton, highly gratified, handed the beautiful letter first to her son, then to Mr Armstrong.

Roger was hardly as taken with it as his mother.

"Civil enough," said he, "and I dare say he means all he says; but I don't warm to the prospect of being cherished by him. Besides, there is something a trifle too neat in the way he invites his whole family to Maxfield. What do you think, Armstrong?"

Mr Armstrong was perusing the letter with knitted brows and a curl of his lips. He vouchsafed no reply until he had come to the end. Then he shook the glass ominously out of his eye and said—

"I'll tell you that when I see him."

Roger knew his tutor well enough to see that he did not like the letter at all, and he felt somewhat fortified in his own misgivings accordingly.

"I wonder what mother will do with them all?" said the boy. "Surely we aren't to have the place turned into a nursery for two years."

"I understand the young people are more than children," said the tutor.

"So much the worse," growled Roger.

On the morning before the "Oriana" was due, Mrs Ingleton suggested to her son that it would be a polite thing if he were to go to town and meet the travellers on their arrival. Roger, not particularly charmed with the prospect, stipulated that Mr Arm strong should come with him, and somewhat shocked his fond parent by expressing the hope that the vessel might be a few days late, and so allow time for a little jaunt in London before the arrival of his new guardian.

Mr Armstrong meekly acquiesced in the proposal, and scarcely less exhilarated than his pupil, retired to pack for the journey.

Roger meanwhile occupied the interval before starting by writing a letter in the study. Since his father's death he had taken quiet possession of this room, one of the pleasantest in the house. A feeling of reverence for the dead had prompted him to disturb its contents and furniture as little as possible, and hitherto his occupation had scarcely extended beyond the arm-chair at the fire, and the writing-table. To-day, however, as he sat biting his pen and looking for an inspiration out of the window, his eye chanced to rest for a moment on a frame corner peeping from behind a curtain. He thought nothing of it for a while, and having found his idea, went on writing. But presently his eyes strayed again, and once more lit upon the misplaced piece of gilding.

He went over mechanically to adjust it, pondering his letter all the while.

"Why ever can't they hang things where they can be seen?" said he as he drew back the curtain.

The last words dropped half-spoken from his lips, as he disclosed the portrait of a certain boy, flashing at him with his reckless eyes, and half-defying him out of the canvas.

Like Mr Armstrong, when he had encountered the picture a month ago, Roger Ingleton instinctively guessed in whose presence he stood.

The discovery had something in it both of a shock and a disappointment. If this was really his elder brother, he was strangely different from what he had in fancy pictured him. He had imagined him his own age, whereas this was a boy considerably his junior. He had imagined him dark and grave, whereas this was fair and mocking; and he had imagined him amiable and sympathetic, whereas this was hostile and defiant.

Yet, for all that, Roger stood fascinated. A chord deep in his nature thrilled as he said to himself, "My brother." He, the young man, felt himself captive to this imperious boy. He wished he knew the mind of the picture, or could hear its voice. What were the eyes flashing at? At whom or what were the lips thus curled? Was it wickedness, or anger, or insolence, or all together, that made the face so unlike any other face he knew?

How long he spent over these speculations, half afraid, half enamoured of the picture, he could not say. He forgot all about his letter; nor did he finally descend from the clouds till a voice behind him said—

"What have you got there, old fellow?"

"Oh, Armstrong," said the boy, turning round hurriedly, like one detected in mischief, "look here at this picture."

The tutor was looking.

"Who is it?" he asked.

"My elder brother, I'm sure. I didn't know we had it."

"There's not much family likeness in it," said Mr Armstrong. "Are you sure it is he?"

"I feel positive of it. Stay, perhaps there's something written on the back," and he lifted the picture from the nail.

The paper at the back was almost black with dust and age. They wiped it carefully with a duster, and took it to the window.

"No," said Roger, "nothing there."

"Yes," said the tutor, "what's this?"

And he pointed out a few faint marks in very faded ink, which, after considerable trouble, they deciphered.

> "R.I., born 3 September 1849, died 186—," (the last figure was illegible).

"That settles it," said Roger, "all except the exact date when he died. Upon my word, I'm quite glad it is my brother after all. I shouldn't have liked if he'd turned out any one else."

"Do you know," added he, as he was about to replace the picture, "I think I shall take it up to my room. I've taken rather a fancy to him."

That afternoon the two friends took the train to London, where, considerably to the relief of both, they heard that the "Oriana" was not expected in dock for three days.

Chapter Four
Acquaintances New and Old

Roger's projected jaunt in London did not turn out as satisfactorily as he had anticipated, as he caught a heavy cold on the first day, which kept him a prisoner in his hotel. Mr Armstrong needed all his authority to restrain the invalid within bounds; and it was only by threatening to convey him bodily home that the boy consented to nurse himself. Even so, it was as much as he could do to shake off his cold sufficiently on the morning of the arrival of the "Oriana" to accompany his tutor to the Dock to greet his unknown kinsfolk.

As he shouldered his way on board over the crowded gangway, he found himself speculating somewhat nervously as to which of the numerous passengers standing about the deck was his new guardian. Was it the ferocious man with the great black beard who was swearing at his Indian servant in a voice loud enough to be heard all over the ship? Or was it the dissipated-looking fellow who walked unsteadily across the motionless ship, and finally clung for support to the deck railings? Or was it the discontented-looking little person who scowled at the company at large from the bridge? Or was it the complacent man with the expansive presence and leonine head, who smoked a big cigar and was exchanging a few effusive farewells with a small group of fellow-voyagers?

Roger accosted one of the stewards—

"Will you please tell Captain Oliphant that Mr Roger Ingleton is on board, with Mr Armstrong, and would like to see him?"

The man gave a look up and down and went straight to the expansive person before mentioned.

The visitors could see the gentleman start a little as the steward delivered his message, and pitch his cigar away as, with a serious face, he walked in their direction.

"My poor dear boy," said he, taking Roger's hand, "this *is* good of you—very good. How glad I am to see you! How is your dear mamma?"

"Mother is very well. Have you had a good voyage? Oh, this is Mr Armstrong."

Mr Armstrong all this while had been staring through his eye-glass at his co-trustee in no very amiable way, and now replied to that gentleman's greeting with a somewhat stiff "How do you do?" "Where on earth did I see you before, my gentleman?" said he to himself, and having put the riddle, he promptly gave it up.

Mr Oliphant displayed very little interest in his fellow-guardian, but said to Roger—

"The children will be so delighted to see you. We have talked so much of you. They will be here directly; they are just putting together their things in the cabin. But now tell me all about yourself, my boy."

Roger did not feel equal to this comprehensive task, and said, "I suppose you'll like to go straight on to Maxfield, wouldn't you?"

"Oh, yes! It may be a day before we get our luggage clear, so we will come to your hotel to-night and go on to-morrow. Why, my boy, what a cough you have! Ah! here comes Rosalind."

The figure which approached the group was that of a young lady about seventeen years of age, tall and slim, clad in a loose cloak which floated about her like a cloud, and considerably encumbered with sundry shawls and bags on one arm, a restive dog in another, and a hat which refused to remain on her head in the wind.

Mr Armstrong was perhaps no great connoisseur of female charms, but he thought, as he slowly tried to make up his mind whether he should venture to assist her, that he had rarely seen a more interesting picture.

Her face was flushed with the glow of youth and health. An artist might have found fault with it here and there, but to the tutor it seemed completely beautiful. The fine poise of her head upon the dainty neck, the classic cut of mouth and nostril, the large dark liquid eyes, the snowy forehead, the short clustering wind-tossed hair, the frank countenance, the refinement in every gesture—all combined to astonish the good man into admiration. Yet, with all his admiration, he felt a little afraid of this radiant apparition. Consequently, by the time he had half decided to advance to her succour, his ward had stepped forward and forestalled him.

"Let me help you, Cousin Rosalind," said Roger.

She turned on him a look half surprise, half pleasure, and then allowing him to take cloaks, bags, dog, and all, said—

"Really, papa, you must go and help down in the cabin. It's an awful chaos, and Tom and Jill are making it ten times worse. Do go." And she sat down with a gesture of despair on one of the benches, and proceeded to adjust her unruly hat. While doing this she looked up at Roger, who stood meekly before her with her belongings.

"Thanks! Don't mind holding them; put them down anywhere, Roger, and do, there's a dear boy, go and help father and the others in that horrid, horrid cabin."

Roger, more flurried and docile than he had felt himself for a long while, dropped the baggage, and thrusting the dog into Armstrong's hands, flew off to obey the behests of his new cousin.

The young lady now looked up in charming bewilderment at the tutor, who could not fail to read the question in her eyes, and felt called upon to answer it.

"May I introduce myself?" said he. "I am Frank Armstrong, Roger's tutor."

"I'm so glad," said she with a little laugh. "I'd imagined you a horrid elderly person with a white cravat and tortoise-shell spectacles. It *is* such a relief!"

And she sighed at the mere recollection of her forebodings.

"There's no saying what we may become in time," said Mr Armstrong.

"I suppose," said she, eyeing him curiously once more, "you're the other trustee, or whatever it's called? I hope you and father will get on well. I can't see what use either of you can be. Roger looks as if he could take care of himself. Are you awfully fond of him?"

"I am rather," said the tutor in a voice which quite satisfied his hearer.

"Heigho!" said she presently, picking up the dog and stroking its ears. "I'm glad this dreadful voyage is over. Mr Armstrong, what do they all think about all of us coming to Maxfield? If I lived there, I should hate it."

"Mrs Ingleton, I know, is very pleased."

"Yes, but you men aren't. There'll be fearful rows, I know. I wish we'd stayed behind in India. It's hateful to be stuck down where you aren't wanted, for every one to vote you a nuisance!"

"I can hardly imagine any one voting *you* a nuisance," said Mr Armstrong, half-frightened at his own temerity.

She glanced up with a little threatening of a blaze in her eyes. "Don't!" said she. "That's the sort of thing the silly young gentlemen say on board ship. I don't like it."

The poor tutor winced as much under this rebuff as if he had been just detected in a plot to run away with his fair companion; and having nothing to say in extenuation of his crime, he relapsed into silence.

Miss Oliphant, apparently unaware of the effect of her little protest, stroked her dog again and said—

"Are you an artist?"

"No; are you?"

"I want to be. I'd give anything to get out of going to Maxfield, and have a room here in town near the galleries. It will be awful waste of time in that dull place."

"Perhaps your father—" began the tutor; but she took him up half angrily.

"My father intends us to stay at Maxfield. In fact, you may as well know it at once, and let Roger know it too. We're as poor as church-mice, and can't afford to do anything else. Oh, how I wish we had stopped where we were!" And her voice actually trembled as she said the words.

It was an uncomfortable position for Mr Armstrong. Once again his mother-wit failed him, and he watched the little hand as it moved up and down the dog's back in silence.

"I tell you this," continued the young lady, "because tutors are generally poor, and you'll understand it. I wish papa understood it half as well. I do believe he really enjoys the prospect of going and landing himself and all of us at that place."

"You forget that it is by the desire and invitation of the old Squire," said the tutor.

"Father might easily have declined. He ought to have. He wasn't like you, fond of Roger. He doesn't care—at least I fancy he doesn't—much about Roger at all. Oh, I wish I could earn enough to pay for every bite every one of us eats!"

To the tutor's immense relief, at this point Captain Oliphant reappeared, followed by Roger with a boy and little girl.

The boy was some years the junior of the heir of Maxfield, a rotund, matter-of-fact, jovial-looking lad, sturdy in body, easy in temper, and perhaps by no means brilliant in intellect. The turmoil of debarkation failed to ruffle him, and the information given him in sundry quarters that he was the *fons et origo* of all the confusion in the cabin failed to impress him. Everything that befell Tom Oliphant came in the day's work, and would probably vanish with the night's sleep. Meanwhile it was the duty of every one, himself included, to be jolly. So he accepted his father's chidings and Roger's greetings in equally good part; agreed with every word the former said, and gave in his allegiance to the latter with one and the same smile, and thought to himself how jolly to be in England at last, and perhaps some day to see the Oxford and Cambridge boat-race.

The little maid who tripped at his side was perhaps ten or eleven—an odd blending of the sister's beauty and alertness with the brother's vigorous contentment. A prophet, versed in such matters, would have predicted that ten years hence Miss "Jill" Oliphant might seriously interfere with the shape of her elder sister's nose. But as no prophets were present, only a fogey like Mr Armstrong and an inexperienced boy like Roger, no one concerned themselves about the future, but voted the little lady of ten a winsome child.

"Well, thanks for all *your* help," said Tom to his elder sister. "I don't know what we should have done without her. Eh, Roger?"

"Upon my word, with *you* in charge down there," retorted the young lady, "I wouldn't have been safe in that awful place a minute longer. I wonder you haven't packed up Jill in one of the trunks."

"Oh, Cousin Roger took care of me," said Miss Jill demurely.

"I hope Armstrong did the same to you, Rosalind," said Roger. "Here, Tom; this is my tutor, Frank Armstrong—a brick. Here, Jill; say how do you do to Mr Armstrong."

Jill horrified Mr Armstrong by putting up her face to be kissed. Indeed the poor gentleman as he shook the glass out of his eye and gazed down at this forward young person in consternation, presented so pitiable a spectacle, that Rosalind, Roger, and Tom all began to laugh.

"She won't bite," said Tom reassuringly.

Mr Armstrong, thus encouraged, took off his hat, and stooping down, kissed the child on the brow, much to that little lady's satisfaction. This important operation performed, Captain Oliphant expressed concern for Roger's cough, and proposed that his ward should take the girls and himself to the hotel, while no doubt Mr Armstrong would not mind remaining to help Tom with the luggage. By which excellent arrangement the party succeeded at last in getting clear of the "Oriana."

The tutor had his hands full most of that morning Tom Oliphant's idea of looking after the luggage was to put his hands in his pockets and whistle pleasantly up and down the upper deck; nor was it till Mr Armstrong took him bodily below, and made him point out one by one the family properties (among which, by the way, he included several articles belonging to other owners), that he could be reduced to business at all.

Then for half an hour he worked hard; at the end of which time he turned to his companion with a friendly grin.

"Thanks awfully, Mr Armstrong. I say, I wonder if you'll be my tutor as well as Frank's? I heard father say something about it! Wouldn't it be stunning?"

Mr Armstrong gave a qualified assent.

"I'm not a bit clever, you know, like Rosalind, but I'd like to have a tutor awfully. I say, haven't we done enough with these blessed boxes? They'll be all right now. Should we have time to see Christy's Minstrels on our way to the hotel, do you think? I'd like it frightfully."

"My dear boy," said Mr Armstrong, "if we are to get all the things properly cleared and labelled and sent off to Maxfield, we shall have no time for anything else. If the way you stick to your lessons is anything like the way you stick to this task, I don't envy your tutor."

This covert threat at once reduced Tom to a sense of discipline, and he made a gallant effort to secure Mr Armstrong's good opinion.

The tutor was right. It was well on in the afternoon when they had the baggage finally disposed of, and were free to follow to the hotel.

Here they found, instead of the party they expected, a hurriedly scrawled line from Roger.

"Dear Armstrong,—

"Oliphant has taken it into his head to go down to Maxfield at once by the two train. So we are starting. I'm sorry he can't wait, so as all to go together. If you are back in time to come by the evening train, do come. If not, first train in the morning.

"Yours ever,

"R.I."

It was too late to get a train that day; so Mr Armstrong, much disgusted, had to make up his mind to remain. Tom, on the contrary, was delighted, and proposed twenty different plans for spending the evening, which finally resolved themselves into the coveted visit to Christy's Minstrels.

The tutor, in no very festive humour, allowed himself to be overborne by the eagerness of his young companion, and found himself in due time jammed into a seat in a very hot hall, listening to the very miscellaneous performance of the coloured gentlemen who "never perform out of London."

The tutor, who had some ideas of his own on the subject of music, listened very patiently, sometimes pleased, sometimes distressed, and always conscious of the enthusiastic delight of his companion, whose unaffected comments formed to him the most amusing part of the entertainment.

"Isn't that, stunning?"

"Thanks awfully, Mr Armstrong, for bringing me."

"Hooray! Bones again!"

"I say, I'm looking forward to the break-down; ain't you?" and so on.

Whatever Mr Armstrong's anticipations may have been as to the rapture of the coming "break-down," he contained himself admirably, and with his glass inquiringly stuck in his eye, listened attentively to all that went on, and occasionally speculated as to how Miss Rosalind Oliphant was enjoying her visit to Maxfield.

The programme was half over, and Tom was repairing the ravages of nature with a bun, when Mr Armstrong became suddenly aware of a person in the row but one in front looking round fixedly in his direction.

To judge by the close-cropped, erect hair and stubbly chin of this somewhat disreputable-looking individual, he was a foreigner; and when presently, catching the tutor's eye, he began to indulge in pantomimic gestures of recognition, it was safe to guess he was a Frenchman.

"Who's that chap nodding to you?" said Tom with his mouth full. "Is he tipsy?"

"He lays himself open to the suspicion," said Mr Armstrong slowly. "At any rate, as I vote we go put and get some fresh air, he will have to find some one else to make faces at. Come along."

Tom did not at all like risking his seat, and particularly charged the lady next to him to preserve it from invasion at the risk of her life.

Then wondering a little at Mr Armstrong's impatience to reach the fresh air, he followed him out.

The Frenchman witnessed the proceeding with some little disappointment, and sat craning his neck in the direction in which they had gone for some minutes. Then, as if moved by a similar yearning for fresh air, he too left his seat and went out.

The band was beginning to play as he did so, and most of the loiterers were crowding back for the second part.

"You go in; I'll come directly," said Mr Armstrong to the boy.

Tom needed no second invitation, and a moment later had forgotten everything in the delightful prelude to the "break-down." He did not even observe that Mr Armstrong had not returned to his seat.

"Well, Gustav," said that gentleman in French as the foreigner approached him, where he waited in the outer lobby.

"*Eh bien, man cher,*" replied the other, "'ow 'appy I am to see you. I can speak ze Englise foine, *n'est ce pas?*"

"What are you doing in London?"

"I am vaiter, *garçon* at ze private hotel. 'Zey give me foods and drinks and one black coat, but not no vage. *Oh, mon ami,* it is ver' ver' 'ard."

"And the old man?"

"*Ah, hélas*! he is ver' ver' ill. He vill die next week. *Moi,* I can not to him go; and Marie, she write me she must leave Paris this day to her duties. It is sad for the poor old *père* to die with not von friend to 'old 'is 'and. Ah! if ze petite Françoise yet lived, *ma pauvre enfant,* she would stay and—"

"Stop!" said the tutor imperatively. "Is he still in the old place?"

"*Hélas,* non! you make ze joke, you. Ve are ver' ver' poor, and 'ave no homes. *Mon père,* he is to the hôpital. Thank 'eaven, they 'ave zere give 'im ze bed to die."

"Which hospital is he at?" said the tutor.

"De Saint Luc."

"I will see him."

The Frenchman gave a little hysterical laugh; then, with tears in his eyes, he seized the hand of the Englishman and wrung it rapturously.

"*Oh, mon ami, mon cher ami!*" cried he, "'eaven will bless you. I am 'appy that you say that. You vill see 'im? Yes? You vill 'old 'is 'and ven he do die? He sall have one friend to kiss his poor *front*? Oh, I am content; I am gay."

How long he would have gone on thus it is hard to say. Mr Armstrong cut short the scene rather abruptly.

"There, there!" said he. "Good-bye, Gustav. I shall go very soon, and will come and see you when I return." And he went back to the performance.

"You've missed it!" said Tom, as he dropped into his seat. "It was the finest 'break-down' you ever saw! That one next but one to Bones kept it up best. We couldn't get an encore out of them. Never mind; perhaps they'll have another to finish up. There's lot's more in the programme."

Mr Armstrong watched it all with the same critical interest as before, but his mind was far away. It wandered to the foreign city, to the gaunt pauper hospital there, to a little low bed where lay an old dying friendless man, tossing and moaning for the laggard death to give him rest. He saw nothing of what went on before him; he felt none of the merry boy's nudges at his side; he even forgot Roger and Maxfield.

The performance was over at last.

"Well, that *was* a jolly spree! I wish it was coming all over again," chirped the boy. "Oh, thank you awfully, Mr Armstrong, for bringing me. Did you like it too? That last break-down wasn't up to the other, but I'm glad you've seen one of them, at any rate."

As they crowded out, Mr Armstrong was surprised and a little vexed to see Gustav still hanging about the lobby waiting for him. He dropped behind the boy for a moment and beckoned him.

"Well, Gustav?" said he impatiently.

"Ah, *mon ami*," said the Frenchman, putting a little bunch of early violets into the tutor's hands, "vill you give 'im zese from me? 'Tis all I can send. But he will love zem for the sake of me and ze little Françoise. Adieu, adieu, *mon cher ami*."

It took not a minute; but in that time Tom had wandered serenely on, never dreaming that his protector was not close at his heels. Nor did he discover his mistake till he found himself half-way up Piccadilly, enlarging to a stranger at his side on the excellence of the evening's performance. Then he looked round and missed his companion. The pavement was crowded with wayfarers of all sorts, some pressing one way, some another. Among them all the boy could not discover the stalwart form of Mr Armstrong. He pushed back to the hall, but he was not there. He followed one or two figures that looked like his; but they were strangers all. Then he returned up the street at a run, hoping to overtake him; but in vain.

He knew nothing of London; he did not even know the name of the hotel; he had no money in his pocket.

He was, in short, lost.

As for Mr Armstrong, not seeing his charge at the door, he had started to run in the direction of the hotel, which was the opposite direction to that taken by Tom. Seeing no sign of the prodigal, he too returned to the hall, just after Tom had started a second time on the contrary tack; and so for an hour these two played hide and seek; sometimes almost within reach of one another; at others, with the whole length of the street between them.

At last the crowd on the pavement thinned, and the tutor, sorely chagrined, started off to the hotel, on the chance of the boy having turned up there. No Tom was there. Tom, in fact, was at that moment debating somewhere about a mile and a half away whether he should not try to make his way to the "Oriana" at the Docks, and remain quietly there till claimed. What a joke it would all be when he *was* found! What an adventure for his first night in London!

It was not very easy even for Tom Oliphant to derive much amusement from these philosophical reflections, and he looked about him rather dismally for some one of whom to inquire his way.

A seedy-looking person was standing under a lamppost hard by, trying to light a cigarette in the wind. Tom decided to tackle him.

"Please can you tell me the way to the Docks where the P and O steamers come in?" said he.

The man let drop his match and stared at the boy.

"Vy," said he with an odd shrug, "that is some long walks from here. *Mais, comment.* Vas you not at ze Christy Minstrel to-night viz a nice gentleman?"

"Rather!" said the boy. "Were you there? I say, wasn't it a clipping turn out? I did like it, especially the break-down. I say, I'm lost. The fellow who was looking after me has lost me."

"Oh, you 'ave lost 'im. I am 'appy you to find. You sall not valk to ze Dock, no. I sall give you sleeps at ze hotel, and to-morrow you sall find zat dear gentleman. Come wiz me."

"Oh, but you know, he'll be looking for me; besides, I've got no tin. Father forgot to leave me any. I'd better go to the Docks, I say."

"You sall not. Zey will be all shut fast zere. No, my dear friend, you sall come sleep at my hotel, and you sall have nothings to pay. It will be all right. I would die for to help ze friend of my friend."

"Is Mr Armstrong a friend of yours?" asked the boy. "I thought you were only cheeking him that time in the Hall. Oh, all right, if you know him. Thanks awfully."

Gustav, as delighted as a cat who has found her kitten, led the boy off jubilantly to his third-rate hotel off the Strand, taking the precaution, as he passed, to leave word at the Hall that if a gentleman called who had lost a boy, he should be told where he would find him.

He smuggled Tom up to his own garret, and made him royally welcome with three-quarters of his scanty supper and the whole of his narrow bed, sleeping himself on the floor cheerfully for the sake of the *cher ami* who had that night promised to go to Paris to hold the hand of his dying father.

About three in the morning there was a loud ringing of the bell and a sound of steps and voices on the stairs, and presently Mr Armstrong entered the room.

Gustav sprang up with his finger on his lips, pointing to the sleeping boy.

"Oh, *mon ami*," whispered he, "'ow 'appy I am you 'ave found 'im. But I keep him ver' safe. I love to do it, for you are ver' good to me and the *pauvre père*. He sall rest here till to-day, vile you (hélas! that I have no two beds to offer you), you sall take one in ze hotel, and at morning we sall all be 'appy together."

Mr Armstrong grimly accepted this proposal, and took a room for the night at Gustav's hotel.

The next morning, scarcely waiting to take breakfast or bid another adieu to his grateful friend, he hurried the genial Tom, who had enjoyed himself extremely, to the station, and carried him down by express train to Maxfield.

Chapter Five
A Churchyard Cough

When Mr Armstrong with his jovial charge arrived about midday at Maxfield, he was struck with the transformation scene which had taken place since he quitted it gloomily a day or two before.

The house was the same, the furniture was untouched, the ordinary domestic routine appeared to be unaltered, but a sense of something new pervaded the place which he could interpret only by the one word—Oliphant.

The captain had made a touching entry—full of sympathy, full of affection, full of a desire to spare his dear cousin all business worry, full of the responsibility that was on him to take charge of the dear fatherless boy, full of that calm sense of duty which enables a man to assert himself on all occasions for the good of those committed to his care. As for his charming daughters, they had floated majestically into their quarters—Miss Rosalind a trifle defiantly, making no secret of her dislike of the whole business; Miss Jill merrily, delighted with the novelty and beauty of this new home, so much more to her mind than the barrack home in India. And Roger, despite all his sinister anticipations, found himself tolerant already of the new guardian, and more than tolerant of his *suite*.

For somehow his pulses had taken to beating a little quicker since yesterday, and when half a dozen times that evening he had heard a summons down the landing to come and hang this picture, or like a dear boy unfasten that strap, or like an angel come and make himself agreeable, unless he intended his cousins to sit by themselves all the evening as penance for coming where they were not wanted,—at all such summonses Roger Ingleton had experienced quite a novel sensation of nervousness and awkwardness, which contributed to make him very uncomfortable.

"Why," said he, as he and his tutor greeted one another again in Mr Armstrong's room, "why, it seems ages since I saw you, and yet it's only yesterday. I wish we could all have come down together. Do you know, Armstrong, I half fancy it's not going to be as awful as I expected."

"That's all right," said Mr Armstrong, who had already begun to entertain a contrary impression.

"Oliphant seems civilly disposed, and not inclined to interfere; and the girls—well they seem harmless enough. How do you like Tom?"

"Tom's a nice, quiet, business-like boy," said the tutor with a grin. "I'll tell you more about him soon, but at present I have no time. I must catch the four o'clock train back to London."

"What! What ever for?" exclaimed Roger, with falling face.

"Urgent private affairs. I shall be away perhaps a week," said Mr Armstrong shortly, in a tone which discouraged Roger from making further inquiries.

"I'm awfully sorry," said he; "I shall miss you specially just now."

"If I could have taken any other time, I would," said the tutor, busily throwing his things into his bag all the time; "but I am going to a death-bed."

"Oh, Armstrong, I'm so sorry. Is it a relation?"

"As I regard relations, yes. Now I must go and make my apologies to your mother. I'll come and see you before I go."

He found the lady sitting in the library in consultation with Captain Oliphant. The table was spread with the late Squire's papers and documents, concerning which the Captain was evincing considerable interest.

The tutor glared a little through his glass at the spectacle of this industry, and disposing of his co-trustee's greeting with a half nod, accosted Mrs Ingleton.

"I must ask you to excuse me for a few days, Mrs Ingleton. I have just received news which render a journey necessary."

"Indeed!" said Captain Oliphant, looking up from his papers. "I am afraid, Mr Armstrong, we must ask you to postpone it, as there are a good many business matters of importance to be gone into, which will require the attention of all the trustees. It is an inconvenient time to seek for leave of absence."

The tutor's mouth stiffened ominously.

"You take unnecessary interest in my affairs, sir. I shall be at your service on my return. Mrs Ingleton, I am sorry for this interruption in Roger's studies. It shall be as brief as I can make it."

"Oh, of course, Mr Armstrong," said the lady, "I hope it is nothing serious. We shall be glad to have you back to consult about things; that is all Captain Oliphant means, I'm sure."

The tutor bowed.

"I really hope," said Captain Oliphant blandly, "Mr Armstrong will appreciate my desire to cooperate harmoniously in the sacred trust laid upon us all by the dying wish of our dear friend."

"I have no wish to do anything else, sir," said the tutor shortly, "if you will allow me. Good-bye, Mrs Ingleton."

Roger was a good deal concerned to notice the grim cloud on his friend's face, when he returned for a moment to his room for his bag. He knew him too well to ask questions, but made up for his silence by the warmth of his farewell.

"Come back soon, Armstrong; it will be awfully slow while you're away. Let's carry your bag down-stairs."

As they passed the end of the lobby, a certain door chanced to open, and Armstrong caught a vision of an easel and a fair head beyond, and beyond that a mantelpiece decorated with all sorts of Oriental and feminine knick-knacks. He might have observed more had his glass been up, and had he not been eagerly accosted by Miss Jill, who just then was running out of the room.

"Mr Armstrong! Mr Armstrong!" shouted she in glee. "Rosalind, he's come back; here he is!"

And without more ado she caught the embarrassed tutor by the arm and demanded a kiss. He compromised feebly by patting her head, whereat Miss Jill pouted.

"You're more unkind than yesterday," she said; "you kissed me then."

"You shouldn't ask Mr Armstrong to do horrid things," said Miss Rosalind, coming to the door.

The tutor, very hot and flurried, replied to this cruel challenge by saluting the little tyrant and bowing to her sister.

"Won't you come in and see the studio?" said the latter. "It's a little less dreadful than yesterday, thanks to Roger. What are you carrying that bag for, Roger?"

"Armstrong's going up to town for a few days."

"How horrid!" said Miss Rosalind, with vexation in her voice; "just while Jill and I are feeling so lonely, cooped up here like nuns, with not a soul to talk to, and knowing we're in everybody's way."

"Armstrong has a sad enough reason for going," said Roger; "but I say, it's not very complimentary to me to say you've not a soul to talk to."

The half-jesting petulance in Rosalind's face had given place to a look almost of pain as she held out her hand.

"Good-bye, Mr Armstrong," said she. "I didn't know you were in trouble."

"It *will* be jolly when you come home," chimed in Jill.

Somehow in Mr Armstrong's ears, as he whirled along to town that afternoon, those two pretty farewells rang continuous changes. When, at evening, he took his seat in the Dover express, they still followed him, now in solos, now in duet, now in restless fugue. On the steamer they rose and fell with the uneasy waves and played in the whistling wind. As he sped towards Paris, past the acacia hedges and poplar avenues, among foreign scenes, amidst the chatter of foreign tongues, surrounded by foreign faces, he still caught the sound of those two distant voices—one quiet and low, the other gay and piping; and even when, at last, he dropped asleep and forgot everything else, they joined in with the rattle of the rail to give him his lullaby. Such are the freaks of which a sensitive musical ear is often the victim.

At Maxfield, meanwhile, he remained in the minds of one or two of the inmates.

The two young ladies, assisted by their cousin, and genially obstructed by their easy-going brother, proceeded seriously in the task of adorning the studio; now and then speculating about the absent tutor, and now and then feeling very dejected and lonely. Roger did his best to enliven the evening and make his visitors feel at home. But although Tom and Jill readily consented to be comforted, Miss Rosalind as stubbornly refused, and protested a score of times that the cabin of the "Oriana" itself was preferable to the misery of being condemned, as she termed it, to eat her head off in this dismal place. She was sorry for Mr Armstrong, but she was vexed too that he should go off the very first day after her arrival, and leave her to fight her battles alone. After that talk on the steamer, she had, in her own mind, reckoned on him as an ally, and it disappointed her not to find him at her bidding after all.

But she was not the only person whose mind was exercised by the tutor's abrupt exodus.

Captain Oliphant felt decidedly hurt by the manner of his going. It argued a lack of appreciation of the newly arrived trustee's position in the household on which he had hardly calculated; and it bespoke a spirit of independence in the tutor himself, which his colleague could not but regard as unpromising. Indeed, when, after the day's labours, Captain Oliphant sought the seclusion of his own apartment, this amiable, pleasant-spoken gentleman grew quite warm with himself.

"Who is this grandee?" he asked himself. "A man hired at a few pounds a year and fed at the Maxfield table, in order to help the heir to a little quite unnecessary knowledge of the ancient classics and modern sciences. What was the old dotard,"—the old dotard, by the way, was Captain Oliphant's private manner of referring to the lamented "dear one," whose name so often trembled on his lips in public,—"what was the old dotard thinking about? At any rate, I should like to know a little more about the fellow myself."

With this laudable intention he questioned Mrs Ingleton next morning.

"He is a good friend to dear Roger," said the mother. "Roger is devoted to him. I am sure you will get to like him, Edward. He is perhaps a little odd in his manner, but he has a good heart."

This was about all Mrs Ingleton knew, except that he was a University man and an accomplished musician.

Captain Oliphant was not much enlightened by this description. He sat down, and for the third time carefully read over the "dear one's" will.

"I think," said he at lunch-time, "I will stroll over to Yeld this afternoon and see Mr Pottinger. Roger, will you walk with me? A walk would do you good. You are looking pale, my boy."

"Oh, I'm all right," said Roger, whose cough, however, was still obstinate. "I'll come with pleasure."

A walk of five miles on a damp afternoon through drenched country lanes may be a good specific for a cough in India, but in England it occasionally fails in this respect. Roger was wet through when he reached Yeld.

"I shall not be long," said the Captain as they reached the attorney's door. "Don't catch cold, there's a good fellow. Remember your health is very precious."

Roger undertook to act on this considerate advice, and occupied his time of waiting by strolling up and down the High Street in the rain, paying a call here and there at one or two shops, and finally dropping in to see his friend Dr Brandram.

The Captain meanwhile was having an interesting chat with the attorney.

After introducing himself and receiving the suitable congratulations, he said—

"Mr Ingleton's will, Mr Pottinger, so far as I can understand it, seems fairly simple, and I am ready and anxious to perform my part of its provisions."

"Yes. You see, after all, it is only a matter of two years' trouble. As soon as Master Roger comes of age you will be released."

"Unless," says the Captain, laughing, "he marries, becomes mad, or goes to prison, isn't that it? What a curious proviso!"

"It is. The old Squire had his peculiarities, like most of us. He set his heart on this boy turning out well."

"Ah! I presume this tutor, Mr Armstrong, has very high qualifications, since so much depends on him."

"Of that I can't say, Captain Oliphant. To tell you the truth, I never quite understood that appointment. But doubtless the Squire knew best."

"Doubtless. He must have had a very high opinion of him to associate him with Mrs Ingleton and me in the guardianship. I take it, by the way, that hardly extends beyond his present duties as tutor."

"That's just it," said Mr Pottinger. "According to the will, he has the right to participate in every action taken by the other trustees, either as regards the boy, or the estate, or anything else."

"How very singular! You don't mean to say that he is to be consulted in matters of finance or the management of the property?"

"Technically, yes—if he claims it. I imagine, however, he is hardly aware of this, and I am not inclined to urge him to claim it. I should be sorry to give you an unfavourable impression, Captain Oliphant, but I do not like this Mr Armstrong."

"He appears to be well thought of at Maxfield," said the Captain.

"My private opinion is—but you must not let it influence you—that he is somewhat of an adventurer. I know nothing of his antecedents."

"Indeed! not even where he lives?"

"No; the Squire was reticent on the matter. He told me he had good recommendations with him, and that he was an Oxford man."

"Surely that should be satisfactory. I hope we shall find him not difficult to get on with, after all. We shall have to wait a week or so, however, before putting the question to the test, as he has just gone off rather abruptly, and at this particular time rather inopportunely, on a journey, for what object I do not know."

"Humph!" said the attorney. "I do not like mysteries. However, I trust it will be as you say."

Dr Brandram, when presently the Captain called in for his ward, was in by no means a good temper.

"I have been blowing Roger up sky-high," said he, puffing his smoke rather viciously in the Captain's direction, "for behaving like a lunatic. The idea of his coming out and getting himself wet through with this cold upon him."

"Dear, dear!" said the Captain; "has he got wet through? Why, my dear boy, what did I tell you?"

"You shouldn't have let him come," said the doctor bluntly. "He's no business to play tricks with himself."

"Really, doctor," said Roger, laughing and coughing alternately, "I'm not a baby."

"You're worse," said the doctor severely. "Don't let it happen again. You must go home in a fly; I won't allow you to walk. Armstrong wouldn't have let you do it."

It grated on the Captain's nerves to hear the tutor thus quoted in what seemed to be a reflection on himself.

"Roger, my boy," said he, "you are fortunate to have somebody to look well after you. I quite agree with the doctor; we must drive home. I hope your things are dry."

"He's made me change everything I had on," said Roger.

"Quite right—quite right!"

The doctor took an opportunity before the fly arrived of talking to the Captain seriously about his ward's health.

"He's not robust, you can see that yourself," said he, "and he won't take care of himself, that's equally evident. You must make him do it, or I won't answer for the consequences."

The Captain laughed pleasantly. "My duties grow on me apace," said he. "I have come over from India to look after his morals, his estate, his education, and now I find I must add to them the oversight of—"

"Of his flannels. Certainly; see they are well aired, that's more important than any of the others. Good-bye!"

The Maxfield household was a dismal one that evening. Mrs Ingleton in distress had prevailed on Roger to go to bed. Miss Rosalind, defrauded in one day of her two allies, sulked in a dignified way in her own room, and visited her displeasure with the world in general on poor Jill, who consoled herself by beginning a letter to her "dear Mr Armstrong." Tom, having wandered joyously over the whole house, making friends with everybody and admiring everything, was engaged in the feverish occupation of trying to find his stamp album, which he had left behind in India.

The only serene member of the party was Captain Oliphant, who in the arm-chair of the library smoked an excellent cigar and ruminated on things at large.

"Poor lad!" said he to himself, "great pity he's so delicate. Not at all a pleasant cough—quite a churchyard tone about it. Tut! tut! I'm not favourably impressed with that doctor; an officious bumpkin, he seems to me. And this Armstrong—I should really like to know a little more about him. Pottinger was decidedly of my way of thinking. Not a nice fellow at all, Armstrong. Wrong sort of companion for Roger. Poor fellow! how he's coughing to-night."

And this kindly soul actually laid down his cigar and went out into the passage to listen.

"Shocking cough," said he as he returned and relit his cigar. Then he took out a document from his pocket—a copy of the will, in fact—and read it again. Which done, he relapsed into genial meditation ones more.

Presently his kindly feelings prompted him to pay his ward a visit.

"Well, my boy, how are you? Better, I hope."

"Oh, yes," said Roger, coughing; "it's only a cold in my head. I'll soon be all right. I'm awfully sorry to desert the girls and Tom, tell them."

"Nothing I can do for you, is there?"

"Thanks very much. I'm all right. I shall get to sleep pretty soon. Good night, Cousin Edward."

"Good night, dear boy. Another time you must take better care of yourself. Remember your life is precious to us all."

With these affectionate words Captain Oliphant left the room, candle in hand. As he passed his daughter's boudoir he looked in. It was empty. The young ladies had long since taken refuge in their bedroom. All the house, in fact, except Captain Oliphant, had done the same.

That gentleman, as he passed another door which stood half open, could not resist a friendly impulse to peep in. It was a snug room, with a piano in one corner, and foils, boxing gloves, Oxford prints, and other tokens of a bachelor proprietorship displayed on the walls. The table was littered with classical exercises, music scores, and letters. A college boating-jacket hung behind the door, and one or two prize-goblets decorated the mantelpiece.

Captain Oliphant displayed a genial interest in everything. He read the inscriptions on the goblets, glanced casually through the papers, read the addresses on a few of the letters, and generally took stock of the apartment. Of course, like an honourable gentleman, he disturbed nothing, and presently, distressed by a sudden fit of coughing from the direction of his ward's room, he hastily stepped out into the lobby again and made his way back to the library.

Before he went to bed this methodical person committed three several matters to paper. In his memorandum-book he wrote the name of a certain college at Oxford, and a date, corresponding, oddly enough, to the name and date on one of the goblets in Mr Armstrong's room.

That done, he scrawled a post card to Dr Brandram, requesting him to call and see Roger, whose cough was still a little troublesome.

After that, he pulled out of his pocket and read with a somewhat pained expression a letter he had received the day before by the Indian mail. It was gather long, but the passage which pained Captain Oliphant particularly ran thus:—

> "The trouble about the mess accounts is not blown over yet. I have done what I can for you. I hope you will make it unnecessary for me to enter into details with the parties chiefly interested in that affair. It depends pretty much on what you are able to tell me, whether I can give you the time you mention in your last. You will consult your own interests best by being quite square," and so on.

The expression which Captain Oliphant mentally applied to the writer as he re-read this pleasant passage was not wholly flattering, and his countenance, as I have said, bore traces of considerable pain. However, after a little meditation it cleared somewhat, and he wrote:—

> "It seems to me a pity you should take up a position which can only end in trouble all round. You know how things

stand, and how impossible it is to hasten matters. At the present moment there seems every probability of my being able to discharge all my accounts—yours among them—considerably earlier than the time first mentioned. It is worth your while, under the circumstances, reconsidering what, you must allow me to say, is a preposterous claim for interest. Of course, if you charge me for the full term, I have very little inducement to settle up sooner. Turn it over, like a sensible man, and believe me, meanwhile,

"Yours truly,

"E.O.

"*P.S.*—I enclose a copy of the clauses of the will most likely to interest you. I am sorry to say my ward is in very bad—I might say seriously bad—health. He has a constitutional complaint, which, I greatly fear, will make this winter a most anxious time to us all."

After this, Captain Oliphant soothed himself down with a cigarette, and spent a little time in admiring contemplation of an excellent portrait of Mrs Ingleton on the wall. Finally, he went cheerfully to bed.

Chapter Six
A Case of Eviction

A week passed and Mr Armstrong did not return. By the end of that time Miss Rosalind Oliphant, for better or worse, had settled down into her new quarters, and made herself as much at home as a fair Bohemian can do anywhere. She still resented the fate which brought her to Maxfield at all, and annoyed her father constantly by casting their dependence on the hospitality of the place in his teeth.

"I wish you had some business, father," said she, "so that we could pay our way. I don't suppose my pictures will ever sell, but every penny I earn shall go to Roger. Couldn't we go and live in the lodge, somewhere where we can—"

"Rosalind," said her father, "you vex me by talking like a child. After the education I have tried to provide for you, I had a right to hope you would at least regulate your tongue by a little common-sense. Do you not know that I have given up my profession, everything, in order to come to do my duty here?"

"I wish you hadn't," said the girl doggedly; "it would have been so easy to decline the trust and remain independent. It's awful to think we've nothing to live on but what we get out of Roger's money."

"Foolish girl," said her father with a forced laugh, "you are a delightful specimen of a woman's incapacity to understand the very rudiments of business. Why, you absurd child, old Roger Ingleton's will bequeathed me £300 a year for acting as the boy's guardian."

"Yes, for two years. And Roger would have been all that richer if you'd declined. I'm sure his mother and Mr Armstrong are plenty to look after him. I'd have liked you so much better, dear father, if you'd stayed in the army."

"I'm afraid, my poor girl, it is useless to argue with you. When you do get a wrong idea into your head, nothing will induce you to part with it, even if it involves an injustice to your poor father."

"Father," said she, "you know it is because I love you and—"

"Enough," said he rather sternly. "I know you mean well."

And he went.

At the door, however, he returned and said—

"By the way, Rosalind, I must mention one matter; not for discussion, but as my express wish. You named Mr Armstrong just now. I desire that you hold no communication with him. I have reason for knowing he is not a desirable person at all."

"If so, you had better take us away from here," said Rosalind, flushing. "You've no right to let us stay."

"Silence, miss, and bear in mind what I tell you. Do you understand?"

Rosalind had taken up her brush and was painting furiously at her picture.

Captain Oliphant having waited a minute for an answer and getting none, stalked out of the room a model of parental anguish. As for Miss Rosalind, she painted away for a quarter of an hour, and then said to herself—

"Is he?"

With which profound inquiry she laid down her brush and went to visit her invalid cousin.

Roger was up, though still coughing, and ensconced in his study.

"How jolly of you to come!" said he.

"I came because I'd nothing else to do," said she, "I'm not jolly at all."

"Why, what's the row?"

"Can't you guess? Don't you know that I owe you already for a week's board and lodgings and haven't earned sixpence to pay you."

"I shall put you in the county court," said Roger solemnly.

"It's no joke to me," said she.

"I know it isn't, and I wish to goodness I could help you out. By the way, though," added he, jumping up from his chair, "I've got it."

"Don't," said she; "you'll only start the cough. What have you got? An idea?"

"Yes. Rosalind, do you know I'm going to get some painting-lessons?"

"Where? Oh, I wish I could afford some too. Is there any one near here who teaches?"

"Yes. Some one who's just starting. A rather jolly girl, only she has an awful temper; and I'm afraid, when she sees what a poor hand I make, she'll have no patience with me."

Rosalind looked at him steadily, and then smiled.

"How nice of you! May I really try? I'll teach you all I know."

"Will you promise to be nice, and never to fly out at me?"

"No, I'll promise nothing of the sort. But if you learn well, I'll be very proud."

"And your terms?"

She looked at him again.

"Would a shilling an hour be an awful lot?"

"No. It's very moderate. I accept the terms. I'll begin to-day."

This satisfactory bargain being concluded. Miss Rosalind inquired how her new pupil's cold was.

"Nearly all right. I'm glad to have got rid of it before Armstrong comes back."

"When will that be?"

"I don't know. He hasn't written a line. I hope he'll come soon."

"Are you awfully fond of him!" asked Rosalind.

"Rather," replied the boy.

"That's exactly what he said when I asked him if he was fond of you."

"Odd," said Roger with a laugh. "But, I say, what do you think of my den? Isn't it rather snug?"

"I like one of the pictures," said Rosalind, pointing to a certain portrait on the mantelpiece.

"I'm awfully glad," said Roger. "Do you know who it is?"

"No."

"A brother of mine who died long before I was born."

Rosalind took the picture in her hands and carried it to the window. The scrutiny lasted some minutes. Then she replaced it on the chimney-piece.

"Well," said Roger, "do you like him?"

"Yes, I do."

"Aren't you a little afraid of him, too?"

"Not a bit. He looks like a hero."

Roger sighed.

"I'm glad there's one in the family," said he.

"Why not two? I say, will your tutor mind your having painting-lessons of me?"

"Mind? Not he. I shouldn't be surprised if he wants to have some too."

Rosalind laughed.

"That would be too terrible," said she. "But I must go now. Will you lend me this picture for a little? I'd like to look at it again."

Roger laughed.

"Oh yes, if you'll promise not to fall in love with him for good."

When Roger presented himself at the appointed hour in his cousin's studio, he found that young lady very much in earnest and not at all disposed to regard her new functions as a jest. Roger, who had come expecting to be amused, found himself ignominiously set down at a table beside the amenable Tom (who had been coerced into joining the class) and directed to copy a very elementary representation of a gable of a cottage which the instructress had set up on the easel. Six times was he compelled to tackle this simple object before his copy was pronounced passable; and until that Rosalind sternly discouraged all conversation or inattention.

"Really, Roger," said she, when at last he meekly submitted his final copy, "for a boy of your age you are an uncommonly rough hand. Tom is a much more promising pupil than you."

"I haven't promised you a bob an hour, though," rejoined that not-to-be-flattered genius, beginning to whistle.

"Silence, sir!" said Miss Rosalind, stamping her little foot with something like temper; "as long as you are in my class you must do as I tell you."

Here Roger protested.

"You're rather strict," said he. "I don't mind working hard and attending to all you say, but I vote we enjoy ourselves too—all three of us."

"You mean," said Rosalind petulantly, "that you come here to play, while I try to work."

"No, I don't. I come to do both, and I want you to, as well."

"Very well then, I withdraw from my engagement," said the young lady, with an ominous flush; "we don't agree about art. Unless you can give yourself up to it while you are about it, it's not meant for you—and—and

I'm very sorry indeed I made such a stupid mistake as to think you meant what you said when you told me you wanted to learn."

And she took the copy down from the easel.

"Look here, Rosalind," said Roger, in unusual perturbation, "I'm so sorry. You're quite right. Of course one can't do two things at once. I'll—"

"You're a dear boy, as I've said before," said Miss Oliphant, brightening up suddenly and accepting her victory serenely. "Now please both of you draw the picture again from memory as exactly as you can."

"What's the long and short of it all?" presently whispered Tom, who had been supremely indifferent to the argument. "Is it larks or no larks?"

"Shut up!—that's what it is," said Roger.

"All right; thanks," said Tom contentedly.

And for a quarter of an hour more the two worked steadily and silently, the only sound in the room being the scratching of their pencils and Rosalind's occasional terse criticisms over their shoulders.

This little incident opened Roger's eyes considerably. He was astonished at himself afterwards for taking his rebuff so meekly, and submitting to what, after all, was rather a preposterous regulation. He was aware that he would not have submitted to any one but Rosalind, or possibly Armstrong. Why he should do so to her he did not particularly know; unless it was because he felt it would be pleasanter on the whole to have her as a friend than as a foe.

When, three days later, Mr Armstrong neither appeared nor communicated with any member of the household, the uneasiness which his prolonged absence caused found expression in several different ways. Miss Jill cried in a corner; Miss Rosalind tossed her head and painted fiercely; Roger, already pulled down with a return of his cough, moped in his own room; while his mother, impressed by the growing indignation of her cousin, began to work herself into a mild state of wrath. Tom alone was serene.

"I expect he's having a jolly time with that French chap," he volunteered at the family dinner.

"With whom?" inquired his father pricking his ears.

"Oh, a chum of his; not half a bad sort of cove, only he dropped all his 'h's.' He turned up at Christy's, you know, but missed the best break-down, while he and Mr Armstrong were hob-nobbing outside. I saw it, though. It was prime."

"Why didn't you tell me this before?" demanded Captain Oliphant.

"I didn't know you'd care about it," said his son in mild surprise. "You see, it was this way. The fellow had wooden shoes on, and when the music began slow he began a shuffle, and gradually put on the pace till you couldn't tell one foot from the other."

Here Miss Rosalind broke into a derisive laugh.

"Really, Tom," said she, "you are too clever. However did you guess that we were all dying to hear how a break-down is danced?"

"I didn't till father said so."

Here Roger and the two young ladies laughed again; whereat Tom, concluding he had said something good unawares, laughed too, and thought to himself how jolly it is to be clever and keep the table at a roar.

In private Captain Oliphant pursued the subject of Gustav and his relations (apart from their mutual connexion with the break-down) with the Maxfield tutor.

He received very little satisfaction from his inquiry. Tom was so full of his main topic that the other events of that memorable evening in town occupied but a secondary place in his memory.

He recollected Gustav as a good-natured foreigner whom Armstrong called by his Christian name, and who talked French in return. He could not remember where he lived, except that it was ten minutes' walk from Christy's Minstrels; nor had he the slightest idea what the two men talked about, except that Armstrong had promised to hold somebody's hand, and that Gustav had tried to kiss him by way of recompense.

Captain Oliphant chose to take a very serious view of this disclosure. It fitted in exactly with his theory that the tutor was an adventurer of "shady antecedents," and, as such, an undesirable companion for the late "dear one's" orphan-boy.

"I should not feel I was doing my duty," said he to Mr Pottinger that afternoon, "if I were not to follow this up. We don't know whom we have to deal with; and the fact of Mr Ingleton having confided in him really, you know, weighs very little with me; old men of enfeebled intellect, my dear Pottinger, are so easily hoodwinked."

"Quite so. Does it not occur to you, Captain, that a simple solution of the difficulty would be for Mrs Ingleton to send her boy to college?"

"Mrs Ingleton," said the Captain, "is unfortunately incapable of regarding this subject in any light but that of her son's likings. And Roger Ingleton, minor, is infatuated."

"Humph!" said the lawyer, "I thought so. Then I agree with you, it will be useful to institute a few inquiries."

"Leave that to me," said the captain. "By the way, what about that piece of land you were speaking of?"

"Ah!" said the lawyer, making as near an approach to a blush as he could muster, "the fact is, Hodder's lease falls in next week. He has had it at a ridiculously low figure, and is not a profitable tenant."

"That is the old dotard who is always croaking about Maxfield in the days before the Flood?"

"Well, almost as remote a period. He was here in the time of the late squire's father. At any rate his lease falls in; and I happen to know a person who is willing to give twenty per cent more for the land than he pays. I can't tell you his name," said the lawyer, looking sufficiently conscious, "but I happen to know he would be a better tenant to Maxfield than the old man."

Mr Pottinger amused himself with making a little mystery about a matter that was no secret to Captain Oliphant. That gallant gentleman knew as well as the lawyer did that Mr Pottinger himself, whose land adjoined Hodder's, was the eligible tenant in question.

"There will be no difficulty about that, Pottinger. Of course, you must give Hodder the option of offering your friend's price. If he does not, it is clearly the duty of the executors to take the better tenant."

He took up his hat and turned to go.

"By the way," said he at the door, "it will hardly be necessary, I take it, to go through the farce of bringing a trifling matter of this kind before the other executors; Mrs Ingleton should really be spared all worry of this sort; and as for the other one—well, he chooses to be somewhere else."

"Quite so, quite so. If you and Mrs Ingleton sign the lease it will be sufficient," said Mr Pottinger.

Unluckily for the pleasantly arranged plan of these two good gentlemen, Miss Rosalind Oliphant took it into her pretty head a day or so afterwards to call at old Hodder's cottage in passing, to ask for a glass of milk. The young lady was in a very discontented frame of mind. She was angry with Mr Armstrong for staying away so long. Not that she cared what he did, but till he came back she felt she did not know the full extent of the forces arrayed against her at Maxfield; and she wanted to know the worst. Besides, although Roger was diligently prosecuting his art studies and displaying the most docile obedience to her discipline, she could not help thinking he would not have taken to art except to please her; and that displeased her mightily. Besides, Tom, her brother, was too silly for anything; he insisted on enjoying himself, whoever else was miserable; and Jill was very little better. Altogether, Miss Oliphant was out of humour, and felt this walk would do her good.

She found the Hodder family in mighty tribulation. The old man sat in his corner with his hat on the floor beside him, crying and boohing like a child. And his two little granddaughters looked on at his grief, pale and half-frightened, knowing something bad had happened, but unable to guess what.

"Why, Hodder," said Miss Rosalind, "whatever's the matter? What a noise you're making! What has happened?"

"Happened!" cried the old man with a voice quavering into a shrill treble. "How would he like it himself? Seventy years, boy and man, have I sat here, like my father before me. I've seen yon elm grow from a stick to what she is now. I've buried all my kith and kin bar them two lassies."

"Of course, I know you're very old. But why are you crying?" demanded Rosalind.

"Crying! Wouldn't you cry, Missy, if you was to be turned neck and crop into the road at threescore years and ten?"

"Nonsense. What do you mean?"

"Come Tuesday," sobbed the old man, "me and the lassies will be trespassers in this here very place."

"What!" exclaimed Miss Rosalind, "do you mean you're to be turned out? Who dares to do such a thing?"

"You go and ask Mr Pottinger, if you doubt it," blubbered the old man. "He ought to know."

Without another word, Miss Rosalind flung herself from the cottage and marched straight for the lawyer's, pale, with bosom heaving and a light in her eyes, that Armstrong, had he been there to see it, would have shivered at.

"Mr Pottinger," said she, breaking unceremoniously into the lawyer's private room, "what is this I hear! How dare you frighten old Hodder by talking about his leaving his farm?"

The lawyer stared at this beautiful apparition, not knowing whether to be amused or angry. It was the first time any one in Maxfield had addressed him in this strain, and the sensation was so novel that he felt fairly taken aback.

"Really, dear young lady, I am delighted with any excuse that gives me the pleasure of a visit from—"

"Mr Pottinger," said the young lady in a tone which made him open his eyes still wider, "will you tell me, yes or no, if what Hodder tells me is true?"

"That depends on what Hodder says," replied the lawyer, trying to look cheerful.

"He says he has had notice to leave his farm next week. Is that true?"

"That entirely depends on himself, if I *must* suffer cross-examination from so charming a counsel."

"You mean—"

"I mean, my pretty young lady, that if he chooses to pay the new rent he is entitled to stay."

"You have raised his rent?—a poor old man of seventy-five?"

"I have no power to do that. But I understand he has had the land for next to nothing. It is worth more now."

"Mr Pottinger," said Miss Rosalind, "let me tell you that if you have any hand in this wicked business you are a bad man, whatever you profess to be. I shouldn't sleep to-night if I failed to tell you that. So is everybody who dares treat an old man thus."

"Pardon me, Miss Oliphant, that is not quite respectful to your own father."

She rounded on him with trembling lips.

"My father," she began and faltered—"my father is not the sort of man to do a thing of this kind unless he were cajoled into it by some—some—some one like you, Mr Pottinger—"

With which she left the room, much to the lawyer's relief, who tried to laugh to himself at the pretty vixen, but couldn't be as merry as he would have wished.

Rosalind, on her return to Maxfield, went straight with flashing eyes to Roger's room, and told him the story.

"Roger," she said, "if you are half a man you will stop it. You are master here, or will be. Are you going to let this poor old man be turned out of his home? You are not the dear boy I take you for, if you are."

"Of course it must be stopped," said Roger, amazed at her vehemence; "and it shall be. I always thought Pottinger a sneak. I assure you, Rosalind, I shall make poor old Hodder happy before we are a day older. So good-bye; I'll go at once."

But he was no match for the lawyer, who politely recounted the circumstances and referred him to his guardians, who, however, as he pointed out, had no choice but to accept the best-paying tenant.

"It is done in your interest, my dear boy," said Mr Pottinger. "We are bound to consider your interests, whether you like it or not."

Mortified beyond measure, both on his own account and at the prospect of facing Rosalind, Roger returned slowly to Maxfield. As he entered, a hand was laid on his shoulder; Mr Armstrong had come back.

Chapter Seven
Mr Armstrong puts down his Foot

Mr Armstrong, as unconcerned as if he had just returned from a half-hour's stroll, had little idea of the flutter which his return caused to the Maxfield family. He could hardly know that Raffles was parading the lower regions rubbing his hands, and informing his acquaintance down there that the season for "larks" was coming on; nor, as he was out of earshot, could he be supposed to know the particularly forcible expressions which Captain Oliphant rehearsed to himself in celebration of the occasion. As for the young people, it did afford him a passing gratification to feel his pupil's arm linked once more in his own, and to encounter the expected boisterous welcome from Tom and Jill. Miss Rosalind was busy, forsooth! and if Mr Armstrong flattered himself she took the slightest interest in his return, he might find out his mistake.

"I'll join you in a minute, Roger," said he to his ward, "but I must go and pay my respects to your mother."

"Oh, she'll keep," said Roger; "I want to hear what you've been up to."

"In five minutes," said the tutor, going to the drawing-room.

Mrs Ingleton was there, looking pale and fragile, pouring out afternoon tea for Captain Oliphant.

"Why, Mr Armstrong," said she, "we had given you up for lost; Roger was getting quite melancholy without you."

"I understood," began the captain, "when you asked leave—"

"Mrs Ingleton, I must ask you to excuse my long absence. I went to see a dying friend, and was unable to return earlier."

"You might have written," said the captain, returning to the charge.

Mr Armstrong screwed his eye-glass round and stared at the speaker.

"I beg your pardon," said he.

"I say, sir, you might have written. Let me tell you, Mr Armstrong, that, as my dear relative's co-trustee and guardian—"

"I am sorry," observed the tutor, addressing Mrs Ingleton, "that Roger's cough is still troubling him. He is waiting for me upstairs, by the bye, but I was anxious to offer you my apologies without delay for my long absence."

"Mr Armstrong," said the captain, stepping between the tutor and the door, "this will not do, sir. When I speak to you, I expect you to listen."

Mr Armstrong bowed politely.

"I repeat, sir, your conduct satisfies neither me nor your mistress. You forget, sir, that you are here on sufferance, and I desire to caution you that it may become necessary to dispense with your services, unless— I am speaking to you, Mr Armstrong."

Mr Armstrong was examining with some curiosity a china group on the mantelpiece. He turned round gravely.

"You were saying—?" said he.

The captain gave it up.

"We shall discuss this matter some other time," said he.

"Pray, pray," said Mrs Ingleton with tears in her eyes, "let us not forget that my boy's happiness depends on our harmony. I am sure Mr Armstrong recognises that I depend on you both."

Mr Armstrong bowed again; and finding that the captain had returned to his chair, he quietly left the room.

When he entered Roger's room, humming a tune to himself, he neither looked like a man who had returned from a funeral or from an altercation in the drawing-room. In five minutes he was in possession of most of what had taken place during his absence—of Roger's cold, of the painting-lessons, of Tom's reminiscences of Christy's Minstrels, and most of all of Hodder's tribulation.

"And what sort of an artist are you turning out?" inquired he.

"Oh, all right. But I say, Armstrong, I want you to make it right about Hodder before anything. Will you come and see him?"

"My dear fellow, Hodder is as safe in his cottage as you are here. Leave that to your responsible guardian. My present intention is to work on the tender mercies of Raffles for some dinner. I have travelled right through from Paris since this morning."

"Your friend died?" inquired Roger.

"Yes. I was in time to be of some little help, I think, but he was past recovery. How is Miss Oliphant?"

"All right; but in an awful state about old Hodder. I'm afraid to meet her myself. She will be relieved to have you back."

"Will she really?" said the tutor, laughing. "I hardly flatter myself her comfort depends on which particular hemisphere I happen to be in."

Miss Oliphant, as it happened, had taken to a spell of hard work in her studio, and was not visible all the evening. She was, in fact, making a copy of the portrait Roger had lent her, and the work interested her greatly.

This bold, fearless, almost insolent, boy's face fascinated her. She seemed to be able to interpret the defiance that flashed in his eye, and to solve the problem which gathered on his half-mocking lips. She was half afraid, half enamoured of this old piece of canvas.

"Why are not you here now?" she muttered as she gazed at it. "You don't look like the sort of boy to die. Should we be friends or enemies? Heigho! I shouldn't care much which, if only you were here. Roger minor is a dear boy; but—you are—"

She didn't say what he was, but worked late into the night with her copy.

At bedtime Jill came in radiant.

"He's come back, Rosalind. Dear Mr Armstrong's come back."

"Oh!" said Rosalind shortly.

"Aren't you glad? Oh, I am!"

"Why should I be glad? I don't care two straws for all the Mr Armstrongs in the world. Go to bed, Jill, and don't be a goose."

Jill obeyed, a little discomfited, and was sound asleep long before the artist joined her. And long before she woke from her dreams next morning Rosalind was astir and abroad. She had resolved to pay an early call on old Hodder, if not to relieve his mind about the eviction, at least to take him some comfort in the shape of a little tea and sugar.

The old man was sitting outside the cottage, smoking and moaning to himself. He cheered up a bit at the sight of his visitor, still more at the sight of the tea. But it was a short-lived gleam of comfort, and he relapsed at the earliest opportunity into the doleful.

"Little good it'll do me," said he, "as have known this place, man and boy, seventy-five years, Missy. Never a word did they say to me till now. The old squire had allers his nod for Hodder, and when times was bad he let the rent stand. And young Master Roger was of the same sort."

"Oh, Roger is your friend still," said Rosalind; "he's doing everything to help you."

"I don't mean *him*. He's good enough; but he's a boy. But young Master Roger as was, he had a will of his own, Missy. Not one of 'em durst stand up to him."

Rosalind became interested. "Do you mean the one who died?" said she.

"Ay, they say he died. They said as much and wrote it on the tombstone."

"Do you mean that there was ever a doubt about it?" said the young lady uncomfortably.

"They said he died, so he must have died," said old Hodder, sipping his tea. "It was all talk to the likes of me. Young Master Roger wasn't of the dying sort."

"He went abroad, I hear?" she asked.

"So they say. It's a score of years or more since. I tell 'ee, Missy, young Master Roger wouldn't have stood by to see me turned out like this; he'd have—"

Here there was a click at the gate and a long shadow fell on the footpath. It was Mr Armstrong in his flannels. He looked somewhat alarmed to find Miss Rosalind in possession. Still more to perceive that she proposed to remain where she was. His impulse was to make a feeble excuse and say he would call again. But his courage revived on second thoughts.

"Ah, Hodder," said he, after saluting the young lady, "what's all this about turning you out of your cottage! What a notion to get into your head!"

"You may call it a notion, Mr Armstrong," said the old man, "but what about this here piece of paper?" And he produced a blue legal document.

Mr Armstrong put up his eye-glass and read it, with a face which, as Rosalind furtively glanced upwards, seemed inscrutable. When he had finished he coolly put it in his pocket.

"I'll see to this," said he. "You choose the best time of day for a walk, Miss Oliphant."

"Shall you really be able to settle this for Hodder?" replied she.

"I've very little doubt about it."

The old man chuckled ungallantly. "He, he," said he, "Missy, you ladies are good enough for tea and sugar, but it takes a man to put the likes of me right with my masters."

Armstrong flushed angrily at this speech and was about to relieve his mind when Rosalind laughingly interposed—

"Poor old Hodder! You're quite right; I should never have been clever enough to help you. Good-bye. I'm so glad."

To tell the truth, Miss Oliphant was a good deal more engrossed with what the old man had let drop concerning the lost Roger than with the tutor and his knowledge of the law of landlord and tenant.

"Suppose he did not die!" she said, half scared at the boldness of the suggestion. "If he were to come back!" And she went back and looked long once more at the picture. Then with less satisfaction she contemplated her own copy. Thus employed Roger found her when he passed her door an hour later.

"Still harping on my brother," said he.

"I've done with him, thank you," said Rosalind, handing him back the picture. "See, I have one of my own now."

"Why, it's better than the original. I like it better."

"That shows how little you know about painting."

"It shows how much you know about my brother," said he. "But if you like to keep the original and let me have the copy, I should consider I had the best of the bargain."

Rosalind tossed her head and locked her own copy up in her desk.

"Roger," she said when that was done, "where did he die?"

"The date is on the picture, if one could only make it out. He was abroad at the time, I believe."

"Where?"

"I never heard."

"Have you never tried to find out?"

Roger looked at her, startled.

"It was before I was born," said he. "Father never spoke of him. But why do you ask?"

"Only a girl's curiosity. I thought, if any one knew, you would. But there is the bell for lunch."

Armstrong meanwhile had been having an interview of a different kind. He strolled into Mr Pottinger's office almost at the same time as that worthy lawyer himself.

"So you are back?" asked the latter.

"Yes, and quite at your service," said the tutor. "I am afraid my absence has been inconvenient. But I am ready for business now. By the way, I have brought you back a document which must have been left on old Hodder by mistake. I certainly did not sanction it."

The lawyer sat back in his chair and gazed at the tutor through his spectacles. Mr Armstrong, leaning against the chimney-piece, put up his glass and gazed leisurely back. The two men understood one another pretty well already.

"The notice is quite in order. I have Captain Oliphant's instructions."

"And mine?"

"You were not here."

"I am here now, and I object to Hodder's being disturbed. Do I make myself clear?"

"But—"

"You must excuse me, Mr Pottinger. I shall be glad to discuss the matter with you in the presence of my co-trustees. Meanwhile, good-morning."

The lawyer jumped out of his chair like a man shot.

"What, sir—you, an interloper, an adventurer, a nobody, a parasite—do you suppose I am going to be talked to by you as if I didn't know my own duty. Do you know, Master Usher, that you can any day receive a week's notice of dismissal—"

"A month's, I think," observed the tutor, taking up his hat. "In that respect, perhaps, I have the advantage of the solicitor to the trust. However, we won't talk of that just now. Good-morning again."

Mr Armstrong looked in on his friend the doctor, whom he found in an opportune moment at breakfast. The two men had a long chat over their coffee, and finally adjourned for a walk along the shore, ending up with a cool spring dip in Sheephaven Cove. After which, much refreshed, and glad to be once more in his familiar haunts, the tutor strolled cheerfully back to Maxfield for lunch. He was quite aware things had undergone a change. He had two new enemies, but he was not afraid of them. He had a new pupil, but he liked him. He had a devoted new champion, in the shape of a little girl, but that was no hardship, Roger, too, despite his new friends, was still loyal to his tutor; and Mrs Ingleton, by all appearances, still regarded him as a useful friend. What then was the difference! It could hardly have anything to do with a certain young person half his own age, with whom the tutor had not had two hours' continuous conversation in his life, and of whose behaviour generally he did not at all know whether he approved or not.

"Ridiculous!" said Mr Armstrong to himself with a smile, as he strolled up the carriage drive.

At that moment the distant hall-door opened, and a light figure stepped out for a moment on to the door-step to pat the great mastiff that lay sleeping on the mat. The apparition, the caress, and the vanishing occupied scarcely half a minute, and when it was past Mr Armstrong was only ten paces nearer the house than he had been when it appeared.

But, somehow, in those few seconds the amused smile on his lips faded away, and the eye-glass dropped somewhat limply from his eye, as he repeated to himself more emphatically than before—

"Ridiculous!"

At lunch, Roger innocently broached the question of Hodder's eviction.

"Mother," said he, "what do you think that idiot Pottinger has been up to? He's taken it into his wise head to threaten to turn old Hodder out of his cottage unless he pays a higher rent in future. I went to row him about it, but he's far too dense to see what a scoundrelly thing it is."

"How shocking!" said Mrs Ingleton. "Poor old Hodder has been in that place all his life. Your father was always fond of him, Roger. I wouldn't have him disturbed for the world."

"You'll have to tell Pottinger so yourself," said Roger. "He says he's bound to screw all he can out of the old chap in my interests, if you please."

The captain had listened to this parley with anything but comfort, and was about at this point to explain, when Mr Armstrong seeing his chance adroitly stepped in.

"You may make yourself easy about the matter, Roger. Evidently Mr Pottinger has acted most unwarrantably on his own responsibility. I have been to see him this morning, and told him in future he is not to take upon himself to do anything about the estate without consulting Mrs Ingleton, and Captain Oliphant, and myself—"

"Then Hodder is not to be disturbed?" inquired Rosalind.

"I have seen that the notice is withdrawn. I, for one, should certainly never sanction it."

"Oh, how delightful you are," said the young lady. "How happy you will have made the poor old man. Father, do get that horrid Pottinger sent away. He's a monster. I told him so yesterday, but he wouldn't believe me."

"Rosalind," said her father, whose lunch was not agreeing with him at all, "it vexes me to see you interfere in matters in which you have no concern. It seems to me, my dear Eva," he added, addressing Mrs Ingleton, whom he had already taken to calling by her Christian name, "that these business questions had much better be left for discussion among ourselves, and not at the family meal."

"Perhaps so," said Mrs Ingleton; "only we are all so interested in poor old Hodder, we hardly regard this as a business question. However, I am delighted to hear it is all right now. I only wish Mr Pottinger had consulted you, Edward, before he took such a step."

"Oh, he did," blurted out Rosalind. "But, as I told him, of course papa not knowing what a villain he was, would believe all he said. It was all the more shame of him to go and impose on papa, who hasn't had time to get to know all the people about the place, instead of going to Auntie or Mr Armstrong, who know all of them. I don't think he'll do it again," said the young lady, firing up like a charming Amazon, at the remembrance of her interview.

Captain Oliphant pushed his chair brusquely back from the table and got up, looking, so Armstrong thought, not as proud of his loyal daughter as he should have been.

"Eva," said he drily, "I shall be in the library if you want me. Will you tell Raffles to bring me in the *Times* when it arrives?"

"I'm afraid papa will be very angry with me," said Rosalind dolefully, as she and Roger walked back across the hall. "But if he won't stand up for himself some one must. I'm quite sure he would give the impression, to any one who did not know him, that he had purposely been harsh to poor Hodder."

As it happened, Captain Oliphant displayed no anger. The question of Hodder was allowed to drop, and no further reference was made to his threatened eviction. Mr Pottinger during the week meekly submitted an agreement to permit him to remain where he was, which the trustees sanctioned unanimously; and when the old man's champions at Maxfield rejoiced in the discomfiture of the man of the law.

Captain Edward Oliphant said nothing in his defence.

After this matters went on quietly, as they will do when one storm has blown over and the next is yet below the horizon. Armstrong settled down to his duties with his two pupils—or rather his three pupils, for Miss Jill made a point of receiving lessons too. Miss Rosalind worked away at her painting, and succeeded in evoking a glimmering interest in art in the Philistine breasts of her two students. The young people divided their leisure between riding, cricket, tennis, and yachting. Mrs Ingleton, as the weeks went by, not only grew more pale, but began to be aware of the attentions of her sympathetic kinsman, and to be sorely perplexed and disturbed thereat. And the Captain himself received his Indian letters regularly by each mail, and confessed to himself that, but for two considerations—one appertaining to love, the other to hate—he had better far have remained in Her Majesty's service abroad.

Chapter Eight
Two Ends of a Rope

The summer passed, and even Captain Oliphant began to grow reconciled to his surroundings. That is to say, he discovered that at present it was his policy to make himself agreeable, even to his co-trustee. Armstrong, with the position he held at Maxfield as Roger's friend and Mrs Ingleton's trusted servant, was not to be disposed of quite as easily as the gallant officer had at first anticipated. At the same time, while he remained where he was, the Captain felt himself decidedly embarrassed in the working out of sundry little projects which floated in his ingenious brain. Besides which, time was getting on. Roger would be twenty in November, and a year later—

Captain Oliphant had reached this pleasant stage in his meditations one morning, as he sipped his coffee in his own room, when Raffles entered with the letters.

"Eightpence to pay on this one, please, sir."

It was a letter with an Indian post-mark, unstamped.

The Captain regarded it with knitted brows; then tossing it on the table, said—

"Give it back. I won't take it in, Raffles." Raffles, reflecting within himself that the Captain must have a vast amount of correspondence if he could afford to chuck away an interesting document like this, took the letter and retired.

"Wait a minute," called the Captain, as the door was closing. "Let me look at it again."

Raffles guessed as much, and brought the missive back triumphantly. The Captain again regarded it with expressions of anything but cordiality, and seemed half inclined to reject it once more. But he took it up again and posed it in his hand.

"You can leave it, Raffles," said he presently; "give the postman the eightpence."

It was some time before Captain Oliphant opened the letter. He sipped his coffee and glared at it viciously, as it lay on the table beside him.

"What game is the scoundrel up to now?" muttered he. "I began to hope I was rid of him. What does he want now?"

He opened the letter and read—

> "Dear Comrade,—You have not answered my last three letters, and I feel quite anxious to know of your welfare. You will be pleased to hear that I have arranged to take my leave home during the coming autumn—"

The Captain put the letter down with an exclamation which startled the sparrows on the window-ledge, and set the breakfast cup shaking in its saucer.

"Coming home!" he gasped. Then he read on.

> "I look forward to inquiring personally after your health and prospects, in which, as you know, my dear fellow, I am much interested. It would be very nice of you, as the only friend I have in England, to ask your old comrade on a visit to you in your comfortable quarters. A particular advantage in such an arrangement would be that it would prevent my coming without being asked. I am due by the 'Nile' about the first week in October. Come and meet me in town. I have no doubt I shall get a line at Southampton to say at which hotel I shall find you. I fear you will find me financially in low water. But I shall have with me papers relating to the regimental accounts previous to your regretted departure from India, which, no doubt, some people would regard as valuable, *Au revoir*, my dear fellow—
>
> "Yours ever,—
>
> "R.R.
>
> "P.S.—Commend me to your charming family, I look forward with particular pleasure to make the acquaintance of the young ladies, of whom I have heard delightful reports over here."

Raffles, when he came in to remove the breakfast things, could not help being struck with the narrow escape Captain Oliphant had had of throwing away, for the sake of a paltry eightpence, a most interesting and appetising letter.

The Captain sat holding it abstractedly in his hand, nor was it till the door opened half an hour later and Rosalind sailed in that he hastily pulled himself together, and crumpled the paper away in his pocket.

"Why, papa, what is the matter? Is there any bad news in that letter."

"On the contrary, it announces the arrival from India of a very dear old comrade."

"Oh," said Rosalind. "You will like to hear all about the people over there. Does he belong to our regiment?"

"No, dear. But I shall expect you to be very agreeable to him when he comes here."

"But he's not coming *here*, is he?" she asked, in amazement.

"Where else do you suppose he would be likely to come to visit me?"

"Oh, but, papa, we cannot—we must not ask people here. As it is, think of all four of us living here on Roger's money. It isn't fair."

"Rosalind, you use expressions which, to anyone but your father, would be positively offensive. Rest assured that I do not require my own child to correct me."

"Oh, of course, dear father, I don't mean that, but—"

"But it sounds extremely as if you did mean it."

"I do hope you won't ask any one here," said she doggedly.

"Rosalind, you offend me. You are incapable, as I have told you before, of appreciating your duty either to me or yourself. Oblige me by going."

"Papa, dear, I am only anxious—"

"Go!" said the Captain brusquely.

She obeyed. Mr Armstrong, as he met her in the hall and marked the bright colour in her cheeks and the light in her eyes, thought to himself how uncommonly well she was looking this morning. He might have thought otherwise had he seen her in her studio half an hour later, with the colour all faded, striving miserably to resume her painting at the point where she had left it off.

Her good father, meanwhile, naturally put out, continued his meditations.

"A most vexing child—no support to me at all. On the contrary, an embarrassment. I might have guessed she would cut up rough. Yet I do so long for a little sympathy. Wonder if I shall get any from my dear cousin

Eva some fine day? Hum. I more and more incline to that venture. It would suit my book, to say nothing of my being really almost in love with the dear creature. But I'm so abominably shy. Let's see, Ratman is due first week in October—a month hence. I shall have to keep him quiet some how. He won't be satisfied with things as they are, I'm afraid. All very well to be heir-presumptive when there's little prospect of presuming. Dear Roger is certainly not robust—not at all, poor boy. Still he seems tenacious of what would be very much more useful to me than to him. Yes, it would strengthen my hands vastly if my dear cousin Eva were to give me the right to regard the lad as a father. There would be something definite in that. It would solve the Armstrong question, for one thing, I flatter myself; and as for Rosalind—yes by the way—"

He took out the letter again and read the postscript carefully.

"Yes—tut, tut—how oddly things do work out sometimes. Evidently it is my duty all round, for the sake of everybody, to cast aside my natural bashfulness and use the opportunities Providence gives me."

With which reflection he lit a cigar, and had a pleasant ramble in the park with little Miss Jill, who had rarely seen her papa more lively or amusing.

His spirits were destined to be still further cheered by an occurrence which took place on the following day.

Roger, despite his delicate health, had managed to get through a creditable amount of work during the summer under Mr Armstrong's guidance. He was shortly to go up for his first B.A. in London, and, with that ordeal in view, had been tempted to tax his strength even more than was good for him.

At last the tutor put down his foot.

"No, old fellow," said he; "if you work any move you will go backwards instead of forward. You must take this week easy, and go up fresh for the exam. Depend on it, you will do far better than if you tried to keep it up till the last moment."

In vain Roger pleaded, threatened, mutinied. The tutor was inexorable, and, fortified by the joint authority of Mrs Ingleton and Dr Brandram, carried the day. He had also an unexpected ally in Miss Rosalind.

"Don't be obstinate, Roger," said she. "The three Fates are too many for you; and don't sulk, whatever you do, there's a dear boy, but make yourself nice and propose to take Tom and Jill and me across to Pulpit Island to-morrow. If you are so wedded to lessons, you and Tom shall have your art class for once in a way on the Pelican's Rock instead of my room."

Roger could hardly hold out after this; and Mr Armstrong, a little envious, set the seal of his approval to the programme.

"I wish you'd come too," said Tom; "can't you?"

"Oh, do," said Jill; "it would be twice as nice."

"Mr Armstrong has enough of all of us on working-days," said Rosalind rather cruelly, "to forego a chance of being rid of us on a holiday."

"Quite so," said the tutor, trying to enjoy the situation; "when the mice are away the cat will play—on the piano."

The next day promised well for the picnic; and Roger had sufficiently warmed up to the proposed expedition to be able to enter eagerly into the preparations.

The Pulpit Island, a desolate cavernous rock three miles from the coast, dominated by a lighthouse, was a familiar hunting-ground of his in days gone by, and he decidedly enjoyed the prospect of doing the honours of the place to his cousins now—particularly one of them.

As not a breath of air was stirring, they decided not to encumber the small boat with mast or sail, but to row leisurely across with just as much energy as suited their holiday humour. The channel was on the whole free from currents, and, as Roger knew the landing-places as well as the oldest sailor in the place, any precaution in the way of a pilot was needless.

Armstrong, as he watched the little craft slowly glide over the glassy water, dwindling smaller and smaller, but sending back the sound of voices and laughter long after it itself had become an indistinguishable speck in the gleaming water, wished himself one of the crew. But as fate had ordained otherwise he retreated to his piano, and succeeded in irritating Captain Oliphant considerably by his brilliant execution, vocal and instrumental, of some of his favourite pieces.

The day, however, was too hot even for music, and after an hour's practice Mr Armstrong gave it up and took a book.

But that was dull, and he tried to write some letters. Worse and worse. The place was stifling, and the pen almost melted in his hand.

What was the matter with him? Why did he feel so down, so lonely. Surely he could exist a day without his pupil, whatever the temperature. Perhaps he had his doubts about the boy's success in the coming examination. No; he fancied that would be all right. He would try a stroll in the park. It could not at least be hotter under the trees than in the house.

Across the passage a door stood wide open—a familiar door, through which he caught sight of a familiar easel on the floor, and over the fireplace one or two familiar Indian knick-knacks. He couldn't help stopping a moment to peep in. It seemed cooler in there. What was the picture on the easel? Might he not just look? A view of the park, with the sea beyond—pretty, but—no, not as good as it might be. Landscape was not this artist's strong point. Ah, there was a portrait on the mantelpiece. That promised better. Why, it was the identical boy's portrait that had once hung in the old squire's library. No—it was a copy, but an extraordinary copy, as if the original had suddenly lived while it was being made. Mr Armstrong had rarely seen a portrait which looked so like speaking and breathing. The original in Roger's room was weak compared with this. And in front of it stood a glass with a rose, whose petals leaned over and just touched the canvas—

Mr Armstrong, feeling very guilty, beat a hasty retreat into the hot passage and made his way down-stairs. He was a little jealous of that portrait, perched there in that cool room, with the sweet rose in front of it.

"Going out?" said Captain Oliphant in the hall. The Captain, by the way, had taken to being civil to his co-trustee, much to Mr Armstrong's annoyance, "Warm, isn't it?"

"Yes," said he.

"Beautiful day for those young people."

"Beautiful," said the tutor.

As he spoke, he casually tapped the barometer at the hall-door, as was his habit. To his surprise, the dial gave a great leap downward. Something was wrong with it evidently, for the sky was as monotonously blue as it had been all day, and not a leaf stirred in the trees. However, Mr Armstrong took the precaution to return to his own room for a moment to consult the barometer there. It, too, answered him with a downward plunge.

The tutor screwed his glass rather excitedly into his eye, and looked at the clock. Half-past three. He touched the bell.

"Tell the groom to saddle 'Pomona' for me, Raffles. I will come to the stables in a minute or two and mount there."

"You need a bit of exercise this weather, you do," remarked Raffles to himself, as he retired, "to keep warm."

A few minutes later the tutor was riding smartly to Yeld. During the half-hour occupied by that journey the signs of the approaching storm became manifest. The blue of the sky took a leaden hue, and out at sea an ominous cloud-bank lifted its head on the horizon, while the sultry air seemed to breathe hot on the rider's cheek.

He pulled up short at Dr Brandram's door.

"What's the matter now?" asked the doctor. "I hate to see you on horseback. It always means bad news. Is Mrs Ingleton poorly? I am not at all comfortable about her."

"No; nobody's ill. But I want you for all that. There's a storm coming on."

"So the glass says. All the more reason for staying indoors."

"The youngsters from the Hall are out in it."

"Well, can I lend you an umbrella?"

"Don't be an ass, Brandram. They are out in an open boat at sea."

The doctor jumped to his feet.

"By Jove!" he exclaimed.

"They went to the island this morning, and will have started back a quarter of an hour ago."

"They've caught it already, then," said the doctor. "Look!"

The horizon was lurid with clouds. Pulpit Island out at sea seemed, instead of three miles distant, to have come in to within a mile. The channel between, still gleaming in the sun, was struck by a bar of shadow which seemed like a scar on the surface. The two men, as they stood in the street looking seaward, could hear already the solemn hum through the breathless air, and feel the first cool whiff of the breeze on their faces, while at their feet there fell with a sudden plash a heavy drop of rain.

"Had they a sail?" asked the doctor.

"No."

"It's coming south-east. They will drive in this side of Sheep Head."

"That's what I thought. An awful coast, and not a boat there."

"Get the horse in the gig," said Dr Brandram, "while I put together what we are likely to want. Look sharp."

Armstrong wanted no encouragement to be expeditious, and had the trap at the door almost before the doctor had his pile of blankets, wraps, with brandy and other restoratives, ready to put in it. In the village they paused to buy a rope and to warn one or two stragglers of their errand. Then in the gathering storm they drove hard towards Sheep Head.

There was no mistake about the gale now. The sky was black with clouds, and the rain and wind struck them simultaneously as they urged on. The warning hum had already risen to a roar, and the wave, as they raced, crest over crest, to the shore, hissed and seethed with a fury which could be heard a mile off.

Neither of the men spoke. Armstrong, with the reins in his hand, kept his eyes stolidly between the horse's ears. The doctor, more agitated, looked eagerly out across the sea.

At last, near the summit of the tall, angular headland, the gig came abruptly to a standstill. The horse was tied up, and the two men, scarcely able to keep their feet, staggered to the cliff edge. There for half an hour they lay, straining their eyes seaward, with the full fury of the blast on their faces. It was hopeless to expect to see anything, for the rain drove blindingly in their eyes, and, though scarcely five o'clock, the afternoon was almost as dark as evening.

"Could they possibly drive clear of the point?" asked the doctor.

"Not possibly, I think. Come down to the shore. We are no use here."

"Wait a bit; it seems to be getting lighter."

It was; but for a long time the glow served only to make the obscurity more visible. Presently, however, the rain paused for a moment, and enabled them to dear their eyes and look steadily ahead. Dr Brandram felt his arm suddenly gripped as his companion exclaimed hoarsely—

"What's that?"

"Something red."

Sure enough there was a speck of red tossed about in the waves, now visible, now lost, now returning. It was all that could be seen, but it was enough for Mr Armstrong.

"It's the boat. She wore a red cloak. Come down, come down."

"No; stop till we see how they are driving. There's time enough."

As far as they could calculate, the boat (if boat it was) was being driven straight for Sheephaven Cove, under the cliff on which they stood—a furious, rugged shore—unless, indeed, a miracle should chance to pitch them into the deep, natural harbour that lay in between the low rocks and the headland.

"Come down," said Armstrong again.

From the sea-level nothing, not even the red speck, was discernible; and for a terrible five minutes they wondered, as they scrambled out on hands and knees to the outmost limit of the jutting rocks, whether, among the wild breakers, the little boat and its precious crew had not vanished for ever.

It was all they could do to struggle to their feet, and, clinging to the rocks, turn their faces seaward. A new paroxysm of the gale well-nigh dashed them backwards, and for a time prevented their seeing anything. But in a minute or two it eased off enough to allow them to open their eyes.

"See—there—look out, look out," cried the doctor, pointing.

He was right. About a quarter of a mile away, buffeted like a cork on the water, was a boat, and in it something red.

"Stand up and wave; it's no use shouting," said Armstrong.

Taking advantage of a temporary lull, they stood and waved their coats above their heads. Whether they were seen or not, they could not tell. No signal came in return; only the boat—as it seemed, stern-foremost—drove on towards them.

"Hold on and get your rope ready," said the doctor.

"Will she clear the rocks or no?"

"We shall see. They've no oars out. Stay there while I wave again."

This time it was not in vain. There was a stir in the boat. The red cloak was seen to wave aloft, and a faint cry mingled with the storm.

"Hold on!" cried the doctor; "they see us, thank God. I'll go on waving."

Presently they could see one oar put out, in an attempt to steer the boat into the cove. But in a moment it was swept away, and she drove on as helplessly as before.

It seemed years while she gradually approached, stern-foremost, now seeming to lurch straight towards the fatal rocks, now to stand clear for the narrow channel. They could distinguish the four passengers at last. She in red sat in the stern looking ahead, holding her little sister at her side. The two lads in the middle were baling out wildly, pausing every now and then to turn white faces landward, but returning at once to their task. And indeed the boat sat so low in the water that it was a miracle how she floated at all.

Armstrong stood up, his friend holding him, and waved his coil of rope above his head. The signal was read in a moment. The two girls retreated to the middle of the boat to make room for Roger in the stern.

On and on they came. For an instant it seemed as if nothing could save them, for an ugly cross wave hurled them straight towards the rocks. But the next righted them as suddenly, lifting them high on its crest and dashing them headlong towards the one spot where help awaited them.

Before they rose again a deft cast from Armstrong had sent the rope across the bows within Roger's reach, while the doctor, with the other end lashed round his body, was running at full speed towards the calmer water of the cove.

For a moment the line hung slack, as a great back-wave lifted the boat on its crest and carried it seawards. But suddenly the strain came, carrying the two men on shore nearly off their feet, and grinding on the gunwale of the boat with a creak which could be heard even above the waves.

"Hold on now!" cried Armstrong, as a forward wave surged up behind the boat.

All obeyed but Roger, who, seeking to ease the strain, began to haul in on the rope. The wave tossed the boat up with a furious lurch, half swamping it as it did so, and flinging it down again headlong into the trough. When it rose once more the rope still held, and three of her passengers were safe. But Roger was not to be seen.

With an exclamation which even the doctor, in the midst of his excitement, could hear, Armstrong flung himself blindly into the chaos of water. For a moment or two it seemed as if he had gone straight to his fate, for amid the foam and lashing spray they strained their eyes in vain for a glimpse either of him or his pupil.

Then he appeared high above their heads on the crest of a wave, striking out to where, for one instant, an upstretched arm and nothing more rose feebly from the water. The next moment, hurled thither as it seemed by the wave, he had reached it, and was battling for dear life with the surf that swept him back seaward.

By this time a few bystanders had ventured out on to the rocks, one of them with a rope, which, after three vain attempts, fell within reach of the exhausted pair. By its aid Armstrong piloted his senseless charge into the calmer water of the cove, and the whole party, a few moments later, were safe on *terra firma*.

Chapter Nine
The Captain relieves Guard

When Mr Armstrong, having with some difficulty taken in who and where he was, proceeded, as was natural under the circumstances, to feel for his eye-glass, he discovered that his right arm hung powerless at his side, and refused to perform its familiar functions. The next thing he was aware of was that Rosalind and the doctor were kneeling on the rocks beside the senseless form of Roger, who lay, white as a corpse, with the blood trickling from a gash on the temple. Then Jill crept beside him, pale and sobbing, and said something, he did not hear what. Finally the ruddy countenance of Tom dawned upon him, and made him aware, even in the midst of his dream, that one person at least had thoroughly enjoyed the day's adventures, and was no whit the worse either for the fright or the drenching.

How they all got up to Maxfield the tutor was never able to say, for the pain of his broken arm became so intense that he was as near swooning as he had ever been in his life, and but for the timely services of the doctor, who was able to give him some little relief, he might have disgraced himself for ever by fainting light off. He remembered seeing Roger lying in the carriage with eyes half open, his head on Rosalind's shoulder. And he remembered feeling his own hand held fast in the two hands of his little champion.

The next thing he was conscious of was that he was in his own bed, with his arm firmly bound beside him, and the friendly face of Dr Brandram bent over him.

"That's better, isn't it, old fellow?" said the latter. "It's a wonder it was only the arm. You must keep quiet now, for you shipped a lot of water, and were a quarter drowned into the bargain."

"What about Roger?"

"He'll do now—at least I hope so. I was concerned about him at first, but he came round. I envy you your plunge. Just my luck! All the big things are done by the other fellows, and I'm left to hold on to the rope and order the physic. Never mind. I never expected to see either of you out of that caldron. I certainly could never have come out myself."

"Miss Oliphant—is she all right?"

"Right as a trivet; and has mounted guard over her cousin already. If he doesn't get well with her for nurse, he's an obstinate, customer."

"Thanks, Brandram. Come again soon."

Captain Oliphant's concern at this untoward misadventure may well be imagined. He shed tears with the mother over their "dear one's" narrow escape, and censured in terms of righteous indignation all who had been parties to the hazardous expedition.

He cross-examined the doctor as to the dangers to be apprehended from the patient's present condition, and shook his head gloomily at the probable consequences of so terrible a shock to his already fragile constitution. He summoned his three children into his presence to be severally kissed in recognition of their deliverance, and sent a message by Raffles to Mr Armstrong to say that he was glad to hear his injuries were only of a slight nature, and trusted he would take what time was necessary from his duties to make a proper recovery. After which, in a passably good-humour, he returned to his room, and wondered what improvements he should make at Maxfield if, by any melancholy dispensation of Providence, the property should fall into his unworthy hands.

Of course there were the usual thorns among the roses. Mrs Ingleton, ill herself, was far too painfully absorbed in her boy's danger to lend an ear to the tender nothings of her sympathetic kinsman. And the whole party were so possessed with the notion that Mr Armstrong was something of a hero, that any suggestion to the contrary was just then clearly inopportune.

The main fact, however, was that Roger Ingleton, Minor—dear lad—was very ill indeed.

"I trust, doctor," said the captain, about a fortnight after the accident, to Dr Brandram, who was quitting the house with a decidedly long face, "I trust our dear young patient is on a good road now to recovery."

"I don't like the look of him, I must confess," replied the doctor; "but, with perfect quiet and nothing to excite him, he will pull round. The one thing to be dreaded is excitement. The lungs we have got well in hand, but that blow on his temple makes an ugly complication."

"Poor fellow. Is there nothing one can do?"

"Let him alone, with your sweet daughter to nurse him. She is an angel, Captain Oliphant, if you'll excuse my saying so."

"She knows, as we all do, how precious his life is. And how is your other patient?"

"Armstrong? Practically well. I have given him leave to get up. He has the constitution of a tiger. I wish we could give some of it to the boy."

"Ah, indeed!" said the captain, with a sigh.

On the following day, a desire took possession of the guardian to visit his dear ward in the sick-chamber. Rosalind, who had clung to her post, defiant of fatigue and sleep, had been prevailed upon in deference to her father's peremptory command to seize an hour's sleep in her own room.

"I will sit with him myself," said the captain. "You must not be selfish, my child, in using your privilege. You forget that what gratifies you may also be a pleasure to others. I am going to town in a few days. Who knows if I may see the dear fellow again."

"Father!" exclaimed Rosalind, seizing his arm almost roughly; "he is getting better. The doctor says so."

"My poor child," said her father, with a forced cheerfulness far more terrifying to the girl than his previous melancholy, "I was wrong to alarm you. Yes, of course he is getting better; of course. Come, we must all be brave."

Rosalind, quite broken down, went to her bed and cried herself to sleep.

When the captain entered the sick-chamber, he found the mother at the bedside.

"My dear Eva," said he, "let me beg you to take a little rest. I will remain here. Do give me the pleasure for once. You know how I shall value the privilege."

Mrs Ingleton, who was in truth fairly worn out, was fain to consent, on condition that she should be called at once if necessary.

Having escorted her affectionately to the door, Captain Oliphant seated himself at the bedside, and looked hard at his ward.

The boy lay in a feverish doze, his large dark eyes half-closed, and his head turning now and again restlessly on the pillow.

"My poor dear fellow," said his guardian, bending over him, "how do you feel this afternoon!"

"Better, I think. Where's Rosalind?"

"Gone to bed. I am really afraid of her becoming ill. She looks so pale and worn."

"She was so good to me," said Roger. "I never thought of her getting ill. How long have I been ill?" he asked.

"Three weeks, my boy. What a narrow escape you had. You know I never heard yet what happened that day in the boat. How did it all happen?"

Whereupon Roger, rousing himself still more, began to go over the events of that memorable day, which at that distance of time seemed to loom out in his mind more terrible than at the time.

His guardian, deeply interested in the narrative, drew him out into a full and particular account of all that passed: the picnic on the island, the sudden storm, the drive before the wind, the awful roar of the surf on the shore, what each one said and thought and prepared for, and then of the crowning excitement of the rescue, the struggle in the water, and the drowning sensations.

When all was told the boy's head fell exhausted on the pillow, his chest heaved, and he lay half muttering to himself, half moaning, a pitiful spectacle of weakness and exhaustion.

When, an hour later, Rosalind glided in, her father walked with finger to his lips to meet her.

"Make no noise," said he, "the dear lad is sleeping. Don't disturb him whatever you do."

That was a bad night in the sick-room. The fever rose higher and higher. Roger tossed and moaned ceaselessly all night, and for the first time wandered in his talk. Armstrong, who looked in once or twice, durst not let himself be seen by the patient for fear of adding to his excitement. A midnight messenger was despatched for Dr Brandram, who came, looking very grave, and remained at the bedside all night. Captain Oliphant was indefatigable in his inquiries and attentions. He denied himself his natural sleep in order to linger near the dear one's door and feed on the crumbs of information which from time to time came out. He insisted on lending Dr Brandram a pair of his own slippers, and besought Armstrong, with his bad arm, to take care of himself and go shares in his brandy and water.

Finally, when the doctor peremptorily ordered every one to bed, he retired in a chastened mood to his own room, where he packed his trunk and smoked his cigar thoughtfully till daylight struggled through the windows.

Then he took a brief nap in his arm-chair, and was astir in time to meet the doctor as he descended to the hall.

"What news?" he asked.

"Don't ask me," said the doctor; "my calculations are completely upset. Something has excited him. Whom did he see yesterday?"

"Only my daughter and his mother, and, for a short time, myself."

"Was he at all disturbed while you were there?"

"On the contrary, he was drowsy when I entered and drowsy when I left. He may possibly have caught sight of Mr Armstrong when he looked in."

"He should not have come near him in his present state. Anything that reminds him of the accident is bad for him."

"Dear, dear, what a pity! No doubt the boy caught sight of him. Tell me, doctor—may I venture up to town for a day or two on important business? If you thought I should stay—"

"No. I hope it's not quite as bad as that; but you should leave word where a message will find you, if necessary. Good day."

"I'm not quite such a fool," growled the doctor to himself as he walked to the stables, "as you think me, my fine fellow. If you were in the room half an hour last night this is all explained. To think that you are the father of that ministering angel, too!"

The captain, in a spirit of subdued cheerfulness, travelled up that afternoon to town. The weather was superb. The country, rich with harvest, looked beautiful. The carriage was unusually comfortable, and the cigars magnificent. Altogether this good man felt that he had much to be thankful for, and quietly wondered within himself whether, on his arrival at the "Langham" Hotel, he should find a telegram from Maxfield already awaiting him.

Instead, he found what pleased him decidedly less, a telegram from Southampton.

> "Business keeps me here for a week—arrive London Friday evening.
>
> "Ratman."

The captain expressed himself to himself as greatly annoyed by this simple message, and for the rest of that evening quite lost his natural gaiety.

Next morning, however, not being a man to waste the precious hours, he decided, like a dutiful son of his *alma mater*, to take a little run to Oxford.

He had still in his pocket a certain memorandum, made long ago, of the name of a certain college at that seat of learning, at which, at a certain date, of which he had also a note, a person in whom he felt interested had been a student. Why not improve the occasion by a few inquiries on the spot as to the academical career of that interesting person? It was a brilliant idea, no sooner conceived than executed.

That afternoon, among a crowd of returning undergraduates at — College, might have been seen the well-dressed military form of a certain gentleman, who politely inquired for the senior tutor.

"I have called sir, on behalf of a friend of mine in India, to inquire respecting a Mr Frank Armstrong, who is, or was a year or two since, an undergraduate here."

"Armstrong, Armstrong?—no man of that name here at present. Ah, I fancy we had a man here of that name some years since."

"Could you conveniently inform me how long it is since he left?"

The tutor referred to his lists.

"He left three years ago. I remember him now—well."

"My friend would be extremely grateful for any information. He has lost sight of him since he was at Oxford."

"Well, the fact is Armstrong was not a particular success here. He was a fairly good scholar, and athlete too, I believe, but his course here ended abruptly."

"Dear, dear! Do you mean to say he was expelled?"

"Hardly so. But he left the place heavily in debt. At the end of his second year he wrote to the authorities to say that the source of supply on which he had depended for paying his college and other bills (which had accumulated to a very considerable extent) had suddenly ceased, and he was unable to meet his obligations. As he was in destitution, he could make no suggestion for meeting them, and requested us to accept an undertaking from him to discharge them if possible at a future time. Under the circumstances he was informed that he was not to come up again, and his name was struck off the books. I believe that since then a few of his debts have been reduced by small instalments."

"I am very grieved to hear what you tell me. Could you very kindly tell me the address from which he last wrote?"

"If I remember, it was from a coffee-house in London, and he mentioned that he was hoping to obtain employment as a private tutor in a family."

"Well, sir, although this is very disagreeable news for my friend. I am sure he will thank you all the same. I suppose you have no idea, beyond this address in London, what became of him?"

"None."

"Or where he lived before he came to Oxford?"

"I was looking for that. I see the address on the entrance form is 3, Blue Street, London."

Captain Oliphant made a note of the address, and after effusive thanks, said good-bye.

He spent two interesting days in Oxford looking about him and enjoying himself considerably. But although he met several men whose names he knew, and made several new acquaintances, he was unable to hear anything further of the defaulting undergraduate of — College.

On his return to town, as he had still a day or two to spare, this industrious gentleman, with a good deal of trouble, found out Number 3, Blue Street. For a person of his refined tastes it was in a shockingly low neighbourhood near one of the docks, and Blue Street itself was one of the shadiest—metaphorically—of its streets.

It consisted mainly of slop shops, patronised by the shipping interest, and displaying wares of which one half at least might be safely counted upon as stolen property. Number Three, which for some unexplained reason was located half-way down the street, was an establishment of this sort, very offensive to the nose and not at all agreeable to the eye. Old clothes of every fashion and antiquity hung exposed in the dingy window, while within a still larger assortment lay piled up on the counter. Nor were the clothes all. Second-hand watches, marlinspikes, compasses, spoons, books, boxes, and curiosities crowded the narrow space, in the midst of which the shrivelled old lady who called herself proprietress was scarcely visible.

"Come in—don't be afraid," cried she, as the captain paused doubtfully at the door.

"Is this Number 3, my good woman?"

"Look over the door—'aint you got no eyes?"

"Number 3, Blue Street—this is Blue Street, is it not?"

"If yer doubts it, go and read the name at the end of the street. What do you want? Clothes or money?"

"Neither—I want information," replied the captain.

"Then yer've come to the wrong shop. Don't sell it 'ere, so clear out. Do you think I don't know what you're arter?"

"Very well," said the captain, "that will be so much saved. I shall have to get for nothing what I meant to pay for."

She looked at him doubtfully and growled.

"Why can't yer say what yer want instead of talking gibberish there?"

"If this is Number 3, Blue Street, and you are the same person who was here five years ago—"

"Go on."

"I may have something to give you from an old lodger; but not till I'm sure you have a right to it."

"What, *him*?"

"Very likely," said the captain, calmly lighting a cigarette. "I shall know if you're right, I dare say."

"Right? Do you suppose I'm made of lodgers! 'Aint you talking about the singing chap—Armstrong he called himself, but at the Hall they called him Signor something—Francisco or the likes of that."

The captain pricked his ears with a vengeance, and in his eagerness rattled the keys encouragingly in his trouser pocket.

"That won't do," said he. "I must have come to the wrong place after all. What sort of looking man was he, and where did he come from?"

"He'd got a pair of arms would knock you into the middle of next week, and when he went down to the Hall—"

"Which Hall?"

"The 'Dragon' Music-Hall—what, don't you know it! go on with you—when he went there he flashed it with an eye-glass. Lor', you should 'ave heard him sing! He'd a made your hair curl; it was lovely."

"Ah! he wore an eye-glass and sang, did he?" said the captain. "And where did he come from, and what became of him when he left you?"

"Come from? I don't know. The other end of the world, I fancy myself. Where he went to I don't know neither. I fancy myself he took up with a bad lot at the Hall, and turned me up. Howsomever, I got my dues out of him, so it's no concern of mine. There you are, mister. Now, what have you got for me?"

The captain looked doubtful and shook his head.

"I'm afraid it's not right after all," said he. "It doesn't correspond with the particulars I have. Had you no other lodgers?"

"What did I tell you," snarled the woman, perceiving she was to be done out of her reward after all. "Come, are you going to give me what you promised or not? If you 'aint, clear out of here, my beauty, or I'll break every bone of your ugly body."

And since, with a stick in her hand, she looked very like putting her threat into execution, the captain beat a hasty retreat, chuckling to himself at the thought of his own excellent cleverness.

"Upon my word," said he to himself as he strolled westward, "I am having a most interesting time. What a versatile genius my co-trustee appears to be—a tutor to an heir, a defaulting and rusticated undergraduate, a penniless music-hall cad. Dear, dear! what a curious settlement of scores we shall have, to be sure—or rather, should have had, had our poor dear Roger remained with us. Heigho! what a curious sensation it will be, to be sure, to own a fortune."

At the hotel the porter met him with a telegram. He expected as much. He could guess what was inside. It really seemed waste of energy to open it.

But he must go through with his melancholy functions, and he therefore took a seat in the hall and composed his face for the worst.

"Thankful to say good night; fever abated, all hopeful.

"Rosalind."

Captain Oliphant turned pale, crushed the pink paper viciously in his hands, and uttered an exclamation which called forth the sympathy of the hotel servants who loitered in the hall.

"Poor gentleman," said the lady manager to her clerk, "he's got some bad news in that telegram."

He had indeed.

Chapter Ten
Robert Ratman, esquire, Gentleman

The next morning, as Captain Oliphant, somewhat depressed by the good news of last might was, attempting to write to his dear cousin expression his thankfulness for the mercies vouchsafed to their precious boy, he was considerably disturbed to feel himself slapped on the shoulder and hear a voice behind him exclaim—

"Got you, my man. How are you, Teddy!"

The captain turned with, a startled face, and confronted a stylishly-dressed man of about thirty-five, who, but for the dissipated look of his eyes and the vulgarity of his ornaments, might have passed for a gentleman. He wore a light suit—diamonds and turquoises blazed from his fingers, a diamond stud flashed from his shirt front, and from his heavy watch chain hung a bunch of seals and charms enough to supply half a dozen, men of ordinary pretensions His light hat was tilted at an angle on his head, his brilliant kid boots sparkled beneath the snow-white "spats," and the lavender gloves he flourished in his hands were light enough for a ball-room.

Once he might have been a handsome man. There were still traces of determination about his mouth, his nose was finely cut, and his lustreless eyes still retained occasional flashes of their old spirit. There was a recklessness in his face and demeanour which once, when it belonged to an honest man, might been attractive; and when he took off his hat and you saw the well-shaped head with its crisp curly hair, you could not help feeling that you saw the ruin of a fine fellow.

It was when he began to talk that you would best understand what a ruin it was. He was chary of his oaths and loose expressions—but when he spoke the words came out vulgarly, with a sleepy, half-tipsy drawl, which jarred on the ear.

Any words from the lips of Robert Ratman, however, would have jarred on the ears of Captain Oliphant.

"Aren't you glad to see me?" said the new arrival, putting his hat cheerfully on the writing-table and helping himself to an easy-chair. "As usual, writing *billets doux* to the ladies! Ah, Teddy, my boy, at your time of life too! Now, for a youngster like me—"

"I thought you would not be able to leave Southampton till the end of the week?"

"Couldn't resist the temptation of giving you a pleasant surprise. Why, Teddy, you look exactly as if you thought it was the arm of the law on your shoulder and heard the rattle of the handcuffs. Never mind. They're all safe. I know where they keep them."

"Ratman," said the captain, "you have a very poor idea of humour. You have made me blot my letter, and I shall have to write it over again."

"Take your time, old boy. No hurry. I shall not be going away for six months or so."

Captain Oliphant came to the conclusion he had better finish the letter with the blot than attempt a new one. Having done so, he put it in his pocket, and turned with a good show of coolness to his guest.

"When do we run down to Maxfield?" inquired the latter.

"Not for some time. There is illness in the house. You must wait."

"Oh, I don't mind if you don't. Who is the invalid? Young Croesus?"

"Yes—dangerously ill. I expect every day to hear that it is all over."

Ratman laughed.

"Order two suits of black while you're about it. But, Teddy, my boy, doesn't it strike you you'd be more usefully employed down there than here? It seems unfeeling of a guardian to be enjoying himself in town while his ward is *in extremis* at home, doesn't it? Who is nursing him?"

"My daughter, chiefly."

Ratman laughed coarsely.

"Ho, ho, clever Teddy! You've left a deputy to look after your interests, have you? Poor boy—no wonder you expect news of him!"

Captain Oliphant, crimson and trembling, rose to his feet.

"Ratman!" muttered he between his teeth, "I may be all you take me for—but don't talk of my daughter. She—she,"—and he almost choked at the word—"she is as good as I—and you—are black. Talk about me if you like—but forget that I have children of my own."

"My dear boy, you are quite amusing. I will make a point of forgetting the interesting fact. So the boy is being well looked after?"

"Too well," replied the captain, pulling himself together after his last outbreak. "The doctor is daft about him; and besides him, as I told you, there is the tutor."

"Ah! I forgot about him. Is he a nice sort of chap?"

"He's your worst enemy as well as mine. While he is about the place there's no chance for either of us."

"Thanks—don't bring me into it. Say there's no chance for you. I can take care of myself. And how about mamma?"

"She is at present too ill and distracted by her son's danger to think of anything else. If the boy dies I shall not need to trouble her. If he gets well, I may find it my duty to become his stepfather."

"Charming man, and fortunate mamma! Meanwhile, what are you going to do for me?"

"My dear fellow, you must wait. I can put you up at Maxfield if you behave decently, but as to money, you will spoil all if you are impatient. I am not the only trustee, remember. I have to be careful."

"That's all very well. Sounds beautiful. But do you know, Teddy, I've not quite as much confidence in you as I should like to have. I can't enjoy my holiday without some pocket-money. The big lump might wait, if properly secured. But the interest would be very convenient to me just now. What shall I give you a receipt for?" added he, taking a seat at the table; "a hundred?"

"Don't be a fool, Ratman! I've nothing I can give you just now," said the captain angrily.

Ratman put down his pen, and whistled a stave, drubbing his fingers on the table. Then he took the pen again.

"A hundred, eh?" he repeated.

The captain ground his teeth in impotent fury.

"No. Fifty."

"Thanks very much. I'll make it seventy-five, if you don't mind."

Captain Oliphant, with black countenance, slowly counted the notes out onto the table, while his friend with many flourishes wrote out the receipt. Before signing it he counted the money.

"Quite right, perfectly right. Thanks very much, Teddy. Now let us go out and see the sights. You forget it's years since I was in town."

"Tell me first," said the captain, going to the window, was turning his back, "about that—you know—that affair in—"

"About your robbing the mess-funds?" supplied his friend cheerfully. "Certainly, my dear boy. Quite a simple matter. Shortly after you left, Deputy-Assistant something or other came with a long face. 'This is a bad job,' says he; 'your friend Oliphant's left the accounts in an awful mess. Doesn't look well at all. Where is he?' 'Nonsense, my dear Deputy-Assistant,' says I; 'must be a mistake. Oliphant's a man of his word. Besides, he's just come into a fortune. Bound to be right if you look into it.' 'Will you make it good if it's wrong?' asks he. 'Don't mind if I do,' says I, 'within reason. He's a young family.' 'Only way of hushing it up. Either that or bringing him back between a file of soldiers.' 'You don't mean that?' says I. 'What's the figure?' '£750,' says he."

"Liar!" growled the captain, wheeling round. "It wasn't half that."

"They're bound to make something out of it—always happens. Well, as you'd told me you'd got the pickings of a cool half million, I felt I couldn't go wrong in covering you. So I came down with five hundred of needful. Got them to promise to let the rest stand till I had done myself the pleasure of a run over here just to remind you that they have you on their mind. You've disappointed me, Teddy, my boy, but I won't desert you. Don't say you've no friends. I'll stick by you, I rather fancy."

The captain was probably able to form a pretty clear estimate how much of this glib story was fact and how much fiction.

Whatever the proportion may have been, he had to acknowledge that this friend of his held him in an uncomfortable grip, and had better—for the present at least—be conciliated.

So the two went out arm in arm for a stroll—the first of many they took during their fortnight's sojourn in town.

The news from Maxfield became unpleasingly damping. Here, for instance, is a letter the doting father received from his son and heir a week after Ratman's arrival.

"Dear Pater,—Isn't it fizzing that old Roger is pretty nearly out of the wood? The fever's come down like anything, and he's getting quite chirpy. I can't fancy how a chap can hang on at all with nothing to eat but milk. It wouldn't fill up my chinks. If ever I get a fever, keep me going on beefsteak and mashed potatoes. It's been a great lark having no lessons. Armstrong's forgotten my existence, I think. He and Rosalind have regular rows about sitting up with him—I mean Roger, and Rosalind generally has to cave in. It does her good to cave in now and then. Armstrong's the only one can make her. I can't; nor can Brandram. Brandram's a stunner. I drive him in and out of Yeld every day, and he's up to no end of larks. And now Roger's pulling round, he's as festive as an owl. Jill's in jolly dumps because she's out of it all. Rosalind sits on her and tells her she's too much of a kid to be any good; and she doesn't get much change out of Armstrong. So she has to knock about with me all day, which is awful slow. I say, go and see Christy's Minstrels when you're in town, and get them to let Jockabilly do the breakdown. It will make you split. If that French chap is hanging about, tip him a bob for me and be civil to him, because he was decent enough to me. Auntie Eva said something about your bringing a gentleman home with you. I hope he's a jolly sort of chap. Rosalind's temper is all anyhow. When I told her a visitor was coming, she shut me up with a regular flea in my ear. Never mind, she's been a brick to old Roger and Auntie Eva, so we must make allowances. Old Hodder calls up nearly every day to ask after us all. He's grown quite young since he was left alone in his cottage, and Armstrong came down like a sack of coals on that beast Pottinger. My dear father, if you would like to know what I most hope you'll bring home for me, it's a football—Rugby—for the coming winter. Armstrong's promised to coach me in the drop kick. Can you do it? I shall be glad to see you home, as I'm jolly low in pocket-money, besides the affection one feels for those who are absent. Jill joins in love.

"Your affectionate 'Tom.'"

"P.S.—Auntie Eva is not nearly so down on her luck now that Roger's taken his turn. If he's well enough she's going to have a little kick-up on his birthday, which will be rare larks."

"A letter!" inquired Ratman, who had watched the not altogether delighted expression on his friend's face as he read it. "Good news? May I read it?"

"If you like," said the captain, tossing it across the table.

Ratman, who evidently had a better appreciation of juvenile vagaries than the father, read it with an amused smile on his face.

"Nice boy that," said he; "he and I will be friends."

"Remember," said the captain, "our bargain. Do and say what you like with me, but before my children—"

"Don't be afraid, Teddy, my boy. Depend on me for doing the high moral business. The innocent babes shall never guess that you owe me three years' pay, and that I could walk you off to the next police station for a sharper. It's amusing when you come to think of it, isn't it? But, I say, it looks as if you'll have to trouble mamma after all. The boy's getting well in spite of his nurses. I'm really impatient to see the happy family. When shall we go?"

"Next week. We must be decent, and wait till he's better now."

"Oh, all right. If we can't go to the funeral we'll go to the birthday party, eh? It's all one to me, Teddy, as long as you don't make a fool of me in the long run."

"You wait, and it'll be all right," said the captain, with a trace in his voice of something like desperation.

At the end of the following week these two nice gentlemen presented themselves at Maxfield. Captain Oliphant had written for the brougham to meet them, and as Tom and Jill were in it, Mr Ratman was spared the embarrassment of meeting the whole household at one time. Before the house was reached he had impressed Tom with the conviction that there was a considerable possibility of "larks" in his father's visitor. But Jill, who had acquired the habit of contrasting every gentleman she saw with her dear Mr Armstrong, was obdurate to his fascinations.

"I don't want to talk to you," said she shortly, when for the twentieth time he renewed his friendly overtures. "I don't like you, and hope you're not going to stay long."

Ratman took his rebuff as complacently as he could; and Jill, having exhausted her conversation with this outburst, put her hand apologetically into her father's, and remained silent the rest of the drive.

At Maxfield, the visitor, who appeared to experience no difficulty in making himself at home, received a polite welcome from the widow, whose style he generally approved, and considered a good deal better than his gallant comrade deserved. Then, as none of the rest of the household put in an appearance, he retired serenely to his comfortable apartment to dress for dinner.

Captain Oliphant's first anxiety was naturally for his dear young ward. He found him sitting up in an arm-chair, with Rosalind reading Shakespeare to him.

"Hullo, guardian!" said he, "you see the place hasn't got rid of me yet—thanks to my kind nurse here."

"I am indeed thankful, my dear boy, for your recovery. And how is my Rosalind?"

She came and kissed him.

"Very well, dear father. But Roger has to keep very quiet still, so you must only stay a minute or two, or I shall get into disgrace with the doctor. He has been so good. Have you seen cousin Eva?"

"Yes, my child. But come with me; I want to introduce you to Mr Ratman."

She looked inclined to rebel, but after a moment closed her book, and, having smoothed the invalid's cushions, followed her father from the room.

The captain felt decidedly nervous as she walked silently at his side. At her own door she paused abruptly and said—

"Won't you come in, father? I want to say something to you."

"A storm brewing," said the captain to himself. "I expected it."

He followed her into her studio and closed the door.

"What is it?"

"I am going to leave Maxfield, father. I cannot stay here any longer, living on other people. I am going to accept an engagement at the vicarage as governess."

"What!" exclaimed her father. "What freak is this, miss? I forbid you to do anything of the kind."

"I am very sorry you don't approve. I thought you would. It will enable me to support myself, and perhaps help to keep Jill. I shall get my board and lodging, and £30 a year, I am going on Monday. I wanted to tell you before any one else knew of it."

"I repeat you must abandon the idea at once. It is most derogatory in one of our family. In addition to which, I particularly desire to have you here during Mr Ratman's visit."

"It is chiefly on that account I have decided to go. It is not right, father, indeed it is not, to go on as we are."

She put her hands on his shoulders and kissed him, and looked into his eyes.

It was an ordeal on which Captain Edward Oliphant had not calculated. The sight of her there, the touch of her hands, the clear flash of her eyes, recalled to him all sorts of unpleasant memories. They reminded him of a day long ago, when the girl's mother had stood thus and pleaded with him for the sake of their children to be pure and honest and self-respecting. It reminded him of his own miserable schemings and follies, and how he had rejected that dear appeal, and ever since slipped and slipped out of reach of any love but the love of himself. It reminded him of the day when he heard that the one prop of his manhood had gone from him; and of how, even then, his sorrow was tempered by the thought that he was a free man to follow his own paths without question or reproof. Now, suddenly, the same hands seemed for a moment to lie on his shoulders, the same eyes to look into his, the same voice to fall on his ear, and he staggered under the illusion.

For a moment at least hope was within his reach. But the sound of a man's voice in the passage without recalled him, with a shiver, to himself.

It was Ratman's voice—the voice of the man to whom he owed money, who held the secret of his crime, who claimed his villainy and—who could say?—might even have to be pacified with a human sacrifice.

He shook her off rudely and said in dry, hard tones—

"Rosalind, I am disappointed in you. I will not discuss the matter with you. You know my wish; I expect you to obey me."

And he left the room.

She remained standing where she was till the bell rang for dinner. Then with a shiver she went down-stairs.

On the stairs she met Mr Armstrong.

"Your father has returned," said he.

"Yes, with a friend. Are you going down, or shall you stay with Roger?"

"May I?" he asked.

"You know how glad he will be."

So the tutor turned back, and thought to himself that Miss Rosalind was evidently anxious that he should not be a witness to her introduction to her father's friend.

Mr Ratman, brilliantly arranged in evening dress, and evidently already very much at home, was comfortably leaning against the mantelpiece in the hall as she descended. He did not wait for an introduction.

"I could tell Miss Oliphant anywhere," said he, advancing, "by her likeness to her father. May I offer you my arm?"

"I am not at all like father," said she quietly, scanning him as she spoke in a way which made even him uncomfortable, and then putting her hand on her father's arm.

Thus repulsed, the visitor cheerfully offered his arm to Mrs Ingleton, congratulating her as he did so on the recovery of her son.

During the meal he was aware that the young lady's eyes were completing their scrutiny, and although, being a bashful man, he did not venture too often to meet them with his own, he was conscious that the result was not altogether satisfactory to himself. His few attempts to talk to her fell flat, and in spite of the captain's almost nervous attempts to improve the festivity of the occasion, the meal was an uncomfortable one.

"Where's old Armstrong?" demanded Tom.

"With Roger," replied Rosalind.

"Have you seen Armstrong?" inquired the boy of the visitor; "he's a stunner, I can tell you. He can bend a poker double across his knee. You'll like him awfully; and he plays the piano like one o'clock. He's our tutor, you know—no end of a chap."

Mr Ratman was fain to express a longing desire to make the acquaintance of so redoubtable a hero.

"Does he lick you?" he inquired.

"Sometimes, when it's wanted; but, bless you, he could take the lot of us left-handed; couldn't he, Jill?"

"Oh, yes," said Jill enthusiastically; "and he saved Roger's life, and prevented Hodder being turned out, and won such a lot of prizes at Oxford."

"He must be a fine fellow," said Ratman, with a disagreeable laugh. "You admire him too, of course, Miss Oliphant?"

"Yes, he's honest," said she.

"Teddy, my boy," said the visitor, when he and his friend had been left alone at the table, "that girl of yours is a treasure. She don't fancy me, but she'll get over that. I like her, Teddy; I like her."

That evening, on his way to say good night to his dear ward, Captain Oliphant stopped at his daughter's door.

She was hard at work over a picture.

"Rosalind," said he, "you have disappointed me. But if your mind is made up, I know it is no use my setting up my authority against your self-will. Therefore, to relieve you of the sin of disobedience to your father's wishes, I withdraw my refusal to your proposal. You may do as you like. Good night!"

Chapter Eleven
Awkward Questions

The sun, when it peeped through the blinds next morning, found Mr Robert Ratman wide awake. His was one of those active minds which do not waste unnecessary time in sluggish repose, but, on the contrary, do a principal part of their most effective brain-work while other people are asleep.

"Snug enough so far," said he to himself, turning over on his side. "The place will suit me after all. Capital table, easy-going hostess, charming young Bohemian to amuse me, money going about, and all that. Teddy wants stirring up. I shall have to flick him a bit. He'll go well enough when he's once started, but he's wasting his time here disgracefully. Eight months since he came, and absolutely nothing done! The boy's not buried, the mother's not married, and the tutor's not had his month's notice, (Like to see this precious tutor, by the way.) Upon my honour, it's about time I came and opened shop here."

And with a grunt he got out of bed, and began to array himself preparatory to a stroll round the park before breakfast.

It was a delicious September morning. The birds, hardly convinced that the summer was over, were singing merrily in the trees. The hum of the not distant ocean droned solemnly in the air. The sunlight played fitfully with the gold of the harvest fields, and the lowing cattle in the meadows added their music to nature's peaceful morning anthem.

Mr Ratman was only half alive to the beauties of nature. He was considerably more impressed with the substantial masonry of the manor house, with the size of the timber, the appointments of the stables, and the acreage of the park. They all spelt money to him—suggesting a good deal more behind.

"Teddy's certainly a man to be looked after," said he to himself. "He's wasting his time scandalously. Yet he's clever in his way, is Edward. He has tucked his family into the big bed snugly, and made the most of his chance that way. Why—"

He had reached this pleasant stage in his reflections when something darted round from a side-walk and collided with him suddenly.

It was Miss Jill, taking an early scamper with her dog, and little dreaming that she was not, as usual, the sole occupant of the grounds.

"Hullo! my little lady," said Mr Ratman, recognising his enemy of yesterday; "you nearly did for me that time. Come, you'll have to tell me you are sorry, and beg my pardon very prettily."

"No, I won't!" exclaimed Jill, and proceeded to run.

Mr Ratman was not beyond a bit of fun himself; besides, he did not quite like to be thus set down by a child of twelve. Therefore, although his running days had passed their prime, he gave chase, and a very exciting race ensued.

Jill, as fleet as the wind, darted forward with little to fear from her pursuer; while the dog, naturally regarding the whole affair as an entertainment got up for his benefit, barked jubilantly, and did his best to force the pace. After a minute or two Mr Ratman began to wonder if the game was worth the candle, and was turning over in his mind the awkward possibility of owning himself beaten, when he perceived that the little fugitive was, by some error of judgment on her part, leading the way into what looked uncommonly like a *cul de sac*. Therefore, although painfully aware of the stitch in his side, he bravely held on, and had the gratification in a minute more of running his little victim to earth after all.

"Aha!" said he, laughing and panting; "you can't get away from me, you see. Now, my little beauty, I'm going to take you back in custody to the place where you started from, and make you beg my pardon very prettily for nearly knocking me over."

In vain Jill protested and struggled; he held her by the wrist as with a vice, and, rather enjoying her wild efforts to escape, literally proceeded to carry his threat into execution.

He had nearly brought her back to the starting-place, and she, having fought and struggled all the way, was beginning with humiliation to feel her eyes growing dim with tears, when a gentleman dressed in boating flannels, with one arm in a sling and an eye-glass in his eye, stepped abruptly across the path.

A moment later Mr Robert Ratman lay on the grass half a dozen yards away, on the flat of his back, blinking up at the sky.

Several curious reflections passed through his mind as he occupied this not very exhilarating position. Jill had escaped after all. That was annoying.

He should have a black eye for a week. That was very annoying. This left-handed individual with the eye-glass must be the tutor. That was most excessively annoying.

And the injured gentleman, neither looking nor feeling at all well, pulled himself together and sprang to his feet.

Jill was there, clinging to her champion. "Run away, Jill!" said Armstrong.

"But you have only one arm," said she. "Go, Jill!" said he, so decisively that the little maid, darting only one look behind her, fled towards the house.

All she saw was the two men facing one another—one flurried, vicious, and noisy; the other curious, silent, disgusted.

"You dog!" hissed Ratman, with an oath, "what do you mean by that?"

"My meaning should have been clear—it was intended to be."

Ratman tried hard to copy his adversary's composure, but failed miserably.

With many imprecations, and, heedless of the tutor's maimed condition, he threw himself upon him.

But Robert Ratman's boxing, like his running, was a trifle out of date, and once more he found himself on his back regarding the clouds as they flitted by overhead.

This time the tutor assumed the initiative.

"Get up," said he, advancing to his prostrate antagonist.

Ratman was surprised at himself when, after a moment's doubt, he obeyed.

"What's your name?" demanded Mr Armstrong, surveying him from head to foot.

Again, by some curious mental process, Mr Ratman obeyed.

"What are you doing down here?"

"I am Captain Oliphant's guest," growled Ratman.

The tutor looked him up and down in a manner which was clearly not calculated to imply admiration of Captain Oliphant's choice of friends.

"Allow me to tell you, sir, that in this part of the world we call men like you blackguards."

And the tutor, whose eye-glass had become uncomfortably deranged during this brief interview, screwed it in with a wrench, and turned on his heel.

"Where's jolly old Ratman?" inquired Tom, when the family presently assembled for breakfast.

"Tired with his journey, no doubt," said Mrs Ingleton.

As no one disputed this theory, and Jill's exchange of glances with her champion passed unheeded, there seemed every prospect of the meal passing off peaceably. But Tom, as usual, contrived to improve the occasion in the wrong direction.

"You'll like him, Armstrong, when you see him. He's no end of a chap — all larks. He'll make you roar with his rummy stories."

"I have met him already," said the tutor shortly.

"Then he is up. Jill, my child," said the captain, "go and knock at Mr Ratman's door, and tell him breakfast is ready."

"I won't go near him," said Jill, flushing up. "He's a horrid, hateful man. Isn't he, Mr Armstrong?"

Mr Armstrong, thus appealed to, looked a little uncomfortable, and nodded.

"Yes," blurted the girl; "and if it hadn't been for Mr Armstrong, father, he might have hurt me very much."

"Explain yourself," said the fond father, becoming interested.

"I don't want to talk about him," said Jill.

"What does all this mean, Armstrong?"

"As far as I am concerned, it means that I took the liberty of knocking Mr Ratman down for insulting your daughter. I am sorry you were not present to do it yourself."

Captain Oliphant turned white, and red, and black in succession.

"You knocked a visitor of mine—"

"Down twice," said the tutor, helping himself to sugar.

"Oh, what a lark!" exclaimed Tom. "Oh, I wish I'd been up too. Was it a good mill, I say? How many rounds? Six? Why ever didn't you come and tell me, Jill?"

"Be quiet, Tom," said Jill.

"Did you get him clean on the jaw, I say?" persisted Tom, "like the one—"

"Hold your tongue, sir," said his father peremptorily. "Mr Armstrong, I must ask you to explain this matter later; this is not the place for such talk."

"Quite so. I regret the matter was referred to. Tom, be good enough to pass Miss Oliphant the toast."

Tom could scarcely be induced to take the hint, and talked at large on the science of boxing during the remainder of the meal with an access of high spirits which, on any other occasion, would have been amusing.

Mr Ratman, later in the day, appeared with a decidedly marred visage, and announced with the best grace he could that an important business letter that morning necessitated his return to London.

In private he explained himself more fully to his host.

"If this is what you call making me comfortable," growled he, with an unusual number of oaths interspersed in his sentence, "you've a pretty notion of your own interests."

"My dear fellow, how could I help it?"

"You can help it now, and you'll have to. I may be only a creditor, but I'll let you see I am not going to be treated in this house like a dog, for all that."

"The awkward thing is that if you had behaved—"

"Shut up about how I behaved," snarled the other. "You'll have to clear that cad out of the way here. I'll not come back till you do; and till I do come back you're sitting on a volcano."

"My dear fellow, you will spoil everything if you take such an absurd view of the matter—really you will. Of course I'll put you right. You are my guest. But remember my difficult position here."

"It will be a precious deal more difficult for you soon. I can promise you," said Mr Ratman, lifting his hand to his swollen eye with an oath. "Now then, I'll give you a month. If you're not rid of this fellow by then, and aren't a good deal nearer than you are now to squaring up with me, you'll be sorry you ever heard my name."

"I'm that already," said the captain. "I can promise nothing; but I'll do what I can."

"You'll have to do more, if you're to get rid of me. How about money?"

This abrupt question fairly staggered the captain, who broke out—

"Money! Didn't you drain me of every penny I had in London?"

The fellow laughed coarsely.

"What did you drain the regimental mess of, I should like to know? You needn't think you're out of that wood. Now, I shall want £200 for my month in town. I mean to enjoy myself."

The captain laughed dismally. "Where are you going to get it from?"

"You. Look sharp!"

"I tell you, Ratman, I haven't any money. You can't get blood out of a stone."

"Then you must give me a bill—at a month."

"No, no! I won't begin that," said the captain, who had fibre enough left in him to know that a bill was the first plunge into an unknown region of financial difficulty. "If you're bent on ruining me in any case, for heaven's sake do it at once and have done with it. Remember, you bring down more than me. Whatever I may be, they don't deserve it."

"For their sake, then, give me the bill. Bless you, any one can put his hand to paper. Consider yourself lucky I don't insist on taking it out in hard cash."

It was no use arguing or protesting with a man like this. The captain flung himself miserably into a chair and scrawled out the ill-omened document.

Ratman snatched it up with a grunt of triumph.

"That's more like," said he. "What's the use of all that fuss? Plenty of things can happen in a month. Order the dogcart in half an hour."

The abrupt departure of Captain Oliphant's guest might have excited more remark than it did, had not another departure from Maxfield that same day thrown it somewhat into the shade.

True to her promise, or rather threat, Miss Rosalind had packed up her things and had them transported to the Vicarage.

It was not without a pang that she uprooted herself from her surroundings in Maxfield, or bore the protests of Roger, the tears of Jill, and the chaff of Tom for her desertion.

"It's not that you're not all awfully kind," said she to the first that afternoon, when the party was assembled in his room. "You are too kind—that's why I'm going."

"If a little of the opposite treatment would induce you to stay," said Roger, "I'd gladly try it. Don't you think it's a little unkind of her to go when we all want her to stay—eh, Armstrong?"

"That depends," said Mr Armstrong diplomatically. "I should be inclined to say no, myself."

"Thank you, Mr Armstrong, I'm glad I've got one person to back me up. Every one else is down on me—auntie, father, Roger, Jill, Tom—"

"I'm not down on you," put in Tom. "I think it's rather larks your going to the Vicarage. No more of that beastly art class for us. But if you want to know who's down on you, it's jolly old Ratman. I've just been to see him off in the tantrums to London. I asked him to be sure and be back for Roger's birthday, and he said he'd try, if his black eye was well enough. That must have been a ripping clean shot of yours, Armstrong. He'll get over it all right, you bet. He was grinning about it already, and said he'd have a return some day. I asked him if he didn't think Rosalind was a stunner (one's got to be civil to fellows, you know), and he said 'Rather,' and envied the kids at the Vicarage. I don't. You always make yourself jolly civil to other people, but I don't come in for much of it, nor does Jill."

"I can't bear your going away," said Jill, with tears in her eyes; "I'll be so lonely. But it would be far worse if Mr Armstrong were to go away too. You'll stay, won't you, dear Mr Armstrong?"

Dear Mr Armstrong jerked his eye-glass by way of assent, and said he was sure everybody would miss Miss Oliphant and— and he would say good-bye now, as he had some letters to get off by the post.

Miss Rosalind, who had just been thinking a little kindly of the tutor, stiffened somewhat at this abrupt exit, and thought Mr Armstrong might at least have offered to escort her over to her new quarters.

To tell the truth, that poor gentleman would have given a finger off his hand for the chance, and retired to his room very dejected about the whole business—so dejected that he fidgeted about his room a good while before he noticed a note addressed to himself, in Captain Oliphant's hand, lying on the table. He opened it and read—

> "Mr Frank Armstrong is informed that his services as tutor to Roger Ingleton will not be required after this day month, the 25th *prox*. Mr Armstrong is at liberty to remain at Maxfield until that date, or may leave at once on accepting a month's wages in lieu of notice.—For the Executors of Roger Ingleton,—

"Edward Oliphant."

The tutor's lips curled into a grim smile as he perused this pleasing document, and then tossed it into the waste-paper basket. He relieved his feelings with a few chords on the piano, and then, after a few more uneasy turns in his room, went off to call on his co-trustee.

On his way down-stairs he met Rosalind and her escort about to take their departure.

"Come along with us, do!" said Tom. "We're just going to trot Rosalind over to her diggings, and then we can have a high old lark in the paddock on our way back."

"The programme is not attractive, Thomas," said the tutor. "Good-bye again, Miss Oliphant."

Captain Oliphant had already bidden his daughter a tender farewell, and was enjoying a cigar in the library.

"Oh," said he, as the tutor entered, "you got my note, did you, sir?"

"I did, thanks."

"Well, sir?"

"That was the question I was about to ask you. Excuse my saying it, but it was a very foolish note for a man in your position to write. Did Mrs Ingleton—"

"Mrs Ingleton has decided, on my advice, to send her son to Oxford. I have recently been there, and made inquiries."

"Indeed! I'll join you in your smoke, if you don't mind," and the tutor drew a chair up to the table and filled his pipe.

Captain Oliphant was considerably disconcerted at this cool reception of his piece of news; but, warned by previous experiences, he forbore to bluster.

"I think the life will suit him. He is wasting his time here."

"If his health improves sufficiently," said the tutor, "there is a good deal to be said in favour of the University."

"You think so, do you?" said his co-guardian drily. "You are an Oxford man yourself, I understand."

"Yes; I was at — College."

"So I heard from a friend of mine there, who remembered your name."

Mr Armstrong twitched his glass a little and puffed away.

"Yes," said the captain, encouraged by this slight symptom of uneasiness; "I heard a good deal about you up there, as it happened."

"Kind of you to take so much interest in me. You ascertained, of course, that I left Oxford in debt and without a degree?"

This was check again for the captain, who had counted upon this discovery as an effective bombshell for his side.

"As regards Roger, however," proceeded the tutor, reaching across for the captain's ash-tray, "I would advise Balliol in preference to—"

"We shall not need to trouble you for your advice."

"But I shall most certainly give it."

By this time Captain Oliphant's self-control was rapidly evaporating. He was beginning to feel himself a little small, and that always annoyed him.

"Look here, Mr Frank Armstrong," said he, leaning back in his chair, and trying hard to look superior, "it is just as well for you and me to understand one another. I have heard what sort of figure you cut at Oxford, and the disgrace in which you left the University. Allow me to say, sir, that it reflects little credit on your honour that you should have imposed on your late employer, and taken advantage of his weak health and faculties to foist yourself upon his family under false colours."

"Will you oblige me with a light?" interposed Mr Armstrong.

"You are under a delusion if you think I am not perfectly well acquainted with your disreputable antecedents. Let me tell you, sir, that a music-hall cad is not a fitting companion for a lad of Roger's rank and expectations."

"I perfectly agree with you. But really this has very little to do with our arrangements for Roger's future."

"Do you mean to deny, sir, that you were a music-hall singer?"

"By no means. I was. On the whole, I rather enjoyed the vocation at the time. I look upon that and the year (about which you apparently have not been fortunate enough to learn anything) during which I was tutor and private secretary in the family of the Hon. James Welcher—the most notorious blackleg in the kingdom—as two of the most interesting episodes in my career."

"I can believe it. And, before you devoted your energies to singing disreputable songs to the blackguards of the East End—"

"Pardon me. I was particular. My songs were for the most part of the classical order; but what were you saying?"

"I was saying," said the captain, now fairly dropping the dignified, and falling back on the abusive, "what were you before that?"

"Really, Captain Oliphant, you have been so acute and successful so far, I would not on any account deprive you of the satisfaction of discovering what little more remains to complete my humble biography by your own exertions. Meanwhile, as to Roger's college; had you leisure when at Oxford to make any inquiries as to that rather important question?"

"Oblige me by addressing your conversation to some one else, sir. I am not disposed to be asked questions by an adventurer and sharper, who—"

The tutor's face blackened, the glass fell from his eye, and he rose to his feet so suddenly that the chair on which he had been sitting fell back violently.

Captain Oliphant turned pale and started to his feet too in an attitude of self-defence and retreat. But the tutor only walked over to the fireplace to knock out his ashes into the fender, and then, resuming his glass, said quietly—

"I beg your pardon; I interrupted you." Captain Oliphant did not pursue the subject, and presently retired, leaving his co-trustee master of the situation.

"Strange," said the latter to himself when the enemy had gone, "what a look he has of his daughter. The resemblance was distinctly fortunate for him five minutes ago."

Chapter Twelve
A Windfall for the Captain

The impending birthday festivities at Maxfield were a topic of interest to others than merely the residents at the manor-house. There, indeed, the prospect was considerably damped by the failing health of Mrs Ingleton and the absence of Rosalind from the scene of action. The burden of the arrangements fell upon the tutor, who only half relished the duties of *major domo*, and heartily wished the uncomfortable date was past. Mrs Ingleton, however, ill as she was, was intent on celebrating the occasion in a manner becoming the hospitable traditions of the house of which her son was now the head, and accordingly, a large party of the neighbouring gentry was invited for the occasion.

Among the uninvited guests one individual was anticipating the event with considerable interest. This was Robert Ratman, Esquire, as he lounged comfortably on a sofa at the "Grand Hotel" in London, and perused a letter which had just reached him by the post.

"I shall have to get you to take another bill in place of the one I gave you, due on the 26th. The fact is, I forgot that was the day of my ward's twentieth birthday, when there are to be celebrations at Maxfield," ("What on earth has that to do with it?" grunted the reader). "If you will take my advice you will postpone your return here till after that date. In any case, please understand I am unable to attend to money matters at present. It may interest you to know that the tutor is under notice to leave," (here the reader uttered a not very complimentary expletive), "also that I am on the best of terms with the fair widow.

"E.O."

"Thinks I'm a fool, does he?" grunted Mr Ratman; "I shall have to undeceive him there."

So he laid down his cigar and wrote—

"Dear Teddy,—It sounds very nice, but it's not good enough. You've mistaken your man, my boy. You'll have to stump up £100 on the day, and I'll wait a month for the rest and interest. I shall be on the spot to receive it and join in the festivities. If you are not lying, you deserve credit for getting rid of the tutor. See he is packed off before I come; and see I get no more impertinence from those brats of yours, unless you wish trouble to their father.

"Yours,—

"R.R."

The receipt of this genial epistle considerably marred the pleasure with which Captain Oliphant looked forward to the approaching festivities at Maxfield.

It had been bad enough to have the Oxford scheme and all it involved fall through. Roger had explained in his pleasant manner that he was not disposed to accept his guardian's advice as to a University course at present; and as his decision was backed up by both Mrs Ingleton and Mr Armstrong, the poor man found himself in a minority, and no nearer a solution to his difficulties than before.

In addition to this, Roger was every day recovering health, and, in Rosalind's absence, devoting himself more loyally than ever to his tutor's direction and instruction.

Altogether Captain Oliphant had a dismal consciousness of being out in the cold. His carefully thought cut plans seemed to advance no further. Mrs Ingleton's ill-health was an unlooked-for difficulty. He even began to suspect that when he did screw himself up to the point of proposing he should make by no means as easy a conquest of the fair widow as he had flattered himself. She, good lady, liked him as her boy's guardian, but in his own personal capacity was disappointingly indifferent to his attentions.

With all these worries upon him it was little wonder if Mr Ratman's letters hurt his feelings.

He was very much inclined to throw up the sponge and vanish from the Maxfield horizon, and might have attempted the feat had not a letter which arrived on the following day suggested another way out of his difficulties. It came from America, addressed to the late Squire, and read thus—

> "Dear Ingleton,—I guess you've forgotten the scape-grace brother-in-law who, thirty-six years ago, on the day you married his sister Ruth, borrowed a hundred pounds of you without the slightest intention of paying you back. He has not forgotten you. Your hundred pounds started me in life right away here, where I am now a boss and mayor of my city. I've put off being honest as long as I can, but can't well manage it any longer. I send you back the money in English

bank-notes, and another hundred for interest. It won't do you much good, but I reckon I'll sleep better at night to have got rid of it. I saw in the papers the death of my sister, and her son, my nephew. Such is life! I got more good from that marriage than she did. I take for granted you are still in the old place, and, like all the Ingletons I ever met, alive and kicking.

"Yours out of debt,—

"Ralph Headland."

Captain Oliphant read and re-read this curious letter, and hummed a tune to himself. He gave a professional twitch to each of the hundred-pound notes, and held them up one after the other to the light. Then he examined the post-mark on the envelope, and failed to decipher the name of the town.

"Very singular," said he to himself, tapping his fingers on the envelope. "Quite like a chapter in a story. Really it restores one's faith in one's fellow-man to find honesty asserting itself in this way after thirty-six years' suppression. Our dear one must have forgotten this debt years ago; or written it off as a gift. I'm sure he would not have liked to accept it now. Very singular indeed!"

Then he hummed on for five minutes, and tried to recall what he had been thinking about before the letter came. He fancied it was about Ratman. Yes, Ratman was a bad man, and must be got rid of, not so much on the captain's account as for the sake of the innocent darlings whose happiness he threatened.

And as if there were some connection between the two ideas, captain Oliphant abstractedly put the two notes into his own pocket, and proceeded thoughtfully to tear up the letter and envelope of the American mayor.

He had hardly completed this function when the door opened and Rosalind sailed in, looking particularly charming after a breezy walk across the park.

She had rarely seen her father in better and more amiable spirits.

"Ah, my dear child," said he; "it does one good to see you again. A week's absence is a long time. And how are you getting on at the Vicarage?"

"They are awfully kind to me," said Rosalind, "and I like my little pupils. I half wish it was harder work. As it is, I get time for a little art in between lessons. I've come over to-day to finish my picture of the old tower for Roger's birthday."

"Ah, to be sure. The dear boy's birthday is getting near. We shall depend on you to help us here on the day, Rosalind. So they make you happy, do they? I am very glad to hear it. Have you all you want?"

"Everything, dear father; and it makes all the difference to me to feel I am supporting myself."

"Brave little puss. See now," added the fond parent, taking out a couple of sovereigns from his purse.

"I want you to take these to get any little trifle which may add to your comfort. I have not been very lavish with pocket-money, but I think just now you may find this useful. Take it, my dear child, and bless you."

"Really, I have all I—"

"You must not refuse me, daughter; it will please me if you take it."

So Rosalind kissed her father gratefully, and said she should be sure to find the money useful, if he could really spare it. And he, good man, only wished it were twice as much.

"I have just had a note," said he, "from Mr Ratman, who announces his return on the 25th. During the few days he remains, my dear Rosalind, I think you should try, even if it cost you an effort, to be friendly. After all, he is an old comrade, and I have reasons for desiring not to offend him."

"Oh, why ever do you let him come back after the unkind way he behaved to Jill? I'm sure he is a bad man, father. Indeed, I wonder at his thinking of coming at all after what has happened."

"I dare say his manner may have been rough; but it was meant only in good-natured fun. Let us think no more about that. I was annoyed at the whole affair; but I must ask you, Rosalind, not to give him unnecessary offence when he comes again."

"I can't pretend to like people I detest," said she; "but if he conducts himself like a gentleman, and goes away soon, there needn't be any trouble about it." And she went off to rejoice Roger with a visit.

During the week that followed, Captain Oliphant impressed the whole family with his chastened good-humour.

He paid a friendly call at the Vicarage, and expressed his obligations to the vicar and his wife for their consideration, and trusted his daughter, who (though he said so who should not), he was sure was a conscientious girl—would do her work well and requite them for their kindness.

He bought Tom his longed-for football, and ordered from town a handsome dressing-case for his dear ward. He delighted Miss Jill by allowing her to drive him in his rounds among the tenantry, when he had a friendly word for everybody.

Jill, in charge of the reins, was as happy as a queen, and quite captivated by her father's cheerful good-humour.

"I wonder what makes you so jolly," she said, as they spanked along the country lanes to Yeld, "dear, dear old daddy? I shall always drive you now, for you see I can manage the pony, can't I? Mr Armstrong taught me. He says I shall make a first-rate whip. I'm sure I was very stupid when I first tried; but he is ever so patient. He scolds sometimes, but he always lets me know when he's pleased; so I don't mind. Do you know, father, I'd give my head for Mr Armstrong any day, I like him so?"

Captain Oliphant shrugged his shoulders. He wasn't equal to coping with a case of sheer infatuation.

"I'm sure," persisted Jill, flicking the pony into a trot, "he's fifty million times as nice as that horrible Mr Ratman."

"Mr Ratman is a friend of mine," said her father, "and I fear he must think you a very silly little girl to object to a bit of fun as you did."

"I don't mind what he thinks. It wasn't fun at all. He hurt me very much. Ugh!"

"Well, he was very much annoyed, and so was I, at what happened; and when he comes here again next week—"

"Is he coming again next week?"

"Yes."

"All right. I shall run away then—or if I can't do that, I shall keep a knife in my pocket. *Please*, father, don't let him come!"

And the child nearly cried in her eagerness.

"Listen to me, Jill," said her father sternly. "Unless you can behave yourself sensibly I shall be very angry indeed. I expect you to be polite to Mr Ratman while he is here."

"He'd better be polite to young ladies," said the irrepressible Jill. "If he doesn't, I know somebody who will make him."

"Be silent, miss, and bear in mind my wishes."

That afternoon Captain Oliphant sent a polite message to his co-trustee requesting the favour of an interview.

Mr Armstrong found him in an unusually balmy frame of mind, anxious to go into the executorship accounts.

Everything was square and exact. The rents and other receipts were all in order, and the amount duly paid into the bank. The tutor quite admired his colleague's aptitude for figures, and the lucid manner in which he accounted for every farthing which had passed through his hands. He was hardly prepared for such precision, and there and then modified the previous bad impression he had formed.

"It is necessary to be particular in money matters," said the captain, "especially where the money of others is involved. Perhaps you will check my figures, sir, and let me know if you agree in the result."

Mr Armstrong spent an afternoon painfully going over the agent's and banker's accounts, and satisfying himself that all was absolutely correct and in order. He countersigned the balance-sheet, and went out of his way to thank Captain Oliphant for taking so much of the labour as to save both him and Mrs Ingleton a great deal of time.

"Thank you," said the captain drily; "a compliment from Signor Francisco is worth receiving. But it is uncalled-for. Good afternoon, sir."

Mr Armstrong flushed, and screwed his glass violently in his eye.

"A civil, pleasant-spoken gentleman," said he to himself as he returned to his room.

A few days later, the day before the birthday, Captain Oliphant received a telegram couched in the following lordly terms—

"Arrive 5.30. Send trap to meet me.—Ratman."

He frowned to himself as he read it. The tone did not betoken peace. It rather called to mind a good many unpleasant reflections, the chief of which was that Mr Ratman would find matters no further advanced as regarded the widow, the heir, or the tutor. The only comfort was that he could hardly make himself disagreeable about the bill.

The coachman was sent down with the dogcart; but if Mr Ratman expected any further demonstration of welcome, he was disappointed. Mrs Ingleton was in bed; Jill was dining at the Rectory; Roger and Armstrong were taking a long ride; Tom was poaching on the Maxfield preserves. Only Captain Oliphant was at home.

"Oh, you're here to receive me, are you?" snarled the visitor. "How long has it taken you to organise this flattering reception, I should like to know?"

"I really have nothing to do with other persons' arrangements," said the captain. "If they happen to be out, it's not my concern."

"But it's mine. You ought to have sent the heir down to meet me—I've not seen him yet—and had those girls of yours here to give me afternoon tea. Where are they?"

The captain attempted to explain.

"That won't do for me," said the visitor, "not by any means. They should have been on the spot. When did the tutor leave?"

"He is still here."

"Still here!" said Ratman, with a curse. "Didn't I tell you he was to be packed off before I came?"

"You said a good many things, Ratman. I expected he would have gone a fortnight ago; but he can't be moved."

Ratman growled out a string of oaths.

"Get me some tea," said he, "and tell them to take my traps upstairs. What time do we dine?"

"I was going to propose that we should dine together in my room at seven," said the captain.

"Not good enough. I'll dine with the lot of you at the big table. And now, about my bill."

Now was the captain's turn.

"What about it?" said he.

"What about it? I want the money for it—that's what's about it."

"All right, keep your temper. You shall have the hundred to-morrow when it's due."

Ratman glanced up at his host with a leer.

"Whose till have you been robbing now?" he said.

Captain Oliphant frowned.

"You haven't a very genial way about you, Ratman. Try a cigar."

"Oh, bless you," said he, "I ask no questions. It's all one to me, so long as it's solid pounds, shillings and pence."

"You wait till to-morrow, and it will be all right," said the Captain; "and meanwhile, my dear fellow, try to make yourself agreeable, and don't spoil sport by being unreasonably exacting. Ah, here's the tea!"

At dinner that evening, Mr Ratman found his only companions Captain Oliphant, Roger, and Mr Armstrong. The talk was difficult, the captain working hard to give his guest a friendly lead; Mr Armstrong trying to appear oblivious of the fact that he had knocked the fellow down twice for a cad; and Roger as head of the house, trying to be affable to a person whom he had expected to find detestable, and who quite came up to expectations.

As the meal went on Mr Ratman showed alarming symptoms of requiring no friendly lead to encourage his powers of conversation. Despite his host's deprecatory signals, he began to tell stories of an offensive character, and joke about matters not generally held to be amusing in a company of gentlemen. Captain Oliphant grew hot and nervous. Mr Armstrong leant back coolly in his chair, and kept his eye curiously on the speaker, an apparently interested listener. Roger, after the first surprise, flushed wrathfully and fidgeted ominously with his napkin ring.

He was nearly at the end of his tether, and an awkward scene might have ensued, had not Tom opportunely broken in upon the party, very hungry and flushed with a good afternoon's sport.

"Hullo, Ratman!" said he, greeting the visitor; "turned up again? Got over your black eye all right? I've told Armstrong to let me know when the next mill comes off, and I'll hold the sponge? Been telling them some of your rummy stories? I roared over that you told me about the—"

"Be quiet, Tom, and go and wash yourself before dinner," said his father.

"All right. But I say, Ratman, you'd better steer clear of my young sister Jill. She's got a downer on you, and so has—"

"Do you hear, sir?" shouted the father.

Somehow this genial interruption robbed Mr Ratman of his ideas, and stopped the flow of his discourse, much to the relief of the remainder of the party.

"Well?" said Mr Armstrong, when he and his ward met afterwards in the room of the latter, "how do you like our new visitor?"

"So badly that I am thankful for once that Rosalind has gone."

Mr Armstrong looked hard at his ward for a moment. Then he twitched his glass uncomfortably, and replied in an absent sort of way—

"Quite so—quite so."

Chapter Thirteen
A Voice from the Dead

Roger Ingleton's reflections, as he lay awake on the morning of his twentieth birthday, were not altogether self-congratulatory. He was painfully aware that he was what he himself would have styled a poor creature. He was as weak, physically, as a girl; he was not particularly clever; he was given to a melancholy which made him pass for dull in society. Ill-health dogged him whenever he tried to achieve anything out of the commonplace. His tenantry regarded him still as a boy, and very few of his few friends set much store by him for his own sake apart from his fortune.

"A poor show altogether," said he to himself. "That boy on the wall there would have made a much better thing of it. There's some go in him, especially the copy that Rosalind—"

Here he pulled up. In addition to his other misfortunes, it occurred to him now definitely for the first time that he was in love.

"She doesn't care two straws about me," said he ungratefully; "that is, except in a sisterly way. Why should she? I know nothing about art, which she loves. I'm saddled with pots of money, which she hates. The only way I can interest her is by being ill. I'm not even scape-grace enough to make it worth her while to take me in hand to reform me. Heigho! It's a pity that brother of mine had not lived. Yes, you," he added, shaking his head at the portrait, "with your wild harum-scarum face and mocking laugh. You'd have suited her, and been able to make her like you—I can't. I believe she thinks more of Armstrong than me. Not much wonder either. Only, wouldn't he be horrified if any one suggested such a thing!"

And the somewhat dismal soliloquy ended in a some what dismal laugh, as the heir of Maxfield assumed the perpendicular and pulled up his blind.

Mr Armstrong, fresh from his dip in the sea, came in before he had finished dressing.

"Well, old fellow," said he, "many happy returns! How are you—pretty fit?"

"I'm not sorry there's a year between each," said the boy.

"What's wrong?" said the tutor.

"Oh, nothing; only I don't feel particularly festive. I've been lying awake a long time."

"Pity you didn't get up. Shocking habit to lie in bed after you're awake."

"At that rate I should often be up at two in the morning," said Roger.

"I doubt it—but what's wrong?"

Roger put down his brush, and flung himself on a chair.

"I don't know—yes, I do. Can't you guess?"

"Cheese for supper," suggested the tutor seriously.

"Don't be a fool, Armstrong, and don't laugh at me; I'm not in the mood for a joke. You know what it is well enough."

The tutor's glass dropped from his eye, and he walked over to the window.

"Quite so. I overtook her in the park a quarter of an hour ago, and she is already in the house, wondering why you are so late down on your birthday."

Roger sprang up and resumed his toilet.

"Has she really come? Armstrong, I say, I wish I knew how to make her care for me."

"I'm not an expert in these matters, but it occurs to me that the sort of thing you want is not made."

"You mean that if she doesn't care for me for what I am, it's no use trying to get her to care for me by being what I am not."

"Roger, you have a brilliant way occasionally of putting things exactly as they should be put."

"That's not much consolation," pursued the boy.

"Possibly," said the tutor; "but, as I say, I am not an expert in these delicate affairs. Much as I would like to prescribe, I rather advise your taking a second opinion—your mother's, say. I was engaged to teach you classics and the sciences, but the art of love was not included among the subjects to be treated of."

Mr Armstrong was late for breakfast that morning. For some reason of his own he wasted ten minutes at his piano before he obeyed the summons of the gong, and the chords he played were mostly minor. But when he did appear his glass was fixed as jauntily as ever, and his pursed lips looked impervious to any impression from within or without.

To his surprise, he found Miss Jill waiting outside the door.

"I didn't mean to go in," said she, "where that horrid man is, till you came. I don't mind a bit now. Come along, dear Mr Armstrong."

Dear Mr Armstrong came along, feeling decidedly compromised, but yet a little grateful to his loyal adherent.

As usual he dropped into his seat at the foot of the table after a bow to Miss Oliphant, and a friendly nod to Tom.

Jill, to her consternation, found a seat carefully reserved for her next to Mr Ratman. Her impulse on making the discovery was to run; but a glance at Mr Armstrong, who sat watching her in a friendly way, reassured her. To gain time she went round the table and kissed every one (including the tutor), and especially the hero of the day, whom she artfully tried to persuade, in honour of the occasion, to make room for her next to himself. But when that transparent little artifice failed, she bridled up and marched boldly to the inevitable.

"Well, little puss," said Mr Ratman, "haven't you got a kiss for me?"

"No," she replied. "Father says I'm to be civil to you, so I'll say good-morning; but I don't mean it a bit; and I still think you're a horrid, bad man, though I don't say so. I'm not a bit afraid of you, either, because Mr Armstrong is here to punish you if you behave wickedly."

Tom, as usual, improved matters with a loud laugh.

"Good old Jilly!" cried he; "let him have it! Sit on his head! He's got no friends! Never you mind, Ratman—she doesn't—"

"Silence, sir?" thundered his father, "or leave the table instantly."

Tom subsided promptly.

"And you, Jill," continued her father, "do not speak till you're spoken to."

Jill looked down at Mr Armstrong to see if he counselled further resistance; but as he was studiously busy with the ham, she capitulated, and said—

"Then I hope no one will speak to me, because I don't want to talk."

Mr Ratman made an effort to turn the incident off with a laugh, and addressed his further remarks to his host. But as that gentleman found some difficulty in being cordial, and as the rest of the party continued to enjoy the meal without paying much attention to him, he was on the whole relieved when the performance came to an end.

On his way to the captain's room, afterwards, he encountered Mr Armstrong.

The two men glared at one another in a hostile manner for a moment, and then the tutor observed casually that it was a cold day.

"It will be hotter before it's much older," growled the late owner of a certain black eye.

"I can well believe that," said the tutor drily.

"Yes, sir, I shall have something to say to you."

"Delighted, I'm sure, at any time that suits you."

"You and I had better understand one another at once," said Mr Ratman.

"Why not? I flatter myself I understand you perfectly already."

"Do you? Now, look here, my fine fellow. It's easy for you to give yourself airs, but I know a good deal more about you than I dare say you would care to own yourself. If you'll take my advice, the sooner you clear out of here the better. You may think you've a snug berth here, and flatter yourself you pass for a saint with your pupil and his mamma, but, let me tell you, I could open their eyes to a thing or two which would alter their opinion, as well as the opinion of certain young lady friends who—"

"Who do not require the assistance of Robert Ratman to keep them out of bad company," retorted the tutor, hotly for him.

"No, but they may require the assistance of Robert Ratman to keep them from being ashamed of their own father, Mr Armstrong."

The tutor glared through his glass. He understood this threat.

"What of that?" said he.

"Merely," said Mr Ratman, "that it depends pretty much on you whether they are to continue to believe themselves the children of an officer and a gentleman, or of a—a fugitive from justice. That's the position, Mr Tutor. The responsibility rests with you. If you choose to go, I shall not undeceive them; if you don't—well, it may suit me to open their eyes; there!"

The tutor inspected his man from top to toe in a dangerous way, which made the recipient of the stare decidedly uncomfortable. Then, pulling himself together with an effort, Mr Armstrong coolly inquired, "Have you anything more to say?"

"That's about enough, isn't it? I give you a week."

"Thanks, very much," said Mr Armstrong, as he turned on his heel.

Roger, after a long ramble in the park with his fair tormentor, returned about noon, flushed and excited.

"Armstrong, old man," said he, "what's to be done? She's kind to me—horribly kind; but whenever I get near the subject she laughs me off it, and holds me at arm's length. What's the use of my name and my money and my prospects, if they can't win her? If I jest, she's serious, and if I'm serious, she jests—we can't hit it. What's to be done, I say?"

"Patience," said the tutor; "it took several years to capture Troy."

"All very well for an old bachelor like you. I expected you'd say something like that. I know I could make her happy if she'd let me try. But she won't even let me tell her I love her. What should you do yourself?"

Mr Armstrong coloured up at the bare notion of such a dilemma.

"I think I might come to you and ask your advice," said he.

Roger laughed rather sadly.

"I know," said he. "Of course it's a thing one has to play off one's own bat, but I sometimes wish I were anything but the heir of Maxfield. She might care for me then."

"You can disinherit yourself by becoming a criminal, or marrying under age—"

"Or dying—thank you," said the boy. "You are something like a consoler. I know it's a shame to bore you about it, but I've no one else to talk to."

"I'd give my right hand to help you, old fellow," said the tutor; "but, as you say, I'm absolutely no use in a case like this."

"I know. Come upstairs and play something."

"By the way," said the tutor, as they reached the study, "I've something to give you. You may as well have it now."

And he went to his desk and took out an envelope.

"It will explain itself," said he, handing it to the boy.

He sat down at the piano, and wandered over the keys, while Roger, too full of his own cares to give much heed to the missive in his hands, walked over to the window and looked out across the park. The afternoon sun was glancing across the woods, and gleaming far away on the sea. "If only she would share it with me," thought he to himself, "how proud I should be of the dear old place. But what good is it all to me if she condemns me to possess it all myself?"

Then with a sigh he turned his back on the scene, and let his eyes fall on the letter.

He started as he recognised the dead hand of his father in the inscription—

"*To be given unopened into the hands of Roger Ingleton junior, on his twentieth birthday.*"

His breath came fast as he broke the seal and looked within. The envelope contained two enclosures, a document and a letter. The latter, which he examined first, was dated scarcely a fortnight before the old man's death, written in the same trembling hand as the words on the envelope.

"My dear son," it said, "this will reach you long after the hand that writes it is still and cold. My days are numbered, and for better or worse are rapidly flying to their account. But before I go, I have something to say to you. Read this, and the paper I enclose herewith. If, after reading them, you choose to destroy them, no one will blame you; no one will know—you will do no one an injury. You are free to act as you choose. What follows is not a request from me, still less a command. It is a confidence—no more."

Roger put down the letter. His head was in a whirl. He only half heard the notes of the tutor's sonata as they rose and fell on his ear. Presently, with beating heart, he read on—

"You had a brother once—a namesake—whom you never saw, and perhaps never heard of. You never mourned his loss, for he was gone before you were born. Twenty-two years ago he was a boy of 16—a fine, high-spirited Ingleton. Like a fool, I thought I could bring him up to be a fine man. But I failed—I only spoiled him. He grew up wild, self-willed, obstinate—a sorrow to his mother, an enemy to his father. The day came when we quarrelled. I accused him unjustly of fraud. He retorted insolently. In my passion I struck him, and he struck back. I fought my own boy and beat him; but my victory was the evil crisis of my life, for he left home vowing he would die sooner than return. His mother died of a broken heart. I had to live with mine; too proud to repent or admit my fault. Then came a rumour that the boy was dead. I never believed it; yet wrote him off as dead. Now, as I near my end, I still discredit the story; I am convinced he still lives. In that conviction, I have made a new will, which is the paper enclosed. As you will see, it provides that if he should return before you attain your majority, he becomes sole heir to the property; if not found before that time, the will under which you inherit all remains valid. You are at liberty to keep or destroy this new will as you choose. Nor, if you keep it, are you bound to do anything towards finding your lost brother. But should you desire to make inquiries, I am able to give you this feeble clue—that, after leaving home, he went to the bad in London in company with a companion named Fastnet, but where they lived I know not. Also, that the rumour of his death came to me from India. I can say no more, only that I am his and your loving father,—

"Roger Ingleton."

Towards the end the writing became very weak and straggling, and what to the boy was the most important passage was well-nigh illegible. When, after reading it a second time, he looked up, it was hard to believe he was the same Roger Ingleton who, a few minutes since, had broken the seal of that mysterious letter. The tutor, lost in his music, played on; the sun still flashed on the distant sea, the park still stretched away below him—but all seemed part of another world to the heir of Maxfield.

His brother—that wild-eyed, fascinating, defiant boy in the picture—lived still, and all this place was his. Till that moment Roger had never imagined what it would be to be anything but the heir of Maxfield.

Every dream of his for the future had Maxfield painted into the background. He loved the place as his own, as his sphere in life, as his destiny. Was that a dream after all? Were all his castles in the air to vanish, and leave him a mere dependant in a house not his own?

He took up the document and read it over. It was brief and abrupt. Referring to the former will, it enjoined that all its provisions should remain strictly in force as if no codicil or later will had been executed until the 26th of October, 1886, on which day Roger Ingleton the younger should attain his majority. But if on or before that day the elder son, whom the testator still believed to be living, should be found and identified, the former will on that day was to become null and void, and the elder son was to become sole possessor of the entire property. If, on the contrary, he should not be found or have proved his identity by that day, then the former will was to hold good absolutely, and the codicil became null and void.

Such, shorn of its legal verbiage, was the document which Roger, by the same hand that executed it, was invited, if he wished, to destroy. Perhaps for a moment, as his eyes glanced once more across the park, and a vision of Rosalind flitted across his mind, he was tempted to avail himself of his liberty. But if the idea endured a moment it had vanished a moment after.

He went up to the piano, where Mr Armstrong, still in the clouds, was roaming at will over the chords, and laid his father's letter on the keyboard.

"Read that, please, Armstrong."

The tutor wheeled round on his stool, and put up his glass. Something in the boy's voice arrested him.

He glanced first at his pupil, then at the paper.

"A private letter?" said he.

"I want your help; please read it."

The tutor's inscrutable face, as he perused the letter carefully from beginning to end, afforded very little direction to the boy who sat and watched him anxiously. Having read it once, Mr Armstrong turned back to the first page and read it again; and then with equal care perused the codicil. When all was done, he returned them slowly to the envelope and handed it back.

"Well?" said Roger, rather impatiently.

"It is a strange birthday greeting," said Mr Armstrong, "and comes, I fear, from a mind unhinged. Your father had more than one delusion near the end. But on the night before he died he told me this elder son of his was dead. This was written before that."

"Tell me exactly what he said."

The tutor repeated as nearly as he could the conversation of that memorable night.

"Is it not more probable that a fortnight earlier his mind might be clearer than at the very moment of his death?"

"It is possible, of course; but the letter does not seem to show it. Besides, the inscription at the back of the portrait (which you have forgotten) is a distinct record of the boy's death. I wish you had not shown me the letter, because the only advice I have to give you is that you do with it what he invites you to do."

"Look here, Armstrong!" said Roger, getting up and walking restlessly up and down the room; "you mean kindly, I know—you always do—but you don't seem to realise that you are tempting me to be a cad and a coward!"

The tutor looked up, and his eyebrow twitched uncomfortably. Roger had never spoken like this before, and the heat of the words took even him aback.

"You asked my advice, unfortunately, and I gave it," said he, rather drily.

"Do you think I should have an hour's peace if I didn't do everything in my power to find my brother now?" retorted the boy. "You're not obliged to help me, I know."

"I am—I am bound to help you; not because I am your tutor or your guardian, but because I love you."

"Then help me in this. My father, I feel sure, was right. Whether he was or not, and whether I have to do it single-handed or not, I mean to find my brother."

"Certainly you may count on me, old fellow," said the tutor; "but be quite sure first that you know what you are undertaking. If it is not a wild-goose chase it is something uncommonly like it. You resolve to waste a whole year. You are not strong, your future is all in Maxfield; the happiness of your mother, your hopes of winning the object of your affections, are involved in the step you take. Even if this brother of yours be living (of which the chances seem to be a hundred to one he is not), he is, as your father says, a man who has gone to the bad; not the boy of the picture, but a man twice your age, of the Ratman order, let us say, probably the worst possible companion for yourself, and a bad friend to the people who already count you as their master. Had he been living with any desire or intention of claiming his title, he would certainly have come forward months ago—"

"I know all that, Armstrong," said the boy; "I know perfectly well you are bringing up all these points as a friend, to prevent my taking a rash step of which I shall afterwards be sorry. I don't care how bad he is, or what it costs, I mean to find him; and if you help me, I'm confident I shall. Only," said he regretfully, "I certainly wish it was the boy in the picture, and not a middle-aged person, who is to be looked for."

Here Tom broke in upon the conference.

"Hullo, Roger, here you are! What are you up to? You and Armstrong look as blue as if you'd swallowed live eels. I say, you're a nice chap. Rosalind has been waiting half an hour, she says, for that ride you were to go with her, and if you don't look sharp she'll give Ratman the mount and jockey you, my boy. Poor old Ratty! didn't Jill drop on him like a sack of coals at breakfast? Jolly rough on the governor having to stroke him down after it. I say, mind you're in in time to receive the deputation. They're all going to turn up, and old Hodder's to make a speech. I wouldn't miss it for a half sov! All I know is I'm jolly glad I'm not an heir. It's far jollier to be an ordinary chap; isn't it, Mr Armstrong?"

"Decidedly," said the tutor demurely; "but we can't all be what we like."

"Tell Rosalind I'll be down in a second; I'm awfully sorry to have kept her," said Roger.

"By the way," said the tutor, when Tom had gone; "about this letter. The communication is evidently made to you by your father as a secret. I am sorry, on that account, you showed it to me, because I object to secrets not meant for me. But if you take my advice you will not let it go further. It would be clearly contrary to the wishes of your father."

"I see that. Lock the will up in your desk again; I'll take care of the letter. Nobody but you and I shall know of their existence. And now I must go to Rosalind."

Chapter Fourteen
What a Horsewhip discovered

Mr Ratman's business interview with his friend was short and stormy.

When Captain Oliphant produced the hundred-pound note, and requested his creditor to accept a fresh bill for the balance, that injured gentleman broke out into very emphatic abuse.

"Likely, is it not?" laughed he. "You, a common thief, bring me, who've saved you from a convict's cell, here to be insulted and made a fool of by your miserable brats and servants, and then have the calmness to ask me to lend you a hundred pounds? I admire your impudence, sir, and that's all I admire about you."

"My dear fellow, how can you blame me—"

"Blame you! You don't suppose I'm going to take the trouble to do that! Come, hand over the other hundred, sharp. I've nothing to say to you till that's done."

And Mr Ratman, digging his hands in his pockets, got up and walked to the fireplace.

Captain Oliphant's face fell. He knew his man by this time, and had sense enough at least to know that this was no time for argument. Yet he could not help snarling—

"I can only do part."

"The whole—in five minutes—or there'll be interest to add!" retorted Mr Ratman.

With a groan Captain Oliphant flung down the second bank-note on the table.

"Take it, you coward! and may it help you to perdition!"

"Thanks, very much," said Ratman, carefully putting away the money. "I'm not going to ask you where the money came from. That would be painful. Ah, Teddy, my boy, what a nice, respectable family man you are, to be sure!"

With which acknowledgment Mr Ratman, in capital spirits, returned to his room. On the way he encountered Tom, who, being of a forgiving disposition, owed him no grudge for the trouble that had occurred at breakfast-time.

"Hullo, Mr Ratty!" said the boy; "going out? Aren't you looking forward to the party to-night? I am. Only I'm afraid they'll make a mess of it among them. Auntie's ill and in bed, Rosalind and Roger are spooning about in the grounds, Armstrong's got the dismals, and the governor's not to be disturbed. I've got to look after everything. The spread will be good enough—only I think they ought to have roasted an ox whole in the hall; don't you? That's the proper way to do things, instead of kickshaws and things with French names that one can swallow at a gulp. I say, there's to be a dance first. I'll introduce you to some of the old girls if you like. It won't be much fun for me, for Jill has made me promise to dance every dance with her, for fear you should want one. But I know a chap or two that will take her off my hands. I say, would you like to see my den?" added he, as they passed the door in question.

Mr Ratman being of an inquiring turn of mind, accepted the invitation, and gave a cursory glance at the chaos which formed the leading feature of the apartment.

"It's not such a swagger crib as Roger's," said Tom; "but it's snug enough. That's Roger's opposite. Like to look?"

Once more Mr Ratman allowed himself to be escorted on a tour of discovery.

"Who is that a portrait of?" asked he, looking at the lost Roger's picture.

"Oh, that's what's his name, the fellow who would have been heir if he hadn't died. He looks rather a tough customer, doesn't he? That's the picture Rosalind painted for Roger's birthday—a view of the park from her window, with the sea beyond. Not so bad, is it? Rosalind thinks she's no end of an artist, but I—"

"When did he die?" inquired Mr Ratman, still examining the picture.

"Oh, ever so long ago—before the old Squire married Auntie. I say, come and have a punt about with my new football, will you?"

"Go and get it. I'll be down presently. I like pictures, and shall just take a look at these first!"

Tom bustled off, wondering what Mr Ratman could see in the pictures to allure him from the joys of football.

To tell the truth, Mr Ratman was not a great artist. But the portrait of the lost Roger appeared to interest him, as did also the sight of an open letter, hastily laid down by the owner on the writing-table.

Something in the handwriting of the letter particularly aroused the curiosity of the trespasser, who, being, as has been said, of an inquiring disposition, ventured to look at it more closely.

"*To be given unopened into the hands of Roger Ingleton, junior, on his twentieth birthday.*"

The coast was conveniently clear for Mr Ratman, as, fired with a zeal for information, he slipped the letter from the envelope and, with half an eye on the door, hastily read it. As he did so, he flushed a little, and having read the letter once, read it again. Then he quickly replaced it in its cover, and laying it where he had discovered it, beat a rapid retreat.

He played football badly that afternoon, so that his young companion's opinion of him lowered considerably. Nor was either sorry when the ceremony was over, and the bell warned them to return to their quarters and prepare for the evening's festivities.

Mr Ratman dressed with special care, spending some time before the mirror in an endeavour to set off his person to the best advantage. As the reader has already been told, Mr Ratman retained some of the traces of a handsome youth. The fires of honour and sobriety were extinguished, but his well-shaped head and clear-cut features still weathered the storm, and suggested that if their owner was not good-looking now, he might once have been.

Perhaps it was a lingering impression of the lost Roger's portrait which made this vain gentleman adjust his curly locks and pose his head before the glass in a style not unlike his model. Whether that was so or not, the result appeared to satisfy him, and in due time, and not till after several of the guests had already arrived, he descended in state to the drawing-room.

It was the first festive gathering at Maxfield since the death of the late Squire, and a good deal of curiosity was manifest on the part of some of the guests both as to the heir and his new guardian.

Roger, nerved up to the occasion by his own spirit and the encouragement of his tutor, bore his inspection well, and won golden opinions from his future comrades and neighbours.

Captain Oliphant also acquitted himself well; and anything lacking in him was amply forgiven for the sake of his charming daughters, the elder of whom fairly took the "county" by storm.

Quite unconscious of the broken hearts which strewed her way, Rosalind, with the duties of hostess unexpectedly cast upon her by Mrs Ingleton's illness, exerted herself for the general happiness, and enjoyed herself in the task.

Despite Tom's forebodings, the evening went off brilliantly. The music was excellent, the amateur theatricals highly appreciated, and the dance all that could be desired. The loyal youth found no difficulty in palming his young sister off on half a dozen partners delighted to have the opportunity, and his head was fairly turned by the sudden popularity in which he found himself with visitors anxious for an introduction to the fair Rosalind.

"Oh, all serene," said he confidentially to one of those glowing youths. "She's booked six or seven deep, but I'll work it for you if I can. You hang about here, and I'll fetch her up."

But the luckless ones hung about in vain. For Tom's progress was intercepted by other candidates for the same favour, amidst whom the young diplomatist played fast and loose in a reprehensible manner.

"Promised *you*, did I?" demanded he of one. "Well, you'll have to square it up with that sandy-haired chap at the door. He says I promised *him*; but he's all wrong, for the one I *did* promise is that little dapper chap there in the window. He's been waiting on and off since eight o'clock. Never you mind; you hang about here, and I'll work it if I— Hullo! here's another one! I didn't promise you, did I? All right, old chappie. You lean up there against the wall, and I'll engineer it for you somehow. She's owing me a dance about eight down the list. You can have a quarter of it, if you like, and the other two chaps can go halves in the rest."

With which the unprincipled youth absconded into the supper-room.

"And who is that talking to your charming cousin?" asked a dowager who had succeeded in capturing Roger for five minutes in a corner.

"Oh, that's my tutor, Armstrong—the best fellow in the world."

"Evidently a great admirer of Miss Oliphant. No doubt the attraction is mutual?"

Roger laughed, and speculated on Armstrong's horror were he to hear of such a suggestion.

"And that gentleman talking to Captain Oliphant? What relation is he?"

"He? None at all. He's a Mr Ratman, an Indian friend of my guardian's."

"Dear me! I quite thought he was an Ingleton by his face—but I'm glad he is not; I dislike his appearance. Besides, he has already had more than is good for him."

"He's no great favourite," said Roger shortly.

Presently Captain Oliphant and his companion stepped up to where Rosalind and her partner stood.

"Mr Armstrong," said the former, "will you kindly see that the band gets supper after the next dance?"

The words were spoken politely, and Mr Armstrong, although he knew that the speaker's solicitude on behalf of the band was by no means as great as his desire to see the tutor's back, felt he could hardly refuse.

"Rosalind," said the Captain, looking significantly at his daughter, "Mr Ratman desires the pleasure of a dance, and will take you into the next room."

Rosalind tossed her head and flushed.

"Thank you; I am tired," said she. "I prefer not to dance at present."

"You are keeping Mr Ratman waiting, my dear."

The colour died out of the girl's face as, with a little shiver, she laid the tips of her fingers on her partner's arm.

"That's right," said that genial individual. "Do as you are told. You don't fancy it; but pa's word is law, isn't it?"

She said nothing, but the colour shot back ominously into her cheeks.

"And so you've run off and left us," pursued her partner, who rather enjoyed the situation, and was vain enough to appreciate the distinction of dancing with the belle of the evening. "So sorry. I quite envy the little vicar boys and girls—upon my honour I do. Very unkind of you to go just as I came. Never mind. Not far away, is it? We shall see lots of one another."

At this moment, just as the band was striking up for a quadrille, Jill came up.

"Have you seen dear Mr Arm— O Rosalind! how *can* you dance with that man?"

Mr Ratman laughed.

"Very well, missy. I'll pay you out. You shall dance with me, see if you don't, before the evening is out."

Before which awful threat Jill fled headlong to seek the tutor.

"Fact is," pursued Mr Ratman, reverting to his previous topic, "ever since I saw you, Miss Rosalind, I said to myself—Robert Ratman, you have found the right article at last. You don't suppose I'd come all the way here from India, do you, if there weren't attractions?"

She kept a rigid silence, and went through the steps of the quadrille without so much as a look at the talker, Ratman was sober enough to be annoyed at this chilly disdain.

"Don't you know it's rude not to speak when you're spoken to, Miss Rosalind?" said he. "If you choose to be friends with me we shall get on very well, but you mustn't be rude."

She turned her head away.

"You aren't deaf, are you?" said he, becoming still more nettled. "I suppose if it was the heir of Maxfield that was talking to you you'd hear, wouldn't you? You'd be all smiles and nods to the owner of ten thousand a year, eh? Do you suppose we can't see through your little game, you artful little schemer? Now, will you speak or not?"

Her cheeks gave the only indication that she had heard this last polished speech as she gathered up her dress and swept out of the quadrille.

"Wait," said he, losing his temper, "the dance is not over."

She stepped quickly to a chair, and sat there at bay.

"Come back," said he, following her, "or I will make you. I won't be insulted like this before the whole room. Come back; do you hear?"

And he snatched her hand.

Rosalind looked up, and as she did so she caught a distant vision of an eye-glass dropping from a gentleman's eye to the length of its cord. A moment after, Mr Ratman felt a hand close like a vice on his collar and himself almost lifted from the room. It was all done so quickly that the quadrille party were only just becoming aware that a couple had dropped out; and the non-dancers were beginning to wonder if Miss Oliphant had been taken poorly, when Robert Ratman was writhing in the clutches of his chastiser in the hall.

Mr Armstrong marched straight with his prey to the kitchen.

"Raffles," said he to the footman, "get me a horsewhip."

Raffles took in the situation at once, and in half a minute was across at the stable.

As he returned with the whip he met Mr Armstrong in the yard, holding his victim much as a cat would hold a rat, utterly indifferent to his oaths, his kicks, or his threats.

"Thanks," said the tutor, as he took the whip; "go in and shut the door. Now, sir, for you!"

HE CONTINUED HIS HORSEWHIPPING TO THE BITTER END.

"Touch me if you dare!" growled Ratman; "it will be the worse for you and every one. Do you know who I am! I'm—I'm,"—here he pulled himself up and glared his enemy in the face—"I'm Roger Ingleton!"

It spoke worlds for the tutor's self-possession that in the start produced by this announcement he did not let his victim escape. It spoke still more for his resolution that, having heard it, he continued his horsewhipping to the bitter end before he replied—

"Whoever you are, sir, that will teach you how to behave to a lady."

"You fool!" hissed Ratman, with an oath, getting up from the ground; "you'll be sorry for this. I'll be even with you. I'll ruin you. I'll turn your precious ward out of the place. I'll teach that girl—"

An ominous crack of the tutor's whip cut short the end of the sentence, and Mr Ratman left the remainder of his threats to the imagination of his audience.

When, ten minutes later, the tutor, with eye-glass erect, strolled back into the drawing-room, no one would have supposed that he had been horsewhipping an enemy or making a discovery on which the fate of a whole household depended. His thin, compressed lips wore their usual enigmatic lines; his brow was as unruffled as his shirt front.

"Dear Mr Armstrong, where have you been?" cried Jill, pouncing on him at the door; "I've been hunting for you everywhere. You promised me, you know." And the little lady towed off her captive in triumph.

The remainder of the evening passed uneventfully until at eleven o'clock the festivities in the drawing-room gave place to the more serious business of the "county" supper, at which, in a specially-erected tent, about one hundred guests sat down.

Tom had taken care to procure an early and advantageous seat for the occasion, and, with one of the vicar's daughters under his patronage and control, prepared to enjoy himself at last. He had had a bad time of it so far, for he was in the black-books of almost every youth in the room, and had been posted as a defaulter in whatever corner he had tried to hide from his creditors.

"It's awful having a pretty sister," said he confidentially to his companion; "gets a fellow into no end of a mess. I wish I was your brother instead."

"Thank you," said the young lady, laughing.

"Oh, I didn't mean that," said Tom. "You're good enough looking, I think. But I don't see why Rosalind can't pick her own partners, instead of me having to manage it for her. Look out! if that chap opposite sees me he'll kick—put the ferns between. There she is next to Roger. Like her cheek, bagging the best place. Do you see that kid there grinning at the fellow with the eye-glass? That's my young sister—ought to be in bed instead of fooling about here. Ah, I knew it! she's planted herself opposite the grapes. If we don't look out we shan't get one. That's my governor coming in; looks rather chippy, don't he? I say, lean forward, or he'll see me. He's caught me in the supper-room five or six times already this evening. By the way, where's old Ratty? Do you know Ratty, Miss Isabel? No end of a scorch. Just the chap for you. I'll introduce you. Hullo! where is he?" added he, looking up and down the table cautiously. "Surely he's not going to shirk the feed? Never mind, Miss Isabel; I'll work it round for you if I can."

Miss Isabel expressed her gratitude with a smile, and asked Tom how he liked living at Maxfield.

"Oh, all right, now I've got a football and can go shooting in the woods. I have to pay up for it though with lessons, and—(thanks; all right; just a little more. Won't you have some yourself while it's here?)—Armstrong makes us stick at it. I say, by the way, do you remember that fellow who died? (Don't take any of that; it's no good. Wire in to a wing of the partridge instead.) Eh, do you?"

"Whom? What are you talking about?" asked she, bewildered.

"Ah, it doesn't matter. He died twenty-one years ago, before Roger was born. I thought you might have known him."

"Really, Tom, you are not complimentary. You can't expect me to remember before I was born."

"What! aren't you twenty-one?" asked Tom, staring round at her. "Go on; you're joking! No? Why, you look twice the age! This chap, you know, would have been the heir if he'd lived. There's a picture of him upstairs."

"And he died, did he?"

"Rather; but old Hodder—know old Hodder?"

"Hush!" said his companion; "the speeches are beginning."

"What a hung nuisance!" said Tom.

The oratorical interruption was a brief one. The Duke of Somewhere, as the big man of the county, rose to propose the health of the heir of Maxfield. They were glad to make their young neighbour's acquaintance, and looked forward that day year to welcoming him to his own. They hoped he'd be a credit to his name, and keep up the traditions of Maxfield. He understood Mr Ingleton was pretty strictly tied up in the matter of guardians—(laughter)—but from what he could see, he might be worse off in that respect; and the county would owe their thanks to those gentlemen if they turned out among them the right sort of man to be Squire of Maxfield. He wished his young friend joy and long life and many happy returns of the day.

Roger, rather pale and nervous, replied very briefly.

He thanked them for their good wishes, and said he hoped he might take these as given not to the heir of Maxfield but to plain Roger Ingleton. He was still an infant—("Hear, hear!" from Tom)—and was in no hurry to get out of the charge of his guardians. Whatever his other expectations might be, he felt that his best heritage was the name he bore; and he hoped, as his noble neighbour had said, he should turn out worthy of that.

As he sat down, flushed with his effort, and wondering what two persons there would think of his feeble performance, his eye fell on the form of Dr Brandram, who at that moment hurriedly entered the room.

He saw him whisper something to Armstrong, who changed colour and rose from his seat. An intuition, quicker than a flash of lightning, revealed to the boy that something was wrong—something in which he was concerned. In a moment he stood with his two friends in the hall.

"Roger, my brave fellow, your mother has been taken seriously worse within the last hour. Come and see her."

The boy staggered away dazed. He was conscious of the hum of voices, with Tom's laugh above all, in the room behind; of the long curve of carriage lights waiting in the garden without; of the trophy of flowers and pampas on either side of the staircase. Then, as the doctor stepped forward and softly opened a door, he followed like one in a dream.

For an hour the dull roll of carriages came and went on the drive, and the cheery babel of departing voices broke the still morning air.

But two guests left Maxfield that night unexpectedly.

One was the soul of a good lady; the other was the horsewhipped body of a bad man.

Chapter Fifteen
Strong Hearts and Weak Tempers

In the sad confusion which followed upon Mrs Ingleton's sudden death, no one appeared to remark the abrupt departure of Mr Robert Ratman. Roger certainly never bestowed a thought on the occurrence, and if any of the other members of the household thought twice about it, they all—even Jill—kept their ideas on the subject to themselves.

To Roger the week that followed his twentieth birthday was the most dismal of his life. When a similar blow had fallen months ago he had been too bewildered and benumbed to realise fully his own loss. Now he realised everything only too vividly.

His own trouble; the loss of the last near relative he had in the world; his own sickly health, chaining him down when he would fain seek comfort in action; the uncertainty of his position as heir of Maxfield; the hopeless task before him of finding his lost brother; Rosalind's indifference to his affection—all seemed now to pile up in one great mountain to oppress him, and he half envied the gentle dead her quiet resting-place.

It was in the second week after the funeral, when Maxfield once more began to assume its normal aspect, and Captain Oliphant was allowing himself to hope that, notwithstanding the removal of his latest "dear departed," things were likely to shape themselves a trifle more comfortably for his own designs in her absence—it was in the middle of November that a letter was handed to Roger as he dressed one morning in his room.

It bore the London post-mark, and looked mysterious enough to induce Roger to lay down his brushes and open it there and then. This is what it said:—

> "Dear Roger,—You'll have been expecting to hear from me, as no doubt your moral friend, Mr Armstrong, has told you who I am. I don't fancy you are specially pleased with the discovery, and it may suit you to turn up your nose at your affectionate brother. You may turn up what you like, but it doesn't alter the fact. I am your brother. When I heard of my father's death I was in India, and made up my mind

to come home on the chance the old boy had forgiven me and left me some of the needful in his will. Your guardian, Oliphant, had little idea that the Indian chum who made such a long journey to pay him a visit at Maxfield was really the man to whom the place ought to have belonged if every one had his rights. Of course I soon found out my mistake. The old man kept up his grudge to the end, and cut me out of his will without even a shilling. So you've nothing to be afraid of. I dare say when you come into the property you will do something for your big brother. Meanwhile I don't expect much out of the pair of hypocrites my father chose to leave as your guardians. But as I am hard up, and you can probably do what you like with your pocket-money, let me have a £10 note once and again, say fortnightly, addressed to Robert Ratman, to be called for at the General Post Office. If I don't get this, I shall conclude the Ingletons are true to their reputation of being a good deal fonder of their money than their flesh and blood.

"I don't know whether I shall turn up again or not. It will depend pretty much on what I hear. No doubt you've set me down as a cad and a blackleg. Perhaps I am. I've not had the advantages you have. But, cad or no cad, I've a right to sign myself your brother,—

"Roger Ingleton, *alias* Robert Ratman."

Roger read this remarkable epistle once or twice, in a state of mind bordering on stupefaction. Robert Ratman, cad, sharper, blasphemer, insolent profligate, his brother! The notion was ludicrous. And yet, when he tried to laugh, the laugh died on his lips. He walked over to the portrait on the wall and looked at the wild, mocking boy's face there. For a moment, as he met its gaze, it seemed to grow older and coarser—the light died out of the eyes, the mouth lost its strength, the lines of shame and vice came out on the brow. Then the old face looked out again—the face of the lost Roger Ingleton.

"Ratman my brother!" he groaned to himself.

Then of a sudden he seemed to see it all. It was a fraud, an imposition, an impudent plot to extort money. But no! As he read the letter again that hope vanished. This was not the letter of an impostor. Had it been, there would have been more about his rights, more brotherly affection, a greater anxiety to appear in good colours. As it was, the writer wrote in the reckless vein of a man who knows he is detested and expects little; who owes a grudge to fortune for his bad luck, and being hard up for money, appeals not to his rights, but to the good nature of his more lucky younger brother.

What a sad letter it seemed, read in that light. And how every word drove the unhappy heir of Maxfield deeper and deeper into the slough of perplexity.

Three weeks ago, when his dead father's letter had come into his hands, he had not hesitated for a moment as to his duty or his desire in the matter. He had cheerfully accepted the task of finding that lost, aggrieved, perhaps hardly-used brother, to whom his heart went out as he gazed on the likeness of what he once had been.

But now! To abdicate in favour of this blackguard. To look for him, to tell him that Maxfield was his, to have to depend on his generosity for a livelihood, to see the good name of Ingleton represented in the county by a drunken profligate. What a task was that. The writer evidently did not know of the second will, or suspect that after all Maxfield was his own. No one knew of that document but Roger and Armstrong. For a moment there returned to the boy's mind the words of his father's letter—

"If after reading the papers you choose to destroy them, no one will blame you; no one will know—you will do no one an injury. You are free to act as you choose."

And Armstrong, the only other being who had seen the papers, had urged him to avail himself of the permission thus accorded. Why not take the advice and save Maxfield and the family name, and himself—ay, and Rosalind—from the discredit that threatened. He could yet be generous, beyond his hopes, to the prodigal. He would pay to get him abroad, to—to—

A flush of shame mounted to the boy's cheeks as he suddenly discovered himself listening to these unworthy suggestions.

"Heaven help me," he said, "to be a man." It was a brief inward fight, though a sore one.

Roger Ingleton, weak in body, often dull of wit and infirm of temper, had yet certain old-fashioned ideas of his own as to how it behoves a gentleman to act.

He cherished, too, certain still older-fashioned ideas as to how when a Christian gentleman wants help and courage he may obtain it. And he was endowed with that glorious obstinacy which, when it once satisfies itself on a question of right and wrong, declines to listen to argument.

Therefore when, later than usual, he joined the family party at breakfast, it was with a grim sense of a misery ahead to be faced, but by no manner of means to be avoided.

For fear the reader should be disposed to rank Roger at once among the saints, let it be added that he took his place in as genuine a bad temper as a strong mind and a weak body between them are capable of generating.

"Roger, my dear boy," said the captain mournfully, as became the weeds he wore, "you are looking poorly. You need a change. We both need one after the trouble we have been through. I think a run up to London would brace us up. Would you like it?"

"I don't know," said Roger shortly. "I don't think so."

"It is trying to you, I am sure, to remain here, in your delicate health, among so many sad associations—"

"I'm quite well, thank you," said the boy. "Tom, how does the football get on?"

"Oh," said Tom, rather taken aback by the introduction of so congenial a theme from so unexpected a quarter, "I've not played very much lately. Jill and I had a little punt about yesterday; but we did it quite slowly, you know, and I had my crape on my arm."

Jill flushed up guiltily. The housekeeper, who since Mrs Ingleton's death had assumed the moral direction of the young lady, had expostulated with her in no mild terms on the iniquity of young ladies playing football, even of a funereal order, and she felt it very treacherous on the part of the faithless Tom to divulge her ill-doings now.

She felt reassured, however, when Mr Armstrong smiled grimly.

"Nobody could see," said she; "and Tom *did* want a game so dreadfully."

"We played Association," said Tom. "Jill got two goals and I got fifty-six."

"No, I got three," said Jill.

"Oh, that first wasn't a goal," said Tom. "You see, she got past me with a neat bit of dribbling; but she ran, and the rule was only to walk, you know, because of being in mourning."

"I really didn't run, I only walked very fast," said Jill.

"I should think you might allow her the goal," said Mr Armstrong.

Mr Armstrong was always coming to Jill's rescue; and if any of her heart had been left to win, he would have won it now. Tom gave in, and said he supposed he would have to let her count it; and was vastly consoled for his self-denial by Roger's proposal to join him in a game that very day.

Before that important function came off, however, Roger and his tutor had a somewhat uncomfortable talk in the library.

"You are feeling out of sorts, old fellow," said the latter when they were left alone.

"I've had a letter," said Roger.

"Another?"

"Read it, please."

"If you wish it, I will. Last time, however, it wasn't a success consulting me."

"I want you to read this."

The tutor took the letter and turned to the signature.

His brow knitted as he did so, and the lines grew deeper and more scornful as he turned to the beginning and read through.

"If I were you," said he, returning it, "I would frame this letter as a good specimen of a barefaced fraud."

It irritated Roger considerably, in his present over-wrought frame of mind—and particularly after the memorable inward struggle of that morning—to have what seemed so serious a matter to him regarded by any one else as a jest. For once in a way the tutor failed to understand his ward.

"It does not seem to be a fraud at all," said Roger. "Why didn't you tell me of it before?"

"I did not regard the statement seriously. Nor do I now. There is lie written in every line of the letter. A clumsy attempt to extort money, which ought not to be allowed to succeed. He gives not a single proof of his identity. I horsewhipped him on the night of your birthday for insulting a lady, and—"

"What lady?" asked Roger.

"Miss Oliphant," said the tutor, flushing a little. "He then, as a desperate expedient for getting off the punishment he deserved, blurted out this preposterous story. And having once published it, it appears he means to make capital out of it. Roger, old fellow, you are no fool."

"I am fool enough to believe there is something in the story," said Roger; "at any rate I must follow it up. If this Ratman is my brother—"

The tutor, who himself was showing signs of irritation, laughed abruptly.

"It may be a joke to you, but it is none to me," said Roger angrily. "It may not concern you—"

"It concerns me very much," said the tutor. "I am your guardian, and it is my duty to protect you from schemers."

The two stood looking at one another, and in that moment each relented a little of his anger.

"I know, old fellow," said Roger, "you think you are doing me a kindness, but—"

"Pardon me—kindness is not the word. I appeal to your common-sense—"

Unlucky speech! Roger, who was painfully aware that he was not clever, was naturally touchy at any reference to his common-sense.

"It doesn't seem much use discussing," said he. "I made a mistake in showing you the letter."

"I heartily regret you did."

"I hoped you would have helped me in my difficulty."

"I will do anything for you except believe, without proof, and in spite of every probability, that Ratman is your brother."

"He is just the age my brother would have been now."

"So is George the coachman, so am I, so are half a dozen men in the village."

"He certainly has some resemblance to the portrait."

"I could find you a score more like it in London."

"The long and short of it is, Armstrong, I cannot look to you to back me up in this."

"To make Robert Ratman into Roger Ingleton?—I fear not. To back you up in all else, and be at your call whether you think well or ill of me—certainly."

They parted angrily, though without a quarrel. Mr Armstrong had rarely felt himself so put out, and crashed away ruthlessly at his piano all the morning.

Roger, perhaps conscious that logic was not on his side, whatever instinct and feeling might be, retired disappointed and miserable to the park, and never remembered his appointment with the eager Tom.

At lunch-time he said to Captain Oliphant—

"When did you think of going to town?"

"At the end of the week, my boy. What do you say to coming?"

"Yes—I'll come."

The Captain darted a triumphant glance in the direction of the tutor. But the tutor was investigating the contents of a game pie in the endeavour to discover a piece of egg for Miss Jill.

After a pause that young lady took up her discourse.

"If father and Roger go to town, Tom, we shall have dear Mr Armstrong all to ourselves."

"Hooroo!" said Tom; "that is, if it's holidays."

"I am thinking of going to Oxford next week," said the tutor, elaborately folding up his napkin, addressing his co-trustee. "Have you any message I can give to any of your acquaintances there?"

"I think it would be a pity for you to leave Maxfield just now. One of us should remain."

"Yes, do stay. We'll have such larks," said Tom. "We'll get Rosalind to come and stay, and then we shall be able to play regular matches, ladies against gentlemen, you know."

"No. Mr Armstrong and I will stand Rosalind and you," suggested Jill.

Even these allurements failed.

"I shall make my visit as short as possible. I have, as you know, a few creditors in Oxford on whom I am anxious to call. Let me give you a little cheese, Roger."

That evening when, as usual, the tutor looked in to say good night to his ward, Roger said rather gloomily—

"I suppose you object to my going to London?"

"On the contrary, I rather envy you."

"Of course you understand I am going up to make inquiries?"

"Naturally. With Captain Oliphant's assistance?"

"No. I'm not inclined to tell him anything at present. He has no idea that Ratman is anything but an Indian acquaintance."

"My address will be '"Green Dragon," Oxford,'" said the tutor.

"By the way," said Roger—both men were talking in the forced tones which belong to an unacknowledged estrangement—"Whether this matter is right or not, I propose to write to Ratman and enclose him £10."

"Naturally," said the tutor.

"I am tied down, as you know, in the matter of my pocket-money, and can't well spare it out of my present allowance. I want the trustees to give me an extra allowance."

"In other words, you want your trustees to keep Mr Robert Ratman at the rate of £250 a year. I shall agree to that the day that he satisfies me he is Roger Ingleton."

"I expected you would refuse. I must ask Captain Oliphant."

"I'm afraid he will require my sanction to any such arrangement."

"What! Do you mean to say that I am at your mercy in a matter like this?"

"I fear that is unhappily the case. I can resolve the matter by resigning my tutorship."

Had it come to that? Roger glanced up with a scared look which for the moment clouded out the vexation in his face.

"Excuse me, Armstrong. All this worry is bad for my temper. I'm afraid I lost it."

"I can sympathise," said the tutor, "for I have lost mine. Good night."

Chapter Sixteen
Roger sees a little too much Life

Captain Oliphant's motive for going to London was primarily to escape for a while from the unearthly dullness of Maxfield. As long as the prospect of a matrimonial alliance with Mrs Ingleton had been in view, it had seemed to him good policy to submit to the infliction and remain at his post. That vision was now unhappily past, and the good man felt he deserved a change of scene and amusement. A further motive was to evade a possible return of his dear friend Mr Ratman, whose abrupt departure from Maxfield had both perplexed and relieved him. The second of that gentleman's uncomfortable bills was falling due in a few days, and as on the present occasion no lucky windfall had dropped in from an American mayor, it seemed altogether a fitting occasion for dropping for a season below the horizon.

When, however, Roger unexpectedly consented to accompany his guardian, the visit assumed an altogether different aspect. The captain had long desired to have his dear ward to himself, and the opportunity now presented was certainly one not to be neglected.

"My dear boy," said he, as the two took their places in the London train, "I hope you are well protected against the weather. Change seats with me. You are so liable to cold, you know, that it is really hardly safe for you to face the engine. We must take great care of you now—greater than ever," and he sighed pathetically.

Roger was getting accustomed to, and a little tired of, these demonstrative outbursts, and quietly took the seat in order to spare discussion. He was already repenting of his journey. No one seemed to commend it. Armstrong made no reference to it.

Dr Brandram stoutly disapproved of it. Rosalind tossed her head when she heard of it, and hoped he might enjoy himself. Tom failed to see why, when there was football in the air at Maxfield, any one could be bothered to travel up to London for pleasure, unless indeed he intended to take a season ticket for Christy's Minstrels. Altogether Roger did not feel elated at the prospect of this visit. For all that, he persuaded himself that duty called him thither, even if it was bad temper which drove him from Maxfield.

"What has become of Ratman?" he inquired of his guardian casually during the journey.

Captain Oliphant looked up from his paper sharply Mr Ratman's whereabouts had been occupying his thoughts that very moment.

"I really do not know, my boy," said he. "He left very suddenly, and in the sad trouble through which we have passed I have hardly had time to think about him."

There was a pause. Then Roger said—

"Is he an old friend of yours, cousin Edward?"

Cousin Edward was a little perplexed by this curiosity.

"I have known him a year or so. The friendship, however, is chiefly on his side."

"I thought he came all the way from India on purpose to visit you?"

The captain laughed uncomfortably at this very correct representation of the facts.

"That is the version he likes to give. The fact is that business brought him home, and as he knew I was at Maxfield, he wrote and proposed the visit. He is no great favourite of yours, I suspect, Roger?"

"No," said Roger shortly, and relapsed again into silence. But before the journey's end he once more returned to the charge.

"Was he in the army in India?"

"Once, I believe. But I have never heard much of his antecedents. Latterly I believe he called himself a financial agent, a very vague profession. He was in our station before our regiment went there."

"I suppose he had lived in India all his life?"

"He had certainly been in England when a young man," said the captain; "and from some of his reminiscences, appears not to have led a very profitable life there. But how comes it you are so interested in him?"

"I have only been wondering what he was, that's all," said Roger, feeling he had been on the topic long enough.

Roger had already written a letter to Ratman, addressed to that gentleman at the General Post Office, London.

"Your letter," it said, "has perplexed me greatly. If you are my brother, as you say you are, why do you not give some proof? That should be easy. There must be some people who can identify you, or some means of satisfying us all about your claim to be the elder son. I should not resist you, if it were so. Only my guardians would require clear proof before recognising you. As to whether I think well or ill of you, that has nothing to do with the matter if you are really and truly my elder brother. I enclose ten pounds in this, not to show you that I am myself fully satisfied, but to let you see that the bare chance of your being an Ingleton makes me feel anxious you should not think we, as a family, do not stand by one another. I do not expect to be able to repeat it, as my allowance is limited, and my guardians are not likely to consent to hand over any money for you till you can prove your claim. Write and give me more particulars, and I promise you I shall not shirk my duty to you or the name I bear."

At any other time Roger would have shown this epistle, the writing of which cost him many anxious hours, to Armstrong. Now, however, that help was denied him. The tutor, he knew, would have screwed his eye-glass into his eye and ruthlessly pulled the document to pieces. No. He must play this game off his own bat, and keep his own counsel.

Captain Oliphant, who had a good notion of doing things comfortably with other people's money, had selected a fashionable hotel at the West End.

"We must see you have every comfort, dear boy," said he; "in your state of health we cannot afford to rough it. I have ordered a private sitting-room and fires in the bedroom. When you feel strong enough we will do a little sight-seeing; but meanwhile your first consideration must be to recover lost tone and spirits by means of rest and care."

These constant reminders of his poor health were very unwelcome to the unlucky Roger, who protested that he was in perfect health; and, to prove it, went out next day, in a cold November fog, with no overcoat. The consequence was he caught a severe cold, and had the mortification of listening to a severe lecture from his solicitous guardian on the iniquity of trifling with his precious health.

Roger, too proud to admit that he could not take care of himself, declined to treat himself as an invalid, and insisted on claiming his guardian's promise to show him a little life in the great city.

It was surprising how many acquaintances Rosalind's father had in London. Some were pleasant enough—military men on leave, and here and there a civilian's family who remembered the captain and his charming family in the Hills.

Roger accepted their hospitality and listened to their Indian small-talk with great good-humour, and when now and then some sympathetic soul, guessing, as a good many did, one of the lad's secrets, talked admiringly of

Rosalind, he felt himself rewarded for a good deal of long-suffering. Had he heard some of the jokes passed behind his back, his satisfaction might have been considerably tempered.

"I always said," observed one shrewd dowager, "that Oliphant would make a catch with that daughter of his. He has done it, evidently. This boy will be worth five or ten thousand a year, I hear."

"Poor fellow! He looks as if it will be a battle with him to reach it. What a cough!"

"I can't understand Oliphant not taking better care of him. He drags him about all over town, as if the boy were cast iron. I met them out twice this week."

"Certainly one cannot afford to play fast and loose with the goose that lays the golden eggs."

The "goose" in question made other acquaintances than these. In his bachelor days Captain Oliphant had "knocked about" in London pretty considerably, and had a notion, now that he was a bachelor again, to repeat the process. Roger—a raw country boy, as the reader by this time will admit—found himself entered upon a gay round of club and Bohemian life, which to an old stager like the captain may have seemed a little slow, but to a susceptible youth was decidedly attractive. The guardian's fast acquaintances made the young heir of Maxfield welcome, and might have proceeded to pluck him had his protector permitted. Roger speedily discovered what hundreds of locks there are which the mere rumour of money will unlock. He had never had such an idea of his own importance before, and for a short time he deluded himself into the belief that his popularity was due wholly and solely to his personal merits.

Captain Oliphant fostered this delusion carefully.

"I hope you are enjoying yourself, my dear boy," he would say, after a particularly festive evening.

"It's an excellent rule to make oneself agreeable in all circumstances. I envy you your facility. You see how it is appreciated. It does an old fogey like me good to see you enjoy yourself."

"It was a pleasant enough evening," said Roger, not quite without misgivings on the subject, however.

"By the way, who was the man, older than the others, who talked loudest and not always in the most classical English?"

The captain laughed pleasantly.

"No. I should have been better pleased if he had not been of our party. He never was select, even in my young days, when I met him once or twice. There used to be a saying among us that Fastnet, if he gave his mind to it—"

"Fastnet!"

The cab was dark, and the boy's pale face was invisible to his guardian. But the tone with which he caught at the name struck that good gentleman.

"Yes. What about it?"

"Only," said Roger, after half a minute, and he spoke with an unusual effort, "it seems a good name for him."

Alone in his room that night Roger came to himself. A week or two ago he had hugged himself into the notion he was resolved to do his duty at all costs and in spite of all discouragement. Here had he been wasting a fortnight, forgetting duty, forgetting that he had a mission, posing as the heir, and accepting the compliments of a lot of time-servers who, now that he thought about them, valued him for nothing but his name and expectations.

And one of these—the least desirable of the lot—had been this Fastnet, the companion in profligacy of his lost brother, the one man, perhaps, from whom he might hope to obtain a clue as to the fate or whereabouts of the man whose rights he, Roger, was usurping!

He was tempted to telegraph to Armstrong to come to his help. But he dismissed the thought. In this quest Armstrong was not with him. He shrank from making a confidant of the captain. There was no one else to help him. He must play the game single-handed or not at all.

Once more his courage failed. Ratman his brother, Fastnet his brother's friend! At what a cost to the good name of his house was this wrong to be put right, this self-sacrifice to be accomplished. But ere he slept the honest man gained a victory over the poltroon. Providence had sent him stumbling into the track. It was not for him to draw back.

Next morning both he and his guardian found letters on the breakfast-table re-directed in Rosalind's hand from Maxfield. The latter, as he glanced at his, scowled, and crushed the missive angrily into his pocket. It was a letter from Ratman, reminding him that a certain bill was falling due on the following day, and requiring him, on pain of exposure, to honour it.

Roger's letter was in the same hand. It was dated London, a day or two back. Ratman said—

"Dear Brother,—I received your letter and enclosure. It is what I expected from you, but I hope it is not to be the last. I don't wonder at your suspecting my story—I don't particularly care whether you believe it or not. No doubt, with your respectable surroundings and the prospect before you, you are not over-anxious to claim brotherhood with a fellow of my sort. As long as you believe in me sufficiently not to leave me in the lurch, I shall be fairly content. But I cannot live on air, and have little else to support me. Don't be afraid I shall turn up again now until you want me. If I did, it would be not so much to see you as to see some one else to whom, rake as I am, I have lost my heart, and to whom I look to you to put in a good word on my behalf. You ask for proofs. I can't give you any that I know of. Everything is changed at Maxfield since I was there. Even the old hands like Dr Brandram or Hodder would not recognise me after all these years. In fact, they have seen me and have not done so. They think I'm dead. That's my fault; for when I was ill in India—goodness knows how many years ago—with, as I thought, not a day more to live, I told a comrade to send home news of my death, and they all believed it. So you see it is easier to talk about proof than give it. The only person who might be able to remember me after I left home—I had a hideous row with my father at the time—was a man called Fastnet, with whom I lodged in London, and who helped to make me the respectable specimen of humanity I have become. I lost sight of him long since, and for all I know he has joined the majority with all the others. I merely mention this to show you how hopeless it is of me to attempt to prove what I say. You may make your mind quite easy on that score. I shall probably return to India as soon as I am in funds. Except for the one reason I have named, I don't want to see Maxfield again—I've had enough of it. Nor do I see any advantage in meeting you, so I give no address. But any letters addressed to the G.P.O. I shall receive.

"Your brother,—

"Roger Ingleton."

This letter dispelled any lingering doubt, or perhaps hope, in Roger's mind that he was on a wrong scent. The writer, in protesting his inability to give any proof of his identity, had mentioned the two very circumstances which the old Squire had referred to in his posthumous letter. He had admitted that he had gone to the bad in London in company with a youth named Fastnet. The news of his death had reached England from abroad. Besides, the reckless, devil-may-care tone of the epistle more than ever convinced the younger brother that this was no fraudulent claimant, but the honest growl of an outcast who little guessed what his name was worth to him. Otherwise, why should he keep out of the way?

Captain Oliphant came to his room while these reflections were occupying his mind. He was too much preoccupied by the unpleasant contents of his own letter to notice the trouble of his ward.

"Roger," said he, "business calls me away from town for a day or two. I am sorry to interrupt our pleasant time together, but I hope it will not be long. Make yourself comfortable here, and take care of yourself."

"Are you going to Maxfield?" inquired Roger.

"No. But an old comrade I find is in trouble and wants my advice. It is a call I can hardly turn a deaf ear to."

Had Roger guessed that the friend on whom so much devotion was to be expended was Mr Robert Ratman, he would have displayed a good deal more curiosity than he did as to his guardian's business. As it was, he was not sorry to be left thus to his own devices.

"You know your way to the club by this time," said the captain. "Make yourself at home there—and keep out of mischief."

That evening Roger went somewhat nervously to his guardian's club. Since last night he had grown to detest the place and the company. But just now it was the one place where he might expect to hear something of his lost brother.

His new friends greeted him boisterously—and, relieved of the restraint of his guardian's presence, made more than usually merry in his honour.

They chaffed him about his expectations, and quizzed him about Rosalind. They laughed at his rustic simplicity, and amused themselves by putting him to the blush. They plied him with wine and cigars, and rallied him on his pure demure face. One or two toadies sidled up and professed a sympathy which was more offensive than the badinage.

He endured all as best he could, for one reason and one only. The loudest and coarsest of his tormentors was Mr Fastnet.

At last, however, when, not for the first time, Rosalind's name had been dragged into the conversation, the blood of the Ingletons rose.

The man who had spoken was a young *roué*, little more than Roger's own age, and reputed to be a great man in the circles of the fast.

"Excuse me," said Roger, abruptly interrupting the laugh that followed this hero's jest, "do you call yourself a gentleman?"

A bombshell on the floor could hardly have made a greater sensation.

"What do you mean?"

"I mean, sir, that you're not a gentleman."

The young gentleman staggered back as if he had been shot, and gaped round the audience, speechless.

"Hullo, hullo," said some one, "this is getting lively."

Another of the party walked to the door and turned the key, and several others hastily finished up the contents of their glasses.

Roger needed all his nerve to keep cool under the circumstances, but he succeeded.

All eyes were turned to the young gentleman, whose move it clearly was next.

He was very red in his face and threatening in his demeanour, but when it came to giving his feelings utterance his courage dwindled down into a—

"Bah! sanctimonious young prig!"

The astonishment was now transferred to the onlookers.

"Hullo, Compton, I say," said Fastnet, "did you hear what he called you? Is that all you've got to say?"

The Honourable Mr Compton's face gradually bleached, as he looked from one to the other.

"He said you were no gentleman," repeated Fastnet, determined there should be no mistake about the matter. "Isn't that so, youngster?" appealing to Roger.

"That is what I said," said Roger.

The lily-livered hero was hanging out his true colours at last.

"It's lucky for him," snarled he, "he is only a visitor in this house."

Fastnet and one or two of the others laughed disagreeably.

"Ingleton," said the former, taking control of the proceedings generally, "are you willing to repeat what you said outside?"

"Certainly," said Roger; "anywhere you like. And I shall be delighted to add that he is a coward."

"There, Compton. Surely that satisfies you?"

Mr Compton, very white and downcast, took up his hat.

"Thank you," said he, with a pitiful affectation of superciliousness; "I take no notice of young bumpkins like him," and he turned on his heel.

Fastnet stepped before him to the door.

"Look here, Compton," said he, "you're a member of this club. Do we understand you funk this affair?"

"I've something better to do than bother my head about him. Understand what you like. Let me go!"

Fastnet opened the door.

"Clear out!" said he, with an oath; "and don't show your face here again, unless you want to be kicked."

"What do you mean by that?"

"What I say. Be off, or I won't wait till you come again."

Whereupon exit the Honourable Mr Compton with colours dipped.

"Now," said Fastnet, when he had gone, "it is only fair to the youngster here to say that we agree with him in his opinion of our late member. Eh, you men?"

General assent greeted the question. Upon which Mr Fastnet suggested that, as the evening had been spoiled, the house do adjourn.

"You'd better come and have supper with me," said he to Roger.

And Roger, feeling his chance had come, accepted.

Chapter Seventeen
"When the Cat's away—"

Maxfield Manor, however cheery a place in summer-time, with its household in full swing, was decidedly desolate in dark November weather, with only a housekeeper in charge—that is to say, to any one but the two young persons on whom the honours of the house devolved, it would have appeared dull.

Mr Armstrong delayed his visit to Oxford for some days after the departure of the Captain and Roger. There was a good deal of business to be done in connection with the estate, and as Mr Pottinger discovered, when the second trustee did take it into his head to look into things, it was no child's play. He had an uncomfortable manner, this tutor, of demanding explanations and particulars with all the air of the proprietor himself, and was not to be put off by any dilatory tactics on the part of the official with whom the explanation lay. As in the present case the business transacted was chiefly in connection with leases and conveyances, the unfortunate lawyer had a rough week of it, and felt at the end very much like one of his own clients after a year in Chancery. However, the inquisitor appeared to be fairly well satisfied when all was done, so that Mr Pottinger, who all along had on his mind the uncomfortable consciousness of a few well-hidden irregularities, was doubly relieved when the tutor dropped his glass finally from his eye and observed—

"I need not trouble you further at present, sir."

It was after this final interview that Mr Armstrong looked in on his friend the doctor.

"I'm off to Oxford for a day or two," said he.

"No attractions here?" asked the doctor.

"Yes—you among others."

"And who's to wash and dress the babies at Maxfield? And who is to keep the wolf from the fold at the Vicarage? and who is to keep an eye on the man of the law across the way?"

"The babes are well qualified to nurture one another. The man of the law is under closer observation than he imagines. As to the wolf, I came to speak to you about that. He may make a descent on the fold, in which case Dr Brandram must go out with swords and staves and give him battle."

The doctor laughed.

"I like your ideas of the medical profession. Its duties are variegated and lively. However, make yourself easy this time. I hear to-day that the young ladies at the Vicarage with their governess are to go on Monday to Devonshire."

"Good," said Mr Armstrong, decidedly relieved.

"When does your ward return?" said the doctor. "I dislike this London business altogether. Oliphant is not to be trusted with a boy of his delicate make. You should have stopped it."

The tutor said nothing, but looked decidedly dejected. He was greatly tempted to confide the difficulties of the situation to his friend. But the dead Squire's secret was not his to give away.

"Unless they come home soon," said he, "I have a notion of returning from Oxford by way of London."

"Do—the sooner the better."

When, on the next day, Miss Rosalind sailed up to Maxfield to bid her brother and sister farewell, it fell to the tutor's lot to escort her back to the Vicarage.

"Mr Armstrong," said she abruptly, as they went, "why have you and Roger quarrelled?"

Mr Armstrong looked round uncomfortably.

"Quarrelled?"

"Yes. Do you suppose he would go away like this for any other reason? Won't you tell me what it is about?"

"Roger and I have agreed to differ on a certain point, Miss Oliphant. We have not quarrelled?"

"You cannot trust me, I see, or you would tell me what the trouble is."

"I trust you completely, Miss Oliphant. I will gladly tell you."

Five minutes ago wild horses would not have extorted the confession from him. But somehow or other, as he looked at her standing there, he could not help himself.

"Roger has got an impression that his elder brother is still living, and is to be found; and, if found, that he ought to be made possessor of Maxfield. I am unable to sympathise in what I look upon as an unprofitable quest. That is the whole story."

"Why cannot you back him up, Mr Armstrong?"

"I believe his fancy is utterly groundless; besides which, if the person he believes to be the missing brother is really Roger Ingleton, to discover him would mean disgrace to Maxfield, and an injury to the name of Ingleton."

"What! Mr Armstrong, do you mean to say—"

"I mean to say that Mr Robert Ratman claims to be the lost elder brother, and that Roger credits the story. Miss Oliphant, I am grateful to you for sharing this confidence with me. You can help Roger in this matter better than I can."

She looked at him with a flush in her face, and then replied rather dismally, "I fear not—for, to be as frank with you as you are with me, I am dreadfully afraid Roger is right. The same fancy passed through my mind when first I saw Mr Ratman. I had recently been studying the lost brother's portrait, you know, and was struck and horrified by the resemblance. Mr Armstrong," added she, after a pause, "if I were Roger's guardian and tutor, I would stand by him all the more that his duty is an unpleasant one. Thank you; here we are at the gate. Good-bye. I hope you will have a pleasant time at Oxford."

And she passed in, leaving the good man in a sad state of bewilderment and perplexity.

He started a day or two later in a somewhat depressed frame of mind for Oxford, where he astonished and delighted most of his old creditors by calling and paying off a further instalment of his debts to them. But his satisfaction in this act of restitution was sadly tempered by the sense of coercion put upon him by the doctor and Rosalind, and the conviction that, wise or foolish, pleasant or unpleasant, his place was at his young pupil's side. No excuse, or pleadings of a false pride, could dispel the feeling. No, he must climb down, own himself wrong, and sue for permission to assist in a quest in which he had little faith and still less inclination.

While he is making up his mind, it may be worth the reader's while to remark what was happening at Maxfield.

Tom and Jill woke one morning to discover themselves lord and lady of the situation. In their lamentations, not unmingled with a sense of injury, at the desertion of which they were the victims, it had not occurred to them to realise that there were alleviating circumstances in their forlorn condition.

The great manor-house was theirs—library, dining-hall, corridors, haunted chamber, roof, cellars—all except the servant's hall and the room where Mrs Parker, the housekeeper, held austere sway. The park was theirs, the woods, the stream, the paddocks, and the live-stock. Nay, when they came to reckon all up, half the county was theirs, and a mile or so of sea-beach into the bargain.

They were absolutely free to roam where they liked, do what they liked, eat what they liked, and sit up at night to any hour that pleased them. Mrs Parker, good soul, though excellent in academic exhortations and prohibitions, was too infirm to put her laws into active practice; and when, a day or two after the place had been left in her charge, she succumbed to a touch of her enemy, the lumbago, and had to take to her bed, these two young persons, though extremely sorry for her misfortune, felt that the whole world lay like a glorious football at their feet.

"Good old Jilly!" exclaimed Tom in his balmiest mood one morning, when these two young prodigals assembled for breakfast in the big dining-room at the fashionable hour of eleven, with Raffles in full livery to attend upon them. "This is what I call a lark and a half. Raffles, pass Miss Jill the honey; and walk about, and make yourself useful. I tell you what, we'll go and have a snap at the pheasants, and try a few drop kicks over the Martyr's oak. What do you say?"

"I can't shoot awfully well," said Jill apologetically. "I'd sooner, if you don't mind, Tom, walk about on the roof, or help you let the water out of the big pond."

"Raffles, old chappie, more toast—a lot more toast for Miss Jill. I'll have a wing of something myself. The fact is, Jilly," said he, when Raffles had departed on his quest, "I wanted to get the beast out of the way while I told you I'd got an idea."

"Oh, *what*, Tom?" asked Jill, in tones of surprised pleasure. Tom glanced round cautiously, and then whispered, "You and I'll give a small kick-up here on our own hooks. What do you say?"

"A party! Oh Tom! how clever of you to think of that!"

"You see," said Tom, accepting the homage meekly, "the other day in the library, when we were turning out all the drawers, I found a whole lot of 'At Home' cards, and the list of fellows that were asked to Roger's birthday party."

"How lovely!" exclaimed Jill; "we'll just—"

But here the return of Raffles, and a significant scowl from Tom, warned her to defer her suggestion.

The meal over, the conspirators met in the library, and put their heads together over Tom's documents.

"That's about the ticket, isn't it?" said he, displaying one of the invitation cards which he had experimentally filled up.

"Dr Brandram—

"Mr and Miss Oliphant at home on Wednesday, December 2, at 7 o'clock. Music, dancing, fireworks, etcetera.

"R.S.V.P."

"But we haven't got any fireworks," suggested Jill; "we'll have to get some. And what about the band?"

"I shall write to the Colonel of the Grenadiers and order it. Anyhow, you can play the Goblin polka if we get stuck up."

Jill wondered whether, after an hour or two, her one piece (even though dear Mr Armstrong liked it) might not pall on a large assembly, and she devoutly hoped the Grenadiers would accept.

"There's a hundred and fifty names down," said Tom. "May as well have the lot while we're about it."

"Isn't two days rather a short invitation?" asked Jill.

"Bless you, no. You see, we're not out of mourning. Besides, Mother Parker may be well again if we don't look sharp, or Armstrong may turn up."

"How I wish he would!"

"He'd spoil everything. Look here, Jill, look alive and write the cards. I'll call out."

The two spent a most industrious morning, so much so that the household marvelled at their goodness, and remarked to one another, "The children are no trouble at all."

Towards the end of the sitting Tom flung down his paper with a whistle of dismay.

"I say, Jill, they ought to be black-edged!"

Jill turned pale.

"What is to be done?" she gasped.

"We'll have to doctor them with pen and ink," said Tom.

So for another hour or so they occupied themselves painfully in putting their invitations into mourning. The result was not wholly satisfactory, for a card dipped edgeways into a shallow plate of ink is apt to take on its black unevenly. So that while some of the guests were invited with signs of the slightest sorrow, the company of others was requested with tokens of the deepest bereavement. However, on the whole the result was passable, and that evening Tom slunk down to Yeld post office with a bundle under his arm. At the last moment a difficulty had arisen with regard to postage, as, between them, the two could not raise the thirteen shillings required to stamp the lot. However, by a lucky accident Tom discovered a bundle of halfpenny wrappers, the property of the estate, which (after scrupulously writing an I.O.U. for the amount) he borrowed.

"Saved a clean six-and-six by that," he remarked, when the last was licked up; "that'll go into the fireworks."

Jill, whose admiration for her brother's genius knew no bounds, felt almost happy.

It was Monday evening when the Yeld post-master was exercised in his mind by hearing a loud rap down-stairs, which on inquiry he found to have proceeded from the discharge of 150 mysterious-looking halfpenny missives, written in a very round hand, into his box. Being an active and intelligent person, he felt it his duty to examine one, addressed, as it happened, to the Duke of Somewhere. After some consideration, and a study of his rules and regulations, he came to the conclusion that the enclosure was of the nature of a letter, and thereupon proceeded to mark each with a claim for a penny excess postage. Which done, he retired to his parlour, relieved in his mind.

Tom and Jill had more to do than to speculate on the adventures of their carefully-written cards.

"Now about grub!" said Tom that evening.

Once more Jill turned a little pale. She had been dreading this fateful question all along.

"What do you think?" said she diplomatically.

Tom, of course, had thought the problem out.

"We must keep it dark from the slaveys," said he, "at least till everybody comes, then they're bound to give us a leg up. I fancy we can scrape a thing or two up from what's in the house. And I've called in at one or two of the shops at Yeld and told them to send up some things addressed to 'Miss J. Oliphant—private.' There was rather a nice lot of herrings just in, so I got three dozen of them cheap. Then I told them at the confectioner's to send up all the strawberry ices they could in the time, and 150 buns. You see everybody is sure not to come, so there'll be plenty to go round."

"Didn't Mr Rusk ask what they were for?" inquired Jill.

"I said Mr Oliphant presented his kind regards, and would be glad to have the things sharp."

Next morning, greatly to the delight of the hospitable pair, the herrings came up in a basket, addressed privately to Miss Jill. Later in the day tradesmen's carts rattled up the back drive with similar missives, not a little to the bewilderment of the servants of the house, who shook their heads and wished Mrs Parker would make a speedy recovery.

Tom adroitly captured the booty, and half won over Raffles to aid and abet in the great undertaking.

"Good old Raffy," said he, as the two staggered across the hall with one of Miss Jill's private boxes between them; "would you like a threepenny bit?"

Raffles, whose ideas of a tip were elastic, admitted that he was open to receive even the smallest coin.

"All right, mum's the word. Jill and I have a thing on, and we don't want it spoiled by the slaveys."

Raffles said that, as far as he knew, the "slaveys" were thinking about anything else than the proceedings of the two young Oliphants. "Besides," said he, "being 'olidays, there's only me and the cook, and a maid—and she's took up with nursing Mrs Parker."

"Poor old Parker! How is she? Pretty chippy? Sorry she's laid up. All serene, Raff. Keep it mum, and you shall have the threepenny. Jolly heavy box that—that's the cocoa-nuts."

"Oh, you're going to have a feast, are you?" said Raffles.

"Getting on that way," said Tom. "We can't ask you, you know, because you'll have to wait. But you shall have some of the leavings if you back us up."

With locked doors that night Tom and Jill unpacked and took stock of their commissariat.

"Thirty-six herrings cut up in four," said Tom, with an arithmetical precision which would have gratified Mr Armstrong, "makes 144 goes of herring. If every man-jack turns up, that'll only be six goes short, and if you and I sit out of it, only four. We might cheek in a head or two by accident to make that up."

"Who will cook them?" asked Jill.

"Oh, we can do that, I fancy, on a tray or something. Then six cocoa-nuts into 150 will be twenty-five. You'll have to cut each one into twenty-five bits, Jill. Then one bun apiece, and—oh, the ice! How on earth are we to slice that up? There's about a soup-plate full. Couldn't get strawberry, so he's sent coffee."

"Ugh!" said Jill; "I'll give up my share."

"I did my best," said Tom. "It's not my fault strawberries are out of season."

"Of course not. You're awfully clever, Tom. What should I have done without you?"

"Good old Jilly! What about plates?"

The consultation lasted far into the night.

Next morning the post brought a dozen or so of polite notes which sent the hearts of the hospitable pair into their mouths. The first they opened was from the Duke of Somewhere, who gravely "accepted with pleasure Mr and Miss Oliphant's polite invitation."

Several of the others were acceptances—one or two refusals.

"Five scratched already," said Tom. "That'll make it all right for the herrings."

In the afternoon Dr Brandram called. He carried his invitation card in his hand.

"What game are you at now?" he demanded.

"Oh, I say, Doctor, keep it quiet! You'll come, won't you? There'll be a tidy spread—enough to go all round; and the Duke and his lot are coming, and we expect the Grenadiers."

"Doctor," said Jill, "we shall depend on you so much. Do come early!"

Dr Brandram drove back to Yeld in a dazed condition of mind. He was tempted to telegraph to the Duke and the county generally; to set a body of police to prevent any one entering the Maxfield gates; to shut the two miscreants up in the coal-cellar; to run away, and not return till next week.

But after an hysterical consultation with himself, he decided that it was too late to do anything but cast in his lot with the other victims, and go dressed in all his best to Miss Oliphant's "At Home," and do what he could to steer her and her graceless brother out of their predicament.

As the fateful hour approached, Tom began to be a little nervous. He had not anticipated the vast number of small details demanding his personal attention.

For instance, there was the cooking of the herrings. Jill had nobly undertaken that task at the drawing-room fire, which was the most capacious. But then, if they ran it too fine, the guests might arrive while the fish were still fizzling on the tray. If, on the other hand, they were cooked too soon, they would be lukewarm by the time the guests came to sit down to them. Again, there were the starlights and Roman candles to get into position outside, and arrangements had to be made for their protection from the damp November mist. Then, too, the faithless Grenadiers had not turned up, which necessitated Jill deserting her herrings and privately practising the Goblin polka, in view of possible emergencies. Further, the table had to be laid, and every guest's "go" of buns, and cocoa-nut, and coffee-ice, doled out in readiness. And at the last moment there arose a difficulty in raising the requisite number of knives, forks, spoons, and plates. Then he discovered that the covers were still on the drawing-room chairs and the dust-cloth on the floor, and much time and trouble was necessary for their removal. Finally, he and Jill had to dress to receive their guests.

"I think it will be a jolly evening," said he somewhat doubtfully, as they hurried to their rooms.

"I'm sure it will," said Jill, whose mind had not once been clouded by a doubt. "The herrings will be cold, that's the only thing. But they may think that's the newest fashion."

"Look sharp and dress, anyhow," said Tom, "because you've got to cut them in fours and stick them round on the plates, and it's half-past six already."

Half an hour later a grand carriage and pair drove up to the door, and Raffles solemnly announced—

"His Grace the Duke of Somewhere, and the Ladies Marigold."

Miss Oliphant's evening party had begun!

Chapter Eighteen
Miss Jill Oliphant At Home

When His Grace, who had been a good deal puzzled by his abrupt, under-stamped invitation, stepped, head in air, into the drawing-room, he was somewhat taken aback to discover neither the captain nor his charming elder daughter, but instead, to be greeted by a little girl, nervously put forward by a small boy, and saying—

"Oh, duke, *do* you mind coming? I hope you'll enjoy the party so much. There'll be some dancing presently, and supper as soon as all the others come."

"You're the first," said Tom. "Never mind, the others won't be long. Like to read the newspaper, or take a turn round?"

Mentally he was calculating how he should manage to squeeze in the duke's two daughters, who hadn't been invited, at his hospitable board.

The duke smiled affably.

"We are rather early, but Miss Rosalind will excuse—"

"Oh, she's away—so is father. This is my party and Tom's. Oh, duke, do try and like it!" said Jill, taking the great man's hand.

The duke cast a scared look over his shoulder at his daughters, who were staring in a somewhat awestruck manner at their two small hosts.

"If the girls would like to begin dancing," suggested Tom, "Jill can play her piece now, and you can take one, and I'll take the other. It'll keep the things going, you know, till the rest turn up."

At this juncture Dr Brandram was announced, greatly to Tom's delight, who, among so many strangers, was beginning to feel a little shy.

"That's all right," said he. "Good old Brandy! you lead off with one of the Marigold girls, while I stop here and do the how-d'ye-do's."

The doctor, with a serious face, led His Grace aside.

"This appears to be a freak of the two young people," said he. "They are the only members of the family at home. I am very sorry you have been victimised."

"Tut, tut," said the duke, recovering his good-humour rapidly, "I don't mean to be a victim at all. I mean to enjoy myself; so do you, doctor. Girls," said he to his daughters, "you must see the youngsters through this. Ha, ha! what is the rising generation coming to, to be sure."

Arrivals now began to drop in smartly, and as Tom looked round on the gradually filling drawing-room, a mild perspiration broke out on his ingenious brow.

Jill had gallantly struck up her polka on the piano, but as no one listened and no one danced, she gave it up and returned to the support of her brother.

"It's going splendidly," said Tom in a stage whisper; "they all seem to be enjoying it."

They certainly were—for as each gradually took in the situation, and received his cue from his neighbour, an unwonted air of humour permeated the room.

A few hoity-toity persons of course felt outraged, and would have ordered their carriages had there been any one to order them from. The honest Raffles was, to tell the truth, secretly busy, on a signal from Tom, preparing for the banquet in the dining-room, and no other servant was to be seen.

"My dear," said Mrs Pottinger, in a severely audible voice to her husband, "I wish to return home. Will you get our carriage? My ideas of amusement do not correspond with those of the young people."

"Oh, don't go yet!" said Tom, with beaming face, for he had caught sight of Raffles' powdered wig at the door; "there's some grub ready in the next room. It would have been ready before, only the herrings—"

"Tom," said Jill, "there's the Bishop just come. He couldn't come for Roger's birthday, you know."

"How do you do, Bishop?" said Tom, grasping the new arrival by the hand. "Jolly you could come this time. I was just saying there's some grub in the next room. Jill, Raff had better ring up on the gong, tell him."

Raffles accordingly sounded an alarm on the gong, which brought the company to attention.

"Supper!" cried Tom encouragingly, and led the way, allowing the company generally to sort themselves.

The Duke behaved nobly that night. He gallantly gave his arm to Jill, and asked the Bishop to bring in one of his daughters. This saved Miss Oliphant's party from the collapse which threatened it. Every one took the cue from the great people. Even Mrs Pottinger accepted the arm of the curate, and the ardent youths, who had all arrived under the delusion that Miss Rosalind was the hostess, forgot their disappointment, and vowed to see the youngsters through with it.

"Oh, Duke!" said Jill, hanging affectionately on her noble escort's arm, "are you liking it? Do try and like it! It's Tom's and my first party, and we want it to be a jolly one."

"I never enjoyed a party half so much," said His Grace.

Jill thought him at that moment almost as nice as dear Mr Armstrong.

"Jill," said Tom, waylaying his sister at the door, "we might have cut the herrings in three after all. Never mind, some of them will be able to have two goes. I'll see you do. Good old Jilly. Isn't it going off prime? And you know, the fireworks are still to come!"

It was too severe a strain on the gravity of some of the guests when they beheld each his "go" of lukewarm herring, cocoa-nut, coffee-ice, and penny bun, with a single plate to accommodate the whole, on the board before him. But the laughter, if it reached the ears of the genial host and hostess, was taken by them as a symptom of delight, in which they heartily shared.

Tom, as he cast his eye down the festive board—object of so much solicitude and physical exertion—never felt happier in his life. More than half of the company would be able to get a second helping of fish and bun!

"Wire in," said he to his guests generally, and to the younger Lady Marigold, his next neighbour, in particular, "before it gets cold. Awfully sorry the cocoa-nut milk wasn't enough to go round, so Jill and I thought—"

Here a guilty look from Jill pulled him up. Dear old Jilly, he wouldn't let out on her for worlds.

A good many eyes turned curiously to where the Duke sat with his "go" before him. Those who were quick at observing details noticed that he had ranged his cocoa-nut and ice on the edge of his plate, and was beginning to attack his herring with every sign of relish. His portion consisted mostly of hard roe, for which he had no natural predilection, but this evening he seemed to enjoy it, helping it down with occasional bites at the bun, and keeping up a cheerful conversation the while.

The Bishop, too, who had a tail, was making a capital meal, as were also several other of the guests near him.

"Capital fish!" said the Duke presently. Then beckoning to Raffles, "Can you get me a little more?"

"Yes, your grace."

Tom felt a little anxious lest Raffles should select from out of the surplus "goes" one of those with the heads which were to eke out in a last emergency. But when he saw that the duke's second helping consisted of a prime "waist" he rejoiced with all his heart.

"Isn't it nice?" asked Jill, who had been busily at work under the shadow of his ducal wing.

"My dear little lady, I never tasted such a meal in my life."

In due time the cocoa-nut and coffee-ice were attacked with quite as much relish as the first course; after which Tom, looking a little warm, rose and made a little speech.

"I hope you've all liked it," said he. "I was afraid there wouldn't be enough, but some of them didn't turn up, so it was all right after all. Jill—that's my young sister here—cut the 'goes' up, and I don't know anybody more fair all round than her. She and I are awfully glad you came, and hope you'll have a good old time. Please don't tell the governor or Rosalind we gave this party. I beg to propose the health of my young sister—good old Jilly. She's a regular brick, and has backed up no end in this do. No heel-taps!"

A good many healths had been drunk in the county during the year, but few of them were more genuinely responded to than this. And no queen ever bore her honours more delightfully than the little heroine of the evening.

"I suppose we'd better cut into the next room now," suggested Tom, when this function was over. "There'll be some fireworks by and by; but any one who likes a hop meanwhile can have one. Jill knows a ripping piece to play."

The invitation was cordially responded to, and when, after sundry repetitions of the "ripping" piece, the eldest Miss Marigold offered to play a waltz, and after her Miss Shafto relieved duty with a polka, and after her one of the ardent youths actually condescended to perform a set of quadrilles, in which His Grace the Duke, with Jill as his partner, led off *vis-à-vis* with the Bishop and the sister of the member for the county, there was no room to doubt the glorious success of Miss Oliphant's party.

Tom meanwhile, joyous at heart, warm in temperature, and excited in mind, was groping on his knees on the damp grass outside the drawing-room window, fixing his two threepenny Roman candles in reversed flower pots, and planting his starlights, crackers, and Catherine-wheels in advantageous positions in the vicinity, casting now and again a delighted glance at the animated scene within, and wondering if he had ever spent a jollier evening anywhere.

It disturbed him to hear a vehicle rattle up the drive, and to argue therefrom that some belated guest had missed the feast. Never mind; he shouldn't be quite out of it.

"Raffles," called he, as he caught sight of that hardworking functionary through the dining-room window removing the *débris* of the banquet, "leave a few 'goes' out on the table for any chaps who come late, and then go and tell Jill I'm ready, and turn down the gas in the drawing-room."

In due time Raffles delivered his momentous message.

"Oh, the fireworks!" cried Miss Jill, clapping her hands, "the fireworks are to begin. Aren't you glad, duke? Do get a good seat before the gas is turned down."

The company crowded into the big bay-window, and endured the extinction of the light with great good-humour. Indeed, a certain gentleman who entered the room at this particular juncture, seeing nothing, but hearing the laughter and talk, said to himself that this was as merry an occasion as it had been his lot to participate in.

The dim form of Tom might be seen hovering without, armed with a bull's-eye lantern, at which he diligently kindling matches, which refused to stay in long enough to ignite the refractory fireworks.

"Never mind," said he to himself, "they'll like it when they do go off."

So they did. After a quarter of an hour's waiting one of the Roman candles went off with vast *éclat*, and after it two crackers simultaneously gave chase to the operator half-way round the lawn. One of the Catherine-wheels was also prevailed upon to give a few languid rotations on its axis, and some of the squibs, which had unfortunately got damp, condescended, after being inserted bodily into the lantern, to go off. Presently, however, the wind got into the lantern, and the matches being by this time exhausted, and the starlights refusing to depart from their usual abhorrence for spontaneous combustion, the judicious Tom deemed it prudent to pronounce this part of the entertainment at an end.

"All over!" he shouted through the window. "Turn up the light."

When, after the applause which greeted this imposing display, the gas was turned up, the first sight which met Miss Jill's eyes was the form of Mr Robert Ratman, in travelling costume, nodding familiarly across the room.

At the sight the little lady's face blanched, and the joy of the evening vanished like smoke.

"Oh, Duke!" she exclaimed, clinging to her guest's arm, "do please turn that wicked man there out of the house. We didn't invite him, and he's no right, really. If dear Mr Armstrong was only here! Please put him out."

The duke looked a little blank at this appeal.

"Why, child, really? Who is he?" he asked.

"A wicked, bad man, that I hate; and I did think you would be kind enough to—"

"What is his name?"

"Mr Ratman; he hurt me awfully once."

The duke, feeling that Miss Oliphant's party was taking rather a serious turn, walked across the room to where Mr Ratman was already engaged in an uncomfortable colloquy with Dr Brandram.

"What are you doing here?" the doctor had asked.

"That's my business," said Mr Ratman. "For the matter of that, what are you doing here?"

"Among other things, I am here to see that the young people of the house are not annoyed by the intrusion of a person called Ratman."

"And I," said the duke, coming up, "am here to advise you to save trouble by leaving the house."

"And who are you, sir?"

"I am the Duke of Somewhere."

"Proud to renew my acquaintance, sir. May I ask if you have quite forgotten me?"

"Sir, you have the advantage of me. I never saw you before."

"Pardon me, my lord, you saw me a month ago, at a birthday party in this very house."

"If so, I was not sufficiently impressed sir, to remember you now. I repeat my request as the friend of the young lady."

"Ah, indeed!" said Ratman; "I am not aware, your grace, of your right to speak to me in the name of Miss Oliphant, or anybody else."

"Oh," said Tom, arriving on the scene at this juncture, "you there, Ratty? you'd better clear out. All the grub's done, and you're not wanted here. We didn't ask you—took care not to. Rosalind's not here. This is Jilly's and my party. Isn't it, you chaps?" The chaps appealed to, His Grace, the doctor, and one or two of the other guests, corroborated this statement.

Mr Ratman leant comfortably against the wall.

"Flattering reception," said he. "I am inclined to take your lordship's advice and go; but before I do, may I ask your lordship again if you really do not remember me?"

"I never saw you before, sir," said His Grace; "and allow me to add, I have no desire to see you again."

"*Dear* Duke!" whispered Jill encouragingly, putting her hand in his.

"Odd the changes a few years make," rejoined Mr Ratman. "I presume your lordship's memory can carry you back a little time — say twenty years?"

"What of that, sir?"

"Merely that if that is so, you probably can remember a lad named Roger Ingleton who lived in this house, son of the old Squire."

There was a dead silence now, and the Duke looked in a startled way at the speaker.

"I see you remember that boy," said the intruder; "and you probably heard the story of my — I mean his quarrel with his father, and also heard of his supposed death. Now, your grace, put twenty years on to that boy, and suppose the story of his death was a myth, then say again you don't remember me."

"What, you mean to say *you* are young Roger Ingleton?"

"At your grace's service."

Tom gave a whistle, half dismay, half amusement. The doctor smiled contemptuously. The duke bit his lip and gazed stolidly at the speaker.

"You are not obliged to believe me," said the latter jauntily; "only you wanted to know my business in Maxfield, and I have told you. I don't say I'm the heir, for I understand my father was good enough to cut me out of every penny of his estate. And as for being a paragon of virtue, or the opposite, that's my affair and no one else's — eh, your grace?"

His Grace was much disturbed. He had once seen young Roger Ingleton, at that time a mere boy, but retained no distinct memory of him. At the time of the quarrel between father and son he had been abroad, and the news of the lad's death had been formally communicated as a matter beyond question. Recognition, as far as he was concerned, was impossible.

"You choose a strange time, sir," said he, "for coming here with this story, when the heir and his guardians are both away."

"I supposed my brother was here," said Ratman. "In any case he knows who I am; so does your friend the tutor, Dr Brandram."

"Oh, why *do* you stop talking to that hateful man instead of coming, and enjoying the party?" pleaded Jill.

"Ah, my little lady, is that you?" said Ratman advancing.

But his passage was intercepted by the doctor.

"Gently, my friend," said he. "Now that you have relieved yourself of your pretty story, let me suggest that the easiest way out of this house is by the door."

"Who are you, sir?" blustered Ratman.

Dr Brandram laughed.

"I must have changed in twenty years as much as you," said he.

"I am not going to ask *your* leave to be in my father's house."

"I am not going to ask your leave to put you out of it."

Tom's spirits rose. There seemed every promise of an unrehearsed entertainment for the delectation of his guests.

"I caution you, sir."

"I will take all responsibility," said the doctor. "Anything more you have to say can just as well be said in Mr Pottinger's office to-morrow morning as here."

"Thank you, sir," said Mr Ratman, with a snarl. "It is never pleasant to have to introduce oneself, but I am glad to have had the opportunity before this distinguished company. It is now the turn of the other side to move. If they want me they must find me. Good night, your grace; you are a nice loyal neighbour to an old comrade's boy. Good night, you, sir; take as much responsibility as you like if it is any satisfaction to you. Good-bye, my pretty little Jill; some day you'll have to call me cousin Roger, and then we'll be quits. Good night, gentlemen and ladies all. The prodigal's return has not been a success, I own, but it's a fact all the same. *Au revoir*."

And he bowed himself out.

"This fellow is either the most impudent villain I ever met," said the Duke, "or there is something in his story."

This seemed to be the general impression. A few, Dr Brandram among them, scoffed irreverently at the whole affair. But the majority of those present felt decidedly disturbed by the incident, and poor Miss Jill Oliphant had the mortification of seeing her party drop flat after all.

Tom and she made Herculean efforts to rehabilitate it. Jill played her polka till she was tired, and Tom, after setting out all the duplicate "goes" in the hall, retired to grope in the wet grass for a few of the unexploded squibs.

Some of the guests did what they could to back their hosts up, and made great show of enjoying themselves, but the Duke was preoccupied, and the Bishop was pensive. The Marigold girls talked in a corner, and Mr Pottinger was out in the hall calling for his carriage.

"Odious man!" said the poor little hostess, "he's spoiled all our fun. No one likes our party now. They'll all be glad to get away; and we did try so hard to make it jolly."

"Never mind," said Tom cheerfully, "it would have been worse if he had turned up before the grub and the fireworks. They didn't miss them. Keep it up, Jilly, I say; it's going off all right."

When it came to saying good night, every one remembered their genial entertainers, and Jill was a little consoled by the assurances she received on all hands that the evening had been a delightful one.

"Try to think it was nice," said she, "and don't go saying it was horrid as soon as you get outside. It's Tom's and my first party, you know."

And she kissed all the gentlemen, from the Duke downward, and Tom, hovering in the hall, pressed his farewell refreshments, as far as they would go, upon them and gave them a "leg up" into their carriages.

Dr Brandram stayed till the end.

"I should have to come and see Mrs Parker in the morning in any case," said he, "so I have told Raffles to make me a shake down in Armstrong's room to-night. I may as well stay here."

The precaution, however, was unnecessary. Mr Ratman had vanished. He did not call on Mr Pottinger next morning, nor was he to be found at the hotel. He had returned by the early morning train to London.

Chapter Nineteen
A Feeble Clue

Mr Fastnet's lodgings were a good deal less imposing than Roger, who had hitherto only met the owner at the club, had pictured to himself. In fact, the small sitting-room, with bedroom to match, commonly furnished, reeking of tobacco, and hung all round with sporting and dramatic prints, was quite as likely a refuge for an unfledged medical student as for a person of the swagger and presence of Mr Felix Fastnet.

"No use to me," he explained, interpreting his young guest's thought, "except as a dog-kennel. I live at the club—breakfast, lunch, dinner—everything; but I was so disgusted with the performance of that young cad to-night that I even prefer the dog-kennel. Have a soda?"

Roger accepted, and sat down by the fire.

"Yes," growled on his host; "I'm father of that club, and I don't like to see it degraded. If he'd gone for you, and kicked you into the street, I shouldn't have lifted a finger to stop him. He could have made hay of you if I'd chosen, a sickly youngster like you."

"I wonder he did not," said Roger; "but, Mr Fastnet, now I have met you, I want to ask you a question."

"Ask away."

"My name, as you know, is Roger Ingleton. Have you never met any one of my name before?"

"Bless me, no. Why should I?"

"I had a namesake once who came to London, and I wondered if you possibly knew him."

"My dear sir, I don't know quite all the young men who have come to London during the last twenty years. What makes you think it?"

"My namesake was a brother—son of my father's first wife. He left home and disappeared. Rumour says he went to London, where he was last heard of in company of a companion named Fastnet."

Mr Fastnet put down his glass.

"Eh?" said he. "The Fastnets are not a big clan. Are you sure that was the name?"

"It was certainly the name that reached me."

"Must refer to some one else then. I never knew or heard of any one of the name of Ingleton in my life."

Roger's countenance fell. The new scent appeared likely to be a false one after all.

"How long ago is all this?" asked his host.

"More than twenty years. My brother left home in a pique, and, I'm afraid, went to the bad in—"

"Twenty years?" said Mr Fastnet, putting down his cigar beside the glass. "What sort of fellow was he? A harum-scarum young dog, with impudent eyes, and a toss of his head that would have defied the bench of bishops?"

"That is he," said Roger excitedly.

"Sit down!" continued Fastnet—"curly hair, arms like a young Hercules, as obstinate as a bulldog, with a temper like a tiger?"

"Yes, yes! that must be the same."

"Left his mother and father in a furious tantrum, with a vow to cut off his head before he showed face at home again? A regular young demon, as honest as the Bank of England—no taste for vice in any shape or form, but plunged into it just to spite his friends, civil enough when you got him on the weather side, and no fool? Was that the fellow?"

"I'm sure you describe the very man," said Roger.

"Man? He was a boy; a raw-boned green boy, smarting under a sense of injustice, a regular, thorough-paced young Ishmaelite as you ever saw. I should fancy I did know him. But his name was not Ingleton."

"What was it?"

"Jack Rogers."

"No doubt he adopted his own Christian name as a disguise."

"Very likely. I could never get him to talk about his people. His one object was to lose himself—body and soul—it seemed to me. Bless you, I had little enough voice in his proceedings. I was wild enough, but I promise you I was a milksop to him. Neck or nothing was his motto, and he lived up to it. The one drawback to success in his particular line was that he would insist on being a gentleman. Fatal complaint to any one who wants to go to the bad."

"Have you any idea what became of my brother?"

"Not in the least. He knocked about with me for about a year, till he suddenly discovered he was living on me. Not that I minded; I had pots of money—it's been my curse. Never had to do a day's work in my life. He pulled up short at that, pawned his watch, and refused to take another crust of bread, and left me without a penny in his pocket. I only heard once of him afterwards. He wrote to enclose a five-pound note."

"Have you got his letter? Can you remember where he wrote from?" asked Roger excitedly.

"I don't believe there was a letter. The note was wrapped up in an old play-bill of some strolling company of actors. I remember it now," added Fastnet, laughing and re-lighting his cigar. "Yes, it was *Hamlet*. Rogers was cast for the ghost in one act, Polonius in another, and the grave-digger in another. I remember how I roared when I read it. Fancy that fellow as Polonius!"

"Can't you remember the town?"

"Not a ghost of an idea. Some little village in the Midlands probably, where *Hamlet* would be appreciated. I remember, by the way, the bill—pity I didn't keep it—mentioned that this enterprising company was going to give a performance in Boulogne, of all places. It occurred to me it would be a source of great consolation to our fellow-countrymen in that dismal colony to witness Jack Rogers in the ghost for one night only."

"That would be eighteen or nineteen years ago," said Roger, with a sigh at the hopelessness of his quest. "You have heard nothing since?"

"Not a syllable. Have some more sherry?"

Roger reached his hotel that night in more than mental distress. The fatigue and anxiety of the last few days had had their inevitable result on his health, and though the penalty had been postponed, it was coming to account at last.

When his worthy guardian returned on the following day, he was much shocked to find his ward really ill. He did his best. He tried to induce the patient to make an effort to "shake off" his ailments. He sat up late in his room at night, talking and attempting to amuse him. He even purchased a few amateur specifics; and finally, when the boy was as ill as ill could be, called in a pettifogging practitioner, who might be trusted to bungle the case.

"Regular bad case," said that learned gentleman, after the third or fourth visit. "May last a week with care."

The good captain naturally grew concerned. Matters seemed to be progressing beyond even his expectations. The practitioner's verdict speedily got wind in the hotel. Visitors came anxiously to inquire after the young gentleman's condition, and urged a second opinion. And one or two were inconsiderate enough to suggest that the patient was not having fair play.

Under these distressing circumstances, Captain Oliphant decided to write a line to Dr Brandram.

"Roger has unfortunately taken a chill. Will you kindly forward me the prescription which benefited him so much last summer, as I am naturally anxious to omit no precaution for the dear fellow's good. He is being well cared for, and will, I trust, be all right in a day or two."

Dr Brandram's reply to this transparent communication was to order his dogcart and take the first train to London. Before starting, he had time to send a telegram to Armstrong to meet him at the hotel the same evening.

Little dreaming of the effect of his message, Captain Oliphant was spending a resigned afternoon in the sick-room. Fate was working on his side once more. Mr Ratman had apparently vanished into space. Mr Armstrong was out of the way. The practitioner's face had been longer than ever when he took his leave a few hours ago. The difficulties and disappointments of the past few months were giving way to better prospects. The good man's conscience accused him of no actual injury to his ward. On the contrary, he could honestly say he had devoted time, money, personal fatigue, to tending him. He had secured him medical attendance, he had advised the family doctor of his indisposition. He had sat up with him day and night. Was it his fault if the illness took a bad turn, and the Maxfield property changed its owner? He should like to meet the man who could lay anything at his door.

Roger turned on his pillow and began to wander—

"Tell him I believe it. I'll go and find the grave-digger. Ask Fastnet, and Compton, and all of them. No more sherry, thanks. Yes, sir, I said you were no gentleman. I repeat it. You have no right to mention her name. Shut the door, Rosalind. There's only eleven months to do it in. He is waiting at the General Post Office. Armstrong has gone away. They expelled him from the club."

"Poor fellow," sighed the captain, as he smoothed the sufferer's pillow; "poor fellow! How absurdly he talks."

So engrossed was he in his ministrations that he failed to perceive the door behind him softly open and a gentleman enter.

Mr Armstrong had outstripped the doctor in the race to town. Without a word the tutor walked to the bed and bent over the troubled form of his pupil. Then with face almost as white as that of his enemy, he turned.

"What brings you here?" gasped the captain.

"How long has he been like this?" demanded the tutor.

"Do you hear my question?"

"Do you hear mine?"

The weaker man capitulated, with a malediction, to the stronger.

"Since yesterday. He is being carefully tended."

"By whom—you alone?"

"By a doctor."

"What doctor?"

"When I know your right to catechise me, I will answer," snarled the captain.

Mr Armstrong rang the bell.

"Light the fire here at once," said he to the maid, "and then send the messenger up."

In the interval the two men stood eyeing one another, while the patient from time to time tossed on his pillow and muttered to himself.

Mr Armstrong hurriedly scrawled two notes.

"Take a cab, and leave this note at — Hospital. Let the nurse I have asked for come back in the cab at once. Then go on with this note to Sir William Dove, and bring word from him the earliest moment he can be here. Don't lose an instant."

"Captain Oliphant," said he, as soon as the messenger had gone, "three is too many for this room. I am here to relieve guard. You need rest. Dr Brandram will be here any moment. Bring him up directly he comes."

Captain Oliphant was certainly deserving of a little sympathy. He had borne the burden and heat of the day, and now another was entering into his labour. But the tutor's tone had an ugly ring about it, which, for the moment, cowed the injured gentleman, and constrained him, after glowering for a moment or two, and trying to articulate a protest, meekly to withdraw.

"My responsibility ends where yours begins," said he, with his best sneer. "I grudge none of the trouble I have taken for the dear boy, but I must decline to remain here as the assistant of Signor Francisco the music-hall cad."

"I can imagine it might be painful," said Mr Armstrong drily; "but the immediate thing to be desired is that you should not consume the oxygen in this room. Explanations will do later."

Captain Oliphant was not at hand that evening to meet the doctors. A business engagement had summoned him to Maxfield, where he rejoiced the hearts of his two children by a sudden arrival at breakfast-time.

A curt note from Armstrong the same afternoon apprised him that his movements had been anticipated.

"Doctors not without hope. Admirable nurse secured. Brandram and I remain here."

Captain Oliphant derived scant consolation from this announcement, and quite forgot his business engagement in his mortification and ill temper. He dropped in during the day to see Mr Pottinger, to discuss his grievance with that legal luminary. But Mr Pottinger, as the reader is aware, had complications of another kind to disclose. He astonished his visitor with an account of the surprise visit of Mr Ratman a few days previously, and of that gentleman's astounding claims to the name of Ingleton.

"What!" exclaimed the captain, "you mean to say that scoundrel actually claimed to be the lost son? I always had a high opinion of his impudence, but I never imagined it capable of that. Why, my dear sir, I have known him as a pettifogging money-lender in India for years."

"Quite so; but did you know why and when he came to India?"

"I can't say I did. Surely you don't credit his story?"

"Well, not exactly. But it strikes me the gentleman will give us some difficulty."

"Why? What good can it do him even if he is what he claims! He cannot upset the will, which emphatically cuts him out of every possibility of benefit."

"No; that leaves him no loophole, certainly. But he may calculate on working on the chivalry of his younger brother, or if that fails, on blackmailing him."

"If so, he will have us to deal with. For once in a way Armstrong and I are likely to be of the same opinion. Surely there is evidence enough to prosecute for conspiracy."

"Hardly. He claims nothing but the name. He admits he has no rights. My opinion, Captain Oliphant, is that we have not heard the end of him."

"Very likely not, especially as I unluckily owe him money."

"That is awkward. The sooner you square accounts and get rid of him the better."

"Easier said than done," remarked the captain, and returned with a decided headache to Maxfield.

Roger, with Armstrong to nurse him, with Dr Brandram to attend him, with his own strong bias towards life to buoy him up, emerged slowly from the valley of the shadow of death, and in due time stood once more on his feet. Weeks before that happened he had told and heard all that was to be said about his lost brother. Dr Brandram had recounted the incident at Miss Jill's party, and he in turn had confided to his tutor his meeting with Fastnet, and the feeble clue in which that conference had resulted.

"Armstrong, old fellow," said he one day at the close of the year, "won't you help me in this? I know you hate the business, and think me a fool for my pains. I must do it, with you or without you, and would sooner do it with you. In ten months it will be too late."

"I hate the business, as you say, but you may count on me; only don't ask me to hail Mr Ratman as Squire of Maxfield, or subscribe a penny to his maintenance, a day before his claim is proved."

"You are a brick; I was a cad ever to doubt it. Let us start next week for Boulogne."

"Quite so," said the tutor, screwing his glass viciously into his eye; "let us go to Boulogne by all means."

Chapter Twenty
The Ghost of Hamlet

It is possible to conceive of a more hopeful task than hunting up and down a large French town for tidings of a strolling player who, for one night only, played the ghost in *Hamlet* twenty years ago. But Roger, as, early in the year, he stepped ashore at Boulogne with Armstrong at his side, felt sanguine and of good cheer.

His recovery had been slow, and not without interruption. As soon as he could be moved he had returned to Maxfield, only to find Rosalind still away, and his guardian obdurate to any suggestion for expediting her return.

As to the proposed journey to Boulogne, the gallant captain looked upon that as a symptom of serious mental exhaustion on the part of the invalid. Roger, however, was in a mood impervious to argument.

When the time actually came, the captain surprised every one by giving in more readily than any one had expected. The truth was, Mr Ratman, though lost to sight, contrived to make himself very dear to his debtor's memory, and already a legal document had reached Maxfield demanding the payment in full of a certain bill within a certain date on pain of certain consequences. And Captain Oliphant felt it would be distinctly convenient, for a while, to be relieved of the presence both of his co-trustee and his ward. He felt himself quite competent to deal with the trust moneys which were shortly about to come in without assistance.

When, therefore, Roger with some hesitation returned to the charge, he said, somewhat severely—

"You are old enough to decide for yourself, my boy. You know my view of the matter. I conclude you are not going alone?"

"No; Armstrong is coming."

"Naturally. I wish you joy. On your return I shall be happy to resume my responsibility for your welfare. I cannot profess to feel oppressed by it in your absence."

This was enough. True, the captain contrived to get in a parting shot by announcing that Rosalind was likely to return shortly to Maxfield. But even that did not suffice to change the lad's purpose.

"Don't be very long away," said Jill to Mr Armstrong. "You are always going and leaving us. Rosalind will be very, very sorry to find you are away. She likes you—she told me so; but she doesn't like you half as much as I do."

The tutor flushed uncomfortably.

"Oh," said Tom, "you're always spoons on somebody, Jill. I heard you tell that Duke chap you liked him better than anybody in the world."

"O Tom! how dare you tell such a wicked falsehood? I told him I liked him *nearly* as much as Mr Armstrong, but not quite. Really I did, Mr Armstrong."

"I am very jealous of the Duke," said Mr Armstrong gravely.

Once across the Channel, Roger's spirits rose. He had a presentiment he was on the right track. Like a knight of old, set down to a desperate task, the fighting blood rose joyously within him. Whatever it cost, whoever deserted him, whoever opposed him, he would find his brother, and give to him his own.

For days they went hither and thither, inquiring at cafés, theatres, cabarets, custom-houses, police stations, and even cemeteries, without success. Most of the persons accosted laughed and shrugged their shoulders to be asked if they remembered the visit of strolling players to the town as far back as twenty years. Others bridled up suspiciously, as if the question were a preliminary to their detection in some old evil deed. Others utterly failed to comprehend the question; and a few pityingly tapped their own foreheads, and shook their heads at the two half-witted English holiday-makers. But no one could tell a word about Rogers.

A fortnight passed, and the thoughts of both, dispirited and worn, turned homeward. Rosalind, a letter had informed them, was back at Maxfield.

Of the two, perhaps Mr Armstrong displayed less disposition to own himself beaten. He had worked like a horse all the time. Roger had been compelled to own that without him his mission would have been a feeble farce. Not a stone did the dogged tutor leave unturned. Not a difficulty did he shirk. Not a man or woman, however forbidding, did he hesitate to tackle, who in the remotest degree might be suspected of being likely to give information. Now that it came to giving in, he hung back, reluctant to dip his colours.

"To-day's Thursday," said he. "Let's give ourselves till Saturday. If nothing turns up by then, I am your man to slink home."

Roger, a little ashamed to find the first last and the last first in the race after all, readily assented. And the two worked unflagging for two days longer.

Friday evening came, and the two sat dismally down to *table d'hôte* with defeat staring them in the face. They said very little, but each knew the mortification in the other's breast.

At last, when the meal was over, Mr Armstrong said—

"I suppose we had better go and get our tickets."

"I suppose so."

But the *bureau* was closed for the night, and the two took a solitary walk along the beach. They walked on further than usual in the clear moonlight, till at last the tutor looked at his watch.

"It's nine o'clock," said he; "we must go back."

"Let's take the country road back."

"It is a mile longer."

"Never mind. It is our last night."

So they struck up by the cliffs, and followed the chalky country road back to Boulogne.

About two miles from the town the cheery lights of a wayside *auberge* attracted their attention.

"Let us get some coffee here," said Armstrong.

This solitary tavern rejoiced in the name of "Café d'Angleterre," but if its owner expected thereby to attract the custom of Mr John Bull, he was singularly mistaken. The chief customers of the place were labourers and navvies, who by their noisy jargon were evidently innocent of all pretensions to a foreign tongue.

Seeing two strangers, presumably able to pay ready money for what they consumed, the old landlord invited his visitors into the bar parlour, where at his own table he set before them that delightful concoction of chicory and sifted earth which certain provincial Frenchmen call *café*. And being a gregarious and inquisitive old man, and withal proud of his tolerable stock of English, he took the liberty of joining them.

"Inglese?" inquired he, with a pantomimic shrug.

"Quite so," said the tutor, putting up his glass, and inspecting the fellow carefully.

"This is the 'Café d'Angleterre,'" said the landlord, "but, *hélas*! it is long since the Inglese gentleman come here. They like too well the great town."

"Ah, Boulogne has grown. Can you remember the place twenty years ago?"

"Can I? I can remember forty years."

"I wonder," broke in Roger, too impatient to allow his tutor to lead up gradually to the inevitable question, "if you can remember some English players coming over here about eighteen years ago and acting a play called *Hamlet* in English."

The landlord blew a cloud of smoke from his lips, and stared round at the speaker as if he had been a ghost.

"Why do you ask me that? *'Amlet*! Can I forget it?"

Here was a bolt out of the blue! The tutor's eye-glass dropped with a clatter against his cup, and Roger fetched a breath half gasp, half sigh.

"You remember it!" exclaimed he, seizing the man's hand; "do you know, we have been a fortnight in Boulogne trying to find some one who did!"

"Would not *you* remember it," replied the Frenchman, with a gesticulation, "if 'Amlet had put up at your inn and gone away without paying his bill?"

"Did one of the actors stay here, then?"

"One? There was twenty 'Amlets, and Miladi 'Amlets, and Mademoiselle 'Amlets. They all stay here, *en famille*. The house is full of 'Amlets. The stable is full. They bring with them a castle of 'Amlet, and a grave of 'Amlet. My poor house was all 'Amlet!"

"And," inquired Mr Armstrong, flushed with the sudden discovery, but as cool as ever, "you had a pass to see the play, of course?"

"*Mon dieu*! it was all the pay I got. 'Amlet come to my house with his twenty hungry mouth, and eat me up, flesh and bone. He sleep in my beds, he sleep on my roof, he sleep in my stable. The place is 'Amlet's. And all my pay is one piece of card bidding me see him play himself."

"And was it well played?" Asked Mr Armstrong.

"Well played? How do I know? But six persons came to see it—I one—and in six minutes it is all done. Your English 'Amlet will not play to the empty bench. He call down the curtain, and bid us go where we please. Not even will he pay us back our money. Then, when he come to leave the hall himself, *voilà*, he has no money to pay his rent. His baggage is seized, and 'Amlet fights. *Mon dieu*, there was *une émeute* in Boulogne that night; and before day 'Amlet has vanish like his own ghost, and I am a robbed man; *voilà*."

"Very rough on you," said the tutor. "So there was a ghost among the players?"

"Why no? It would not be *'Amlet* without."

"Did the ghost stay here too?"

"*Hélas*! yes. He eat, and drink, and sleep, and forgets to pay, like the rest."

"What did you lose by him?" asked Roger, with parched lips.

"Ah, monsieur, I was a Napoleon poorer for every 'Amlet in my house that night."

Roger put down two sovereigns on the table.

"That is to pay for the ghost," said he, flushing. "He was my brother."

The landlord stared in blank amazement.

"Your brother! Monsieur le Ghost of *'Amlet* was—*pardieu*!" exclaimed he, looking hard at his guest, "and he was like you. It was no fault of his *'Amlet* did not take the favour, for he play in the first act and make us all laugh. If the other 'Amlets had been so amusing as him, the house would have been full—packed. Ha! now you say it, he was a gentleman, this poor Monsieur le Ghost. He held himself apart from the noisy company, and sulk in a corner, while they laugh, and drink, and sing the song. They were afraid of him, and, *mon dieu*! they might be—for once, when Monsieur Rosencrantz, as I remember, came and threw some absinthe—my absinthe, messieurs—in his face, Monsieur le Ghost he knocked him down with a blow that sounded—oh, like a clap of the thunder. And this pauvre ghost," added the man, "was monsieur's brother! *Hélas*! he was come down very poor—his coat was rags, and his boots were open to the water of heaven. He eat little. Ah, monsieur, I have deceived you. He cost me not five franc; for, when I remember, he ate nothings—he starve himself."

"Was he ill?" asked Armstrong.

"Worse," said the landlord, lowering his voice; "he was in love. I could see it. She laugh and make the mock at him, and play coquet with the others before his face. It nearly killed him—this pauvre ghost. He would have give his hand for a kind glance, but he got it never."

"Who was the girl?" asked Roger.

"But a child, the minx—fifteen, perhaps sixteen, years, no more. She played the part of a page-boy, and only so because monsieur, her father, was manage the play. He was Frenchman, this monsieur, but mademoiselle was English like her mother. *Hélas*! monsieur, your brother was deep in love. But there was no hope for him. A fool could see that."

This was all the host could tell them. He had never heard since of any member of the ill-fated company. He could introduce them to no one who remembered their visit. A few there might be who when appealed to might have recalled the disturbance on the night of the performance, and the absconding of the players. But who they were and what became of them no one could say.

On their return to the hotel at Boulogne at midnight they found a telegram and a letter awaiting them.

The former was from Dr Brandram to Mr Armstrong—

"Come at once."

The letter was a missive addressed to Roger at Maxfield from London, and forwarded back to Boulogne. It was from Mr Fastnet.

"Dear Ingleton,—Oddly enough I stumbled yesterday across the very piece of paper I spoke to you of. Here it is for what it was worth."

Roger eagerly opened the yellow sheet. It announced a performance of *Hamlet* at Folkestone by a celebrated company of stars under the direction of a Monsieur Callot. Among the actors was a Mr John Rogers, who took the part of the ghost in the first act. Further down was mentioned a Miss Callot, who acted the part of a page. And the bill announced that after the performance in Folkestone the company would perform for two nights only in Boulogne. More important, however, than any other particular was a footnote that Monsieur Callot was "happy to receive pupils for instruction in the dramatic art at his address, 2 Long Street, London, W. Terms moderate. Singing and dancing taught by Madame Callot."

Here at last seemed a clue. The pulses of the two friends quickened as they read and re-read the time-worn document.

"The boat sails in two hours," said Mr Armstrong, "I must leave you in town. Brandram would not telegraph for me like this unless he meant it."

"I suppose it means my bro— Ratman, has turned up again. If so, Armstrong—"

"Well?" inquired the tutor, digging his glass deep into his eye.

Roger said nothing.

On the following afternoon Mr Armstrong had a pleasant game of Association football with Tom on the Maxfield lawn, and Miss Jill, who volunteered as umpire, gave every point in favour of the tutor.

Just about the time when he kicked his final goal, Roger Ingleton, minor, in London arrived at the dreary conclusion, after an hour's painful study of directories and maps, that there was no such street as Long Street, London, W.

Chapter Twenty One
Sharks by Land and Water

Mr Brandram's abrupt summons to Mr Armstrong was not due to the reappearance on the scene of the mysterious Robert Ratman. It was, in fact, at the instance of Miss Rosalind Oliphant that the doctor sent his message.

That young lady had returned a week ago to find everything at Maxfield awry. Her father was gloomy, mysterious, and haggard. The rumour of Mr Ratman's extraordinary claims had become the common property of the village. Roger and his tutor were away, no one exactly knew where or on what errand.

On the day following her return she walked across from the Vicarage to visit her father.

He sat in the library, abstracted, pale, and limp. The jaunty, Anglo-Indian veneer had for the time being dropped off, unmasking the worried exterior of a chicken-hearted man.

At the sight of his daughter he pulled himself together, and crushed in his hand the letter which he had been reading.

"Why, my child," said he, with unusual cordiality, "this is a pleasant apparition. Cruel girl, to desert us for so long. We have hardly existed without you, Roger and his tutor are away in France holiday-making, while I remain here on duty with no one to cheer me up."

"Dear father," said Rosalind, kissing him, "how worried you look! What is the matter? Won't you tell me?"

The father's eyes dwelt for a moment on her fair earnest face—so like her mother's, so unlike a daughter of his—then they fell miserably.

"Worried?" said he. "Do I show it as plainly as all that? I flattered myself I kept it to myself."

"Any one can see you are unhappy, father. Why?"

"I am in difficulties, my child, which you could not understand."

"I could. Do tell me."

"The fact is," said the captain, taking up his pen and dotting the blotting-pad as he spoke, "that when on former occasions I have tried to claim your sympathy I—well, I was not quite successful. I do not want the pain of a similar failure again."

"I would do anything, anything to help you, if I could!"

He took her hand and held it in his.

"I am in great straits," said he. "An old Indian debt has followed me here. I cannot meet it, and ruin stares me in the face. You know I am a poor man; that I am living on other people—you have reminded me of that often enough; that of all the money which passes my hands, scarcely enough to live on belongs by right to me. You know all that?"

"Yes; I know that we are poor. How much do you owe?" she asked.

"I cannot say. Not long ago it was some hundreds, but by this time it is nearer thousands. Nothing grows so rapidly as a debt, my child—even," added he, with an unctuous drop of his voice, "a debt of honour."

"And will not your creditor wait?"

"My creditor has waited, but refuses to do so any longer. In a month from now, my child, your father and those he loves best will be paupers."

"Is there no way of meeting it? None whatever?"

"I cannot pay; I shrink from borrowing. The trust funds in my charge are sacred—"

"Of course!" said she, astonished that he should name them in such a connection. "Is there nothing else?"

"My creditor is Robert Ratman—or as he calls himself, and possibly is, Roger Ingleton. As you know, he claims to be the elder brother of our Roger, and I—"

"Yes, yes," said she; "Roger told me about that. He is your creditor?"

"He is. I got into his clutches in India, little guessing who he was, and he is crushing me now. There is but one way, and one only, of escaping him—and that way is, I fear, impossible, Rosalind."

"What is it?" said she, with pale face, knowing what was to come.

"He loves you. As my son-in-law he would be no longer my creditor."

She drew away her hand with a shudder.

"Father," said she, in a dry hard voice which startled him, "do you really mean this?"

"Is it a time for jesting?" said he. "I ask nothing of you. I merely state facts. You dislike him—there is an end of it. Only remember we are not now dealing with Robert Ratman, but with an injured man who has not had a fair chance. The good in him," continued the father, deluded by the passive look on his daughter's face, and becoming suddenly warm in his championship of the absent creditor, "has been smothered; but for aught we know it may still be there. A wife—"

She stopped him with a peremptory motion of her hand.

"Please do not say anything more. Your debt—when does it fall due?"

"In a week or ten days, my child. Consider—"

She interrupted again.

"No more, please," she said, almost imploringly. "I will think what can be done to help you in a week. Good-bye, dear father."

She stooped, with face as white as marble, and touched his forehead with her cold lips.

"Loyal girl," said the father, when the door had closed behind her; "she will stand by me yet. After all, Ratman has his good points—clever, cheerful, good man of business—"

Here abruptly the soliloquy ended, and Captain Oliphant buried his face in his hands, a miserable man.

To Rosalind, as she walked rapidly across the park, there came but one thought. Her father—how could she help him? how could she save him, not so much from his debts as from the depths into which they were plunging him?

"My poor father," said she. "Only a man in desperate plight could think of such a remedy. He never meant it. He does not really suppose—no, no; he said he did not ask anything. He told me because I asked. Poor darling father!"

And with something very like a sob she hurried on to Yeld.

She went straight to Dr Brandram's.

"Well, my dear young lady, it does one good to see you back," said he; "but bless me, how pale you look."

"Do I? I'm quite well, thank you. Dr Brandram," said she, "do you know anything about this Mr Ratman?"

The Doctor stared at this abrupt inquiry.

"Nothing more than you and every one else does—that he is a rank impostor!"

"I don't mean that. I mean, where is he? I want to see him very much."

"You want to see him? He has vanished, and left no track. Is it nothing I can help you in?"

"No," said she, looking very miserable. "I hoped you could have told me where to find him. Good-bye, and thank you."

She departed, leaving the doctor sorely disturbed and bewildered. He stood watching her slight figure till it disappeared in the Vicarage garden, and then shrugging his shoulders, said, "Something wrong, somewhere. Evidently not a case for me to be trusted with. It's about time Armstrong came home."

Whereupon he walked over to the post office and dispatched the telegram which, as the reader knows, procured Tom Oliphant the unspeakable pleasure of a game of football on the following afternoon.

"Well," said the tutor to his friend in the doctor's parlour that evening, "what's all this about?"

"That's what I'm not likely to know myself," said the doctor; and he narrated the circumstances of Miss Oliphant's mysterious call.

"Humph!" said the tutor. "She wants to see him in his capacity of Robert Ratman, evidently, and not of Roger Ingleton, major."

"So it seemed to me."

"And you say she had just come from visiting her father at Maxfield?"

"Yes."

"On the principle that two and two make four, I suppose we may conclude that my co-trustee is on toast at present," said the tutor.

"And further, that that co-trustee being somebody's father, you are the man to get him off it."

The tutor's face clouded, and his glass dropped with a twang from his eye.

"Don't make that mistake again, Brandram—unless," and here his lips relaxed into a quiet smile, "you mean by somebody, Miss Jill."

Dr Brandram read a good deal in this short sentence, and, like a good friend, let the subject drop.

"As Tom has gone to the Rectory to dinner," said the tutor, "I take it the neighbourhood for twenty miles round will know of my return by this time."

Meanwhile I must go back and possibly find out some thing from Oliphant himself."

Captain Oliphant, however, was in no mood for confidences. The sudden return of his co-trustee was extremely unwelcome at this juncture—indeed so manifestly unwelcome that Mr Armstrong was convinced he had come back not a day too soon.

The captain professed great annoyance and indignation at what he termed the desertion of his ward, and demanded to know when the tutor proposed to return to his duties.

"In fact, sir," said he, "I desire to know what brings you here in this uncalled-for manner."

"Business, my dear sir," replied the tutor. "It need not incommode you."

"Your proper place is with your pupil. Where have you left him?"

"In London, prosecuting a search which neither you nor I consider to be very hopeful. I should not be surprised to see him back any day."

"And may I ask the nature of the very pressing business which forms the pretext of this abrupt return? Am I to understand you and my ward have quarrelled?"

"No, sir; we are excellent friends. It's getting late; I'll say good night."

"By the way," said he at the door, "while I am here, there are a few small matters connected with the accounts which seemed to my unpractised eye, when I went through Pottinger's books, to require some little elucidation. If you have an hour or so to spare to-morrow, I should like to go through them with you. Good night."

He did not stay to notice the sudden pallor of his colleague's face, nor did he overhear the gasp which greeted the closing of the door.

The captain did not go to bed that night. For an hour he sat motionless in his chair, staring blankly into the fire; then, with a sudden access of industry, he went to the safe, and producing account-books, bank books, cheques, and other documents, spent some troubled hours over their contents. That done, for another hour he paced the floor, dismally smoking a cigar. Finally, when the early March dawn filtered through the blinds, he quitted the house, and surprised Mr Pottinger by an unexpected visit at breakfast-time. Thence he proceeded to the bank; and after transacting his business there, returned easier in mind, but exhausted in body, to the seclusion of his room at Maxfield.

The tutor meanwhile was abroad on horseback with Tom and Jill. The three took a scamper over the downs, and returned by way of the shore. Biding with Tom and Jill, as may be imagined, was a series of competitive exercises, rather than a straightforward promenade. Tom was an excellent rough horseman; and Jill, when Mr Armstrong was at hand, was not the young lady to stick at anything. They had tried handicaps, water-jumps, hurdles, and were about to start for a ding-dong gallop along the mile of hard strand which divided them from Maxfield, when the tutor's eye detected, perched a little way up the cliff, the figure of a young lady sketching.

"I'll start you two," said he, "I scratch for this race. Ride fair, Tom; and Jill, give the mare her head when you get past the boulders. I shall go back by the downs. Are you ready now? Pull in a bit, Tom. Now—off you go!"

Not waiting to watch the issue of this momentous contest, he turned to where Rosalind sat, and reining up at the foot of her perch, dismounted.

She came down to meet him, palette in hand.

"Mr Armstrong, I am so glad to see you. I want to speak to you dreadfully. Are you in a great hurry?"

"Not at all. Brandram told me you were in trouble, and I was wondering when and where I should have the opportunity of asking how I can help you."

He tied his horse to a stake, and helped her back to her seat on the cliff.

There was an awkward pause, which he occupied by examining her picture with a critical air.

"Do you like it?" said she.

"I don't know. I'm no great judge. Do you?"

"I did, before you came. I'm not so sure now. Do sit down and let me say what I want to say."

The tutor, with a flutter at his breast, sat meekly, keeping his eyes still on the picture.

"Mr Armstrong, it's about Mr Ratman."

"So Brandram said. What of him?"

Rosalind told her father's story, except that she omitted any reference to the desperate proposition for satisfying his claims.

"I am sure it is a fraud, or blackmail, or something of the sort. For all that, he threatens to ruin father."

"What does the debt amount to?"

"Father spoke of thousands."

"Does the creditor offer no terms?"

Rosalind flushed, and looked round.

"None; that is, none that can be thought of for a moment."

"I understand," said the tutor, to whom the reservation was explicit enough.

"The difficulty is, that he has disappeared. If we could find him I would—"

"You would allow me to go to him," said the tutor. "No doubt the opportunity will soon come. He wants money; he is bound to turn up."

"But why should you be mixed up in father's troubles?" asked Rosalind after a pause.

"Your father's troubles are yours; your troubles are—shall we say?—Roger's; Roger's troubles are mine."

There was another long silence, during which Rosalind took up her brushes and began work again on the picture, Mr Armstrong critically looking on.

"Have you no troubles of your own, then, that you have so much room in you for those of other people?" she said at last.

"I have had my share, perhaps. Your picture, with its wide expanse of calm sea, was just reminding me of one of them."

"Tell me about it."

"It was years ago, when, before I was a singer in London— You knew I followed that honourable vocation once, don't you?"

"I have heard father speak of it. Why not?"

"No reason at all. But before that I worked at the equally honourable profession of a common sailor on a ship between New York and Ceylon. At that time I was about as wild and reckless as they make them, and deluded myself into the foolish belief that I enjoyed it. How I had come to that pass I needn't tell you. It wasn't all of a sudden, or without the assistance of other people. I had a comrade on board—a man who had once been a gentleman, but had come down in the world; who was nearly as bad as I, but not quite; for he sometimes talked of his home and his mother, and wished himself dead, which I never had the grace to do."

"Are you making this all up for my benefit," asked Rosalind, "or is it true?"

"The story would not be worth telling if it were not true," said Mr Armstrong, screwing his glass into his eye and taking a fresh survey of the picture. "One very hot summer we were becalmed off Colombo, and lay for days with nothing to do but whistle for a wind and quarrel among ourselves. My mate and I kept the peace for a couple of days, but then we fell out like the rest. I forget what it was about—a trifle, probably a word. We didn't fight on deck—it was too hot—but jumped overboard and fought in the water. I remember, as I plunged, I caught sight, a hundred yards away, of an ugly grey fin lying motionless on the water, and knew it belonged to a shark. But I didn't care. Well, we two fought in the water—partly in spite, partly to pass the time. Suddenly I could see my opponent's swarthy face become livid. 'Good God!' he gasped; 'a shark!' and quick as thought he caught me by the shoulders and pushed me between him and the brute. I heard it swish up, and saw it half turn with gaping jaws. In that moment I lived over my life again, with all its folly and crime, and for the first time for years I prayed. How it happened I cannot tell; the shark must either have made a bad shot at me or else I must have ducked instinctively, for I remember feeling the scrape of his fin across my cheek and being pushed aside by his great tail. Next moment my mate's hands let go their grip of me and there was a yell such as I pray I may never hear again. When at last they hauled me on board I was not the same man who three minutes before had dived into the water. That was the scene your picture reminded me of, Miss Oliphant. You have told me one of your troubles, and I have told you one of mine, which makes us quits. But my horse is getting fidgety down there; I must look after him. Good-bye."

Mr Armstrong was a little surprised, when he came to go through the accounts with his co-trustee that afternoon, to find that he must have been mistaken in his previous supposition that they were not all correct and straightforward. Everything appeared quite plain and properly accounted for, and he agreed with the figures, rather abashed to feel that, after all, he was not as acute a man of business as he had flattered himself. Mr Pottinger and the captain rallied him about his deserted mares'-nest, and bored him with invitations to go through all the items again, to give him a chance of proving them wrong. He declined with thanks, and signed the balance with the best grace he could summon.

"Odd," said he to himself, as he strode home after the interview; "either you must be very clever or I must be very stupid. I should greatly like to know which it is."

Chapter Twenty Two
Mr Ratman visits his Property

"Dear Armstrong," wrote Roger from London about a week after the tutor's return to Maxfield, "you will be surprised to hear I am just off to Paris to look for a Mr Pantalzar. This is how it comes about. Long Street does not exist, as I told you, nor any trace of the family Callot. But old Directories are still available, and in one of these I found that fifteen years ago there was a Long Street, and that Number 2 was then occupied by a person of the uncommon name I have mentioned. The name seemed too promising a one to be let drop; so I tracked it down to the year before last, when I found a Pantalzar was proprietor of a cook-shop in Shoreditch. Of course, when I went to inquire, my gentleman had vanished. I'm sick of asking the interminable question, 'Does So-and-so live here?' The present cook-man, however, remembered the queer name as that belonging to his predecessor, and informed me that, not having made the business pay over here, he had decamped two years ago without saying good-bye to his creditors, and announced his intention of starting a *café* in Paris. This, then, is my off-chance. Unless he has changed his name, I should be able to discover him in Paris; and if he turns out to be the man who once lived at Number 2 Long Street, he may be able to tell me something about the Callots; and the Callots, if by a miracle I can find them, may be able to tell me something about Rogers, the Ghost in *Hamlet*. I only wish you were coming to back me up, but, from what you say, I would ever so much rather you remained on the spot at Maxfield. I hope it will be possible to help Oliphant out of his fix. Try. You'd better write to the *Poste Restante* at Paris. Remember me at home.

"Yours ever,—

"R. Ingleton."

The tutor read this letter with a somewhat troubled countenance. It proved to him that his ward was desperately in earnest in his uphill quest, and it filled him with some concern to feel that he himself was not, where he should have liked to be, at the boy's side.

But to leave Maxfield at present seemed impossible. Rosalind claimed his help on behalf of her father; and the possibility that any day Mr Ratman might turn up and court exposure decided the tutor to remain where he was. Another motive for this step was a haunting perplexity as to the hallucination under which he had apparently laboured with regard to the estate accounts. He never flattered himself he was a particularly good man of business, but it puzzled him to explain why a few weeks ago there should have appeared to be discrepancies and irregularities to the tune of several hundred pounds, whereas now everything was in startling apple-pie order.

Much to Mr Pottinger's annoyance, he took to visiting the honest lawyer's office every other day, and spent hours in trying to discover where it was he had made his great mistake. Mr Pottinger was unable to render him any assistance; and the captain, when once he referred to the subject, only smiled pityingly and advised him to take a few lessons in the elements of finance; which advice, to do him justice, the tutor humbly proceeded to take. The result was to deepen his perplexity and cause him to regret that he had so compliantly countersigned an account which, every time he studied it in the light of his new wisdom, appeared to bristle with problems.

Faithful to her promise, at the end of a week Rosalind presented herself at Maxfield.

"Well, my child?" said the parent blandly, laying down his newspaper.

"I said I would come and speak again about what you were saying the other day. Have you heard any more from your creditor?"

"Things remain, as far as he is concerned, in *statu quo*; and I am no nearer being able to satisfy him to-day than I was a week ago; unless, indeed—"

"All I have to say," said Rosalind nervously, "is, that I would work like a slave to help you, if I could."

"Is that all?" asked the captain with falling face.

"You know it is, father. You knew it a week ago. You knew I would even go to this man and on my knees beg him to be merciful."

Her father laughed dismally.

"In other words," said he, "you can do nothing. I do not complain; I expected nothing, and I have not been disappointed. I was foolish to think such a thing possible; Heaven knows I have been punished for my folly."

She tried hard to keep back the tears, and rose to go.

"Stay!" said he sternly; "I have a question to ask you. A week ago you seemed to hold a different mind to this. What has changed it?"

"No," said she, "it was out of the question; you said so yourself."

"I ask you," repeated he sternly, and not heeding her protest, "what has changed it? Have you taken counsel with any one on the subject? Have you spoken to any one of this wretched business?"

"Yes; I have spoken to Mr Armstrong."

"Exactly. I thought as much. I understand. Leave me, Rosalind."

"Father, you are wrong— Oh, but you must hear me," she said, as he raised his hand deprecatingly and took up his newspaper. "You must not misunderstand. I told Mr Armstrong of your difficulties, and who your creditor was. I told him no more. My only object was to see if there was any way to help you."

"You mean to tell me," said he, interrupting in an angry voice, "that you considered it consistent with your duty as a daughter to gossip about my private affairs with a scoundrel who—"

"No, father," she said. "Mr Armstrong is a gentleman—"

"Naturally *you* say so. But enough of this. I forbid you, as I have already done, to hold any communication with Mr Armstrong. Know that, of the two men, the man you affect to scorn is infinitely less a villain than this smug hypocrite. Go!"

She made no reply, but went, choking with misery and a smarting sense of injustice. No longer was it easy to hug herself into the delusion that this was all a horrid dream. Her father stood on the brink of ruin, and she could not help him.

"If only," said she, "it had been anything else! O God, pity my poor father!"

The captain's thoughts were of a very different kind. He had clung to the hope that Rosalind would after all solve his difficulties by undertaking the venture he had set before her. He had already in imagination soothed his own conscience and smoothed away all the difficulties which beset the undertaking.

"It might be for her good, after all, dear girl! She will reclaim him. A fortune lies before them; for Roger will be easily convinced, and will surrender his claim to them. Ratman is too long-sighted not to see that I can help him in the matter, and that on my own terms. We shall start fresh with a clear balance-sheet, and live in comfort." Now, however, these bright hopes were dashed, and to the captain's mind he owed his failure, first and last, to Mr Frank Armstrong. Had he not come home, he said to himself, Rosalind would have yielded.

With him still at Maxfield everything came to a dead lock. Ratman could not be propitiated, still less satisfied. The accounts would be restlessly scrutinised.

Rosalind, and in less degree Tom and Jill, would be mutinous. Roger, at home or abroad, would be beyond reach.

All the grudges of the past months seemed to culminate in this crowning injury; and if to wish ill to one's fellow is to be a murderer, Captain Oliphant had already come perilously near to adding one new sin to his record.

But where, all this while, was the ingenuous Mr Ratman? Why had he not, true to his word, come to claim his own—if not the Maxfield estate, at any rate the little balance due to him from his old Indian crony?

The captain, after a week or two of disappointed dread, was beginning to recover a little of his ease of mind, and flattering himself that, after all his creditor's bark was worse than his bite, when the blow abruptly fell.

Mr Armstrong had gone for the day to visit one of his very few old college friends on the other side of the county, and Tom, released from his lessons (the captain's animosity for the tutor, by the way, stopped short at withdrawing his son from the benefit of the gratuitous education of which for the last year that youth had been the recipient) was trundling a "boneshaker" bicycle along the Yeld lanes, when he perceived the jaunty form of Mr Ratman, bag in hand and cigar in mouth, strolling leisurely in the direction of Maxfield.

Tom, who was only a beginner in the art of cycling, was so taken aback by this apparition, that, after one or two furious lurches from one side of the road to the other, and a frantic effort to keep his balance, he came ignominiously to the ground at the very feet of the visitor.

"Hullo!" said that worthy; "as full of fun as ever, I see."

"Hullo, Ratty!" said Tom, picking himself up; "got over your kicking?"

This genial reference to the circumstances under which the so-called lost heir had last quitted Maxfield grated somewhat harshly on the feelings of the gentleman to whom it was addressed.

"Look here, young fellow," said he, "you'd better keep a civil tongue in your head, or I shall have to pull your ear."

"Try it," retorted Tom.

Mr Ratman seemed inclined to accept the invitation; but as he was anxious for information just now, he decided to forego the experiment.

"Is your father at home?" he demanded.

"Rather. You'd better go back the way you came. We know all about you up there," said Tom.

"That's all right. And how are your pretty sisters, Tommy?"

If any insult more than another could disturb the temper of Master Oliphant, it was to be called "Tommy," as many of the rustic youths of the neighbourhood knew to their cost. He therefore replied shortly, "Find out," and proceeded to address himself to the task of remounting his machine.

"That's what I'm going to do. Here, let me hold it for you, or you'll break your neck."

"Look here," said the outraged Tom, thoroughly roused by this crowning indignity, "I don't want to be seen out here talking to cads. I don't mind fighting you. If you don't care for that, keep your cheek to yourself, and go and talk to somebody who's fond of rot. I'm not." And the young bruiser, who had an uncommonly broad pair of shoulders, looked so threatening that Mr Ratman began to feel a little concerned.

"Ha, ha!" said he, "how well you do it! I always liked you, Tommy, my boy. I'll let your tutor know what a credit you are to him."

"I wish to goodness Armstrong was at home," growled Tom; "he'd make you sit up."

This was just the information Mr Ratman had been anxious to get. The prospect of encountering Mr Armstrong had interfered considerably with his pleasure in arranging this visit. But if he was out of the way—well, so much more the luck of Mr Ratman. Therefore, without wasting time in further parley with this possible brother-in-law, he proceeded jauntily on his way.

"You won't fight, then?" said Tom by way of farewell.

"Some day."

"All right. Coward! Good-bye, Mr Roger Ingleton, major!"

Having relieved himself of which appropriate sentiment, Tom felt decidedly better, and walked his bicycle down the hill, determined to keep clear of Maxfield till the evening.

Mr Ratman, somewhat ruffled, but on the whole cheerful, swaggered on to his destination.

The captain was luxuriously smoking a cigar and solacing himself with a sporting paper, when Raffles sent his heart to his mouth by announcing—

"Mr Ingleton, sir, to see you."

"Ah, Ratman!" said he with a forced air of welcome as his creditor entered. "I didn't recognise you by your new name. You're keeping it up, then?"

"What do you mean?" demanded Mr Ratman, taking an easy-chair and helping himself to a cigar from the captain's box. "It's you who are keeping it up, I fancy. I'll trouble you to drop the Ratman."

The captain laughed unpleasantly.

"As you like," said he.

"Now to business. Of course, you're ready to make good these little bills," and he pulled four or five blue slips from his pocket.

"No, I'm not. You may as well know it at once."

"Hum! What do you propose, then? Do you know there's a writ out?"

"I propose nothing. I want to know what you propose."

The two men regarded one another in silence; one insolent and sneering, the other desperate and scowling.

"What do I propose?" said Ratman, puffing away cheerfully. "Scarcely anything—only to make a little communication to the War Office, give a few instructions to the Sheriff, write a paragraph or two to the county papers, and tell a few interesting anecdotes to your charming daughters."

Captain Oliphant started to his feet with a smothered exclamation.

"Not the last, Ratman! I'm in your clutches; but for Heaven's sake don't bring them into it!"

Ratman laughed.

"You *will* insist on forgetting my name, my dear fellow. Yes, that's my little programme. I fancy I may as well begin at the end."

"Look here," pleaded the victim; "I know it's no use appealing to your pity, for you have none; or your honesty, for you've less of that than I have. But doesn't it occur to you that it would be decidedly against your interest to ruin me just now?"

"What do you mean?" said Ratman with a yawn.

"Why, you claim a certain name, and you have to prove your claim. Roger has got the romantic notion into his head that if his elder brother can be found, that brother shall have the property. He is more than half inclined to credit your story already. You have to satisfy two other persons, of whom I am one. Do you understand?"

"Perfectly," said Mr Ratman, who began to be interested. "I anticipate no difficulty there."

"You forget that at present only a sickly boy stands between myself and the property. It would surely mean something on my part for me to admit a second life between."

"What is the use of talking nonsense?" said Ratman. "Even if you did, for the sake of a little longer credit I might give you, own my right to my own name, what's the use of that, when this man Armstrong has to be satisfied too? If you could crack that nut there might be something in it."

The captain groaned. He knew that every project would be pulled up short at this sticking-point.

"Come," said Ratman encouragingly, "if you could work things in that direction, it might be worth my while to give you time."

"I can do nothing. The fellow is immovable. In six months—"

"In six months everything will be too late. And now, what about the other matter? Is that all right?"

Once more the captain groaned. "I can say nothing about it yet. She knows my wishes, but as Robert Ratman she will not hear a word of it. As Roger Ingleton, the elder, you may depend on it the matter will take another view. All depends on your success there. When that's achieved, the rest will come if you give her time."

Mr Ratman sneered.

"You are a glib talker, Oliphant. I admire you. Now listen. You want credit, and you know how to buy it. One way or another, this business must come to an end. I'll take new bills with interest at three months. By that time everything must be square and smooth; otherwise you'll be sorry you and your children were born, my boy. Order dinner. I'm going back by the six train. Pass me that paper, and don't disturb me any more by your talking."

As Mr Ratman, very well satisfied with his day's business, strolled serenely back through the park that afternoon, he was surprised to hear light footsteps behind him, and, on turning, to discover that his pursuer, of all people, was Miss Rosalind Oliphant.

"Hullo!" said he, "this is flattering, with a vengeance."

"Mr Ratman, I want to speak to you, please," said Rosalind, very pale and nervous.

"Excuse me," said he, "that's not my name; my name is Roger Ingleton. What's the matter?"

"It's about my father. Have you seen him?"

"Just left the dear man."

"He says he owes you money, and that you threaten to ruin him. Is that so?"

"Upon my word, if you want to know, it is."

"How much is it, please?"

Ratman laughed.

"Nothing. A trifle. Fifteen hundred pounds or thereabouts."

"Fifteen hundred!" faltered she. "Does he owe you all that."

The little she had to offer was a drop in the bucket only.

"Look here," said he; "Miss Rosy, your father's in a fix. I don't want to be hard on him, but I must have my money or its equivalent. Now, I should consider it a very fair equivalent to be allowed to call him father-in-law. I may not be up to your mark in some things, Miss Rosalind, but I've a good name, and I flatter myself I know beauty when I see it. Now, think over it. It's the only chance your father's got, and you might do worse for yourself than become the mistress of Maxfield. Good-bye. Shake hands."

She drew herself up with an air and a flush of colour which redoubled his admiration, and without a word, turned away with rapid steps.

Mr Ratman was sorely tempted to follow this beautiful creature, who, in all his chequered career, had been the only human being to discover the few last dregs of affection in his nature. As much as it was possible in such a man, he was in love with this debtor's daughter. The sensation was novel and exhilarating enough to afford him food for cheerful reflection as he walked on towards the station.

So engrossed was he in his day-dreams that he forgot that even country trains are occasionally punctual, and that, at least, he had not much time left him to catch the one he aimed at. Indeed, it was not till, within a few minutes of the station, he caught sight of the train already standing at the platform that it occurred to him to bestir himself. He ran, shouted, and waved his arm all at the same time, but to no effect. The whistle blew as he entered the yard, and as he reached the platform the guard's van was gliding out of the station.

Thoroughly ruffled—for this was the last train to town—Mr Ratman vented his wrath on the world in general, and the railway officials in particular, even including in his objurgations an unlucky passenger who had arrived by the train and shared with him the uninterrupted possession of the platform.

"Easy, young man," said the latter, a substantial-looking, bony individual with a wrinkled face, and speaking with a decided American twang. "You'll hurt yourself, I reckon, if you talk like that. It's bad for the jaws."

Mr Ratman took a contemptuous survey of the stranger and quitted the platform.

His first idea was to return to Maxfield and demand entertainment there for the night. But since he would have to walk all the way, and the first train in the morning left Yeld at eight, he decided to put up at the little hotel of the village instead, and with that object threw himself and his bag into the omnibus of that establishment which waited on the trains.

Somewhat to his disgust, the stranger, after collecting his baggage, entered the same vehicle and took a seat opposite him.

"Wal," said he, "you'll have time to cool down before the next train, young man. Putting up at the hotel?"

"Where else should I put up?" growled Ratman. "What business is it of yours?"

"I guess it's my business to get all the information I can on this trip. I came over this side to learn."

"You've come to a queer hole to do it," said Ratman, beginning to feel he might as well resign himself to circumstances.

"Just so. It's changed a bit since I was here last. We had to drive from Barbeck then."

"So you know the place, do you?" inquired Ratman.

"That's so," was the laconic rejoinder. "A resident, likely?"

"Well, not at present, or I shouldn't be going to the inn."

"Down here on business, I reckon? I was a bagman myself once."

"You're wrong again. I've been down to see my property, if you want to know."

"Large estate, no doubt? Anywhere near my friend Ingleton's plot, now?"

Mr Ratman stared at the stranger with something like consternation.

"Ingleton!" he exclaimed. "What do you know of Ingleton?"

Here the omnibus pulled up.

"Wal, I reckon I should know something of my own family," drawled the stranger as he alighted. "What say?—shall we have a snack of something in the parlour! Come along."

The landlord led the way into the coffee-room. He knew Mr Ratman by this time.

"Sorry we can't give you and your friend the private room, sir, but there's only one other gentleman in the coffee-room, and he's going directly."

As they entered, the other gentleman, who was drying his boots at the fire, turned round, and Mr Ratman had the rapture of finding himself face to face with Mr Armstrong.

Chapter Twenty Three
Captain Oliphant pays one of his Debts

Mr Ratman's natural modesty prompted a precipitate retreat from the embarrassing vicinity of the gentleman whom he had last seen with a horsewhip in his hand; but prudence and the presence of the stranger, and the lack of any other place to go to, prevailed upon him to remain.

The stranger, apparently unaware of the presence of a third party, continued his conversation where it had been interrupted.

"Yes," said he, "I reckon I should know something of my own family, although it's a generation since I set foot in these parts."

"Yes; all right," said Ratman uncomfortably. "I'll go and order dinner."

But the entrance of the landlord prevented this manoeuvre.

"The gig from Maxfield is in the village, Mr Armstrong," said he, addressing the tutor. "I've sent word to Robbins to call for you in half an hour. Maybe, if Mr Ratman is going up, you could give him a lift."

"Mr Ratman is not going up," said Mr Armstrong.

The stranger here took notice of the tutor.

"Friend of my friend, eh?" said he. "Pleased to know you, sir. Resident in these parts, I presume? What?"

"Quite so," said Mr Armstrong, putting up his glass, and honouring the speaker with a minute survey.

"As I was saying to our young friend here, there's been changes in this locality since I was here about the time of Noah. You named Maxfield just now, sir. Likely you know Squire Ingleton, my relative, at the manor-house there?"

The tutor's glass dropped abruptly.

"Your relative? What relation were you to the old Squire?"

"*Was* I—is he dead, then?"

"More than a year ago."

"Sir," said the stranger, with some excitement, "that man was my sister's husband. I guess I've come here a trifle late. Dead? He didn't look to have it in him. What say?"

It said a good deal for Mr Ratman's nerve that in the tutor's presence he took upon himself to reply boldly—

"My father died rather suddenly a year since. So you are my uncle?"

The American mayor stared at the speaker in bewilderment, which was not lessened by an abrupt laugh from the gentleman at the fireplace.

"I guess I'll take a seat and work this out," said he. "I'm your uncle, am I? I never should have known it, if you hadn't been so obliging as to tell me, young man. Which branch of the family tree do you hang on to?"

"Your sister had a son, Roger Ingleton. That's my name."

"Is that so? And you're the present Squire of Maxfield? Well, well. When did you come to life again?"

"There was a false report of my death," said Ratman, glancing a little nervously at the tutor, who was diligently removing the mud from his riding-boots.

"Wal, it's singular. I never expected to see a nephew of mine again. Why, how long is it, now, since I went over? Thirty-seven years if it's a day."

"I can't remember that," said Ratman tentatively.

"Seeing you weren't born, you'd find it hard," said Mr Headland. "But, say, by all accounts you were a troublesome boy."

"I was not all I might have been," replied Mr Ratman, beginning to wish this cross-examination was over.

"Put it that way, certainly. You ran away, and left your mother, my sister, with a broken heart, I've heard say."

"My father and I quarrelled, and I left home—yes."

Here the tutor quitted the fire and came to where the two men sat.

"Excuse my interrupting you, sir," said he to the stranger, "but your conversation interests me. The fact is, the Squire married a second time, and left a son, whose guardian I happen to be. By the old man's will my ward is the heir. You will allow I have a right to feel interested in this gentleman, who only discovered six months ago that he was the lost elder brother."

The good American sat back in his chair and looked from Ratman to Armstrong, and from Armstrong back to Ratman, in a state of painful bewilderment.

"Now," said the tutor, "my ward feels a little curiosity about his elder brother—only natural, is it not?—and I, as his legal guardian, naturally share that curiosity."

"Why, certainly," said the Mayor, beginning to be interested.

Mr Ratman began to lose countenance, and fidgeted uncomfortably with the forks and spoons.

"I have heard a little of this gentleman's romantic career," continued the tutor, with his half-drawl. "He has been good enough to tell us, in fact, that when he left home—by the way, when was that, Ratman?"

"When I know your right to ask me questions," growled Ratman, "I'll see about answering them."

"Seems to me," said the Mayor, assuming judicial functions for the time being, "unless you've disgraced yourself, you can't hurt much by saying. You say you're the Squire's son; this gentleman—I didn't catch your name, sir?—Armstrong?—Mr Armstrong says he's not as sure as you are. Seems to me, if you tell one thing, you may as well tell another. It's all one story, and if it's true, it's a good one."

Mr Ratman did not like the turn affairs were taking. If he refused to reply to the questions put to him, he was aware that he was damaging his own claim. If he answered, how was he to know if the risk was not even greater? And yet, what more was Armstrong likely to know about the lost son than he himself? He might as well go through with it. So he replied, sullenly—

"I left home a year before my mother died. He can get the date of that from the tombstone, if he wants it."

"Thanks; I'll look at it," said the tutor with aggravating cheerfulness. "You went up to London, didn't you?"

"I've told you so, and that I lived there with a man called Fastnet."

"And then you went abroad, I think you said?"

"Yes; to India."

"Just so; that's where you died, is it not? You stayed in London long enough to go to the dogs, I understood you to say?"

"That didn't take long. I spent all my money in six months, and then enlisted," said Ratman, feeling fairly launched by this time.

"Quite so. And you died, I believe, in India?"

"I was supposed to have died in a skirmish; and they sent news home that I had. I never corrected it."

"Whereabouts was the skirmish, if it's a fair question?"

"On the frontier. I forget the name."

"That's unfortunate. By the way, to go back to London, do you recollect where Mr Fastnet lived? I should like to call on him."

"You won't find him; he died before I went abroad—drank himself to death."

"I'm sorry to hear that. And you enlisted under your present name of Ratman, of course?"

"My present name is Ingleton. If I called myself Ratman, that was because I didn't want my father to hear of me. I never told any one my real name."

"Seems to me," said the Mayor, "it's odd how your medical adviser on the field of battle found out where to write home to say you were dead."

"It is still more odd, sir," said the tutor, fixing the claimant with his glass, "that this Mr Fastnet (who, you will be glad to hear, has also come to life again, was still in good health when my ward saw him a few weeks ago) retains a vivid recollection of the runaway son having entertained him for a year at his own lodgings; at the end of which time the prodigal, so far from enlisting, took to the stage, and spent another year, at least, with a company of strolling players.

"We have your unfortunate's nephew's story," proceeded the tutor, "carefully traced up to a certain point, and if either you or Mr Ratman are interested in the matter, we can produce our witnesses. Your memory is a treacherous one, Robert Ratman. It is no use asking you, I fear, what became of you after a certain riot in Boulogne when you, as the Ghost in 'Hamlet,' and your fellow-tragedians were mobbed for not paying the rent of your hall?"

Mr Ratman, who during this cross-examination had passed through all the stages from blustering rage to abject discomfiture, sank back on his chair and turned a livid face to his questioner. He had sense enough to see that the game was up; and not being an actor himself, he was at a loss to conceal his defeat. The tutor's cold, keen gaze took the heart out of him.

"Lying dog!" snarled he, "I've had enough of your questions. You think yourself clever, but I'll be even with you yet. I'll ruin the lot of you—you and your fellow-scoundrel and his brats, who don't know yet what it is to have a felon for a father. You'll be sorry for this."

So saying, he took up his bag, and with the best swagger he could assume slunk from the room.

"See—stay here, young man," said the Mayor excitedly; "there's something else."

But he was gone. The outer door slammed to and his footsteps died gradually away down the street.

Mr Armstrong and the stranger exchanged glances in silence. Then the Mayor turned to Mr Armstrong with a stern face.

"Seems to me, sir," said he, "that if that young man's the knave, you're uncommon like the fool. You'll excuse me mentioning it after the service you have just rendered to the cause of veracity, but it's a solemn fact."

"I have heard the same opinion expressed by other authorities, and I have no doubt it is true. You mean to tell me I should have extorted from him a written recantation of his claim?"

"That's so; you guess right. Consequence is, I'm bound to stay now as a witness to see this quarrel through. Here have I come on a pleasure-trip to see my relatives, and it seems I've got to combine business and pleasure after all."

"You forget I've no hold over this man. He does not claim the property, although he guesses that my ward will hand it over to him if he proves his identity. I can only show him to be a liar."

"You seem pretty sure of that."

"I am myself; and I hope, for everybody's sake, that your nephew, if he should turn up, will be a better credit to the name than this land-shark."

"Well, sir, I don't thank you for dragging me into the business; but, since I am here, I stay to see it out."

"I am relieved to hear you say so."

"Tell me now," said the Mayor, "what the story is; and what does our young friend mean by his farewell threats?"

Thereupon Mr Armstrong gave his new ally a faithful account of the family difficulty: of Captain Oliphant's embarrassing relations to the claimant, of Miss Rosalind's dilemma, of Roger's quixotic determination to find his lost brother, and of his own—the tutor's—conviction of the hopelessness of the quest.

The visitor by no means shared the last conclusion.

"I rather calculate that lost young man ain't as dead as you think," said he. "By all accounts he wasn't born to be drowned, and he's not hung yet. You bet, the young brother will come up with him before time's called."

"Well, by the last accounts he seems to have a vague clue as to his whereabouts fifteen years ago," said the tutor; "we shall hear what he makes of it. To-morrow you must come up to Maxfield and see my co-trustee."

The presence of this unexpected friend of the family, in the capacity of impartial umpire, struck the tutor as particularly opportune at this juncture. He had been a witness to Ratman's virtual admission to his imposture, and his natural interest in the discovery of his own nephew was not likely to warp his determination to see fair play for Roger.

Captain Oliphant, when he heard next morning of the new arrival, by no means shared his co-trustee's satisfaction. The news, indeed, agitated him to a remarkable degree, and he astonished the tutor by his ill-concealed reluctance to meet him.

"It is important that you should see him," remarked the tutor. "As the uncle of the lost elder brother he is entitled, I think, to our confidence. I can imagine no reason why you should be afraid to see him."

"Afraid! Who says I am afraid to see him?"

"I can think of no other explanation of your reluctance—"

"Please, sir, Mr Headland to see you," announced Raffles.

Captain Oliphant changed colour as he turned to greet the visitor.

"You'll pardon the early call," said the latter, "but they gave me such a shocking supper at the inn, that I resolved to try my luck up here for breakfast. Captain Oliphant, I presume?—friend of my friend Armstrong. Pleased to know you, sir. Pity you weren't with us last night to see the decline and fall of your ingenious friend, R. Ratman. Your colleague, sir, put that young man to bed in a way that would have made you enjoy yourself. Seems to me, captain, you are well rid of him."

"I fail to understand all this," said the captain. "If you refer to Mr Ratman's claims to be the lost Roger Ingleton—"

"My nephew," interposed the American.

"All I can say is, that I am not at all satisfied the claim is not a just one."

"Well, sir," said Mr Headland, "if that's your opinion, it's more than that young man thinks himself by this time. But never mind that."

"I do mind it, sir; and I should like to know what right any one has to decide the matter for me? I would suggest that, though we are pleased to see you, you should allow us to attend to our own business."

"I not only allow you, sir, but I expect it of you. And that reminds me of a question that has been puzzling me ever since I heard of the Squire's death. I wrote him a letter in the fall of last year."

The captain was seized with a sudden impulse to stir the fire, and as he stood thus with his back turned, Mr Armstrong could not help wondering what there was in the operation so violently to agitate the operator's frame.

"Yes, sir, a letter dated November 9th, which must have been delivered, as I have made inquiries, and find it was not returned. It contained money, and as it was never acknowledged, I had fears it was lost."

"Any letters for the Squire have been opened by his executors. I recollect none from abroad—do you, Captain Oliphant?" said the tutor.

The Captain, still with his back turned, said— "No; it never came into my hands."

"Mrs Ingleton would hardly be likely to have opened it. It would be only a short time before her death."

"It's singular," said the Mayor. "My clerk posted it. He should have registered it, but omitted."

"How was it directed?" asked the captain, turning at last, and pale after his exertions.

"Roger Ingleton, senior, Maxfield, England."

"Hum! Did your clerk know it contained money?"

"Which means, did he purloin it? Well, sir, we shall see. An English bank-note can be traced. That's one advantage you have over us on the other side."

Mr Armstrong during this short colloquy experienced a curious depression of spirits. He was thinking, not of the bank-notes, or the American mayor, or even of Captain Oliphant, but of Rosalind and Jill and Tom; and the thought of them just at this moment made him feel very melancholy.

As for the captain, if his thoughts for a moment turned in the same direction, they came back instantly, with a strong revulsion of hate against the man who stood in his way at every turn; who seemed to read him through, to unmask him silently whenever he sought to take refuge in a lie, to pin him ruthlessly down to the consequences of his own delinquencies. But for Armstrong he might have been a free man—free of his debts, free of his frauds, clear in his children's eyes, able to hold up his head to all the world. As it was, everything seemed to conspire with his enemy to pinion him and hold him fast, a prey to the Nemesis that was on its way! What would he not give to have this stumbling-block out of the path, and feel himself free to breathe and hope once more?

In such a mood he spent the morning; and about midday, shaking off his visitor, wandered out into the park for fresh air and space to think. As he paced, there returned to him memories of old half-forgotten days, of faces that once looked into his trustfully, voices that once made his heart glad, children that once ran to welcome him; visions of vanished hopes, ambitions, ideals. Where were they all now? Who believed in him to-day? Who would believe in him a week hence? What voices rejoiced him now? Into whose life did he carry strength and cheer? The park stretched bleak and desolate before him; the earth lay sullen under his feet, the very trees drooped around him, and the great restless ocean beyond moaned at his coming. It was nothing to him that the smell of spring was in the air; that the lark was carolling high overhead; that the declining sun was darting his rays through the trees.

Near at hand rose a sound of laughter. He durst not turn that way, lest he should meet his own children.

Far away, through a break in the trees, he could catch a glimpse of the old church at Yeld with the Vicarage beside it, where dwelt the one being he dreaded most—his own daughter. From behind wafted a sound of music through an open window, where sat the man who had found him out and could ruin him by a word.

Which way was he to turn? Which way shall a man turn who would escape from himself?

For two long hours he wandered on caring not which way he took, and feeling himself step by step closer beset by his dismal forebodings. Presently he found himself beyond the park boundaries on the open downs which stretched to the edge of the cliff. The touch of the salt sea-breeze on his fevered brow startled him and made him shiver. The last gleam of daylight was fading in the west, and when presently it flickered out and left him in the dark, he felt that the last ray of his own hope had vanished too. And yet, strange as it may seem, this man had never been quite as honest with himself as he was now. The game was fairly up. He had long since given up deluding himself that he was better than he seemed. Now the time was come when it hardly seemed worth while to delude other people. It was no use. Nor, to such a pass had he come, did it seem much use to be a coward. The dog whose last hope has gone will gather himself together for a final fling at his persecutors; the poltroon driven back against the wall, unable to retreat farther, will sometimes turn and make a stand such as he never deemed himself capable of before. And so Captain Oliphant, because he could do nothing else, plucked up a little courage and groped about in the dark for some new fragments of his lost manhood.

He would go back and face the worst. If he was to be ruined, he would pull the mask off himself, and not leave it to Armstrong or any one else to do it. Whatever befell, nothing could well be more wretched than the plight in which he now stood. He had no amends to make, but he could at least simplify the labours of those whose business it was to expose and punish him. With which poor spark of resolution he turned dismally to go back to Maxfield.

As he did so he became aware of footsteps close at hand on the cliff-path. Whoever the passenger might be—at such an hour and place it was not likely to be any one but a coastguard or a fisherman—Captain Oliphant was in no mood for company. He therefore stepped off the path and sat down on a seat on the edge of the cliff till the intruder had passed.

It was not so dark but that the latter perceived the movement, and halting suddenly, said—

"Who's that?"

The voice was that of Mr Ratman. What brought him here at this moment, to extinguish, perhaps, the little gleam of courage that flickered in the breast of his wretched dupe?

For a moment the captain was tempted to run like a thief from a policeman; but his very desperation came to his rescue.

"What do you want here, Ratman?"

"Hullo, it's Oliphant! Here's a piece of luck. You're the very man I wanted to see. I've changed my mind since I said good-bye yesterday, my boy, and mean to remain here on the spot and see the end of this business. I was on my way to see you. Come along."

"You'd better say what you want to say here. You won't find any admirers of yours up at the house."

"Ah! then you've heard of last night's business? What on earth brings this Yankee idiot here at this time to spoil everything? Now, Teddy, the long and short of this business is, that you must stir yourself. You've shuffled long enough. First of all you were going to marry the widow; you boggled that. Then you were going to succeed to the property; you've boggled that. Then you were to clear the tutor out of the way; you've boggled that. Then you were to raise the wind and pay me off, and you've boggled that. I've given you long enough rope, goodness knows. I mean to haul in now."

Captain Oliphant rose from his seat with a dismal laugh. "I'm tired of hearing you say that, Ratman. I wish you'd do it and be done with it."

Ratman peered through the gloom at the speaker in surprise. "Hullo!" said he, "that's a new tune for you. Now look here; I suppose you've not forgotten our talk yesterday?"

"Well?"

"You've two things to do; you've to recognise me as Roger Ingleton when the time comes. There'll be proofs and witnesses. They must satisfy you, mind. Make no mistake of that. Then I must have Rosalind. I love her. On the day I'm your son-in-law you shall have back every bill I hold against you. Now, is it a bargain? It's a cheap one for you, I can tell you."

The blood rose to Captain Oliphant's brow. A few hours ago he would have faltered and evaded, half whined, half promised; now sheer desperation made him reckless.

He laughed bitterly.

"Recognise you—you shark! Never! And if you ever dare to speak of my daughter, I'll shake you like a cur. There now, do as you like; you've got my answer."

Ratman dropped his jaw in utter amazement. For a minute the words would not come. Then, with a face so livid that Oliphant could see its whiteness through the night, he hissed—

"You mean it? You defy me?—me, with these papers in my hand, and the whole story of your villainy in my keeping? You—"

As he held up the bills a wild impulse prompted the wretched captain to make a grab at them.

There was a short struggle. Oliphant, with his back to the cliff, kept his hold for a moment; then a fierce blow sent him reeling backwards to the edge, with the torn half of the documents in his hand. There was a gasp, a half cry, and next moment only one man stood in the place, peering with ashen face into the black darkness below.

Chapter Twenty Four
The Billiard-marker at "l'Hôtel Soult"

In the *salon* of a small dilapidated hotel in one of the southern suburbs of Paris sat Roger, three weeks after the event recorded in the last chapter. He had the dull place, apparently, to himself. The billiard-room, visible through the folding-doors, was deserted. In the dining-room the waiter dozed undisturbed by a single guest. The landlady in her *bureau* yawned and hummed, and had not even a bill to make out.

She had already made out that of the young English gentleman, and a pretty one it was! A guest such as he was worth a season to the landlady of "L'Hôtel Soult." Three weeks ago, half dead with cold and weariness, he had come and asked for a bed; and in that bed till yesterday he had remained, feverish, coughing, sometimes gasping for breath. Compared with the attack he had had in London in the winter, this was a mild one; but in this dreary place, with not a friend at hand, with a doctor who could not understand a word he said, with a voluble landlady who, when she visited him, never gave him a chance of getting in a word, and with a few servants who stared at him blankly whenever he attempted to lift his voice, it was the most miserable of all his illnesses.

He was as close a prisoner as if he had been in jail. The doctor, who took apartments at his expense in the hotel, would not allow him to move. No one to whom he appealed could be made to understand that he had friends in England with whom he desired to communicate. One letter to Armstrong which he had tried to write the landlady impounded and destroyed as waste-paper, perhaps not quite by accident. This well-to-do young guest was worth nursing. His friends would only come and fetch him away; whereas she, motherly soul! was prepared to take him in and do for him. The pocket of the coat which on the day of his arrival she had carried off to her kitchen to dry contained satisfactory proof that Monsieur was a young gentleman who could pay; and although she was too honest to recoup herself for her services in advance, she had kept the coat hanging up in her room for a week, as a pleasant reminder of the joys of hospitality.

Only yesterday the invalid had recovered sufficiently to rout the doctor and stagger down to the telegraph-office; and to-day, propped up with pillows on the uncomfortable stuff-sofa, he was expiating his rashness with a day of miserable coughing.

At the sound of his handbell, the landlady, a buxom dame of forty-five autumns, hastened to the couch of her profitable visitor.

Roger was too weak to oppose the flood of her congratulations and compliments on his recovery, and allowed her to talk herself breathless before he put in his word.

"Madame has not been many years in these parts?" he inquired in his best French.

Madame threw up her shoulders and protested she had lived in those parts from a child, when the dull suburb was once a festive little rustic village, and the great city now gobbling it up once loomed mysteriously in the north, with acres and miles of green fields and woods between.

"But this hotel," said Roger, "has not stood here so long?"

"*Ma foi!*" said she, "since I can remember, when I used to visit my good uncle here every Sunday, I remember 'L'Hôtel Soult.' Why, when I married my cousin and became *Madame l'hôtesse*, it was all fields between us and Paris. Yes, and little enough change about the house. We cannot afford, Monsieur, to build and decorate. By a miracle we escaped the German shells. Ah! a merry time was the year of the war! France suffered, alas! but the 'L'Hôtel Soult' prospered. 'Twas the year I was left a widow! I had ten waiters then, Monsieur, and two billiard-markers, a *chef* from the best kitchen in Paris, and stables, and *chambrières*, and—why, Monsieur, the wages of one week were twenty—twenty-five napoleons!"

"That was after the war?" asked Roger.

"Yes. Before that I had more. But, alas! they left me for the field, and came no more."

"Were all your waiters Frenchmen?" asked Roger.

Madame stared curiously at the questioner.

"Why do you ask? I have had many kinds. Some English, like Monsieur."

"A year or two after the war," said Roger, "there was an Englishman, a relation of mine, who was a waiter in an hotel in one of the suburbs south of Paris. I want to hear of him. I have hunted for weeks. I could hear nothing of him. I came here before I gave it up as a hopeless search, and, as you know, I've been laid up ever since. You have been kind to me, Madame; something makes me think I was not kept here for nothing. Can you help me to find my friend?"

The landlady began to have inward misgivings that she had not behaved to this pleasant-spoken young guest of hers as nicely as she might have done, and she secretly resolved to revise the bill in his favour before presenting it.

"Why, Monsieur, I had plenty English in my time. The year after the war I had—let me think—two or three. Your friend—was he the little lame one who waited beautiful at table, but that he cough, cough, till I must send him away?"

"No; that's not the one."

"Then it was the fat one?—John Bull, we call him, who eat more than he served, never used a fork when he had his fingers. Ah, he was a dirty one, was your friend!"

"No," said Roger; "that's not he. My friend was not much older than I am, and a gentleman."

"A gentleman—and a waiter!" laughed the landlady. "But tell me, what was his name?"

"He used to call himself Rogers."

She shook her head.

"No one of that name was here. I had English, one or two—Bardsley, and Jackson, and Smith; he was a gentleman, but he was not young. He was fifty years, Mr Smith—a good servant. Also there was Monsieur Callow."

"Callot!" exclaimed Roger, starting at the familiar name. "Was he an Englishman?"

"Surely. C-a-l-l-o-w—Callow. Ah! he was a droll one, was Monsieur Callow, and a gentleman too. I never had a billiard-marker like him. He could play any man, and lose by one point; and he could recite and sing; and oh, he eat so little! Every one laughed at him; but he laughed little himself, and thought himself too good for his fellow-waiters."

"What was he like?" asked Roger, flushing with excitement.

"A fine young man, with long curly hair, and whiskers and a beard. He was afraid of nothing, tall and strong. Ah me! I have seen him knock a man down at a blow. He was a wild, reckless man, was Monsieur Callow; but a good servant, and oh! a beautiful billiard player. He always knew how to lose a game, and oh! it made my table so popular!"

"Had he any friends in Paris?"

"Yes; he went often to see his father—so he told me—an actor who gave lessons. I never saw *Monsieur le père*."

"How long did he stay with you?"

"Callow? For five years he served me well. Then there was a *fracas*, a quarrel; I remember it now. An English officer was here, and played with him, and was beaten. 'Twas the only time I ever knew Callow win a game; but he lost his temper this time, and won. Then Milord called him a cheat, and without a word Monsieur Callow knocked him down. The police came, and Monsieur Callow knocked *him* down. Then he put on his hat and walked, and I never saw him more. He always said he would go to sea, and I think he would keep his word. Ah, a telegram! 'Tis long since telegrams came to my hotel. *Hélas*! not for me; for you, Monsieur."

It was from Armstrong.

"Shall be with you, ten to-morrow morning."

The three weeks which had passed at Maxfield had been terrible.

The discovery of Captain Oliphant's body at the foot of the cliff, with the clear traces of a struggle on the brink above, had created a profound sensation at Maxfield and the country round.

For a day the air was full of wild conjectures of suicide, incident, foul play; until the last-named theory was finally confirmed by the discovery in the tightly-clenched hand of the dead man of a fragment of a promissory note bearing the signature of Robert Ratman.

To the tutor, as he held the paper in his hand, everything became startlingly clear. This was the last act of a tragedy which had been going on for months; and now that the curtain had abruptly fallen, he could not help, in the midst of this horror, owning to a sense of thankfulness, for the sake of others, that the troubled career of his rival and enemy had stopped short at a point beyond which nothing but disgrace and scandal and misery awaited it.

From that disgrace it was his business now, by every means in his power, to shield the innocent brother and sisters who still honoured the dead man as their father.

Many a grievous task had been thrown upon the tutor in his day, but none cost him more effort than this, of breaking to the children of his enemy the news of their father's death. But he went through it manfully and ably.

Rosalind, on whom the blow fell hardest, because on her spirit the burden of her father's cares had lain heaviest, rose, with a heroine's courage, to the occasion, and earned the tutor's boundless gratitude by making his task easy. She said little; she understood everything. She remembered nothing but the father's love—his old caresses and confidences and kindnesses. The tears she shed blotted out all the anxieties and misgivings and heart-sinkings of recent weeks. All that remained was crowded with love.

Tom, dulled and stunned, took the story in gradually, and got used to it as he went along. He came and slept at night in the tutor's room, and felt how much worse things might have been had it not been for the stalwart protector who put hope and cheer into him, and filled the blank in his heart with sturdier views of life than the boy had ever harboured there before.

As for Jill, for a week all was blackness and darkness to her. She felt deserted—lost. She cried herself to sleep at night, and by day wandered over the house, peeping into her father's room, and half expecting to see him back. Then her gentle spirit took courage, and she looked up, and her eyes lit with comfort and hope on Mr Armstrong. Everything could not be lost if he was there; and when he sometimes came, and took her little hand in his, and invited her to be his companion in his rides, or sought her out in her lonely walks and made her teach him the haunts of her favourite flowers or read to him from her favourite books, she began to think there was still some joy left on earth.

"Dear Mr Armstrong," she said one day when, by invitation, she came to make afternoon tea for him in his room, "you are so awfully kind to me! If I was only as old as Rosalind, I would marry you."

This rather startling declaration took the tutor considerably aback. He laughed and said—

"You are very nice as you are, Jill."

"You think I'm silly, I know," said she, "but I'm not. Would you hate me if I was older?"

"I don't think I could hate you, not even if you were a hundred."

"I love you ever so much," said she. "Please don't believe what Tom said about the Duke. I don't like him a millionth part as much as you."

"Poor Duke!" said the tutor.

"Really and truly. And oh, Mr Armstrong, if you would only wait I would love to marry you some day! How soon shall I be big enough?"

This was getting embarrassing. But the tutor was in a tender mood, and had it not in his heart to thwart the little Leap-year maid. "Time flies fast," said he; "you'll be grown up before we know where we all are."

She sighed.

"I know you'd sooner have Rosalind. But she doesn't care for you as much as I do. She likes Roger best; but I don't; I like you fifty thousand times better. Would it be an *awful* bother, Mr Armstrong?"

"What! to have Jill for my little wife?" said he. "Not a bit. If ever I want one, she's the first person I mean to ask."

With this declaration Jill had to rest content. It solaced her sorrow vastly; and even though Rosalind, to whom she confided the compact under a pledge of secrecy, scolded and laughed at her alternately, she felt a new prospect open before her, and set herself resolutely to the task of growing up worthy of Mr

Armstrong's affection.

But amid all these troubles and hopes at Maxfield, two questions were on every one's lips: "Where was Roger? Where was Robert Ratman?"

Roger had written once after reaching Paris, a letter full of hope, which had arrived a few days before Captain Oliphant's death. He had succeeded at last in tracking the man Pantalzar to a low lodging in the city, and from him had ascertained somewhat of the history of the Callot family. They had lodged with him at Long Street in London, where they had given lessons in acting, elocution, and music; and Pantalzar clearly remembered the lad Rogers as a constant visitor at the house, partly in the capacity of a promising student of the dramatic art, and partly as a hopeless lover of his preceptor's wayward daughter.

After a year, his troubles in the latter capacity were abruptly cut short by the illness and death of the young lady; a blow which staggered the parents and broke up the establishment at Long Street. It failed, however, to drive Rogers from the party, who, with a romantic loyalty, attached himself to the fortunes of the old people, and became like a son to them in their distresses.

Eventually the bereaved family migrated to Paris, whence Pantalzar had once heard from the father, who had found employment as stall manager of a third-rate theatre in one of the *fauxbourg*. Hither Roger tracked him, and after dogged search, often baffled, sometimes apparently hopeless, discovered some one who remembered the reputed son of the old couple, who, as far as this witness could remember, was thought to have hired himself out as billiard-marker in an hotel in one of the southern suburbs of the city.

Thus far he had succeeded when he wrote home. What transpired subsequently, and how he dropped for a season out of all knowledge, the reader already knows.

The suspense occasioned by his sudden disappearance, as may be imagined, added a new element of wretchedness to the situation at Maxfield. Telegrams, letters, inquiries, alike failed to discover his whereabouts or the secret of his silence. As post after post came and brought neither message nor tidings, the hearts of the watchers grew sick. To the tutor especially, tied as he was to the scene of the tragedy, those three weeks were a period of torture. He urged Dr Brandram to go over to Paris to make inquiries; but the Doctor, after a fortnight of fruitless search, returned empty-handed.

Mr Armstrong thereupon resolved at all hazards to quit his post and go himself. He knew something of Paris. He had old associations with the city, and once, as the reader has heard, possessed acquaintances there. If any one could find the boy, he thought he could; and with such trusty substitutes as the Doctor and Mr Headland, who remained at Yeld, to leave behind, he felt that he might, nay rather that he must, venture on the journey.

It was on the morning of his departure, as he was waiting for the trap to carry him to the station, that Roger's telegram was put in his hand:—

"Come—have been ill—better now—Hotel Soult—no news."

Twenty-four hours later the tutor was at his pupil's side, with a heavy weight lifted from his heart, and resolved, come what would, not to quit his post till he had the truant safe back at Maxfield.

The news he brought with him served to drive from Roger's mind all thoughts of continuing his sojourn a day longer than was necessary to recover his strength.

"It seems pretty certain," said he, "that my brother, when he left here, returned to England, and probably went to sea very soon after. There is no object in staying here. Look in that room there, Armstrong. That's the billiard-room in which he spent most of his time, and that's the very table on which he let himself be beaten regularly for the good of the house."

The tutor walked across to the folding-doors and surveyed the dingy room with critical interest.

"And that must have been little more than twelve years ago," said he. "Do you still hold to your theory that Ratman is your brother?"

"I have no theory. I must find my brother, even if he is a—a murderer," said the boy with a groan. "But, I say, has nothing been heard of him?"

"The police have traced him to London; there the scent ends for the present. He is probably in hiding there, and one may have to wait weeks or months till he gets off his guard and is caught."

About ten days later they started, by slow stages, on the homeward journey. Whether Madame received all she expected for her hospitality is doubtful. Mr Armstrong undertook the duties of cashier, and used his eye-glass considerably in scrutinising the figures. He craved an interview with Madame in her parlour to discuss her arithmetic, and although he appeared eventually to arrive at a satisfactory understanding with the good lady (so much so, that she shed tears at his departure), he did not complain that her charges were extortionate, as French hotels go.

The home-coming of the heir of Maxfield created a welcome flutter of excitement among the desolate occupants of the manor-house and their neighbours. But the flutter in their hearts was nothing compared with that in the heart of the heir himself as he walked across the park on the day after his return to call at the Vicarage and invite Rosalind to accompany him in a ride. What passed—whether the flutter was contagious, what brought back the deserted colour to Miss Rosalind's cheeks, why they rode so slow and left so much of their course to the decision of their steeds,—all this and many other matters for wonder, history recordeth not, as is quite proper. But it does record that when, on their return, Mr Armstrong chanced to come out on to the door-step, where the two stood unmounted, Roger said—

"Armstrong, Rosalind has promised to be my wife."

The tutor flushed a little at this not unexpected announcement; then taking his pupil's arm, he said—

"It means great happiness for you both. I am glad—very glad."

But why, if he was so glad, did he slink off to his study forthwith and play a dirge on his piano, and there sit listlessly in his chair for the rest of the morning staring out of the window through his glass, till Jill tripped in and fetched him down to lunch, saying—

"Dear Mr Armstrong, try not to be too awfully sorry. *I* think no one is as nice as you."

Chapter Twenty Five
The Heir of Maxfield comes of Age

It wanted but a month to Roger's majority, that important day on which the fate of so many persons was to be decided, when a letter was delivered to the heir of Maxfield as he sat at breakfast.

The weeks that had passed since Captain Oliphant's sudden death had been uneventful. To Rosalind and Roger the discovery that they loved one another went far to lighten the sorrow which had befallen both—one in the death of a father, the other in what appeared to be the hopeless loss of a brother.

Roger had by no means yet abandoned his search. Twice already had he and Armstrong been up to London to make inquiries, but without avail. The billiard-marker of "L'Hôtel Soult" had vanished as completely as—well, as Mr Ratman.

"You know, of course," said the tutor once, with the rather unsympathetic drawl in which he was wont to allude to the lost Ingleton—"you know, of course, that if the man you want is Ratman, you are having the assistance of the police in your search. A warrant is out against him, and heaven and earth is being moved to capture him."

Roger sighed.

"I am looking for no one but my brother," said he, "Even if he turns out to be this miscreant, I cannot help it."

"Quite so. Only it is right to remember that to find Ratman means to hang him. That at least is the object the police have in view. But you need not disturb yourself on that score. Roger Ingleton, major, if we find him, may be a villain, but he won't be the murderer of Miss Oliphant's father."

They returned presently, baffled, to Maxfield. No one at the depots, or recruiting head-quarters, or pension offices could tell them a word of a soldier or a sailor named Callot who might have enlisted or gone to sea about twelve years ago. How could they expect it? Nor did the most careful search among the old Squire's papers lead to the discovery of any record of the supposed report of the lad's death.

As a matter of fact, if the billiard-marker at "L'Hôtel Soult" was the man, they had already traced him down to a date long subsequent to that of his rumoured death.

Together they ransacked the memories of Dr Brandram, the Vicar, old Hodder, and one or two other inhabitants who might be supposed to know something of the matter. Very few there were who had seen the boy at all. He had spent most of his time at school, and during his occasional holidays had usually found all the amusement he needed in the ample confines of the park.

No one had seen in black and white an announcement of his death. The Squire had told the Doctor that news of it had arrived from abroad; where and when and under what circumstances he never said. Old Hodder remembered the story of the quarrel between father and son, and identified the portrait as that of the missing lad. But, despite his boasted "threescore years and ten," the old man was absolutely useless in the present inquiry.

And so, thwarted at every turn, not knowing what to hope for, too proud to own himself beaten, Roger abandoned the search, and awaited his majority very much as a debtor awaits his bankruptcy.

Mr Armstrong, who chanced to look up at the moment when Raffles delivered the letter, concluded at once from the startled look on the lad's face that it was a missive of no common importance.

It was from Ratman, and bore on its envelope the London post-mark:—

> "Dear Brother,—For the last time I claim your help. I know quite well that I am being hunted to death by you and those you employ. Without a shred of evidence you are willing to believe me a murderer. I suppose I have no right to complain. It would be convenient to you to have me out of the way, and the best way of getting rid of me is to get up this cry against me. A nice brotherly act, and worthy of an Ingleton! It is no use my telling you that I am innocent—that till I had been two days here I never so much as heard of Oliphant's death. You would not believe it. Nor, I fancy, is it much use telling you that the scoundrel owed me money, that I was shielding him from the consequences of an old felony for which he might have had penal servitude, and that the little he did pay me was stolen from your property. Of course you wouldn't believe it. It is only about your brother, who has been a slung stone all his life, who never had a friend, never knew a kind look from any one, that you are ready to believe evil. I am nearly at the end of my tether here. In a day or

two you will probably hear that I am arrested, and then you will have your revenge on me for daring to be your flesh and blood; and you will have no difficulty in convincing a judge and jury that I have committed any crime you and your saintly tutor choose to concoct between you. Pleasant to be rich and influential! I could escape if I had money. Fifty pounds would rid you of me almost as effectively as the gallows. But it would cost you something; therefore it is absurd to imagine it possible. When, three days hence, I make my last call at the General Post Office, and hear once more that there is nothing for me, not even a message of brotherly pity (which costs nothing), I shall know my last hope is gone. And you, in the lap of luxury, counting your thousands, and monarch of all you survey, will be able to breathe again. Either you will hear of my arrest, or, if my courage befriends me, you may read in an obscure corner of the paper of a wretch, hounded to death, who escaped his pursuers after all, and preferred to die by his own hand rather than that of his brother. Good-bye till then.

"Your brother,—

"Roger Ingleton.

"*P.S.*—The Post Office know me, or my messenger, as 'Richard Redfern.' No doubt you will show this letter to your tutor, who should have no difficulty in using the information I am obliged to give as to my whereabouts to run me down."

The flush on Roger's face had died down into pallor by the time he reached the end of this savage yet dismal letter. Till he came to the postscript he had reckoned on demanding Armstrong's advice as to its contents. Now, somehow, his hands seemed tied. Here was a man, claiming to be his brother, practically placing his life in his hands. Whether the story were true or false, the writer had calculated astutely on the quixotic temper of his correspondent. The appeal, insultingly as it was made, was one which Roger Ingleton, minor, could not resist.

"I have had a letter from Ratman," said he when the two friends were alone together.

"I am not surprised," said the tutor. "He wants money, of course?"

"I can't show you the letter, simply because it contains a vague clue as to his whereabouts, which you would feel bound to follow up."

"I undoubtedly should," said Mr Armstrong. "Shall not you?"

"No. He gives it in confidence, in the hope I shall send him money. I don't intend to do that, but it would hardly be fair to use this letter against him."

"He is Captain Oliphant's murderer."

"He denies it, and once more calls himself my brother."

The tutor shrugged his shoulders.

"As you please. Burn the letter. It probably does not tell more than the police know already."

Roger dismally obeyed. Had he felt sure that this man was his brother, he would have, at all risk and in spite of all, tried to help him. Even so, to help him with one hand would mean to ruin him with the other. If he found him, it would be to hand him over to the police. If he procured his escape, it would be to oust him irrevocably from his inheritance.

There seemed nothing for it but to do nothing and wait.

In other quarters the policy of inaction found little favour. Mr Headland called up the same evening at Maxfield and demanded an interview with the tutor.

"Wal, young man," said he, "I calculate those two hundred-pound notes of mine didn't travel so far astray after all."

"You have traced them, then?"

"I've been three weeks doing it, but I have so."

"And with what conclusion?"

"Just this, that Captain E. Oliphant fell over that cliff just about the right time, sir. Yes, sir, my notes are lying snug at the English Bank at this present moment, and I know their pedigree. Number 90,356 came there from a bank in Fleet Street. The bank in Fleet Street received it from a hotel. The hotel received it from a gentleman who slept in bedroom Number 36, and that gentleman's name was Ratman. Number 90,357 came to the bank later from Amsterdam. Amsterdam had it from an English diamond merchant, the diamond merchant had it from a stock jobber, and the stock jobber had it from a sporting club, who had it from a temporary member in December last in payment of a gambling debt, and that temporary member's name was Ratman. That's not all, sir. My letter was posted in America, November 9. On November 17 the post-master at Yeld, an intelligent man, sir, received a letter with an American stamp, sir, addressed to Roger Ingleton, senior, at Maxfield. A Yankee stamp was a novelty to your intelligent post-master, and he took a note of date, and sent it up here for delivery. It was delivered here November 17, and your footman remembers giving it to your colleague. Three days after, Mr Ratman visited his friend Captain E. Oliphant here. Two days later he reached the hotel in London with a Yeld label on his trunk. A week after that he passed note Number 90,356 to settle his bill. There, sir; the Americans are born explorers. I flatter myself there's not much more to know about my two notes."

"Quite so," said the tutor. "You have done a great deal in three weeks. What reparation can be made you?"

"Sir, you are an honest young man. You believe in shielding the memory of a dead enemy. You are right. Continue on that tack and you'll do yourself credit. As executor of my late kinsman, I will trouble you to place this cheque for £200 to the credit of the estate, and never to say a word about the sum that was lost. Notes get lost every day; at least they do in America."

Mr Armstrong's gratitude was beyond words. He had set his heart, for the sake of the children of his late colleague, and even for Roger's sake, on covering with a cloak of oblivion the crime of which chance had made him the detector. This American had it in his power to aid or thwart him, and had chosen the former course; and a great weight was lifted off the tutor's mind in consequence.

On the following day he was calling at the Yeld bank to transact some business (part of which was to pay in Mr Headland's cheque), when the manager invited him into his parlour. This functionary was a respectable, middle-aged person, who had held his appointment for five or six years, keeping pretty much to himself, and, as is the lot of bank managers, being made a great deal of by clients who chanced to be, or desired to be, under obligations to his bank.

"Mr Armstrong," said he, "you will pardon me, but there's a little matter—"

"Hullo!" thought the tutor, "has the bank stopped payment, or the Maxfield securities been robbed?"

"Well, sir?"

"It's a private matter, and I should not mention it if it were not for the talk which is going to and fro about young Mr Ingleton's lost brother. I understand there's a claimant for the title, and not a very eligible one."

"On the contrary, most ineligible," said the tutor. "And it seems likely that he will, under present circumstances, keep far enough away from these parts?"

"Naturally. The coroner's jury have given him a pressing invitation, which he feels compelled to decline."

"Well, about this lost boy. You'll think me impertinent, but I think I can tell you something about him."

The tutor started, and looked hard at the speaker. "Yes," said the latter mildly. "As you know, I've not been here long. My predecessor, Mr Morris, was a friend of the family. I remember his once mentioning an elder son of the Squire who had been reported dead, and that was all I ever heard of the matter from him or anybody else. But only last week, in a bundle of documents relating to Mr Morris's own affairs, which, as his executor, it was my duty to examine, I came upon a letter which, though evidently private at the time, seems as if it ought at least to be seen by you and your ward now. It proves that ten years ago the elder son was alive, and being in his handwriting, it may be important evidence if you have to deal with the claim of an impostor."

The tutor expressed considerable discomfort at this new complication, and regarded the document in the banker's hand as if it were an infernal machine.

"It's private, you say. Would it not be better to regard it as such?"

"I think it should be seen. If you prefer I will submit it to Mr Pottinger."

This settled the business. The tutor stretched out his hand for the letter. It was dated from on board the ship "Cyclops," off Havana, ten years ago, and, by the unsteady character of the handwriting, which rendered some words almost illegible, had evidently been written in a high sea. Mr Armstrong could scarcely help smiling at the banker's naïve suggestion as to the use of the document as evidence of handwriting.

The note was as follows:—

> "Dear Mr Morris,—I write to you in strictest confidence. My father probably has given me up for dead. I hope so. On no account must he know that I have written to you. My object is to enclose a twenty-five dollar note which I owe him. Once, before we quarrelled, he lent me five pounds. I want to pay it back without any one knowing of it, because I'm determined not to owe anything to anybody, especially to one who has told me I'm not honest. Please put it into his bank account.

He probably will never notice it; anyhow, please, whatever you do, don't tell him or any one alive where it came from, or that you ever heard a word from me or of me. I trust you as a gentleman.

"Yours truly,—

"Roger Ingleton."

"Well, sir," said the banker, who had watched the reading curiously, "does it not seem an important letter?"

"I think so. It appears to be genuine, too, on the face of it. If you will allow me I should like my ward to see it. It will interest him."

The tutor was not wrong. With this strange missive in his hand all Roger's yearnings towards his lost brother returned in full force. The object of his search seemed suddenly to stand within measurable reach. Ten years appeared nothing beside the twenty which only a few months back had divided them. If he could but postpone his majority another year! Then came the miserable doubt about Ratman. If, after all, his unlikely, discredited story should prove to have a grain of truth at the bottom of it! But he dismissed the doubt for the hope.

"Armstrong, I must go to town to find out about the 'Cyclops.' Come with me, there's a good fellow. In three weeks it will be too late."

The tutor was prepared for this decision.

"By all means," said he. "We will go to-morrow to inquire after a passenger or sailor who was on board a sailing-vessel, nationality unknown, which happened to be off Havana in a heavy sea on October 20, ten years ago."

"I know it's absurd," said Roger, "but I can't help it. I never seemed so near my brother before. I should despise myself if I sat idle here."

So it happened that, just when Maxfield was preparing in a quiet way to celebrate the coming of age of the heir; just as the gloom which had followed on Captain Oliphant's tragic death was beginning to lift a little and allow Tom and Jill decorously to think of football; just as Rosalind was beginning to make up her mind that she was not destined for ever to teach the elements of art and science to the Vicarage children; just when everything seemed to be settling down for the last scene of the drama, Roger and his tutor vanished once more on their familiar wild-goose chase.

Dr Brandram grumbled; the county gentry shook their heads; Mr Pottinger breathed again. No one thought well of the expedition; some went so far as to make a jest of it.

Roger cared nothing for what people thought. With Armstrong to back him, with Rosalind to bid him a brave God-speed, with his own stout heart to buoy him up, and with his lost brother only ten years distant, he could afford to start in good cheer, and let the world think what it liked.

But the cheer was destined to failure. They heard of one or two vessels called the "Cyclops," but respecting the crew or passengers, of none of them was it possible to glean a word of news. The vessel in question might have been ship, schooner, or barque; she might have been English, American, Indian, or Australian; she might have foundered, or changed her name, or been broken up for lumber. Lloyds knew her not. West India merchants had never heard of her. Of all their quests, this seemed the most vague and hopeless.

Up to the last, Roger stuck doggedly to it. Even if he spent his majority in the London docks he would not turn tail. The tutor backed up loyally, did most of the work, made most of the inquiries, never grumbled or gibed or protested. When Roger looked most like giving in, it was the tutor who put fresh heart into him.

"To-morrow," said Roger on the eve of his birthday, "I will give it up. But there is a day yet."

And sure enough, on the last day, a vague ray of light came in the shape of a telegram from the port-master at Havana, to whom, at the tutor's suggestion, a message of inquiry had been sent:—

"*Cyclops known. Writing.*"

Writing! A letter would take weeks to come, and they had but a day! They hurried to the telegraph-office and sent an urgent message begging particulars by wire whatever the cost. Late that day, indeed it was nearly midnight, the reply came:—

"*Sailed Ceylon, West Indies. Name Ingleton unknown. Ship now here.*"

Roger staggered from the office a beaten man. Through the deserted City streets the clocks were booming the hour of midnight and ushering in his majority. His brother! All along he had persuaded himself this quest was to end in victory, that before now he should have met his brother face to face and given him what was his. To-day it was no longer his to give. The race was already over, and the clock had won. His brother was not there.

"Take my arm, dear old fellow," said Mr Armstrong, "and cheer up."

Chapter Twenty Six
Missing Links

For three hours that night the two friends, arm-in-arm, paced the empty streets, saying little, brooding much, yet gaining courage at every step. The touch of his guardian's arm thrilled Roger now and again with a sensation of hope and relief in the midst of his dejection which almost surprised him. He had lost his brother; but was not this man as good as a brother to him? Would life be quite brotherless as long as he remained at his side?

The tutor, for his part, experienced a strange emotion too. The opening day had brought a crisis in his life as well as in that of his ward. It was a day to which he had long looked forward, partly with the dread of separation, partly with the joy of a man who has honestly done his work and is about to render up his trust. But was it all over now? No longer now was he a guardian or governor. Was he therefore to lose this gallant comrade, to whom all the brotherhood in his nature went out?

With reflections such as these it is scarcely to be wondered at that little was said during that long aimless walk.

At last Roger shivered.

"Let's turn in," said Mr Armstrong.

They were in a street off the Strand, a long way from their hotel, and no cab in sight.

"Any place will do," said Roger. "Why not this?" and he pointed to the door of a seedy-looking private hotel, over which a lamp burned with the legend—"Night porter in attendance."

The tutor surveyed the house curiously through his and then said—

"Quite so; I stayed here once before," and rang the bell.

The door was opened by a person of whose nationality there could be little doubt, particularly when, after a momentary inspection of his belated guests, he uttered an exclamation of joy and accosted the tutor—

"*Mon ami*! Oh! I am glad to see you, my good friend. Friend of my *pauvre père*!—friend of my youth! It is you. Ah, Monsieur!" added he, addressing Roger, "for your friend's sake you are welcome. *Entrez*!"

"Be quiet now, Gustav," said the tutor. "Bring us come coffee in the coffee-room, if you can get it made, and light a fire in the bedroom. We will talk in the morning."

Gustav gesticulated delighted acquiescence in any demand his hero made, and ushered them into the coffee-room.

"What a queer fellow!" said Roger when he had vanished in search of the coffee.

"Queer but good-hearted fellow is Gustav," said the tutor. "I have known him a long time; to-morrow I'll tell you— Hullo!"

There was but a single candle in the room, and by its dim light, and that of the half-expired fire, they had not at first been able to see that they were not the sole occupants of the apartment. On the sofa lay curled the figure of a man breathing heavily, and, to judge by the spirit-bottle and glasses on the table at his hand, expiating a carouse by a disturbed and feverished slumber.

The tutor raised the candle so that the light fell more clearly on the sleeper. Something in the figure had struck him. The man lay with his face turned towards them. He was stylishly though cheaply dressed. His age may have been forty, and his features were half obscured by a profuse and unkempt sandy beard. This was not what had struck the tutor. In his frequent turnings and tossings the sleeper had contrived to betray the fact that his hirsute appearance was due not to nature but to art. A wire hook had been displaced from the ear, leaving one side of the wig tilted so as to disclose underneath the smooth cheek of a clean-shaven man.

The examination was still in process when Gustav re-entered the room. The clatter with which he put down the cups on the table, aided by the glare of the candle and the tutor's sharp ejaculation, wakened the sleeper with a start. He was sober enough as he raised his head sharply and sprang to his feet. In doing this the treacherous wig slipped still farther. Before he could raise his hand to replace it Mr Armstrong had stepped forward and torn the mask from his face, disclosing the livid countenance of Mr Robert Ratman!

The surprise on either side was at first beyond reach of words. The miscreant stood staring in a dazed way, first at Armstrong, then at Roger, then at Gustav, who, being a Frenchman, was the first to come to his use of his tongue.

"*Mon dieu*! Monsieur, this is no bedroom for the gentleman. It is forbidden to sleep all night in the *salle à manger*."

"Silence, Gustav! Go for a policeman," said Armstrong in a tone so strange that the faithful Gustav slunk away like a dog with his tail between his legs.

"Now, sir!" said the tutor as the door closed.

The wretch made one wild effort at escape. He might have known by this time with whom he had to deal. Mr Armstrong held him by the wrist as in a vice.

"It won't do, Ratman," said he. "The game is up. The best thing you can do is to stand quietly here till the police come."

The prisoner sullenly abandoned his struggle, and turned with a bitter sneer to Roger.

"So you've run me down, have you? You've found your lost brother at last? I expected it. I was a fool to suppose you would lift a finger for me. There's some chance of escaping from an enemy, but from a brother who has set himself to hound a brother to death, never. Never mind. Your money's safe now. Have me hung as soon as you like; the sooner the better for me."

Roger, stupefied and stung to the quick by these taunts, winced as though he and not the speaker were the miscreant. He looked almost appealingly at his accuser, and tried to speak to justify himself, but the words refused to come.

Suddenly he seemed to detect in the prisoner's eye some new sinister purpose.

"Take care, Armstrong; take care!" he cried, and flung himself between the two.

It was not an instant too soon. With his free hand Ratman had contrived while talking to reach unheeded a pocket, from which he suddenly whipped a pistol, and, pounding on his captor, fired.

The shot was badly and wildly aimed at the tutor's face. Even at so short a distance it might have missed its mark altogether. Roger's sudden intervention, however, found it an unexpected target. The lad's up-flung hand caught the pistol at the moment it went off, and received in its palm the ball which had been intended for his friend.

The sight of this untoward accident completely unnerved the prisoner. He sullenly let the weapon drop from his fingers, and with the air of a gambler who has played and lost his last stake, sank listlessly on the sofa on which not ten minutes before he had been sleeping.

"Luck's against me," he said with an oath. "Look to the boy; I shan't trouble you any more. I've done him harm enough without this. I wish I'd never heard of his elder brother."

The tutor, busy binding up his ward's hand, only half heard the words; but Roger, amidst all his pain, heard it and looked up.

"Then you are not my brother?" he said faintly.

"Brother? No. And if you hadn't left the papers about in your room a year ago I should never have known it was worth my while to pretend it."

When, a few moments later, Gustav entered with two constables, Mr Ratman welcomed the visitors with a sigh almost of relief, and placed himself quietly in their hands. As he passed the chair where Roger sat, half faint with pain and loss of blood, he stopped a moment and said—

"Your brother! No. If I had been I shouldn't have come to this."

About ten days later a small party was gathered in Roger's cosy den at Maxfield.

The young Squire was there, with his hand in a sling, still pale and weak, but able to sit up on the sofa and enjoy for the first time the society of a few choice friends. Among those friends it was not surprising to find Rosalind. That young lady had recently exchanged the duties of governess at the Vicarage for those of temporary sick-nurse at the manor-house, and to-night, in her simple mourning, with a flush of pleasure on her cheek as now and again she turned her eyes to the patient whose recovery did her care such credit she looked—at least Roger, an impartial witness, thought so—more beautiful than ever. But as Roger made the same discovery every time he and his nurse met, the opinion may be regarded as of relative value. Tom was there, enjoying himself as usual, indeed rather more than usual, because in the stable hard by, munching his oats, was a horse (the gift of the Squire) who owned him, Tom, as lord and master. Jill was there too, a little pensive as she looked round for some one who was not there, but trying hard to enjoy herself and seem glad. Besides these intimates there was Mr Headland, feeling like a father to everybody; Dr Brandram, in professional attendance; and the Vicar himself, accidentally present to congratulate his young parishioner on his recovery.

The absentee of the evening was Mr Armstrong, who had gone to London the previous day on matters connected with the approaching assizes.

"I wish Armstrong was here," said Tom. "Won't he open his eye when he sees 'Crocodile'!"

"Crocodile" was the name of the horse before mentioned.

"It hardly seems like a party without him," said Jill, blushing a little.

"You were telling us about the letter written at sea," said the vicar. "Of course, you heard nothing of the ship in London?"

"Yes, I did," said Roger. "After no end of disappointment, Armstrong suggested telegraphing to the post-master at Havana, off which the letter was written, you know, and we heard that there had been a ship called the 'Cyclops' ten years ago trading between the West Indies and Ceylon, but that nothing was known of any one of the name of Ingleton."

Rosalind looked up suddenly.

"Ceylon and the West Indies?" exclaimed she. "Roger, did Mr Armstrong never tell you a story he once told me of a shark adventure which happened to him when he was a sailor on a ship trading between Ceylon and the West Indies?"

The sudden silence which followed this inquiry was only broken by a low whistle of wonder from Tom.

Roger, with a flush of colour on his pale cheeks, sat up and said, "What is the story?"

Rosalind told it as nearly as possible in the tutor's own words.

"He did not tell you the name of the ship?" asked the doctor.

"No."

"Or the name of the man who was killed?"

"No."

There was another silence; it seemed as if they were sitting as witnesses to the completion of some curious tunnelling operation, when the party on one side suddenly catches sound of the pick-axe stroke of the party on the other. Step by step the lost Roger Ingleton had been tracked forward to the deck of this West India trading-ship; and backward, step by step, the tutor's history went, till it almost touched the same point.

"I expect," said Tom, with a cheerfulness hardly in accord with the spirits of the company generally, "the fellow who was had by the shark was the one, and Armstrong never knew it."

The profound young man had dropped on the very idea which was present in the minds of each one.

"Wal," said the American mayor, "it may be so; but the question I'm asking myself is this: If so, it's singular Mr Armstrong did not mention the coincidence when you got the cablegram."

"Oh," said Roger, "at the time I was so cut up to find I'd failed after all, that I didn't care to talk; and directly after that we met Ratman. He had no chance."

"I calculate I'd like to ask your tutor one or two pertinent questions," said the Mayor.

The meeting was fully with him, when Tom broke out again—

"I say, I know. Let's ask Gustav. He's no end chummy with Armstrong. He might know a thing or two. He's the chap I told you about at Christy's minstrels," continued Master Tom, warming up at the genial reminiscence.

"Is that the French waiter down-stairs who helped bring you down from London?" asked the doctor.

"Yes. I'm keeping him here as valet for the present. Armstrong mentioned, I remember, that he knew him."

"Ring him up," said Tom.

Gustav appeared, all smiles and shrugs and compliments.

"*Eh bien*! my good gentleman," said he, "I am 'appy to see you well. I was *mortifié* for your mishap; but Mademoiselle—ah, Mademoiselle!"—here he raised his fingers gracefully to his lips—"ze angel step in where ze *pauvre garçon* may not walk. You could not but be well with a nurse so *charmante*. Ah, my friend, 'ow 'appy will be my good, kind friend when he return!"

"You mean Mr Armstrong. Have you known him long?" asked Roger.

"*Pardieu*! Ten, fifteen, twenty year; I know not how long. He is brother to me, your kind governor. He is to the *pauvre père* a son, and to the *petite Françoise—ah! quelle est morte*!"

"What was the name of your father?" demanded Roger, his hand tightening on Rosalind's as he spoke.

"Ah, Monsieur! a poor name; he is called like me, Gustav Callot."

The poor valet was thunderstruck by the sensation which his simple words caused. Surely the English gentlemen and ladies are beautiful listeners; no one ever paid him so much attention in his own country.

The American mayor took up the examination.

"I reckon," drawled he, "that young man did not go by the name of Armstrong when you knew him."

"Ah, no! He has many names, my good, kind friend. It was Monsieur Rogers when we knew his finest. Ah! he act the comedy beautiful! Then when to came to cherish the *pauvre père* in Paris, and mourn with him the death of *la petite Françoise*, he call himself by our poor name. Ah! gentlemen, he was good to us. All he save at 'L'Hôtel Soult' he share with us—and *après* from the sea he even send us pay."

"What was his ship, do you remember?"

"Shall I forget? He told us it had but one eye, and called itself 'Cyclops.' Ah! *mes amis*," continued Gustav, delighted with his audience and amazed at his own oratorical gifts, "he was much changed when I saw him next. 'Tis six, seven, eight years since. The beard is all shorn, the curl is cut off, the eye looks through a glass, and the laugh—*hélas*! gentlemen, the gay laugh of the boy Rogers is turned to the knit brow of the great man Armstrong."

The company had had enough of elocution for one evening, and dismissed the orator with flattering marks of consideration.

The doctor and the vicar rose to go. Close friends of the family as they were, even they were superfluous at a time like this.

But the American mayor remained.

"I guess," said he, "my nephew—"

"Oh!" cried Jill, "then you are his uncle—dear, dear Mr Headland!" and the little maid flung herself into the astonished gentleman's arms and relieved her emotions with a flood of tears.

"Seems to me," said he, looking down and kindly patting the fair head, "my nephew's a hundred miles too far away at this minute."

American mayors are not as a rule endowed with gifts of prophecy, but it seemed as if there was an exception to the rule in the case of Mr Headland; for a moment later the door opened, and the tutor, eye-glass erect, and blissfully unconscious of the interest which his entry excited, strolled jauntily in.

"Ah," said he, "you're still up, then. I just caught the last—"

He stopped short, and the glass dropped abruptly from his eye. Roger had staggered to his feet and was standing with face aglow, stretching out his hand.

The tutor comprehended all. He advanced and placed his arm in that of his brother.

"You have found him at last, then, old fellow?"

"Yes, and without your help."